# THE HOMECOMING

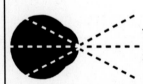

This Large Print Book carries the
Seal of Approval of N.A.V.H.

A SHELTER BAY NOVEL

# THE HOMECOMING

## JOANN ROSS

**KENNEBEC LARGE PRINT**
*A part of Gale, Cengage Learning*

GALE
CENGAGE Learning

Detroit • New York • San Francisco • New Haven, Conn • Waterville, Maine • London

GALE
CENGAGE Learning

**LIBRARY OF CONGRESS CATALOGING-IN-PUBLICATION DATA**

Ross, JoAnn.
    The homecoming / by JoAnn Ross. — Large print ed.
      p. cm. — (A Shelter Bay novel ; no. 1) (Kennebec large print superior collection)
    Originally published: New York : Signet, 2010.
    ISBN-13: 978-1-4104-3032-8 (pbk.)
    ISBN-10: 1-4104-3032-4 (pbk.)
    1. Large type books. I. Title.
PS3568.O843485H65 2010
813'.54—dc22                           2010026180

Published in 2010 by arrangement with NAL Signet, a member of Penguin Group (USA) Inc.

Printed in the United States of America
2  3  4  5  6      14 13 12 11 10
ED294

To Jay — who took me to our beloved Oregon Coast (where I've set my Shelter Bay books), bought me saltwater taffy, then proposed.

After all our years together, I'm even more glad I said "Yes!"

And in memory of Marine Cpl. Jimmy Floren — classmate, neighbor, friend. A true hero, Jimmy was cited for "extraordinary heroism," posthumously receiving the Navy Cross and Purple Heart after sacrificing his life for his fellow Marines and country during the Vietnam War.

# ACKNOWLEDGMENTS

As always, to the incomparable team at NAL, who makes writing a joy, especially my editor, Laura Cifelli, who somehow manages to deftly juggle more balls than anyone I know. Also, matchmaker extraordinaire, my fabulous agent, Robin Rue, for bringing us all together.

Thanks to former high school classmates Jim Flynn and Ron Bonham, who paid good money in a fund-raising auction to have their names included in this book. I know neither of you would ever actually get into the trouble your characters did. (Well, probably not.) At least I didn't make you murderers!

Again, with heartfelt appreciation to all the servicemen and -women who put themselves in harm's way so the rest of us don't have to. Along with their families, who await their safe return home.

And finally, for my sweetie Oregon State University alumnus husband — Go, Beavs!

We should remember that one man is much the same as another, and that he is best who is trained in the severest school.

— Thucydides

Anyone who looks with anguish on evils so great must acknowledge the tragedy of it all; and if anyone experiences them without anguish, his condition is even more tragic, since he remains serene by losing his humanity.

— Augustine of Hippo

# 1

Sax Douchett had heard about people who didn't dream.

Unfortunately, he wasn't one of them. Sometimes he even dreamed while he was awake.

Like he might be doing now, as he felt a familiar prickling beneath his skin. Hair rose on his arms and at the back of his neck. A jolt of fight-or-flight adrenaline hit his bloodstream like a Patriot missile.

He bent over. Put his hands on his knees and drew in several deep breaths.

"You are not in the frigging Kush." Sometimes saying the words out loud gave them more power.

The thick fog on this lonely stretch of beach he was walking on at sunset with his adopted dog turned ordinary things — seaweed, wind-bent cypress, stacks of driftwood — into shadowy objects of mystery. Unlike the placid blue waters of nearby

11

Shelter Bay, the rocky Oregon coastline had claimed scores of ships and their crews over the centuries.

When he'd been trudging through the snow up a steep Afghan mountainside with bad guys blasting away at him and his SEAL teammates, memories of home had kept him putting one boot in front of the other.

When he'd spent another six days all alone on those desolate peaks in the Hindu Kush, wounded, half out of his mind and presumed dead, anticipation for the Dungeness crab jambalaya he intended to fill up on once he got stateside had kept him battling the Taliban assassins sent to finish him off.

And during that lost time when he'd been held prisoner in an enemy village, fantasies of sitting on the porch of the cliff house, an icy bottle of Doryman's Dark Ale in his hand, listening to the rain on the roof, had kept him sane.

After a few frustrating weeks held prisoner again — this time in Bethesda Naval Hospital — like Odysseus, he'd finally made his way home. Physically healthy and, well, *mostly* sane.

And determined to put war behind him and get on with his life. Which was turning out to be a lot easier said than done. Especially with this weekend's damn welcome-home parade the Shelter Bay council and local VFW chapter had planned.

Although everyone in town might have insisted on elevating him onto some gleaming marble pedestal, if there was one thing Sax knew he wasn't, it was a hero.

"Maybe I'll get to kiss me a beauty queen," he said, trying to find something positive about the experience he knew would mean a lot to his parents. Which was the only reason he'd agreed to go along with a celebration that, if reports were true, and he feared they were, was threatening to outdo the annual Whale Watch Weekend and Kites and Crab Fest combined. "That might be cool."

It had been an age since Sax had kissed any woman. Let alone a current Miss Shelter Bay, who'd been crowned during a Whale Watch Weekend he'd had to miss. Given that he'd been tied up. *Literally.*

Just happy to be along for her evening walk, the Irish wolfhound mix he'd named Velcro answered with an enthusiastic bark that startled a heron that had been wading along the tide line, causing the bird to disappear into the fog with a flurry of wide blue wings.

The home he'd grown up in — located over Bon Temps, his parents' sprawling Ca-

13

jun restaurant and dance hall — had taken a hit two years ago by a vicious winter ice storm. Two months later, it was given a knockout blow when hurricane-force winds triggered by a Pacific typhoon came barreling through. Which was when Maureen and Lucien Douchett had thrown in the towel and retired.

Sort of.

Currently they were running a bait shop on the harbor and seemed content with how things had turned out. Mostly, Sax thought, because they were so content with each other. They were also proud. And stubborn. It had taken every ounce of Sax's considerable powers of persuasion to talk them into accepting the money to build a new house in town.

Meanwhile, when Sax had returned home, his grandparents moved in with his parents, giving him the keys to their house overlooking the sea, which had become too large for them to keep up. Although he was still toying with the idea, the thought of rebuilding Bon Temps was growing more and more appealing. A lot of people in Shelter Bay could use the work. Along with the opportunity to eat themselves a good meal, kick up their heels, and have some fun, which seemed in short supply these days.

In the distance, lightning flashed, turning the whitecapped water shimmering neon green. Although she didn't seem afraid of storms, the dog suddenly took off like a shot down the beach, her strident barks being ripped away by the wind.

Velcro appeared to have made it her responsibility to rid the coast of the ubiquitous gulls.

"Good luck with that," Sax said as he climbed the stone steps to the top of the cliff.

He'd just reached the house when she came racing back with what appeared to be a bleached-out piece of driftwood in her mouth.

She dropped it at his feet and began wiggling her fuzzy black butt — her canine way of letting him know it was time to play fetch. Having nothing vital to do at the moment, Sax bent to pick it up.

Since she hadn't exactly gotten the idea of "fetch" down yet, she took off running again with her prize.

Finally, when she realized he wasn't going to chase after her, she returned, dropped it beneath a nearby tree. Then barked an invitation.

After retrieving a flashlight from the house, Sax sauntered over.

Then paused.

"Hell," he muttered.

He'd left the Navy and returned to Shelter Bay determined to put death behind him. Only to have feckless fate — and a clingy, ninety-five-pound mutt — deposit a human bone at his feet.

# 2

"It was a murder most foul," the crime victim insisted for the umpteenth time since Kara Conway, Shelter Bay's sheriff, had arrived at her home.

"That's from Sherlock Holmes, right?" Kara's deputy asked.

"No." The elderly woman shook a head covered in foam rollers that matched her Pepto-Bismol pink chenille bathrobe. "Really, John O'Roarke, if you'd paid more attention to my lectures in your senior-year English class you'd recognize the description as being written by none other than the Bard himself. It's from *Hamlet.* Where the ghost, musing over his own death, states, 'Murder most foul as in the best it is. But this most foul, strange and unnatural.'

"And murdering my poor, innocent mailbox," she said on a burst of annoyance, "for the second time in a month is definitely strange and unnatural."

They all looked down at the mailbox in question, bathed in the glow of the security lights the woman had set up around her house. It had been beheaded, knocked off its post with what Kara would guess had been a baseball bat.

Stifling a sigh, Kara reminded herself that she'd moved back home from southern California to take over her father's job in order to provide a safer environment for her eight-year-old son. A small town where roots went deep into the sandy soil, where everyone knew your name, where people looked out for one another, and children could play in the town park without anxious helicopter parents feeling the need to hover protectively over them.

And where a crime spree consisted of misdemeanor offenses such as barking dogs, jaywalking, and the occasional brawl at the Cracked Crab, the local watering hole favored by hardworking, hard-drinking fishermen.

And, apparently, mailbox bashing.

*Be careful what you wish for.*

Before John had called to let her know that Edna Lawton was demanding to have the sheriff herself check out the crime scene, Kara had finished dinner, overseen her son's homework assignment and been looking forward to a long soak in a bubble bath with a feel-good romance novel where, unlike real life, despite various trials and tribulations, characters and readers were guaranteed a happy ending.

"See those tire tracks?" Edna pointed a gnarled finger at the tread marks that had been left in the mud at the side of the road. "You'll need to take a casting of those right away. While they're still fresh. Then run a DMV computer check on all the vehicles in the county and you'll find the culprit. Then bring the criminals to justice."

"It doesn't exactly work that way." Kara reached down deep for patience.

The woman tossed up her chin. "I've seen it on *CSI*. And *Law and Order*."

"What Sheriff Conway's saying," her deputy broke in before Kara could point out that the television shows were, in fact, fiction, "is that our crime scene techs are currently working with the feds on an important joint task force up in Salem."

*Feds? Crime scene techs?* Since when did her department of three deputies and two dispatchers have any crime scene techs? And what could those imaginary techs possibly be doing in the state capital?

"But it doesn't look like it's going to rain tonight." He deftly cut off any comment

19

Kara might be planning to make.

Studiously ignoring her questioning look, John O'Roarke rocked back on the wedged heels of his cowboy boots and glanced up at the star-studded sky.

"So, Sheriff Conway will send a tech out first thing in the morning to take the casting. Won't you, Sheriff?" he asked.

"I guess," Kara said. And was immediately hit by a razor-sharp look that reminded her of stories of how the elderly woman had once run her classroom with an iron hand. "Sure." She tacked more enthusiasm onto her tone. "Absolutely."

"Well, I'm glad to see you're taking this seriously," the older woman said.

"I always take crime seriously," Kara said. It was the unvarnished truth.

"Your father was a good man," Edna volunteered suddenly. The curlers bobbed as she shook her head with regret. "It was a crying shame, what happened to him, getting shot that way."

"Yes." Her father's too-early death in what had been ruled a hunting accident — eighteen months after Kara had been widowed — still hurt. She suspected it always would.

"A terrible tragedy." Edna looked a long way up at O'Roarke. "You never found the shooter."

"No, ma'am." Kara knew this was a sore point with the man who'd not only been her father's deputy, but his best friend for nearly three decades. The two had gone hunting together in the fall, fishing together in the spring and summer, and argued about sports year-round, although the one thing they could both agree on was that the best place to spend a Friday night was at a Shelter Bay Dolphins high school football game.

"But you're not going to close the case?" Edna pressed.

"No, ma'am." His deep, cigarette-roughened voice was firm with resolve, but Kara knew they were both thinking the same thing: that unless the hunter who'd mistaken her father for a deer came forward, all they had was a spent shell — the same kind sold in gun stores, sporting-goods stores, and even Walmart — all over the country.

"Good." Edna aimed her flashlight down at the flower bed overflowing with pink and purple petunias that surrounded the mailbox post. "That beer bottle wasn't there when I brought my mail in this afternoon. Do you know what that means?"

Not having realized when she'd gotten the call to come out here that she'd be facing a pop quiz, Kara said, "It could have been thrown out of the car by whoever bashed your mailbox?"

"Murdered it," Edna corrected briskly. "Thing's a goner. You should take it in. The bottle, not the mailbox. Get DNA off it. Throw the little miscreant in the slammer."

"That's a good idea," John O'Roarke jumped in again. "Would you happen to have a pair of gloves we could use to pick it up? Wouldn't want to destroy trace evidence."

"As a stroke of luck, I just bought myself a new pair of Rubbermaids while doing my marketing today. So we won't have to worry about contaminating the evidence with any dish detergent residue." Turning on a bunny-slipper-clad foot, she marched back to her weathered gray house.

"DNA tests?" Kara asked with an arched brow once they were alone. "Tire tread print castings? What did I miss while I was home working on long division problems with Trey? Did Shelter Bay's sheriff's department suddenly win the lottery? Which is the only way we'd have enough bucks to buy all that equipment."

"Doesn't take any equipment or all that much time to have Lonnie come over here in the morning and lay down some plaster

22

of Paris," John said with a shrug of his wide shoulders.

Although her deputy was in his sixties, his body was as lean and rangy as back in the day when he'd worked on trawlers. His deeply tanned face was lined, but in a comfortable, lived-in way that made people immediately trust him. Another thing he'd had in common with her father.

"As for the DNA, my niece Sydney — that'd be my brother Webb's middle girl — comes in once a week to tidy up for Edna. She says the old lady TiVos every damn one of those crime shows."

"Which explains why she's constantly calling the sheriff's office," Kara guessed.

"Could be. Though mostly I think she's lonely. But whatever, since she considers herself a criminality expert, it shouldn't be that hard to blame any delay in results on the state police crime lab's being a little busy with major crimes and port terrorism stuff these days."

They watched as Edna came back out of the house, moving with exceptional purpose and vigor for a woman who had to be pushing ninety.

"You're a good man, Deputy O'Roarke," Kara said.

Another shrug that told her he was uncomfortable with personal compliments. "Our job is to protect and serve the community. Way I figure it, serving's just what we're doing out here tonight."

"Here are the gloves," Edna announced. "Right out of the package. And I brought you a Ziploc bag to put the evidence in."

"That was good thinking, Miz Lawton." He struggled to shove his large hands into the bright yellow rubber gloves. "Lonnie will be bringing you out a new box in the morning. Once he gets done taking that plaster casting of the tire tracks, he'll put it up for you."

"I do appreciate that, John," she said. Taking no heed of the formality of the badge he wore on his khaki shirt, she reached up and patted his cheek. "You always were a good boy. Even if you did skip school the first day of deer hunting season every year."

"I always had a note," he claimed, sounding genuinely surprised.

"Which you forged your mother's handwriting to," she countered.

The chuckle rumbled from deep in his chest as he didn't even attempt to deny the accusation.

As he bagged the empty brown beer bottle, Kara's cell phone trilled. The caller ID display read her office.

24

"Conway," she answered.

"Sheriff." The young night dispatcher's voice sounded excited. "Someone just called in a possible crime."

"Well, we *are* the law."

"But this is a *real* crime." Yes, that was definitely excitement causing the tremor in Ashley Melson's voice. "You know about Sax Douchett coming back home, right?"

"I believe I heard something about that."

It would've been difficult not to, since the entire town was abuzz with celebration plans for their local military hero. Knowing and liking his parents, and having a personal reason to be grateful to his brother, Kara hoped the town's most infamous bad boy hadn't fallen back into old habits.

"Well, he's gone and gotten himself a dog. Some oversize mutt he supposedly bought from bikers up in Portland."

Hanging out with bikers wasn't exactly hero behavior. Then again, maybe they weren't the Hell's Angels type, but some regular guys who just happened to ride bikes. Or maybe even the Rolling Thunder group, who showed up at vets' funerals all around the country.

"The dog dug up a bone down on the beach below Douchett's house." There was a long, dramatic pause. Then her voice

25

dropped to a near whisper. "A *human* bone."

Despite having assured herself that she'd happily left the fast lane of police work behind in the rearview mirror of her patrol car, Kara experienced a little zing of excitement at Ashley's breathless announcement.

"I'm leaving now," she said. "Meanwhile, tell Douchett, along with whoever else might be out there with him, to stay put and not move around the area. And tell him to lock the dog in the house."

If, by any chance, it *was* an actual crime scene, Kara didn't need civilians screwing it up.

After saying good night to Edna, who'd been openly eavesdropping on the one-sided call, Kara left John to wrap things up.

Then, after calling her mother, with whom she and Trey lived, and letting her know she'd been delayed, Kara headed her black-and-white Crown Vic cruiser out of Shelter Bay toward the coast. And the cliff house that held so many bittersweet memories.

# 3

Sax was sitting out in a rocking chair on the porch, staying put, as he'd been instructed by the dispatcher — who'd sounded as if she should've been home playing with Barbie dolls rather than answering the phone — when he saw the headlights cutting through the dark.

"Looks like we've got ourselves some company," he told the dog whose collar he was holding on to. Not that she needed that much restraining, since she was pressed against his leg.

Velcro barked in happy agreement.

"Let's see how enthusiastic you are when you're locked inside and have to miss all the fun." He took a pull on the bottle of beer, then pushed to his feet. "Let's go."

The mutt, always eager to please her benefactor, raced inside.

Feeling like a traitor, Sax shut the door behind her, then ambled down the steps toward the gravel driveway.

Having expected John O'Roarke, he was momentarily surprised to see the long female leg come out of the driver's side of the car. The leg, currently covered in a really ugly pair of khaki trousers, was followed by a girl he remembered well.

No. No longer a girl, he considered as Kara Conway strode toward the house. During the decade since he'd last seen her, along with ditching those glasses that had given her the look of a studious owl, she'd shed her gangly teenage frame for a woman's slender curves.

Her hair, which she'd once worn to the middle of her back, was pulled shorter, accentuating her long neck.

*Sweet.*

Her face, like her body, was fuller than it had been back when she was in high school, but her cheekbones could still cut crystal, and as she entered the circle of light created by the porch lamp, the yellow glow caught sparks in almond-shaped eyes nearly the same deep, burnished reddish gold of her hair.

Damn. Until Jared's death, Sax had almost managed to put Kara Blanchard Conway out of his memory. Even on the rare occasions he'd think of her, he'd assured himself that she was no longer that seventeen-year-old girl who'd kissed him silly the night of the prom. She'd been married a long time. Had a kid. Spent the intervening years as a cop, and although he knew those doughnut stories were a cliché, lots of cops seemed to get butt spread riding around in a patrol car all day.

Not this one.

"If I'd known an old bone would get me a visit from a beautiful woman, I'd have started digging up the beach a long time ago," he said in his best bad-boy drawl. Which would probably piss her off. Which would undoubtedly be a good thing. Because getting mixed up with any woman right now wasn't in the cards. Getting mixed up with *this* woman would be a mistake of major proportions.

She paused for just a heartbeat, obviously surprised by such a personal opening gambit. Hell, he'd surprised himself. Then again, as he'd discovered that long-ago night, not only had Kara always had him acting in ways he'd sure as hell never planned, but she was also an enticing surprise wrapped in an enigma.

He'd never been able to figure her out. Which, he admitted as she squared shoulders clad in a shirt every bit as unattractive as her pants, had been part of her appeal.

"I sincerely doubt you have any problem getting women to visit." Her tone was as dry as the Iraqi sandbox where he'd spent way too much time.

The same sandbox where her high school sweetheart husband had survived two tours, only to join the police department and get himself shot to death by a hotheaded wife beater back home.

"Maybe I'm choosy."

Because he was male, and to please himself, he took a slow, masculine appraisal: from the top of her head down to those unbelievably ugly black cop shoes. Then back up again.

And really found himself really wishing she'd gotten doughnut-dumpy.

"I'm five-six," she told him briskly. "One hundred and twenty-five pounds. Hair red. Eyes brown. No distinguishing scars or tattoos. Just in case you were wondering."

"Your eyes — which, by the way, are fabulous now that they're not covered up with those Coke-bottle glasses you wore back in the day, are more amber than brown," he corrected. "Though they *do* have an intriguing little rim of mahogany around the iris. And being sidetracked by those way-sexy gold flecks in them, I hadn't gotten to thinking about tattoos yet.

"Though it's an intriguing possibility," he allowed. "You're looking well, Kara." Even if it was downright strange seeing that nine-millimeter strapped on the hip of his graduating class's valedictorian. Then again, there was definitely something to be said for a woman who carried her own handcuffs on her belt.

"Thanks. But brown's brown and flowery descriptions don't fit in those narrow little driver's license boxes." His compliment didn't exactly appear to have her heart going all pitter-pat as she subjected him to the same judicial study he'd given her. "You're not looking so bad yourself, Douchett. And now that we've both passed muster, how about you show me your bone?"

The unintended double entendre hung in the air between them. Deciding it was too easy — and too dangerous — Sax didn't pick up on it.

"It's not mine," he said. "But you're welcome to it." He pointed toward the tree. "It's over there."

As they walked over to it, Sax got a whiff of that glossy hair. Her scent reminded him of something fresh and pure. Like an ocean breeze. Or his grandmother's sheets hanging out on the line in the sun.

Reminding himself how much their lives had changed since the last time they'd spent the night out here at the beach, he said, "I was damn sorry to hear about Jared. I would've come to the funeral, but —"

"Cole explained you were on some top-secret black-ops SEAL mission. But thanks for the condolences."

Her smile, while not as dazzling as he knew it could be, appeared genuine.

"I appreciated your brother coming down to Oceanside to help bring Jared's body back home."

"Cole's a Marine. Even if he and Jared hadn't had that Semper Fi thing going, no way would he have left that up to you to handle by yourself."

"He's a good guy."

"The best," Sax agreed.

And hadn't everyone in Shelter Bay always said the same thing? Eagle Scout Coleridge Douchett, named after the great Jamaican jazz bassist Coleridge George Emerson Goode, had been a damn tough act to live up to. Which was why Sax had quit trying during middle school and taken out on his own, often rocky path.

By the time the third Douchett son, J.T., named for blues trumpeter Jack Teagarden, had come along, the roles of overachiever and bad boy had already been taken. Which was why, Sax had always believed, J.T. was the most easygoing of the three brothers.

"I was surprised to hear Cole's getting married."

"So they say."

She arched a tawny brow in a way that reminded him of her mother. "Is there a question about that?"

"Nah. As much as he loves Kelli, I just suspect he'd rather face a horde of terrorists armed with AK-47s than put on his dress uniform and jump through all the hoops a wedding seems to require."

"I wouldn't know about hoops. Jared and I eloped to Tijuana, so I guess he got off easy."

Not so easy in the long run, Sax thought. Given that the former Marine turned cop had gotten himself killed responding to a damn domestic dispute.

"How are you doing, Kara?" he asked. "Really?"

They were close enough to the porch light he could see her eyes widen momentarily and guessed she was surprised by such a personal question. Hell, being a guy who'd always been more interested in getting a girl into the backseat of his Camaro than sharing confidences, Sax was surprised himself.

But then again, Kara Conway hadn't been just *any* girl. She'd been the high school sweetheart of his big brother's best friend.

But she'd also been the girl who'd spent an entire night after the spring prom sitting by a fire down on the beach with him. Just talking.

Well, mostly talking. There'd been tears involved, as well. And . . .

Sax wondered if she remembered that hot, impetuous kiss they'd shared. Wondered even more why he should give a damn one way or the other.

She shrugged. "It's been over two years since Jared died."

"I know that. But I was asking about you. Not him."

"I've been through all the appropriate stages of grief. Denial, anger, bargaining, depression, acceptance. So I guess I'm where I'm supposed to be."

Perhaps realizing that she sounded just a little lost at that declaration, she squared those slender shoulders again. Lifted her chin. Met his gaze with a no-nonsense, just-the-facts-ma'am stare he suspected probably worked dandy when she was interrogating criminals.

"I was told that you called me out here because you had evidence of a possible

34

crime. Not to chat about my personal life, which, no offense, Sax, is none of your business."

She sure wasn't the shy bookworm she used to be, who'd pretty much clung to Jared the way Velcro did to him.

Sax figured being a military wife left to fend for herself for months at a time, following her father into law enforcement, losing a husband to violence, and becoming a single mom struggling to make ends meet would make any woman a lot stronger. And as sorry as he was about Jared Conway's death, the intriguing thing was, that edge she'd acquired looked good on her. As good as those curves.

"Jared was my friend, too," he reminded. "Maybe he and I hadn't done the Tom Sawyer–Huck Finn finger-pricking, blood-brother thing, like he and Cole did that summer when they were eleven. But your husband was the guy who taught me how to pitch a curveball. And go in for a layup."

Because the memory of that balmy summer day when Jared and Cole had trounced him on the basketball court tugged yet more emotions he'd rather keep locked in that boiling cauldron inside him, Sax turned his thoughts to another memory.

"He also treated me to my first look at a

naked woman — outside the ones in *National Geographic* — from the *Penthouse* magazine he bought from Jake Woods."

Woods, who'd run the bait shop Sax's parents had bought from Jake's kids after the old man had passed on, had rented out girlie magazines and soft-porn videos to half the high school guys in Shelter Bay. It was probably a good thing he'd keeled over from a heart attack a few years ago, because these days he'd undoubtedly be arrested. Maybe even by the woman standing in front of Sax.

"Jake Woods was a pervert."

Yep. She would've had the porn entrepreneur in handcuffs within days of taking over her dad's job.

"Some might call him that. But others might merely consider him a connoisseur of the female form. If he'd been taking all the boys from Shelter Bay on a field trip to Portland to check out the nude paintings at PAM, he could've well been considered a good citizen."

"There happens to be a big difference between a nude by Cézanne at the Portland Art Museum and pornography."

"Art's subjective," he pointed out. "Though, for the record, the stuff he was renting out probably wouldn't have rated a double X these days."

Then, because they'd gotten offtrack, he decided it was time to change the subject. Not wanting to push her any more about her feelings regarding widowhood, since he really didn't want to give a shit, he pointed his flashlight beam toward the bleached bone he hadn't touched since Velcro had dropped it at his feet.

"Here it is."

"Well." She looked down at it. "I have to agree. That sure looks human to me. You told my dispatcher your dog dug it up?"

"I'm not sure." Speaking of the dog, he could hear Velcro whining on the other side of the door. Too bad the dog couldn't really talk and let him know a few more details. "We were on the beach when she took off like a shot and brought it back up here with her."

Despite the possible seriousness of the topic, Sax almost smiled. "Crazy mutt has a major jones for fetching."

"I appreciate your stopping her from chewing it up."

"No problem. It looks old."

"Yeah. It does." She crouched down to study it closer. "I've got some gloves in the car. I'll take it in and send it to the OSP lab for DNA analysis."

"Isn't there some kind of time limit on DNA?"

"I'm no expert, but when I was on the Oceanside PD, I worked a joint case with the San Diego sheriff's department. The forensics guy the DA brought in to testify had done research on skeletal remains dating back as far as 1000 B.C."

"Well, I'd guess this one's nowhere near that old."

"Hardly. From what I learned, DNA preservation is very dependent on where and how tissue or a sample is stored. Stored cool and/or dry, DNA can last a very long time."

"Which, conversely, means that moisture's going to cause bones to age, so DNA would degrade a lot faster here."

"That'd be my guess. Though I'm certainly no expert on the subject, and again, according to that witness, appearances can be deceiving and don't always predict typing success. Even the best in the business can't look at a sample and know whether it still harbors DNA. So we'll send it in, see if anything pops. I'll also run a check on missing persons, so if we do get a hit the lab can try matching."

He watched her bag and label the evidence with all the care he would have expected from someone who'd always paid attention to detail. But, if he'd given the matter any thought, he would've guessed that Kara would've ended up a doctor, like her mother. Or maybe, given how she'd always been hanging around her dad's sheriff's office, working as a district attorney somewhere.

"I never would've figured you for a cop," he said.

"Like I said, appearances can be deceiving. I never would've guessed you'd end up a hero with a chestful of medals."

"We're only talking two. And one's for getting shot, which any idiot can do. I'm no hero."

She stood up, holding the bag in her left hand. A hand on which, he noticed, she still wore the simple gold wedding band Cole had helped Jared pick out. "Tell that to the town council."

"I tried. They're a little hardheaded."

"Tell me about it. When I came home for Dad's funeral, I sure hadn't intended to end up bagging beer bottles and old bones here in Shelter Bay."

"Beer bottles?"

"There's a chance the miscreants who battered Edna Lawton's mailbox left behind trace evidence she wants sent to the lab."

"Probably be quicker just to ask around."

"Which is exactly what I intend to do. Stuff like that doesn't stay a secret for long. Which you undoubtedly remember."

He rubbed his temple. "Funny. I'm drawing a blank."

They both knew it was a lie. Her own father had picked him up for the same crime one Halloween and kept him overnight in one of the jail's two cells. No charges were ever filed, and the punishment Sax had faced from his parents when he'd arrived home that next morning was probably harsher than anything Sheriff Ben Blanchard could've dished out.

"Selective memory is a handy thing." Her tone was dry, but he thought he detected a touch of humor. "Do me a favor and keep that dog on a leash when you take him —"

"Velcro's a her."

"Velcro?"

"She had a hard start, which has her sticking to me like, well, Velcro. Seemed to fit."

"My dispatcher said you got her from some bikers?"

"There was a little scuffle over turf between the Mongols and the Gypsy Jokers outside a bar in Portland. Shots were fired. Velcro freaked and ran off, dragging a concrete barricade her owner had chained her to behind her. I just happened to be there."

"And took her."

"Liberated her," he corrected, having to raise his voice over the door scratching the dog had added to her whining repertoire at hearing her name.

She smiled at that. A quick, unexpected flash that — oh, hell — hit him like a sucker punch in the solar plexus.

"Yay, you." The smile was gone as quickly as it had appeared. Horizontal lines appeared in her forehead. "You do realize you could have gotten yourself shot."

"They were a little busy trying to beat one another's brains out at the time," he said mildly. "Not that any of them appeared to have that much in the way of gray matter. And from the way the mutt's ribs were sticking out, and all the fleas and ticks using her as their very own happy-hour buffet, I figure whoever owned her didn't much care if she took off with a stranger.

"So I brought her back here, where the vet cleaned her up, gave her shots, and made sure there won't be any pups in case some gentleman dog comes calling."

He didn't mention his hefty contribution to Dr. Charity Tiernan's no-kill shelter. The veterinarian seemed to be on a personal crusade to find every dog and cat in the county a home. It hadn't been easy, but he'd managed to escape her clinic without the box of mewling kittens she'd been trying to push on him to go along with his new dog.

"Trey — that's Jared's and my son — has been after me to get him a dog," Kara revealed. "But we're living with Mom, and she isn't exactly a dog person."

"Bring him over here," he heard himself calling out to her as she moved with purpose toward the black-and-white cop car. "There's plenty of Velcro to share."

She paused long enough to shoot him a look over her shoulder. "Thanks. But I don't take my son along on crime scenes."

*Here's your out. Take it. Do not make this personal.*

"I was talking about some other time." *Shit.* He'd never been that good about taking anyone's advice. Even his own. "Maybe you could bring him by, let him throw a ball to the dog, who'd probably go nuts over having herself a boy to play with, while you and I catch up over a pot of gumbo and a couple of beers. Or wine."

Most women, even brisk professional cops, probably preferred wine. Not that he had any in the house, and, since his home had suddenly turned into a possible crime scene, it sounded like he was going to be stuck here a good part of tomorrow.

Fortunately, Chapman's Harbor Market delivered. Even better, Mary Chapman had always liked him, pinching his cheeks and slipping him sweets from the candy jar she kept on the counter back when he'd been a kid.

"Are you talking about a date?"

It wasn't the most encouraging response he'd ever had from a woman. In fact, she sounded as if he'd suggested they tear off all their clothes and go skinny-dipping with sharks.

"Well, I was thinking along the lines of a meal and conversation. But if you'd prefer to jump a few steps ahead to an actual date —"

"That's not what I was saying." She turned fully toward him, arms folded beneath pert breasts she sure as hell hadn't had back in high school. The badge winked in the light, reminding Sax that Kara wasn't some SEAL groupie looking to pass time, but a law enforcement officer. Along with being a single mom who, from what he could tell, didn't exactly appear to be a merry widow.

She sighed. Dragged a hand through that shiny hair in a gesture he remembered well.

43

"Look, I don't mean to sound unapprecia-
tive of your offering to let my son visit your
dog. But I've got a lot on my plate these
days, so free time's more a fantasy than reality. Besides, thanks to this" — she raised
the bag — "we may find ourselves involved
in a case. So any interpersonal interaction,
no matter how innocent, wouldn't be appropriate."

Because he knew she was as serious as a
heart attack, and also, dammit, probably
right, Sax managed, just barely, to keep the
smile off his face. "Wouldn't want folks
talkin'."

"People always talk. What I wouldn't want
is to risk some defense attorney using any
relationship we might have — past or
present — against me in court."

"Wow." He rocked back on his heels. "And
here I'd thought SEALs were the champs of
thinking through possible outcomes of any
situation."

"You're laughing at me."

"Never." He decided, *What the hell.* "You
were always a pretty girl, Kara, but you've
definitely grown into one fine-looking
woman. And since you brought up fantasies
—"

"Not *that* kind."

"Since you brought them up," he repeated,

44

"a man would have to be dead both between the ears and below the waist not to enjoy himself a few fantasies while looking at you."

He held up a hand when she opened her mouth to argue again. "But when I invited you to dinner, the invitation to your son was absolutely legit. And while I'm being honest here, worrying about losing a hypothetical case because you might have shared a pot of gumbo with someone even remotely connected to that case, especially here in Shelter Bay, where you'd be hard-pressed to find even two degrees of separation between folks, seems a bit of a hard line to take."

He paused. "Unless you're considering me a suspect."

"No." She shook her head. "Of course not. It's just that things are, well, complicated."

"Life's complicated. Which is what keeps it interesting."

"I'm beginning to remember why no girl ever said no to you."

He'd bet his left nut *she* would have, if he'd followed his teenage body's demands back then and asked. Which no way would've happened. And not just because Jared and Cole would've whaled the tar out of him. Because some things a guy, even one with the rep he'd had back then, just didn't do. And poaching another man's

45

woman was up there at the top of the list.

She'd been forbidden fruit.

Which had probably been part of what had made her all the tastier.

"That's an exaggeration," he answered her accusation. Admittedly not by much. Sax had always enjoyed women. Who, fortunately, had always seemed to enjoy him right back. Even better, the ones he tended to hook up with hadn't been into forever-afters any more than he was. "Besides, times change. People change."

"Do you honestly believe that?"

"Sure. Look at me. A guy who was voted most likely to miss his tenth high school class reunion because he'd be in prison is about to be given a big parade down Main Street."

"You were also voted most likely member of our class to be a rock star," she remembered.

"I guess I missed my chance at that when I turned down the Navy's offer to put me in their band."

"Cole told me you'd become a SEAL."

Which didn't sound as if it had surprised her as much as it probably had the rest of the town. "Seemed like a good idea at the time."

A not uncomfortable silence settled over

them. Utilizing a patience that had been drilled into him during BUD/S training, Sax waited her out.

"I'm living with my mother."

"So you said."

"I guess my son inherited some of his father's genes, because he's been after me to let him sign up for a Pop Warner team this coming fall. But neither his grandmother nor I know anything about playing football."

"I was more into baseball, myself. But Jared and Cole used to use me as a tackling dummy, so I learned a few moves I could maybe pass on to him. Enough that at least he'd have some confidence when they start picking teams."

"Jared told you to watch out after me, didn't he?" she asked in that straight-talking way he remembered. The woman had never been one to play coy or beat around the bush. If she was thinking something, she told you. Flat-out. "Back then," she qualified. "After he and Cole left town and joined the Marines."

Not knowing what she'd been told, Sax decided not to lie. "Watching you was no hardship, Kara."

"I suspected it at the time," she said. "And now you feel responsible for watching out for his son."

"You can look at it that way, if that's what'll get you to cross that line you're trying to draw between us in the sand."

Another silence.

"I'll think about it," she said finally as a lonely foghorn sounded somewhere in the night. Then she turned around again and climbed into the cruiser.

Although covering that very fine ass in such an ugly pair of pants was a crime in itself, Sax decided that the scenery around Shelter Bay had definitely improved.

# 4

Dr. Faith Hart Blanchard was waiting up at the kitchen table when Kara slipped into the house from the garage. Despite the late hour, not a blond hair was out of place in her mother's chin-length bob, and her subtly applied makeup looked as fresh as it had when she'd left the house early this morning.

"I thought you might enjoy some tea," her mother said in greeting.

What she'd enjoy was falling into bed and sleeping for the next three days. But Kara forced a smile. "Tea sounds terrific."

"I kept the water hot after you called saying you'd been delayed." Faith took the kettle from the range top and poured it into a blue china teapot.

"I also told you not to wait up."

"A mother worries." She brought the pot and two flowered cups over to the table. Along with cloth napkins and sterling silver

49

spoons Kara knew had been a wedding gift from the Hart side of the family. "Especially when she doesn't know the nature of the emergency call."

"I'm sorry." *Damn.* She should've called once she arrived on the scene. Didn't she know, better than most, how a cop's often routine work could turn deadly? "I didn't have any details when dispatch called. By the time I got out to the Douchett house, I didn't want to risk waking you up to let you know what was happening. In case you had surgery in the morning."

"Well, I don't. And even if I had, I wouldn't have been able to sleep."

The tone was familiar. Kara couldn't count how many times she'd heard it back in high school when she'd tried to sneak into the house after curfew.

"Besides," Faith said, "I've been dying of curiosity about what that Douchett boy's got himself into now."

"He's not a boy anymore, Mama."

During his time away from Shelter Bay, Sax Douchett had definitely turned into a man. Since she hadn't yet made a decision about whether or not to get personally involved with him by taking Trey over to play with the dog she'd yet to see, Kara decided not to share his invitation with her mother.

Nor did she want to even get into the possibility that the town's former bad boy might actually have a date in mind. An idea that proved even more terrifying than facing off against a gang of drug dealers armed with automatic weapons.

She'd started falling in love with Jared when they'd met on the playground when she was eight years old. A childhood friendship had slipped into teenage love as easily as slipping into a warm bath, then deepened as they'd become lovers, then man and wife.

Thinking about it on the drive back from the coast, Kara realized the pitiful fact was, she didn't possess a single dating skill.

"And Sax didn't get himself into anything." She picked up the conversation, ignoring the low hum of nerves. "His dog found a bone that, while it hasn't been tested, definitely appears to be human."

Unlike many women might have, Faith didn't so much as flinch at that news as she poured the tea into the cups. She did, however, wince as Kara stirred in two spoonfuls of sugar. "Do you think someone could have been murdered? Here? In Shelter Bay?"

"It's impossible to say. The bone looked

51

old, though. My bet is that it's probably from someone who drowned. Maybe on a boat that sank."

Taking her cup with her, Kara went over to the counter and took a loaf of bread from the keeper. She'd learned long ago that making her son's lunch before going to bed made for an easier morning.

"I ran into Sherry Archer at the salon this morning," Faith said.

Sherry Archer had been head cheerleader Kara's senior year. She remembered her as having a lot of hair and bonded teeth. After marrying, then divorcing a wealthy mill owner, she'd taken up selling real estate, and, according to her mother, was as generous with her favors now as she'd been when screwing her way through half the football team back in high school.

Which had Kara wondering if Sherry had been waving her pom-poms at Sax. Then she assured herself it was none of her business whom the former SEAL shared his bed with, since, while she was willing to consider some sort of casual friendship solely for Trey's sake, she had no intention of tangling any sheets with the man.

"And?"

"And she pushed one of her fancy, gilt-edged business cards on me. To give to you."

52

"To me? Why on earth would she do that?"

"So she can help you find a new home."

Kara glanced around the kitchen she'd grown up in. "I have a home."

"You're an adult. Maybe you'd have an easier time getting on with your life if you weren't living with your mother."

"Is that you speaking? Or Sherry?"

Her mother frowned without furrowing her forehead, something she'd always somehow managed to do even before anyone had thought to invent Botox. Despite her being fifty-eight years old, her mother's complexion, like everything else about the woman, neared a perfection Kara had years ago given up ever achieving.

"She might have a point," Faith said, dodging the direct question as she lifted the cup to her lips. "Two women in one house isn't always the easiest living environment."

Which was true enough. Especially given that this immaculate house, with its antiques and crystal collection, definitely wasn't kid-friendly. Just last week Kara had watched her mother physically cringe after witnessing a Hot Wheels demolition derby taking place on her waxed-to-a-mirror-sheen living room floor.

"I think the situation is working out well." Again she wondered if this was her mother's

53

way of suggesting she and Trey move out. "At least for now. And I'd say that even if you weren't proving a huge help with Trey."

"I'm his grandmother. And if I weren't here, you'd simply find someone else. Like that nanny you hired in California."

Kara resisted pointing out that while she had been growing up, her own mother had spent more time at the hospital than at home, leaving Kara to the care of their live-in housekeeper.

"But Marguerite wasn't family." Trey's nanny had been a warmhearted, caring immigrant forced to leave her own three children back home in Honduras with relatives while she took care of Kara's son for nine hours a day. Which had always left Kara feeling a little guilty. "And anyone I hired here wouldn't be, either."

Kara spread a thick layer of peanut butter on the bread. If left to her son, the entire food pyramid would consist totally of PB and J. He'd begun eating it every day for lunch, since, unlike in his former school, peanut products weren't banned at Shelter Bay elementary. "Sherry suggested you needed space."

"Sherry's wrong." Grape jelly, which was the only kind Trey would eat these days, went on the other piece of bread. "Besides, this place isn't exactly a cottage." It was, with the exception of the stone-fronted Tudor McMansion Sherry had won in her divorce, the largest house in Shelter Bay. "We've tons of space."

"She also said, in front of half my book club, who were all there getting their roots done for Sax Douchett's welcome-home parade, that you and I are acting as codependents, keeping each other from moving on with our lives."

"She's not only wrong — she's an idiot. What the hell does that mean, anyway?" Kara slapped the pieces of bread together with more force than necessary, leaving fingerprint dents in the surface. "I hate it when people, especially people who have no earthly idea what they're talking about, say that."

"It's not as if I've spent the past six months wearing black crepe and hiding away in my home," Faith agreed briskly as she began brushing bread crumbs off the shiny black granite counter into her palm. "I was back at the hospital the day after your father's funeral. And haven't missed a day of work since then."

Nor shed a tear, from what Kara had been able to tell. And couldn't she identify with that?

"You've always been a pillar of strength," she said now, shaking off the memories of those dark, depressing days when she'd struggled to be strong for the precious son she and her husband had made together. "Which is only one of the things I admire about you."

After dumping the bread crumbs into the garbage disposal and sending them down the drain, Faith glanced back over her shoulder. "You admire me?"

"Of course. Who wouldn't? You're a remarkable woman."

"You were always your daddy's girl." Kara detected what sounded like a surprising hint of hurt in those words. "After all, you *did* choose to follow him into law enforcement. Even taking over his job as sheriff after the accident."

Which was definitely not something that Kara had ever considered doing. But she'd also never foreseen having her husband murdered. Or, twelve months to the day after Jared's death, being nearly killed herself during what should have been a routine traffic stop.

Nor had she expected, when returning to Oregon for her father's funeral, to feel a tug of emotional cords to this place she'd thought she'd broken once she'd become a military wife only weeks after her high school graduation.

Which was why, when the mayor had approached her at the funeral supper and asked her to temporarily fill in until they could find someone to take big Ben Blanchard's job, she'd accepted.

That had been six months ago. And so far, from what she'd seen, no one was out beating the bushes searching for anyone else to take her badge.

"I never planned to go into police work. But with Jared deployed so much, I needed a job, and in the beginning, getting a job as a police dispatcher was not only something I knew how to do, but I could work while Trey was asleep."

Then it had just sort of escalated from there when she'd gotten an opportunity to go to the police academy and graduate to patrol duty.

"And my following in Dad's footsteps doesn't mean I don't admire all you've achieved. But even if I hadn't gotten pregnant with Trey I never would've had the patience to go through college back when I was younger. Let alone med school like you did."

Despite her graduating with honors, all she'd really wanted to do was become Mrs.

Jared Conway. During Jared's final deployment, she'd managed, by cobbling together credits from community college, online courses, plus night school, to earn a degree in criminal justice.

"Besides, I think there's sometimes an easier bond between fathers and daughters and mothers and sons because they're different genders. Jared was always Trey's hero, but in many ways Trey was closer to me."

"Perhaps because your husband chose to spend so many years in the military, playing soldier all over the world instead of stepping up to the plate as the child's father," Faith snapped uncharacteristically.

Then immediately she held up a slender hand that looked as if it belonged more at home on the keys of the ebony grand piano she liked to play in the evenings after work than wielding a scalpel with such skillful precision as a neurosurgeon.

"I'm sorry. That was thoughtless."

"But true. To a point." Kara slipped the sandwich into a Baggie, which she put into Trey's Spider-Man lunch box. "I loved Jared from third grade and never had a single doubt he loved me back. But I also realized, during our first year of marriage, that I'd never be the center of his universe. That the Marines would always be his mistress."

"I don't believe I could have accepted that," Faith surprised her by admitting. Her mother had always appeared to be the most independent woman Kara had ever met. "At least your father was already a Vietnam vet when we met, so I wasn't forced to make that decision."

Kara shrugged. "Every marriage is different. Military marriages are a world unto themselves, but as the saying goes, the only thing tougher than a U.S. Marine is his wife."

It still hurt. Even worse was the all-too-familiar guilt as she recalled their argument the day her husband, who'd survived tours in both Afghanistan and Iraq, died. How could she have foreseen that those angry words she'd thrown at him as he'd left for the police station would be the last he'd ever hear from her?

They'd had their problems. Serious problems Jared had brought back home with him from the war that had escalated, endangering their marriage. The same skills that had made him a warrior — the ability to lock emotions away — had eroded away any sense of intimacy in their marriage.

But, just when Kara had thought she'd reached the end of her rope, he'd left her a voice mail message before going out on patrol that day to assure her that she and their son were the most important, valuable people in his life. And, because he honestly wanted to save their marriage, he said, as soon as his shift was over he was going to call the VA and make an appointment to get some help for the PTSD that had been keeping him from sleeping and making him too edgy.

Unable to believe that they wouldn't have worked things out together, as they'd always done in the past, Kara forced her mind back to happier memories.

"Besides, there's nothing sexier than a guy in uniform," she said. Or out of it, with that ripped warrior's body. "And watching Jared run up and down the beach in those red PT shorts was definitely a perk."

"The first time I saw your father sitting on top of that police horse in his blue uniform during Portland's Waterfront Blues Festival, I fell like the proverbial ton of bricks."

Faith sighed at the memory. Then she turned away, but not before Kara saw her pressing her fingers against her eyes.

How strange that the first thing that she and her mother might have ever had in common would turn out to be widowhood. Especially since the former socialite who'd been born into a family of Philadelphians whose roots harked back to the original Quakers had seemed determined to get through the grieving process in her own stoic Main Line way.

Kara imagined that there must be women somewhere out there who had uncomplicated, easy relationships with their mothers. She was not one of them.

Faith Hart Blanchard had never been one to indulge in mother-daughter confidences. She'd always kept her thoughts to herself and had encouraged Kara to do the same.

"When Jared was killed, I was afraid that if I allowed myself to cry, I'd never be able to stop. Like one of those widows in the tragic myths whose tears filled entire seas." It was something Kara had never admitted to anyone. She decided it was only the lateness of the hour and this odd, unaccustomed near intimacy with her mother that had her saying it out loud now.

"When Jason accidentally slew Cyzicus, after the ruler had welcomed the Argonauts with a banquet, Cyzicus's wife's tears flowed all year round," Faith murmured.

Rather than major in the sciences as an undergraduate, like so many neurosurgeons, her mother had gravitated toward liberal arts. With an emphasis on the classics. Proving herself to be a true Renaissance woman, along with being a practicing surgeon she was also administrator of Shelter Bay Memorial Hospital.

She turned around and met Kara's eyes. "But Cyzicus's widow killed herself from grief."

"That was fiction." Kara wondered if her mother could possibly be considering suicide. She certainly had the medical means, if she were so inclined. But the idea, so alien to the other woman's suck-it-up Yankee nature, was impossible to wrap her mind around. "Real life is more complicated. Besides, we're made of tougher stock, you and I."

"Absolutely."

Her mother shook her head, as if shaking off the uncharacteristically reflective mood. Then she physically stiffened her spine. "I'll finish cleaning up in here. You go on up to bed."

It was more order than suggestion. Since there was no way her cleaning skills could ever live up to her mother's operating room standards, regretting the loss of what might have been a longer moment of intimacy Kara went upstairs, stopping at her son's room.

Moonlight slanted across a narrow mattress crowded with stuffed animals and action-hero figures. Trey had always flopped around like a fish in bed and had, as usual, kicked off his sheets, revealing Batman underpants. One slender arm was flung over his head and his hair — blond, like his father's — gleamed like spun gold in the muted light.

Above the bed, posters of Spider-Man, Wolverine, and the Hulk shared wall space with a Marines recruiting poster; on the table beside the bed was a framed photo of Jared, looking for all the world like a Hollywood superhero himself, so incredibly handsome in his snazzy dress-blue uniform.

Kara pulled the bedding back over his body, and allowed herself the indulgence of brushing her fingers through his hair. He stirred, but didn't wake.

She never went to bed without checking on him. After Jared's death, she'd become obsessive, getting up in the middle of the night just to reassure herself that her son was still safe. Because she'd discovered that even giving your mind and heart and soul to someone wasn't always enough to keep them alive.

She hadn't been the only one whose life had been shattered that day. It had taken weeks for Trey not to believe that whenever she left him to go to work, she — like his father — would not return home. For the first few months, she'd left the house in street clothes, changing into her patrol uniform in the Oceanside police station locker room.

And then making things even worse was her being attacked and nearly killed. Which was when Kara had traded in her patrol car for a desk, hoping that it would ease her young son's troubled mind.

They'd both come a long way, she considered as the eight-year-old mumbled and rolled over onto his stomach, hugging his plush English bulldog, Chesty — named for the Marines mascot — close.

Obviously their lives had been inexorably changed by that man who'd shot Jared, then his wife, before committing suicide by cop in an hours-long standoff. But they were managing better with each passing day. Possessing his father's "never met a stranger" nature, Trey had slipped well into his new school and had even spent the night away on a sleepover last weekend. Which had been a major step for both of them.

Kara brushed her lips against the back of his head, then went across the hall to her own room. After washing her face and brushing her teeth in the adjoining bathroom, she pulled one of the faded gray T-shirts Jared had worn for PT over her head. She might be moving on, but this way of still sleeping with her husband continued to provide some measure of comfort.

It also focused her mind on dreaming about him. Which was proving more and more important as she found it increasingly difficult to picture him during the day.

The police counselor had told her that memories of Jared would begin to fade. It was only natural, an inevitable part of the healing process. At the time, she hadn't believed the idea could be possible.

From the first time she'd met him, on the Shelter Bay Elementary School playground, his essence had infused into every cell in Kara's body until, if asked, she'd never have been able to tell where she left off and he began.

Together they'd made thousands — no, *millions* — of memories together.

Memories that had provided such necessary comfort during all those lonely months — years — he'd been away on deployments.

So how could they be fading?

So much had already been stolen from her. Her husband, her son's father, the life she and Jared had created together, not to mention the marriage she'd been convinced that, despite their troubles, they'd been destined to continue.

And she'd lost everything in a blink of an eye. Or more accurately, with the rapid-fire speed of a nine-millimeter bullet.

And now her memories were being taken away, too?

It wasn't fair, dammit!

"Newsflash," she muttered, as she climbed between the sheets that smelled of the lavender her mother always put in the rinse water. "Life doesn't come with a money-back guarantee that it's going to be fair."

Lying in the same bed she'd slept in as a child, the bed she'd sneaked Jared into the night before he'd left for the Marines, the bed in which she'd conceived their son, Kara drifted into a fitful sleep.

But for the very first time since Jared's murder, the man who visited her dreams was not her husband, but Shelter Bay's very own bad boy turned all-American hero, sexy SEAL Sax Douchett.

# 5

They came to him in the dark of night, with
mud-streaked faces and bullet-riddled,
bloodied bodies. The first time Velcro had
seen his ghosts, she'd gone nuts trying to
decide whether to leap to her rescuer's
defense or cower beneath the bed. Despite
her obvious adoration of her new owner,
fear had won out, and Sax wouldn't have
been surprised if she'd run away, leaving
behind a dog-shaped hole in his outside
wall.

But as soon as she realized that he wasn't
unduly upset, like him she'd grown used to
their visits. In fact, tonight her huge furry
tail thumped a greeting on the hand-pegged
floor.

"So that's her?" Cody — Cowboy —
Montgomery asked in his Western drawl.
"The little gal your big brother's best friend
knocked up?"

"They were going to get married anyway."

Sax rued that day they'd all gotten drunk after surviving BUD/S, when he'd told them about the hometown girl who'd been out of his reach from the get-go. "Her getting pregnant right before Jared left for the Marines just upped the timetable."

"But the jarhead husband isn't in the picture anymore," Jake the Snake — nicknamed for his ability to slither into the smallest of places — pointed out.

Did they know that because they'd somehow run into Jared Conway? Like maybe in some big barracks in the sky? Was heaven, or wherever they'd ended up, like earth, where there was a huge gulf between military and civilians?

*Don't go there. Since you don't want to know anyway.*

Having Velcro dig up that bone, then suddenly having what the nuns would've called "impure thoughts" about Kara Conway had been enough surprises for one damn day.

"He's not in the picture because some shit-for-brains wife beater killed him." It frigging wasn't fair. A guy getting through two tours in the sandbox damn well didn't deserve to get blown away while standing on some front porch in what should've been a safe suburban neighborhood.

"Smart move, making the dinner invitation sound like it was about her kid," Randy — who didn't need a nickname, since his real one had fit him to a T, him being the player of the team — said.

"It *was* about her son," Sax said. Randy's face had been peppered down to bone from the Taliban bad guys shooting bullets into it after they'd killed him, but Sax had no trouble imagining the arched, argumentative black brow. "It was," he insisted. Admittedly with a bit less conviction than he'd intended.

"Maybe you meant that in the beginning," Cowboy allowed. "But by the time that sheriff sashayed back to her black-and-white, you weren't thinking about tossing football passes to her boy."

"More like passes to the boy's mama. Your tongue was dragging so far on the porch floor I'm flat-out amazed you didn't step on it," Jake agreed with Cowboy.

"Better put in a good supply of latex helmets, Sax Man," Randy advised, "because you are so going to get lucky."

"Terrific. That's all I need. Worrying about you characters slinking around my bedroom if things do get serious."

Not that they were going to get serious. He wouldn't let them.

"Who said anything about serious?"

69

Randy challenged. "We're just talking about getting your rocks off."

"And we don't slink," Cowboy complained.

"No. You just show up. Without any damn warning."

"Well, excuuuse me," Jake shot back. "For your information, Sax Man, the afterlife doesn't exactly give a guy superpowers. But maybe if we all put our minds together, we can come up with some way to call you up on your cell phone to let you know we're on our way. Just in case you wanted to make us some milk and cookies."

"Hell with milk. I'd kill for an ice-cold Bud," Cowboy said, suggesting the afterlife also didn't come with alcoholic beverages.

Which, if true, was really the pits.

"Maybe we could try something with nature. Like a rumbling thunder sound," Cowboy continued thoughtfully, as if he were giving the idea serious consideration. "Trouble with that is, you'd probably get us confused with all the storms you get out here on this godforsaken coast."

"I like the coast. The way you always said you liked your mountains," Sax said. "Speaking of which, since you're obviously no fan of the ocean, why don't you consider going to haunt someone back home in Montana?"

"Wyoming," the SEAL corrected, as he always did when Sax purposely got the name of his home state wrong. "And I can't do that. At least, not yet. Not till we accomplish our mission."

Sax still hadn't decided whether he was glad to see the guys or not. He'd missed the missions, and shooting the bull with them, but every time they showed up, memories of that day they'd died, and he'd been wounded and captured, flashed through his mind as if they were playing on a big-screen high-def TV. And guilt slashed at him like a jagged-edged, rusty knife.

"A mission you still haven't bothered to share with me."

"Sorry, dude. It's on a need-to-know basis," Jake said.

"And I don't need to know."

"Got it in one."

Christ, it was like playing *Who Wants to Be a Millionaire* with these guys. Unfortunately, Sax didn't have a phone-a-friend to help him with the answer. "I don't suppose this alleged mission comes with a timetable?"

"That's up to you," Randy said obliquely. "Meanwhile, good luck with the cop chick."

"And don't worry," Jake said. "We can, on occasion, be discreet. You want to do the horizontal get-down boogie with the hot widow, you're not going to have an audience."

"Unless you want one," Randy suggested, the humorous leer in his voice making up for the one missing on his face. "Then we'll bring along some popcorn and sit ourselves down in the front row."

"If you jokers don't mind, I'd like to get some sleep," Sax said. "Because, in case you were too busy staring at Conway's widow's ass to pay attention, in just a few hours I'm going to have cops crawling all over this place."

"Hey, man," Cowboy said. "You only had to ask."

And with that they were gone. Like morning mist over the beach.

Two hours later, the sky outside the window had gone from oh-dark-thirty black to the pearly pink of predawn.

*Hell.*

His ability to sleep eroded by his night visitors, Sax lay on his back and stared up at the ceiling as Velcro's soft snoring provided a rumbling accompaniment to the roar of the tide beating away at the basalt cliff, as it had for aeons.

And strangely, instead of reliving that deadly mission, as he'd always done in the past after the guys had come calling, he found himself wondering what, exactly, Sheriff Kara Conway had been wearing under that shit-ugly khaki uniform.

## 6

"Mom!" The sound of sneakers thudded on the stairs. "I can't find my library book. And if I'm late, sour-faced Mrs. Bernard is going to freak. Again."

"It's not polite to speak insultingly of your teacher," Faith said.

"She's not my teacher. She's the school librarian. And not even the *real* librarian, because she only started substituting when Mrs. Roberts, who was really cool, had to take time off to have her baby.

"Besides, it wasn't an insult, Gram. It's an adjective." He'd been learning parts of speech. "She really does look like she sucks lemons all day. Doesn't she, Mom?"

"What have we discussed about not judging a book by its cover?" Kara asked.

"She's not a book." With total disregard for both his body and his grandmother's furniture, Trey Conway threw himself into the heavy scrolled iron chair.

"But the same holds true for people." She placed a bowl of cinnamon-spiced oatmeal topped with granola and a sliced banana along with a glass of milk in front of her son. "That's exactly how prejudices get started."

"I know." He blew out a long-suffering sigh, then frowned down at the breakfast. "Jimmy Brown's mother gives him Froot Loops and Pop-Tarts for breakfast. And they have this entire great big, huge pantry where they keep all their snack foods."

"Sounds as if Mrs. Brown needs a few lessons in nutrition," Faith observed.

"Strawberry Pop-Tarts are the best. I had some the morning after our sleepover."

"Maybe because it was a special occasion," Kara suggested, attempting to placate her physician mother.

"Nah." Despite claiming to prefer more sugary cereal, he dug into the oatmeal. Trey had been born with a huge appetite, causing Jared to claim he had a hollow leg. "Jimmy says he gets good stuff like that all the time."

"Mrs. Brown's family dentist must love her," Faith murmured.

"Different families do things in different ways." Kara poured coffee into a thermal cup to take with her out to the beach. Hav-

75

ing spent a restless night chasing sleep, being troubled by those damn dreams of Sax, she was in desperate need of caffeine. "And in this family we believe that breakfast is the most important meal of the day."

"So when Jimmy stays over tonight, he's gonna have to eat oatmeal?"

"I suppose we could fix something else. Like waffles or pancakes."

"With chocolate syrup and whipped cream? Like Mrs. Brown makes?"

"Might as well eat sugar straight from the box," Faith muttered.

"I suppose that could be arranged," Kara agreed. "If you get an A on your spelling test."

"Spelling's easy," he said with a grin that was missing a tooth. "I can ace that. Can we have pizza, too?"

"What's a sleepover without pizza?" Kara asked, drawing a sigh of resignation from her mother, who'd always been as rigid about nutrition as she was about everything else.

"All right!" He pumped a small fist in the air.

"Your library book's on the counter," Faith informed him. "I found it in the den while dusting last night."

Kara wasn't sure, but she would've bet an

entire month's salary that her mother was one of the only people on the planet who dusted and Swiffered before going to bed every night. There probably wasn't a flat surface in the house Dr. Blanchard couldn't perform surgery on.

"Thanks, Gram," he said around a mouthful of banana.

"You're welcome. And don't talk with your mouth full, young man."

That earned an expressive eye roll, but he did finish chewing before he brought up the next topic. "Mom?"

"Yes?" Kara knew that tone. It was one that he pulled out only for the big stuff. One that preceded relentless wheedling.

"Can I take the box to school?"

"May I," Faith said automatically.

As she felt the familiar clenching in her stomach, Kara didn't have to ask which box. One of the suggestions of the family grief counselor the police department had assigned them was that together they choose possessions of Jared's that meant the most to each of them. Those were kept in a box, with the rules being that Trey would not get them out unless they were both together. That way, the counselor had said, Kara could keep in closer touch with her son's feelings of loss and abandonment.

"Oh, honey."

The request had come from left field. She also didn't need it right now. Such a sensitive topic required time. Trey had always been an easy child and she knew he wouldn't ask if it didn't mean a great deal to him. But he was also a typical eight-year-old boy. Which, as the third misplaced library book in a month showed, meant he could be careless.

"I promise I'll take good care of it. And not lose it," he insisted.

Kara resisted, just barely, taking a look at her watch. As sheriff, she felt it was important that she be the first on what could well turn out to be a crime scene. On the other hand — and wasn't there *always* another hand? — her role as mother trumped that of sheriff.

She sat down in the chair across from him. Studied his small, earnest face, which was exactly like looking into Jared's back when her husband had been the same age.

"We made the box for the two of us," she said. "Why would you want to share it with the kids at school?"

"Because some of them don't believe Dad was a hero. So, since today's Take Your Dad to School Day, I wanted to bring his medals. Because it'd be kinda like he was there with me. And they'd prove I'm not making it up."

More than one of the reporters in the news clippings Kara had collected had described the action that had won Jared the Navy Cross and Silver Star for "conspicuous gallantry and intrepidity in action against the enemy."

Only after his death had she learned that when his platoon had been ambushed in Fallujah, he'd charged through enemy gunfire, knocked out one machine gun, disarmed an improvised bomb, and, along with three other brother Marines he'd enlisted in the attack, killed a dozen insurgents in close-range fighting; then, under yet more fire from a second wave of the enemy who were shooting from rooftops all around them, the four men had carried three wounded Marines to safety and recovered two bodies.

Jared, unsurprisingly, had been nonchalant about the medals, refusing to make a big deal of them, stating that everyone there that day should be recognized and he'd merely been doing the job the Marines had trained him to do.

And it was his absolute humility, more than his act of heroism during the firefight, that Kara thought of every time she looked at the medals. And even if Jared had shrugged them off, she knew that Trey would appreciate them even more once he grew up. Which was why she was reluctant to allow him to take them to school.

What if he lost one? The way he had his Hot Wheels Hummer just last week?

Also in the box was a police Medal of Valor, awarded posthumously by the Oceanside PD. Kara knew Jared would have been equally embarrassed by being singled out for that honor.

"Of course you're not making it up." She stalled as her whirling mind scrambled to come up with some sort of compromise. "And I don't recall your mentioning anything about bringing fathers to school." *Damn.* If she'd only known, she would have rounded up a surrogate. Or at least spoken with his teacher beforehand to warn her that Trey might be ultrasensitive today.

Thin shoulders, clad in the gray T-shirt he'd begun to outgrow but would not give up that read MY DAD WEARS COMBAT BOOTS, shrugged. "I didn't want to make you feel bad. It's not like you can bring Dad back just for a stupid school event."

It hurt. And, dammit, although she'd do anything for her son, Trey was unfortunately all too right about this: She couldn't bring

Jared back.

"Why don't I drive Trey to school," Faith suggested, "instead of having him take the bus today? Then we can give the box to his teacher for safekeeping until he can show off his father's medals. Then, depending on our schedules, either you or I can drive him home."

Relief flooded through Kara. "That sounds like a perfect solution." She tousled her son's corn-silk hair. "Why don't you run upstairs and get it?"

"Thanks, Mom!"

"Thank your grandmother."

"Thanks, Gram!" The older woman seemed to freeze as he flung his arms around her waist and gave her a huge hug.

As her eight-year-old son clambered up the stairs after the precious box they'd decorated with Marine Corps emblems, Kara crossed the kitchen and laid her head on her mother's shoulder.

"Thank you," she said.

Kara's father had always been a toucher. Faith Blanchard was not. But in a rare physical display of affection, she stroked the back of Kara's head. "It was the logical solution."

Logical, yes. But it also, for some reason, made Kara's eyes mist up.

"Don't you have surgery this morning?"

"It's an easy day." Faith extracted herself from the light embrace and began bustling around the kitchen again. "Rounds this morning, then what should be a simple TLIF — transforaminal lumbar interbody fusion — at eleven."

"That sounds serious."

"The patient's a crab fisherman with recurrent herniated disks due to the physical nature of his work. I'm merely going to join two vertebral segments together, which will eliminate the movement in those joints. The ideal solution would be if he'd stop fishing, but since he also needs to feed his family, and fishing is not only what he does, but all he knows and wants to do, hopefully this will reduce the pain caused by movement and the associated compression of the nerve roots."

She said it so casually. The same way Kara might talk about writing up a speeding ticket. But with a self-confidence that had always seemed to be bred in her mother's bones.

"Then I have appointments at the office with a few patients whose referrals don't indicate any serious problems," she continued, "so I should be done by three thirty. If you're still stuck out there at Douchett's, my bringing Trey home shouldn't be a problem."

"I appreciate that."

Faith shrugged shoulders elegantly clad in a cream silk blouse. "I'm his grandmother. It goes with the territory."

Then, as if realizing she'd made it sound like a duty, she tacked on, "And, of course, he's an absolute delight. Did I tell you the other day that he said he might want to be a doctor when he grows up?"

"That's great." Of course, last week he'd been determined to be a comic book artist. And before that, a superhero who had the power to blow things up with his nuclear glare.

"I'm thinking of buying him one of those toy doctor kits. Not to put any pressure or expectations on him, of course. But if a child shows interest —"

"He'd love it." At the very least he'd probably love using the plastic hypodermic to inject killer poison into the bad guys when playing with his Transformers.

Five minutes later, after Kara had seen her mother and son off on their way to the school, the doorbell rang.

"Damned if I didn't flat run out of coffee," John O'Roarke said when she answered it.

His jeans, Kara noted with a cop's eye for details, had been pressed to a knife-edged crease, which wasn't exactly necessary for digging around in wet sand searching for more body parts. "Thought maybe I might be able to pick up some here before heading out to the beach."

Not mentioned was the fact that he'd passed two minimarts and the Harbor Market, which had recently added a coffee bar, between his house and hers. *Interesting.*

"I'm sorry. Mom cleaned the pot. But if you'd like, I can make more."

"That's okay." His weathered face took on the look of a depressed bloodhound. He glanced past Kara into the house. "So she's left for the hospital already?"

"You just missed her."

"I thought she didn't have early surgery."

Again, Kara found it interesting that he'd know that. "She volunteered to take Trey to school."

"Oh. That's nice."

"Although she said it's a grandmother's job, I thought so, too."

"She sure as hell don't look like anyone's grandmother," he blurted out. Kara watched in amazement as the tips of the older man's ears flamed as scarlet as a boiled rock crab.

"We're in full agreement there. Sorry I

couldn't be of any help. But there's a Union 76 station on the way. I hear you can even get coffee with cinnamon there now."

"Humph." He scraped a hand over the crew cut he'd been wearing as long as Kara had known him. "If things keep going on the way they are, next thing you know, they'll be tearing down the Crab Shack and putting in a damn Starbucks. I just want a cup of plain old black joe."

"Well, I'm sure the gas station still has the regular old-fashioned kind, too," she assured him.

It wasn't like John O'Roarke to complain about anything. He'd always been, along with her father, the most upbeat man she'd ever known.

Then it dawned on her: John had been a guest at dinner enough times over the years that he'd have to know that Faith didn't ever do anything plain. Including her coffee, which was, these days, always an organic free-trade blend done French-roast style.

Using all the detective skills she'd learned while attending the San Diego Regional Law Enforcement Academy, *and* putting together all those markets he'd passed, *plus* his out-of-character frustration, Kara realized that John O'Roarke hadn't come here, mug in hand, for coffee at all.

But to see her mother.
*Interesting.*

# 7

Although Sax wasn't exactly surprised, given that she'd graduated top of her class and was probably the smartest woman he'd ever met, Kara turned out to be damn good at her job.

He *was* surprised to discover that efficiency and focus could be really, really hot.

She was definitely in her element. Within minutes she'd had the beach, along with the steps going down to it, cordoned off and had instructed her deputies, using stakes and string, to establish narrow lanes. Having conducted searches himself, Sax knew it was the best way to search with limited manpower. Such as a SEAL team. Or a small, local police force.

Apparently the state guys — conspicuous in their absence — weren't all that excited about an old bone showing up. If he'd been in their place, Sax probably wouldn't have been, either.

After the searchers, which included volunteers from Shelter Bay's search-and-rescue unit, finished working the lanes, finding nothing, a grid pattern was established and they resumed working the area at right angles to their original lanes.

Sax would've preferred working the lanes himself to standing on his porch observing the action, but he also understood that while she might know he wasn't some sort of crazed killer who'd buried bodies on the beach below his house, she also didn't want to risk having to explain his presence in the event that anything possibly incriminating did turn up.

Which meant that, like most cops, she didn't really trust anyone.

And couldn't he identify with that?

Word spread. The search drew the inevitable lookie-loos. Townspeople and vacationers flocked together like noisy seagulls outside the barricades. The possibility of a crime seemed to trump even whale watching.

As the hours dragged on, deciding that he might as well make himself useful, Sax went into the house, got busy in the kitchen, put together some spicy crab po'boys, and heated up some jambalaya and dirty-rice leftovers.

"That's nice of you," Kara said, as the searchers dug into the food he put out on a wooden table. "Of course, the county will reimburse you for the meal."

"That's not necessary. All it'd do is create more paperwork for you, and I already had the food. If they weren't eating it, I'd just have to toss it out eventually."

"It's illegal for cops to eat for free."

He laughed at that. Maybe he was perverse, but he found her hot even when she got all earnest and official. "Maybe down in the big city, sugar, but you've been gone too long if you don't remember that the line between legal and illegal is a lot more fluid in a small town."

"That doesn't make it right."

She might be hot, but damn if he wasn't beginning to feel as if he was eating lunch with Jiminy Cricket. "Fine." He pulled a stubby pencil out of the pocket of his jeans and scribbled an amount on a paper napkin. "Here's your invoice."

She shook her head. "A dollar doesn't even cover the cost of the paper plates."

"It's Friday."

"I'm well aware of that. But how does which day of the week it is fit into this discussion?"

"Friday is always Chez Douchett's all-you-can-eat discount buffet. Luckily Velcro didn't find that bone on Wednesday, or these guys chowing down on po'boys could be putting a big dent into the town's budget."

Kara shook her head. "Arguing with you is futile, isn't it?"

"You always were a quick study." She'd been the smartest girl in town. But all those book smarts hadn't had her realizing that he'd been carrying a major torch for her most of their senior year.

She glanced over the areas sectioned off with string as she took a bite of her sandwich. "I'm beginning to think that bone really was an anomaly."

"Maybe part of a body that washed down the cliff from some family plot around here." Although the legal burying of bodies on private land had fallen out of favor, the practice — recently dubbed green burial — was gaining in popularity.

"I suppose that's possible." She took another bite. "Did you cook this yourself?"

"Not much to it," he said with a shrug. "Toss some Dungeness into a pot with a couple lemons, garlic, red pepper, and some crab boil, and a few minutes later you got yourself a mess of tasty crab."

"My mother cooks, but nothing like this.

Being a health-freak doctor, she's more into grilled chicken breasts and steamed veggies. I pretty much nuke. This is really, really good."

"Everyone has their skills. For me, growing up over the family business, learnin' to cook was pretty much a rite of passage."

"Jared cooked sometimes. When he was home. On special occasions." She scooped up a forkful of the dirty rice. He'd never before realized how arousing it could be to watch a woman actually enjoying eating. Most of the ones he'd ever gone out with would end up ordering a salad, then pick at it all evening. "He'd have enjoyed this."

Sax was about to tell her that adding the lemon into the jambalaya had been Jared's idea, the last time they'd hung out with Cole in Bon Temps' kitchen before the two best friends had shipped off to boot camp. But he didn't really want to talk about Kara's husband.

"How much longer are you gonna be out here?" he asked instead.

"As long as it takes." She took a napkin and dabbed at the corner of her mouth. When he found the casual gesture achingly sexy, Sax began to understand what a guy felt like when he took his first step into quicksand. "Why?"

91

"I just was wonderin' whether or not to call Dad and ask him to keep the mutt overnight." Knowing that it would be difficult, if not impossible, to keep Velcro in the house while everyone was out on the beach, he'd called his dad at first light and asked him to keep the dog at the bait shop.

"We should be finished soon." Her amber eyes scanned the area. "I sure wish we knew where, exactly, she found the bone, because then we could work outward from there looking for the rest of the skeleton."

"If the body did wash up onto the beach from a wreck, odds are the wildlife have scattered it around."

"Isn't that a lovely thought," she murmured. "But true. The thing is, heads are usually the first to detach from the body. And that's a much larger part of the body for some animal to carry off. So there's still a chance of finding something useful."

"You know your job."

He also knew that fact about bodies, because he'd called Quinn McKade, an old SEAL teammate, first thing this morning. The fellow sniper he'd once spotted for had married himself a former FBI special agent.

Sax had wanted to talk to Cait McKade not because he didn't think Kara would be up to her job. But because he wasn't sure how many details of the case she'd be willing to share. And given that the bone *had* ended up on his property, Sax figured he had a personal stake in finding out where it came from.

"Oceanside PD sent me to a course at the FBI Academy. I picked up a bit of stuff."

"Naturally, you aced the course."

Her eyes smiled, just a bit, at that. "You bet." There was a rumble of thunder out over the ocean. "Storm's coming," she said. "Which is all we need." She stood up, tossed her cleaned-off plate and napkin into the wastebasket he'd brought outside. "Back to work," she called out to the others.

There were a few grumbles. When they'd all first arrived, everyone had reminded Sax of the mood at an OSU Beaver Nation's Saturday-afternoon football game tailgate party. As the day had worn on without as much as a tooth having been discovered, enthusiasm visibly flagged.

Until ten minutes later, when a fresh-faced deputy who didn't look old enough to have a driver's license came running over to Kara.

"You gotta come, Sheriff," he said, reminding Sax a lot of Velcro. If the deputy had had a tail, it would've been wagging to beat the band.

Ignoring Kara's instructions to stay put, Sax followed them into a shell-strewn cave the tides had carved into the stony cliff.

"Bingo," Kara said as the three of them looked down at what was obviously a human skull.

Having never claimed to be a monk, Sax had known a lot of women over the years. But he'd never met one like Kara Conway, who was looking at that empty-eyed, bleached-out skull with its grimace of broken teeth the way another woman might look at a sparkly diamond bracelet.

Definitely quicksand, he reminded himself as the blaze of light in her eyes hit him directly in the heart, then sent heat flooding downward.

# 8

Although death certainly was never anything to smile about, Kara couldn't suppress the burst of excitement that zinged through her at the young deputy's discovery.

Odds still were that the bones were old, possibly belonging to a victim of one of the many boats that had capsized off the coast. And since there hadn't been any reports of anyone having gone missing from Shelter Bay since she'd arrived in town, if the death was the result of a crime, it would undoubtedly be a very cold case.

But it *was* a case. Not just a bashed-in mailbox or some graffiti sprayed on the bridge crossing from the bay to the coast, but a real case to be solved.

Someone was dead, by either a violent act of nature, natural causes, or someone else's hands. Whichever the results would turn out to be — if they could even determine the cause of death — it was her job to identify the body. To give it a name and hopefully return it to those who'd once cared about him or her.

That was one thing she'd discovered while working the Oceanside streets: Everyone, no matter how low they'd fallen, no matter how alone their existence appeared to be, had at least one other individual, somewhere, who cared that they'd lived. And even for those estranged from their families, no one lived on an island. Lives touched others; relationships were created.

Now the thing to do was to connect the dots and find out whom this skull belonged to, and how he or she had died, so this victim could at least be awarded the dignity in death everyone deserved in life.

One problem with that goal was that when she'd called the state police this morning about the bone find, they hadn't exactly turned cartwheels in glee at being invited down here to help. The fact of the matter was that while the detective she'd spoken with hadn't exactly laughed out loud (though that had definitely been a smirk Kara had detected in his tone), he'd turned her down. Flat.

Which wasn't that surprising. She remembered, long before color-coded terrorism threats and other increases in the usual crimes caused by drugs, poverty, and simple bad behavior, her father complaining about much the same thing.

But Ben Blanchard had handled his problems the same way he'd handled every other difficult thing in his life: He sucked it up and did his job.

Which was precisely what Kara intended to do.

She carefully wrapped the skull, tagged it, and boxed it, trying not to even think about how long it would take for anyone in the state lab — needless to say there were probably high school science labs with more equipment than her department's — to begin an investigation. Especially since the state of the skull and last night's bone pointed toward a cold case. And as the detective told her when she'd called this morning, didn't they have enough active cases to solve?

"It's probably going to be the next century before OSP gets anyone on this," Sax, who'd unsurprisingly ignored her instructions and followed her out here, suggested.

"Try millennium. And although I've never had a reason to check it out, I suspect the state isn't at the top of the list for sending dental records of missing-persons cases into NCIC." The National Crime Information

Center, while not entirely reliable, was still the only nationwide dental database. "What I really need is a forensic reconstructionist."

"I know someone who can help with that."

"You know a reconstructionist?" Anyone who'd ever watched *Bones* knew that having an expert re-create what the person whose skull this was once looked like could be a huge help. Unfortunately, crime fighting wasn't as simple as it was on TV.

"No. But I know someone who undoubtedly does. Cait's a former FBI agent who married an old teammate. They both work for this private agency funded by a guy who just happens to have made himself about a bazillion bucks before the markets went south. And he's more than willing to spend it if the cause is right."

Kara speared him a look, wondering what his angle was. Years as a cop had taught her there was *always* an angle. "I can't imagine my skull would interest him."

Sax shrugged. "Truth be told, it probably wouldn't. But Cait already offered to help when I called her this morning —"

"You called a civilian?" Kara fought for patience. Cops who allowed themselves to lose their cool were cops who lost control. Which was never a good thing. "About a possible crime my department hasn't gone public with yet?"

"I called someone with contacts to just about everyone — at all levels — in law enforcement," he corrected mildly, seeming to ignore her uncharacteristic flash of temper. "Who also can get her hands on way more resources than Shelter Bay's sheriff's department could ever dream of having."

She sensed that work had stopped while everyone began watching them with interest, but kept her gaze on his. "And she would be willing to help me why?"

"Because she likes puzzles, which this is. Also, she likes me."

Was there a female on the planet who wouldn't? Years ago Sax Douchett had been a walking, talking testosterone temptation. The years since had only upped his babe-magnet quotient.

Not that she was personally interested.

But that hadn't kept her from noticing.

"And," he continued, "as it happens, *I'm* interested in you. Which makes her interested in your possible crime treasure hunt."

*There* was the angle she'd been expecting. Kara folded her arms. "That's emotional blackmail. Using my need to solve a crime as a way to get closer to me."

"It's being a good citizen," he countered

in that frustratingly reasonable male tone that triggered a headache. "The way I see it, assisting our local police force is along the same lines as not littering and pickin' up after Velcro when I take her onto the beach. A civic responsibility.

"As for your implying I have an ulterior motive, for the record, Sheriff, I've never had to use coercion to get a woman into bed. And I'm sure as hell not going to begin with you."

"We're not going there," she insisted, wondering which of them she was trying to convince. Sax? Or herself?

She rubbed her throbbing temple as she looked down at the box. Thought about some family out there waiting for a lost loved one. Some family who deserved the right to a proper burial. As this man's brother had helped her do for Jared.

"Call your friend," she said. It wasn't her only choice. But it was the right one. When her tone sounded too sharp and brisk even to her own ears, as if she were channeling her mother, she added more contritely, "And thanks, Douchett. I really do appreciate it."

He shrugged. "No problem."

Was it only yesterday that she'd been finding life boring? Kara asked herself as she walked back to her cruiser.

Which just went to show how much could change in twenty-four hours.

# 9

The light was fading from a sky crisscrossed with birds when Sax finally pulled up in front of his parents' house, parking in the drive between a stand of fir trees and his brother's new vehicle.

As yet more proof Cole had succumbed to estrogen poisoning from all the girlie wedding preparations, he'd traded in his fire-engine red dually diesel pickup truck. And the Escape wasn't just green in color; it was a tree hugger's dream hybrid. Not that Sax had anything against saving the planet, but this shiny new SUV was just screaming for a couple of booster seats.

Sax liked kids. Which was why he'd suggested Kara bring her son over to play around with Velcro. But the idea of his big, tough jarhead bro becoming all domesticated was more than a little scary. Because if Cole could fall, what hope was there for the rest of the single guys out there?

At least it was a Ford. Shelter Bay, like many small towns, tended to be traditional. Which meant that if you didn't want to be ragged until doomsday and beyond, you'd best be buying American. Especially when it came to cars.

Sax's own vehicle was the same '97 anniversary Camaro he'd had in high school. White, with hugger orange SS hood stripes, it had been a Mustang killer in local (and illegal) drag races. His dad had kept it in shape for him during the years he'd been in the Navy, declaring that you didn't let a classic car rust.

Which was true enough, but Sax's mom had clued him in on the most important reason Lucien Douchett had babied the muscle car like it had been one of his own children. Apparently Sax's dad had believed that as long as the car was waiting for Sax to come home from the war, his middle son *would* come home.

Velcro, who'd learned the sound of the Camaro's engine, bounded out of the screen door and came racing toward him, ears flapping, tail wagging. She was followed by Laffitte, the coonhound his parents had adopted from the shelter after their previous Laffitte died of cancer.

When Velcro started barking like a seal

and doing the happy dance in crazed circles, Sax caught hold of the mutt's collar and headed up the steps into the house. The much better-behaved hound followed on their heels.

His parents and brother were in the kitchen, which in every Cajun home was the heart of the house. His father was standing at the stove stirring up a pot of gumbo while his mother chopped peppers.

Wearing an old WHO'S YOUR CRAW-DADDY? T-shirt, Cole was sprawled in a chair at the scarred table that still bore the initials Sax had carved into its wooden top back in middle school.

"Saw that pea-soup green SUV out there," Sax said to his brother as he went over to the stainless-steel refrigerator his mother had fussed about him spending money to upgrade to. But from the way she was always polishing it with a dish towel, Sax knew she took great pride in having something that ordinarily would've been beyond their means. "Still hiding out from your beloved?"

"I'm not hiding out from anyone. And it's not pea-soup green. It's kiwi."

"Maybe it's time we staged an intervention," Sax suggested. "Because the fact that a Marine even knows kiwi's a damn color shows you're in a world of hurt."

He pulled out a bottle of beer, pausing on his way over to the table to nuzzle his mother's neck. "Damn if you don't smell good."

Maureen Douchett laughed and pushed at him. "Only if you like peppers. And don't be trying to sweet-talk your mother, Sax Douchett, because I know you too well for it to work."

"Funny, that's not the first time I've heard something along the same lines today," he said, snatching a pepper and pulling his hand away to pop it into his mouth before he got smacked. "So, where's Gramps and Grandmère?"

"Ever since the tasting day for the wedding cupcakes Kelli decided to have instead of a traditional cake, your grandmother's had a craving for a lemon coconut cupcake," Maureen said. "So they left right before you arrived to get her one."

"Do you think that's a good idea?" His grandmother's memory had faded dramatically since the last time he'd been home.

"It's only three blocks to Take the Cake. With no side streets to confuse her. Plus, it's not as if she's alone. Your grandfather's with her."

"I could've stopped and picked some up

on the way, if you'd called."

"It's a good sign that she's been thinking about something that happened two days ago. Meanwhile, as much as we love having them move in with us, it's also good for them to get out and have some private time together."

It still concerned him. But, deciding his parents knew best how to handle the situation, since they'd been the ones dealing with it, Sax turned toward his brother.

"Now that the cupcake-versus-cake issue appears to have been settled, how are things goin' in matrimony land?"

"Gotta admit the cake tasting was pretty fine. At the moment, Kelli's sister's over at the apartment planning the bachelorette party. I was told to make myself scarce."

"And naturally you followed orders like an obedient jarhead."

"Hey." His mother waved a wooden spoon at him. "No one's allowed to disparage Marines. Especially beneath my roof."

"And especially not some *sailor*." Cole heaped an extra amount of scorn on the word.

"SEAL," Sax corrected. "There's a world of difference." He took a pull on the bottle. "What, exactly, do females do at a bachelorette party? String lots of pink hearts

106

from the ceiling and dance with one another, like back in junior high?"

"It's obvious you've been away from real life too long," Maureen said. "These days women cut loose. In fact, the plan is for a girls' night on the town."

"With Bon Temps still shut down, there isn't much nightlife," Sax pointed out.

"They're not talking about Shelter Bay," Cole volunteered. "They're going into the big city."

"Portland?" Sax decided a girlie buff-and-wax spa day must be on the agenda.

"Well, not Tillamook," his mother supplied. "Of course we're going to Portland. The Chippendales are playing there."

Sax nearly choked on his beer at that announcement. "*You're* going to go to a male strip show?"

"Are you suggesting you've never been to an establishment where *women* took off their clothes?"

"Sure. But I'm a guy. A SEAL. You're a . . . well, hell, a *mom*."

The idea of his mother watching some guys in G-strings grind their pelvises was too much to handle. Even worse was the image of her getting a lap dance from some sweaty guy younger than her own three sons.

"I'm sorry," she said sweetly. Too sweetly.

All the Douchett males had learned to recognize — and fear — that sugary tone, which was, in its own way, a lot like the ominous steam rising from Mount Saint Helens.

"Did you happen to have suffered a head wound no one told us about while you were off fighting terrorism?" she asked.

"Not that I recall. Why?"

She flashed him a dazzling smile that he'd seen bring grown men to their knees. She might be in her fifties, but the sheen hadn't worn off the Maureen O'Hara (for whom she'd been named) charisma back from when she'd been Maureen Alice Duffy, second runner-up to Miss Oregon.

"Because that's the only reason I can think of that would have you coming home expecting to see Mrs. Cleaver in the kitchen. I was singing onstage up until the day you were born," she reminded him.

"Then she was back to singing at Bon Temps five days later." Lucien confirmed the story Sax had heard so many times before.

His grandparents had moved from Louisiana in the fifties, after Hurricane Audrey devastated the shrimping business for a time. Hearing that crab boats in the Pacific Northwest were hiring, they'd packed their few remaining possessions and their only son, Lucien, into an old Ford pickup and moved to Shelter Bay.

Shortly after his parents had gotten married, his mother, having learned Cajun cooking from her mother-in-law, had opened up Bon Temps as a take-out joint in a building about the size of a broom closet. It hadn't taken long for the place to expand and become so successful that by the time Sax was born, Lucien had been able to leave his days of fishing, except for pleasure, behind.

"We kept your cradle in the dressing room," Sax's father said. "Your mother used to nurse you between sets."

Okay. Maybe he was being overly sensitive, but even the mention of his mother's breasts, along with that vision he needed to get out of his head about her maybe getting a lap dance, had Sax's brain on the verge of exploding.

"I was just saying that it might not exactly be appropriate," he mumbled, feeling like he was seven years old, when he'd been called on the carpet for hitting a baseball through the kitchen window.

"And, gracious, if I had a sudden desire for etiquette lessons, the first person I'd turn to would be a Navy SEAL." His mother's lips, darkened to the color of a cardinal's wing, which set off her fair skin and glossy black hair in a way that was not the least bit maternal, smiled. Her green eyes, threatening with that fiery Irish temper that could blow them all out to sea, did not.

"She's got you there," Cole crowed. Then damned he if didn't go over and fist-bump their mother.

"One of these days, when you get yourself a wife of your own, you'll discover that the problem with men insisting on putting women up on pedestals is that they give orders better from up there," Lucien said with wink.

"Sounds like Cole's already whipped," Sax said grumpily. "And if I'd wanted a woman to argue with me, I'd get in my car and drive over to the sheriff's office."

"You always did have a thing for that girl," Maureen said.

"He did not," Cole jumped in before Sax could open his mouth. He shot a hard look at his brother. "Everyone, including you, knew she was Jared's girl."

"The heart often ignores what the head knows," his mother said. "Why else would I have turned down that offer to move to Hollywood to marry your father?"

"You would've been a big star," Lucien

said magnanimously. The way his eyes still gleamed when he gazed at his wife of forty years had Sax thinking that if he ever found a woman who made him feel that way, he might up and marry her on the spot.

"It was a very small offer." She returned his smile, then leaned over and brushed her mouth against his. "More than easy to turn down. While, yours, *cher,* was impossible to resist."

Sax's dad patted her butt. His parents had always been open with their affection, which had embarrassed the hell out of Sax back in high school, when they'd slow-dance down at Bon Temps, twined around each other like snakes. But Sax had grown up a lot since then, and although the idea of the male strippers still irked, he'd also discovered what most Cajuns seemed born knowing: that life could be short and often hard, so you might as well live it to the fullest.

*Laissez les bon temps rouler.*

Let the good times roll. Something he sure as hell hadn't been doing a lot of lately.

"Before things besides the gumbo heat up to boiling in here," Cole said, suggesting his mind was running along the same track as Sax's, "what happened out at the beach? Did they find the rest of a skeleton?"

"Not an entire skeleton. But they did find

111

a skull."

"No!" The knife she'd been using to slice the peppers clattered to the granite countertop as Maureen made a quick sign of the cross. "Not on Douchett property?"

"Fortunately not. It was in a cave on the beach right below the house, though."

"Could've washed up from a storm," Lucien suggested thoughtfully.

"That's a possibility." Sax took another pull on the bottle.

"Any outward signs of murder?" Cole asked.

"If you're talking about an ax blade stuck in the back of the head, no. But the teeth still seemed to be there —"

"We're about to have supper," his mother objected.

"Sorry. Anyway, I told the sheriff that I know someone who might know someone who might be able to help her identify whoever it was."

"I wouldn't have been able to sleep at night if I thought anyone was murdered on family land," Maureen said.

"It looked like it's real old." Sax shrugged. "Bad things happen."

"Not in Shelter Bay," his mother insisted. "Which is why, I recall, Ben Blanchard moved his family here from Portland in the first place."

"Not much crime around here — that's the truth," Sax agreed, even as he remembered the way Kara's eyes had lit up at the sight of that skull.

Being a single mom, she'd probably moved back home from California partly for much the same reason her father had brought his family from Portland so many years ago. To build a safe, boring life for her child. Which Sax could understand, having grown up being able to run free with his brothers without some stranger-danger pervert grabbing them while they were out digging up clams.

But now a mystery had landed in her lap.

And, while he could tell she took her job damn seriously, he also knew that on some level she was jazzed at having herself a possible crime to dig those pearly white teeth into.

What would it take, Sax wondered, to have Kara Blanchard Conway look at him the way she'd been looking at that bleached-out old skull?

# 10

Kara had completed the search just in time. The thunder and lightning that had been threatening out over the water had turned into a storm that brought a hard, driving rain inland.

Fortunately she'd put all the evidence in a plastic tub secured with a padlock; in the event this did turn out to be a murder case, no way did she want some dickhead defense attorney getting the killer off on a chain-of-evidence technicality.

Holding the handles on each side, she dashed through the rain into the one-story building that held a reception area, bullpen (such as it was) for her deputies, her own office, a coffee/lunch/conference room, and two jail cells, which usually served only as free motel rooms for drunks sleeping it off.

Her day dispatcher/receptionist/secretary, who'd seen her coming, opened the glass door, saving her from having to set the box down.

"Got a real duck strangler out there." Maude Dutton was seventy-three years old, round as a berry, with a towering Marge Simpson beehive dyed to a flaming Lucille Ball red. The employee Kara had inherited from her father was also a champ at stating the obvious.

As Kara hung her slicker on the hook by the door, Maude poured her a mug of coffee from the carafe she always diligently kept filled. The one thing all cop shops — big city or small town — had in common was that they ran on caffeine.

Maude studied the box over the top of the half-framed granny glasses she'd been using to work on the computer. "John said you'd finished out at the Douchett place before the storm hit."

"Just barely." Kara took a paper napkin from the stack and wiped her wet face.

"So, the dead guy's head's in there?" Maude was eyeing the box as if Jack the Ripper himself were about to leap out of it.

"Can't tell if it's a male or female. But it is a skull, though not all bloody, like some slasher horror movie. Time and weather have washed it down to a slick, smooth skull."

"Still creepy, if you ask me," Maude stated with an exaggerated shiver. Then she shook her head, sending the dangling painted totem-pole earrings that were a jarring accessory to her khaki uniform — starched so stiff Kara suspected it could probably stand on its own — bouncing. "Never used to get things like that happening in Shelter Bay."

Kara thought she detected just a hint of accusation in the dispatcher's tone. It wasn't the first time Maude had seemed to suggest that Ben Blanchard's replacement had brought big-city problems with her from California.

"Well, if the leg bone and skull turn out to be as old as they appear, this person didn't exactly die yesterday."

She took a sip of the coffee, which was smooth and dark as black silk. The woman might be a trial from time to time, but along with being as efficient as a Swiss clock, she also made one great cup of coffee.

"Your father had begun working some cold-case files before he died," Maude said.

"I didn't know that."

"No reason why you should. Since you weren't working here at the time."

"I didn't even know he *had* any cold cases."

"You solve all your cases down there in

California?" It wasn't the first time she'd made the name of the state south of the Oregon border sound like Gomorrah. Kara suspected it wouldn't be the last.

"No. But it's a different environment. People aren't as connected as they are here."

"Folks still go missing. End up dead on occasion. Like your father."

"He was shot in a hunting accident."

"Still haven't found the shooter, though, have you?"

No. And it wasn't for a lack of trying. God knew she and John O'Roarke had worked overtime to find the person who'd killed her father. But, not wanting to get offtrack by even trying to explain and defend her criminal investigation techniques, she asked, "Dad had missing-persons cases?"

Maude shrugged. "A few."

"Did he keep them separate from his other files?"

"Sure." Her expression, along with her tone, suggested she was talking to the village idiot. "In a cold-case file."

"I've gone all through his files. I didn't see anything labeled 'cold case.' "

"Maybe he took it home. Used to do a lot of work there."

That was true. Some of Kara's fondest memories growing up were of playing in his study while he worked at his desk. Sometimes he'd be writing up reports. Other times he'd be sitting in his worn-out La-Z-Boy, reading up on the latest in crime-fighting methods. Shelter Bay might not be a crime hot spot, but if bad guys ever did come to his town, Sheriff Ben Blanchard would be ready.

After locking the box in the walk-in closet laughingly referred to as an "evidence room," Kara went into her office and placed a call to her mother.

"You know your father," Faith said over the phone. "He never tossed away anything. We'd worked out a deal that he'd keep his study door closed and I'd ignore the fact that his dust bunnies had undoubtedly banded together and created entire armies."

"But everything's gone from his study." Her mother had wasted no time in tackling those dust bunnies immediately after the funeral. By the time Kara had packed up her rented California town house and returned to the coast, Ben Blanchard's study could've appeared in the pages of *Better Homes and Gardens.* "Did you throw all his things out?"

"Of course not. Oh, I was admittedly tempted to. But although we might not have much crime here, I found logbooks dating all the way back to his days in Portland. You never know when some criminal's going to get an appeal accepted and details of the case might be needed in court, so I felt obliged to keep them."

Her mother was not only the tidiest, most organized person Kara had ever known — she was also the most practical. And far-thinking. Which made Kara wonder if her father had ever discussed cases with her. Jared hadn't talked about his work, but that was different — he'd been a Marine deployed in some of the deadliest places in the world, which didn't exactly make for scintillating dinner conversation.

But even back in high school the boy who would become her husband had been one of those strong, silent types, keeping things inside him. Although she'd never doubted for a moment that he loved her and Trey, Jared had never been comfortable expressing feelings.

Which made him the flip side of Sax Douchett, who'd never been reticent about sharing his thoughts.

Which, in turn, had her thinking of him when she should be focused on this case — not on a man whose electric blue eyes could draw and hold hers like a magnet. Despite what she'd told her mother, Sax had always been trouble.

Yet another thing about Shelter Bay that hadn't changed.

Shaking off thoughts she shouldn't be indulging in, she dragged her mind back to the conversation. "So I guess you must have rented a storage locker?"

"No. I didn't have to."

"Why not?"

"Because before I could even get everything boxed up, John came over and offered to take them off my hands."

"John O'Roarke?"

"Of course. He was, after all, Ben's chief deputy. Do you think I'd just hand over a lifetime of your father's work to any stranger who walked in off the street?"

"No." Her earlier headache had returned with a vengeance. After telling her mother she might be late to dinner, Kara hung up.

The shift was changing. Maude was shrugging into the yellow county sheriff department slicker that made her look like an oversize lemon just as Ashley Melson came running in the door, tottering on the high-heeled boots she insisted on wearing instead of proper cop shoes. Because, as the Malibu Barbie look-alike insisted, it wasn't as if her job was to chase criminals down herself.

"Did John log out?" Kara asked Maude.

"Right before you came back from Douchett's," the day dispatcher said, sending the beehive tilting as she vigorously nodded her head. "Said he was going to pick up take-out fried clams at The Fish House, then go home and watch himself a baseball game on that new big-screen TV he overpaid for."

"Thanks."

Kara decided to drop by John's house on her way home. Fortunately, she couldn't see her mother just dumping the files into boxes without first sorting them into proper date order. Which meant, she hoped, that she'd be able to locate the cold-case files before the next decade.

And if there just happened to be some missing persons included in them, knowing her father's penchant for detail — which was one of the things he and her mother had in common — there'd undoubtedly be dental records. Which might at least help her put a name to the skull.

"I told Ashley here about the head." There was a wicked glint in the older women's raven bright eyes. "Not sure as she's gonna be much good tonight, given that she near had herself an attack of the vapors."

"I did not." The young blond dispatcher tossed up a chin that made a perfect point to her heart-shaped face.

"You turned white as bleached driftwood and were on the verge of keeling over."

Kara could count on one hand the times she'd seen Maude enjoying herself. This was one of them.

"I may have gotten a little light-headed for a minute. But that's just from the allergy medicine I'm taking," Ashley insisted. "The pollen out there is just awful this time of year."

All three of women knew the excuse was a lie. But at least it was a small, white one.

Kara would never forget the first time, as a green, wet-behind-the-ears patrol cop, that she'd seen her first body. Coincidentally, it had been a young woman decapitated in a drunk-driving accident.

Kara had grown up with cop stories, but had discovered her first week on the job how many gory details her father had kept from her. It had taken every ounce of willpower she'd possessed not to hurl the Egg McMuffin she'd eaten twenty minutes earlier all over the crime scene.

"It's not what you're probably thinking," Kara said again. "It's just a skull. No hanging flesh, no bloodshot eyes. In fact, it looks a lot like those plastic ones people buy to decorate for Halloween."

"Not me," Maude and Ashley said together. Apparently, the two disparate people had finally found something they agreed on.

"Well, just leave it in the evidence closet and you won't have to worry about it," Kara suggested, slipping into her own slicker. Not that Ashley could get in there anyway, since there was only one key, which, as her father had, she kept on her own key ring.

The driving rain had settled down to a mist, which hopefully meant that her sole night-shift deputy wouldn't be called out to an accident. Last time it'd poured like it had earlier, Marvin Miller had driven off the narrow, twisting cliff road on his way home from his job washing dishes at The Fish House.

Since Marvin lived alone, had a drinking problem, which made him unreliable about showing up for work, and, except for a few barflys down at The Cracked Crab, hadn't been all sociable to begin with, he and his truck hadn't been found until a fisherman had gotten his line tangled up on the radio antenna the next day. Amazingly, while crashing down the cliff the pickup had become wedged between a boulder and a wind-bent cypress tree. When Kara's father had arrived with the fire department rescue squad, Marvin had still been alive. Hung-over as hell. But alive.

"Want me to call John and tell him you're on your way out there before I leave?" Maude asked, apparently not trusting such details to her night replacement.

"No. That's okay."

"You want to surprise him? Makes it sound like you think he's got something to hide."

"Of course I don't. I just know you want to get home in time to watch *Wheel of Fortune.*"

"I do like to see what that Vanna White girl's gonna be wearing," Maude agreed. "I read in the *Star* that she's worn five thousand dresses since she started, with nary a single repeat. Can you imagine the size closet that would take? And do you figure she picks out her own clothes for every show? Or does she have some assistant do it for her?"

"All the TV stars have professional stylists," Ashley piped up. "All they have to do is show up and their clothes are right there in their dressing room waiting for them to put on."

"Must be nice," the woman whose entire wardrobe seemed to consist of her uniform, several pairs of elastic-waist jeans, and boxy bowling shirts said as she left the office.

After making sure Ashley was feeling steady enough to handle whatever calls might come in, Kara left the office as well.

Fog was rising up from the water, creating a white wall that her headlights bounced off of as she drove out to John O'Roarke's house at the edge of town.

She thought about Maude's accusation and decided against the possibility that her chief deputy had purposely hidden police business from her. He had, after all, been her father's best friend. And had been invaluable helping her settle into her new job.

Still, another thing, along with an addiction to coffee, that most cops had in common was that they didn't trust easily. Which made sense, given that it didn't take them long to learn that everyone lied.

But although suspicion ran in her veins, Kara wasn't the least bit suspicious of John.

Yet, as she turned down the gravel driveway, she couldn't help wondering why he'd never mentioned that her father had started digging around in a cold-case file.

And why that file now seemed to be, not in the sheriff's office, where it rightfully belonged, but in the home of Deputy O'Roarke.

Who, dammit, hadn't mentioned its existence.

# 11

"Well," Sax asked his brother, "what do you think?"

"I think you'd better drop by St. Andrews and light a bunch of candles asking for a miracle," Cole said. "Because that's what you're going to need to get this place back to the way it was."

Sax shoved his hands in his back pockets as they both stood in the rain in the pitted parking lot of the dance hall and studied the building, which was definitely the worse for wear.

"It's not that bad."

"It's a wreck. Which is too bad, because although Kelli's willing to settle on the VFW hall, she told me she'd always dreamed of having her reception here."

"The wedding's what? A month away?"

"Three weeks. And two days."

"I'm still having trouble imagining you hitched with a bunch of rugrats."

"You, of all people, should understand how, once a guy's had his life on the line enough times, he tends to think about what's really important. Which would be relationships."

"You can have all the relationships you want without getting married, *cher.*"

"Been there, done that. Enough to know it's not the same."

" 'Forever and ever, amen,' " Sax quoted the country song lyrics, "is a really long time."

"Which is why it's important to find the right person to spend that forever-and-ever time with."

"And Kelli's the right one?"

"You bet."

His brother put so much emotion into those two words, for a moment Sax found himself oddly envious.

"Three weeks would be a push," he said.

"No. Like I said, three weeks would be a frigging miracle."

"It's not like I'm doing a whole lot else at the moment."

The roof had lost some shingles, but fortunately the plywood and tarpaper had stayed on, which had kept the inside from getting totally flooded by coastal rains. The Sheetrock would have to be replaced, Sax decided as they entered the abandoned building. But that would allow him to re-configure the place anyway.

After seeing Ireland from the air on a refueling stop at Shannon Airport on the way to the Middle East, Sax had decided to return to his mother's ancestral country on his own. Which he had, several times, vastly enjoying his visits to local pubs, where he always ended up joining in a *seisiún,* playing the Martin backpacker guitar he'd dragged with him all over the world.

The pubs he'd played in weren't dark and dreary bars designed for customers to get quietly and seriously drunk. They were gathering places for the entire community, including the children, to come together for a spicy gumbo of music, dancing, and *craic,* which was Irish for having a bunch of fun. The same sort of thing Cajuns had always called a *fais do-do.*

One thing he'd brought back from those pub visits was the idea of snugs, small rooms off the main one that seated a few customers and allowed for private parties. And, he'd thought when he'd first seen one, places to put kids to sleep while the adults kept partying, something he remembered happening a lot during the parties held at Bon Temps.

"Seems like a lot more guys are out of work these days," he said as he and his brother got busy measuring the floor space.

Maybe he'd add an Irish music night each month. Or maybe even once a week if it proved popular. There were enough Celtic musicians in the state that he probably wouldn't have any problem finding groups willing to take a gig in one of the most spectacularly scenic locations on the planet.

"It's always been hard here," Cole broke into his thoughts. "Which is why so many folks end up moving away to the cities."

His tone suggested he thought this was something akin to hell. Which made sense, since of the three Douchett brothers, Cole had always been the most rooted to this place. He'd spent his teens working on tourist fishing boats. Like Sax, he'd put his money aside while in the service, allowing him to buy a boat of his own from one of his former employers, who'd escaped the rain to retire in the dry desert heat of Arizona.

"Probably wouldn't be hard to find construction workers," Sax said.

"Put a sign on any corner in town and you'll have a line going around the block an hour later. Especially given that they'd be working with a hero."

"Which I'm not."

"Try telling the town council that. The same council who's all jazzed about this weekend's parade."

"Which I'm only doing for Mom and Dad, dammit."

"I know. I also know how uncomfortable I'd feel if I were in your shoes. But the country — and especially this part of it — needs heroes right now. So, baby bro, looks as if you're elected."

"Lucky me." Sax had no sooner said the words than a chill suddenly came over the place.

They were here.

He tried to remain casual as he glanced around. He couldn't see them lurking in the shadows, but they were damn well inside Bon Temps. And visiting in the daytime, which was a first.

"Do you ever think about those days?" he asked, again with as much casualness as he could muster.

"Which days would that be?" Cole had taken a rag and was rubbing away at some window grime. When clean, the window framed a view of the arched bridge and harbor right off a picture postcard.

Sax rubbed the back of his neck, smoothing the hairs that were standing up. "The war days."

"Sure."

"And?"

"And what?" Cole shrugged. "I *think* of them. Think of some of the stuff I did. Fun stuff. Bad stuff. Stuff I saw. I think about friends who died. Then I thank my lucky stars I made it back home.

"Which is why you can rag me until the devil himself shows up and starts throwing snowballs here in Shelter Bay, but I'm not going to regret, for one single solitary moment, marrying the woman I love."

That was nice. Sappy, but nice. Although they'd had their share of sibling rivalry growing up, they were different enough that Sax couldn't remember ever envying his big brother over anything. Until now.

"Those dead friends. You ever dream about them?"

"I did, in the beginning. But then they, and I, eventually moved on." He shot Sax a sharp look from beneath lowered brows. "You having nightmares?"

"No. Not exactly. Just sorta dreams." Though they resonated with more clarity than any dreams he'd ever experienced before.

He decided that if he mentioned having conversations with his dead battle buddies, which apparently only he and Velcro could see, Cole would drag him into some sort of PTSD counseling. Which Sax thought was a good idea for people who needed it. He just didn't think he was one of those people. Yet.

"Any flashbacks?"

"Not a one." Which was a relief, because the regular type of memories could get tough enough.

"Blackouts?"

"Nope."

"Of course, if you're blacking out, you might not realize it. Being blacked out and all."

"I'd realize it."

"If you say so." Cole rubbed his jaw. "You gotten laid lately?"

"Isn't that a little personal? Even for a brother to ask?"

"Our mama used to give us baths together. We shared a double bed until Dad expanded the upstairs out over the garage when we were in middle school. Suffered chicken pox together and that pregnancy scare your junior year of high school after the condom broke while you were doing the horizontal hustle with Emily Denning in the backseat of your Camaro."

"Nobody ever told me the damn things

got old," Sax muttered.

He'd been carrying the condom around in his pocket since his freshman year, after his mother had set him to doing the wash and he'd found a Trojan shoved deep into the pocket of Cole's jeans. Figuring that if Cole had needed it, he wouldn't have let it get into the wash, Sax had commandeered it. Because a guy just never knew when opportunity might arise.

Which it had, two years later, with less than happy results. But he'd lucked out that time. So had the lushly hot Emily, who, his mother had told him, was now happily married to a crab fisherman, with three kids. None of which — *thank you, Jesus!* — were Sax's.

"Haven't heard of you hooking up with anyone since you got back," Cole said.

"It's only been a few weeks."

"Still, factor in all that time you were deployed, maybe that's your only problem. Guy has sex, he sleeps better. And if he dreams afterward, he's more likely to dream about sex than war."

"Thank you, Dr. Ruth." Though he figured that when it came to having sex on a regular basis, Cole probably knew what he was talking about.

"That little blonde from Take the Cake is

as sweet as the cupcakes she bakes. Maybe you might want to give her a swing."

"Yeah, that'd work. The baker and I hook up, she gets mad at Kelli because I'm the brother-in-law-to-be who doesn't call, and she poisons the cute little wedding cupcakes for revenge. Or puts laxative in them, like we did Mr. Kiley's fudge." That had been more than twenty years ago, and Sax could still remember the look on the guy's face when the stuff hit.

"Kiley deserved it. Damn sadist was definitely born in the wrong time, because he would've been a natural to run a Hitler Youth camp. But how do you know it'd just be a one-night hookup? She's easy on the eyes. And smart. Graduated in accounting from Willamette and used to be a CPA. Kelli says she worked herself up an actual profit-and-loss business plan before she came here from Eugene to open up her bakery."

"Anyone who does that much preplanning to sell cupcakes probably isn't into spontaneous, casual sex."

"Good point. You also have a point about not risking pissing her off, since Kelli would kill both of us if you acted like a butthead and screwed up her big day. But now that I think about it, Kelli's got a cousin who

135

moved down here from Astoria six months ago. A night bartender down at Finn Mc-Cool's. A redhead with a rack out to here." He held up his hands a good two feet from his chest.

"If that's true, I'm amazed the woman can stand upright to pull the pints."

His brother ignored his comment. Which wasn't that unusual. There were times it sucked being the younger of the two. "Though she may be a little below average on the intelligence meter," Cole mused, "seeing as how she actually likes you."

"That does show an intel problem," Sax agreed, "given that she's never *met* me."

"She's seen you around. And she must also have a vision problem, given that, according to Kelli, she apparently likes what she saw."

"I don't need a fix-up from my big brother. I'm also not going to have sex just to get rid of some dreams. Which aren't all that bad in the first place."

*Hell.* Sax was sorry he'd brought the damn subject up.

"Of course you're not having sex because of the dreams," Cole agreed with a wicked grin. "You're going to have sex because it's fun. The dream thing is just a bonus."

"Christ, can we just get back to the

topic?" Sax felt the air, which they always stirred, settle. His ghosts had just left the building. "Which would be fixing up Mom and Dad's Bon Temps."

"Since they're happy as clams spending their semiretirement running their bait shop and making music for free with their friends, that would mean the place would then become yours."

"That's the plan. Unless you want a stake in it."

"Hell, no. In case Mom's right about your having suffered a wartime brain injury you haven't mentioned, you might be able to recall that I'm the only person on both sides of several generations of our family who's tone-deaf."

"Yeah." Sax sneered, beginning to feel at ease again. "I seem to remember something about dogs howling all the way up the coast to Astoria whenever we'd all sing 'Happy Birthday' to Mom."

"Ha, ha. So I guess that means you're sticking around?"

"I guess so." Sax, who'd joined the Navy to see the world, was probably as surprised as his brother at that revelation.

Cole gave him another of those deep, probing looks. The big-brother kind he'd subjected Sax to on more than one occasion growing up.

"You're not hiding out from anything?"

"No." Sax had developed a pretty tough stare himself over the years during the special-ops war on terrorism. He shot it back at his brother. "Are you?"

"Good point." Cole nodded, apparently decided to drop the subject, and glanced around again. "If you're serious about fixing this place up, Kelli's brothers and father would probably help. Being the youngest child, not to mention the only girl, she's pretty much the family princess."

"Okay, so finding workers shouldn't be a problem," Sax said. "But, except for Kelli's family, even if I'd be willing to play the hero card, which I wouldn't, that still wouldn't be enough incentive for folks to work for free."

"Probably not. People here might be bighearted. But they also need to eat."

"So I'll be needing some construction bridge financing," Sax mused. Maybe he should go have a talk with Kelli's wedding baker. Even if the woman wasn't an accountant anymore, maybe she'd be willing to make some extra bucks taking on a freelance business client to help him out with the books. How much money could there be in cupcakes, anyway?

The place needed a new stage. Not like the high dinner club one where his mother had once sung like a lush-throated nightingale; more of a platform raised just a bit above the dancers. But big enough for a piano. After doing some research online, he had his eye on a snazzy black ebony electronic baby grand.

"Unless you wanted to go to the cities, getting financing would mean paying a visit to Gerald Gardner," Cole said.

"Yeah." Sax reminded himself that every adventure had a downside. "Dad said he'd inherited the bank."

"Along with the Ford dealership where I bought that SUV you ragged me about. And just last week he snatched up Genarro's funeral home when Tony got behind in paying off the loan he'd taken out to update the place and pay his wife's heart-bypass medical bills."

"That's our boy Gerald," Sax said. "Mr. Bleeding Heart."

"His father wasn't any better."

Which they both knew firsthand because Old Man Gardner had once nearly foreclosed on this place when their father had fallen behind on a loan he'd taken to buy a new commercial stove he'd needed to meet county restaurant codes.

Sax had been about ten at the time, Cole eleven, and although they'd pitched in their paper route money, Lucien had been forced to take on an extra job framing cottages designed to be rented out to tourists. Working along with him after school and on weekends was how both boys had learned their own construction skills.

"Can't see many people wanting to buy that funeral parlor, given all the stories about its being haunted." He'd never believed those stories. Until the guys had started showing up.

"Two things surely certain are death and taxes," Cole said. "Since it's the only mortuary in town, sooner or later everyone's going to end up being a customer. And it turns out that Gardner's not going to try to sell it."

"He's not going to run the place himself?"

"Nah. He might be a damn bloodsucker, but there's gotta be a learned skill to embalming folks. So, out of the goodness of his stone-cold black heart, he's allowing Tony to stay on and keep burying folks. But now, instead of owning the store, Tony will be working for the bank."

"The Genarro family's been handling funerals in this county for the past four generations. That's gotta sting."

"Imagine so. There was talk of getting up a collection to help, but a lot of folks were still hurting from the storms before the recession hit. Which was what helped give Tony the knockout punch. Not much of a market for fancy, satin-lined mahogany caskets when people are having trouble stretching out their food budgets to the end of the month."

Sax stood in the middle of the abandoned building, slowly turning around. Instead of the boarded-up windows, he saw lights shining through the cleaned windows out into the bay, welcoming people to the new, improved Bon Temps.

Ignoring the spiders the size of his fist that had set up homes in the corners, he saw cozy booths filled with happy families enjoying an inexpensive night out.

He imagined the ceiling rafters, which had become home to two birds' nests, stained a deep, rich ebony.

And rather than the scarred floor still swamped in mud and green gunk, he viewed boots scooting over plank wood polished to a gleaming shine.

"We'll need to completely redo the kitchen." He stated the obvious after opening the oven door and finding a pile of pink insulation and droppings that suggested

141

some mice or rats had set up house.

"What's this *we,* kemo sabe?"

"Kelli's your fiancée," Sax reminded him. "A *princess,* I believe you said. You want her to know you bailed on helping achieve the wedding she's been dreaming of ever since she was a little girl playing with bridal Barbie?"

"You fight dirty."

"You're the one who taught me. So, what do you think? Want to give it a shot?"

When his brother didn't immediately answer, Sax went in for the close.

"Giving your bride-to-be her dream reception would be one hell of a wedding present. A big enough one that you'd probably get really, really lucky on your honeymoon night."

"I'm already lucky," Cole said mildly. He shook his head, as if questioning his sanity to even be considering Sax's offer, as his gaze scanned the wreck of a building that had once been a second home to all three brothers.

Being an empathetic kind of guy, Sax understood why, despite the incentive of making the woman he loved happy, Cole wasn't exactly doing cartwheels to jump on board the Bon Temps bandwagon.

"What the hell," Cole said with a shrug.

"Two guys who survived all those years in the Kush and the Iraq sandbox oughta be able to whip a few spiders."

"Hooyah," Sax said.

# 12

John O'Roarke's small shingled house was located just out of town. While no one would be doing surgery on his floors or countertops, neither was it as messy as her dad's study had been.

Though it was missing the woman's touches she remembered from when his wife had been alive. The flowered curtains looked as if they could use a good vacuuming, and a layer of dust had settled on top of the furniture and picture frames.

"A cold-case file?" He frowned as he scratched his crew cut. "You sure he was working on cold cases?"

"That's what Maude said."

"Guess she'd know. Funny he never told me."

"Maybe he was just looking through them. See if any case looked worth digging into again."

"That could be it. Ben had settled real

well into Shelter Bay, but I always got the feeling that part of him missed being in the middle of the action."

She followed him into a room that boasted a pool table, a large-screen TV, and an old recliner even rattier than her father's had been. Duct tape covered the holes worn into the leather arms. The pool table was currently piled high with boxes.

"You could've brought those to the office," she said.

"Figured if Ben had wanted them there, he'd have kept them there," John said, digging into the first one. "Besides, not like there's a lot of room there, either."

That was true enough. "Mom just could've stored them in the attic."

"She wanted them out of the house." John shrugged. "I was glad to help."

"Protect and serve," Kara said, remembering what he'd said about Edna's mailbox.

"Absolutely. Speaking of which, I found the kids who bashed in the box. They've agreed to apologize in person, then spend four hours over the next month weeding Miz Lawton's garden patch and driving her back and forth to the market every Saturday."

"Is that legal? Being a cop and, essentially, the judge *and* jury?"

"Don't know. Don't really care, since it works. Yeah, in some places you'd probably get parents all riled up and calling their lawyers. But here justice doesn't always have to go through so many layers.

"Your dad's the one who thought it up first, years ago, when Steve Granger, who always used to drive like a bat out of hell, was speeding, took the curve too fast, and drove his Caddy across the lawn and into the Mitchells' house. Ben wrote him a ticket for reckless driving and sentenced him to repairing the damage.

"As Steve worked on fixin' the place up, he got to know the Mitchells personally and came to realize the seriousness of what he'd done. That if he'd smashed through one room over, he would've hit the baby's crib and killed her. That sank in, and neither your father nor I ever caught him speeding again."

"That's a nice story." And so like her father.

"I always thought so. Learned a lot from your old man. All of it good."

"Yet you didn't want to take over his office." She'd worried about that in the beginning. Still did, from time to time.

"Oh, hell, no." He took a cigarette from a hard pack in his shirt pocket, broke it in half, which was his alleged method of cutting back, and lit the end. "Too much responsibility for my taste. I'm a good cop. Good with people, and smart enough to close a bashed-mailbox case."

With the cigarette stuck in his mouth, he went back to digging in the box. "But I'd also rather be fishing than politicking for more funds with the town council, not to mention running for election every four years.

"Plus, I don't have the big-city training you and your dad had, so if, God forbid, a serious crime ever happened here — like maybe that skull belongs to a murder victim — I know I'm not the guy to be in charge."

"I think you underestimate yourself."

"And I think you're too generous." He shook his head. "This is a lot of stuff to go through. Why don't I just work on it tonight and see what I can dig up?"

The offer was tempting. Especially since, between dreams about Sax, and the possibility of a felony having been committed in her town, she'd gotten only about an hour of decent sleep last night.

But, as he'd said, he hadn't had the training she'd had. Including spending four weeks at the FBI Academy. Being a control freak, while she really just wanted to go home and soak in the tub with a novel, she also was afraid that he might overlook something. Something that could prove important.

Besides, if Maude could be believed — and there was no reason not to believe her — her father, who admittedly lacked a toss-away gene, might have found something in one of those files in one of those boxes that had piqued his attention.

"Maybe," John suggested, "your dad was just bored and thought he'd like the challenge of solving an old case. Maybe even one from before he came and took over the office."

"That could be."

Although she'd been here only a few months herself, Kara could understand how her father might have been ambivalent from time to time about his decision to leave Portland.

"That's okay," she said. "It's not like I have anything better to do tonight."

"Pretty woman like you should have a hot date on Friday night." He rubbed his chin. Eyed her thoughtfully. "I've got me a nephew. Maybe you remember him. Danny Sullivan?"

"Played soccer. Then moved to baseball. Third base," she recalled. "Made State, scored the championship run, then was drafted by Baltimore, right?"

"That's him. He made it to Triple-A and his name was being bandied around as being next on a short list to be called up to the big leagues when he got hit in the head by a wild pitch."

"I'm sorry. Is he all right?"

"Oh, he's good enough. Gave him a hell of a concussion." He tapped a long ash into an empty coffee mug on the pool table. "Which might not have been any big deal, except it wasn't his first. Got a couple back when he was playing soccer. So, when his double vision took a long time to go away and he still had some memory loss, the club sent him to a specialist, who said that he couldn't play anymore."

"That must have been a terrible disappointment." Kara remembered him now. Cute, with shaggy brown hair, brown eyes, and dimples. In fact, he'd always reminded her of Donny Osmond.

"It sure wasn't what he'd been hoping for. It also didn't help that his mom — my sister — and dad died in a plane crash over the Cascades about the same time. When he came back home, sorta at loose ends, I had your mom check him out. Just in case the first doctor was wrong."

"And?"

"She said he's suffering from somethin' called postconcussive syndrome, which keeps him from being able to play. He was willing to keep training on his own and hoped to get back, but she said that if he plays and gets hit again, he could die. Which got his attention."

"I'm sorry," she said again, knowing that sounded insufficient. But she also knew that disappointment was a lot better than death.

John shrugged. "So was he. Especially when his wife dumped him for the team's catcher."

"I'm sorry."

"Well, though I don't like to bad-mouth anyone, I can't say I didn't see it coming. I could tell from the get-go that she was a baseball Annie. Once he couldn't play, it was just her nature to go looking for a new guy who could give her the lifestyle playing in the majors could provide.

"Truth be told, I think losing his dream hit Danny harder than losing his wife. Although he was always an easygoin' boy, he sure didn't take that well. Then your mom, who's never been one to beat around the bush —"

"Tell me about it," Kara said.

"Well, she had a come-to-Jesus talk with

150

him and laid it out on the table. He's always been a smart boy, so, although he didn't like it, he saw the light. Now he's teaching history, coaching ball at the high school, and seems to have gotten over the hurt and moved on."

"That's nice."

"Yeah. He's real good with kids."

"Having watched his uncle in action, I'm not at all surprised he'd have excellent people skills."

"He's also got himself a house. It's one of them Craftsman bungalow models that Corvallis developer is building up on Hill Road. Three bedrooms, two baths, a nice front porch with a view of the bay, and a good-size backyard. Room enough for a swing set, when he's ready to start a family."

"Definitely sounds as if he's getting his ducks in a row."

"He sure enough is. Which is why I suggested he might want to ask you out. Maybe start with a crab dinner at The Fish House, then maybe a movie at the Bridge Bijou. See how things go from there."

Kara looked up at her deputy. "John O'Roarke. Are you trying to fix me up?"

Color flushed his already ruddy Irish cheeks. "Danny's a good-looking boy. And a good man. A hard worker who doesn't smoke or drink, and I've never heard him lose his temper once in his life. Did I mention he's also good with kids?"

Left unspoken was the fact that she just happened to have a kid. Who, as she'd just told Sax yesterday, was admittedly in need of a male role model. But still . . .

"A woman could do a lot worse," John suggested slyly. "And I wouldn't want to be telling tales out of school, but he's definitely interested."

The Danny Sullivan she remembered had been hugely popular. And outgoing. "Does he know you're talking to me about him?"

"Hell, no. But I know, since Glory died of the cancer, how lonely life can get. . . .

"Like I said, Danny's a nice man. You're a nice woman. Neither one of you has anything, from what I can see, of a social life. If you're not careful, you're going to end up like me: eating takeout every night in front of the TV, letting life pass you by."

Well, wasn't that an appealing scenario?

"You're a good man." Kara went up on her toes and kissed his cheek. "But I think you ought to give that good-looking, smart nephew of yours more credit. If he's got as much going for him as I remember, he won't have any trouble finding someone on his own."

"Hmph. Gotta be looking to find someone."

"I've heard it said that sometimes the right person comes along when you stop looking."

"Yeah, I heard that, too. And you know what?"

"What?"

"I think it's a damn crock."

She laughed at that.

Although she was more than capable of carrying a few boxes, possessing an old-fashioned chivalry that seemed to have disappeared over the generations, John insisted on carrying the files out to her cruiser.

Which, for some reason, had her thinking about him showing up at her house this morning. Had it only been this morning? It seemed a lifetime ago.

She wondered if he'd been looking for her mother. The way he said Danny Sullivan needed to go looking for a woman. Wondered if her mother had noticed he'd been looking.

Wondered if, just maybe . . .

*No.* If she wasn't willing to accept matchmaking from the man who'd always been like an uncle to her, she wasn't going to interfere with anyone else's life.

Distracted by intriguing thoughts of this

salt-of-the-earth man and her perfectionist, New England–cool mother together, Kara failed to notice the shadowy form intently watching them from a nearby stand of Sitka spruce.

# 13

Kara was on her way home when she got a call from Ashley.

"Kyle got called out on a family fight," she revealed, naming one of Kara's deputies. "Maude told me that I should never let an officer handle one of those alone. So I'm calling you."

"You did the right thing." Didn't Kara know firsthand how deadly such a call could be? "Did the caller sound in immediate danger?"

"No. Mostly she sounded pissed. Uh, angry," the dispatcher corrected. "I did what you and Maude taught me — listened for shouting or things breaking or something, but it sounded quiet on her end."

"Did you ask about weapons in the house?"

"Yes, Sheriff. She said no."

"Okay. Give me the address; I'm headed out there. And tell Kyle not to approach the door until I arrive. Unless it sounds as if someone's in imminent danger."

"Yes, Sheriff."

The address was located in Shelter Bay's only gated community. As soon as she pulled up in front of it, Kara recognized the home as belonging to the town's wealthiest family. Which once might have proven a surprise, but unfortunately, domestic violence didn't limit itself to any specific social class. The rich, she'd discovered, were often just better at keeping the problem under wraps.

Gerald Gardner, car dealer, banker, and local real estate tycoon, opened the front door.

"Kara?" He seemed surprised to see her and Kyle standing there. "What are you doing here?"

"Dispatch received a nine-one-one call," she said. "From this address."

"That's impossible." He shook his head. "Your system must not be working correctly."

"The dispatcher spoke with your wife, Mr. Gardner." As Sax had pointed out, there were very few degrees of separation in Shelter Bay. Having gone to high school with Gerald, and having had him ask her out before he got married last month, Kara thought it seemed a little strange calling him *Mr. Gardner,* yet she wasn't here as a former classmate, but as sheriff. Kara glanced past him into the foyer. "May we come in and speak with her?"

He stood in the doorway, blocking the entry. "I believe she's sleeping."

"Then perhaps you could wake her?" It was not a request, and they both knew it. Kara also knew that legally Gerald could refuse her entrance to his home. But she doubted he'd want to take things that far.

She was right.

"Of course." He stepped aside and waved them into the two-story foyer. The floor was a flow of white marble; oil paintings hung on gold silk–draped walls. "Wait here," he instructed them. "I'll go get her."

"Wow," Kyle said, looking up at a chandelier the size of a Volkswagen that hung from a ceiling painted with a fresco of the historic Shelter Bay Gerald's ancestors had settled. "These are some digs."

"I wouldn't want to be the one who had to clean all those crystals," Kara said.

Margaret Gardner approached dressed in an ice blue silk robe, which backed up Gerald's story about her having at least been getting ready for bed. She was carrying a glass of red wine.

The blotchy red mark on the side of her face suggested she'd been the one to call 911.

"Mrs. Gardner." They'd met just last week, when the woman had headed up a fund-raiser for domestic violence victims. Which now had Kara wondering if her decision to volunteer had been based on personal experience. "As I told your husband, we received a call regarding a situation here at your home."

"That was a mistake." She weaved a bit on the satin-heeled mules that matched the robe. "Gerald and I had an argument."

"May I ask what it was about?" Kara asked carefully.

"Cars," Gerald answered before his wife had a chance to respond.

"Cars?"

"Margaret has her heart set on a BMW convertible as a wedding gift."

"My first car was a BMW," she explained. "Daddy bought it for me for my sixteenth birthday." She shot her husband a sharp look. "He appreciated German craftsmanship."

Gerald flushed at that, making Kara wonder how often he found himself being compared to his wife's father. Who, she remembered, was some über-wealthy stockbroker in Portland.

"I tried to explain how it would be inappropriate for us to drive a vehicle I don't sell," he said. "Especially a foreign one."

"I see." Kara turned back to his wife. "Did this argument become physical?"

"Of course not." Margaret lifted her chin. "Surely you're not suggesting we'd come to blows over something so trivial? Not that there's anything trivial about having a car that fits our status," she couldn't help telling her husband.

"Yet you called nine-one-one," Kara pressed on. "And spoke to my dispatcher."

"Oh, that." She waved the glass, causing a bit of burgundy wine to slosh onto the snowy floor. "That was an unfortunate mistake."

"A mistake?"

"I was angry at Gerald. And I'll admit to perhaps having a bit too much wine. So when he said buying me a foreign car would be professionally embarrassing for him, I decided to show him how real embarrassment would feel."

"The nine-one-one system wasn't created as a vehicle to punish spouses," Kara pointed out, "but to protect."

"I realize that." Margaret's lips turned down in a moue. "And I apologize."

159

"We'll be writing a check for a generous contribution to the department first thing in the morning," Gerald assured her.

"That's not necessary." It irked her that he thought she'd take a bribe. But she kept her expression, and her tone, professionally smooth. "But I do have one more question." She turned back toward his wife. "May I ask how you got that mark on your face?"

"My face?" The woman raised a hand laden with a diamond the size of Alaska to her cheek. "Oh, now, that's truly embarrassing. I'm afraid, as our argument progressed, I had a bit too much to drink. When I decided to go to bed — alone" — she shot Gerald another look — "I stumbled over the cedar trunk at the bottom of our bed and hit my face on the wooden bedpost."

Every instinct Kara possessed told her it was a lie. She'd seen too many cases where wives, for varying reasons, backed up an abusing spouse.

She decided to try again. "You're sure that's what happened."

"Absolutely." Margaret Gardner's eyes widened. "Surely you don't suspect Gerald of striking me?"

"We're here because you called nine-one-one," Kara reminded her yet again. "The mark on your face would suggest that could be a possibility."

"My husband may be unreasonable. But he'd never strike anyone." She shook her expertly streaked ash blond head. "I'm sorry, Sheriff. The call was unfortunate. I've learned my lesson and I honestly apologize for causing you and your deputy to come out here."

There was nothing Kara could do. This time. She truly hoped there wouldn't be another.

"They were playing us, weren't they?" Kyle asked as they walked back out to their cars. "Mrs. Gardner just wanted to get back at her husband."

"It could've gone down like she said," Kara allowed.

"But you don't think so?"

"I honestly don't know."

"But you're going to write it up."

"You bet." The days of cops giving such calls a pass were, she hoped, long over. "So, if Gerald does turn out to be an abusive husband, at least his wife will have a record of this call."

"That sucks if she lied for him."

"One thing you learn in this job," she said, "is that you can't fix everything."

"I know that. But it still sucks."

Kara couldn't disagree.

# 14

"Oh, my God!" Kara put her hand above her eyes, as if blocking out the morning's bright early-June sun. "I think I've just been blinded for life by the dazzle that would be a Navy SEAL in dress whites."

"Very funny," Sax drawled as he sauntered into her office the morning after the discovery of the skull with a sexy, easy-hipped stride that would have any woman with blood still running in her veins wanting to scoop him up with a chip. "And putting on these choker whites I never intended to wear again wasn't exactly my idea."

Kara reached into her top drawer and took out her shades — partly to play along with the blinding metaphor, but also to keep him from seeing the out-and-out lust that had to be flashing in her eyes like the light bar at the top of her patrol car.

"Funny. I have a problem envisioning anyone forcing you to do anything you don't want to."

"It was the parade committee's idea," he muttered, throwing his body into a wooden chair on the visitor's side of the desk. "When I reluctantly agreed to go along with this cockamamie parade, I'd planned to wear my cammies. But then the whole thing escalated into a big deal and the damn committee and, God help me, my mother started pushing for the whites."

"The town wants a hero."

"I'm no hero."

"So you keep saying. But nevertheless, to paraphrase a certain politician, you've got to hold a parade with the hero you've got. Who would be you. So you've got to expect them to go full-out. Besides, during tough times, something like this celebration gives everyone something to smile about."

"Everyone but the guy stuck in the damn convertible waving to the crowd and feeling like a fool." He ran his finger around the high, tight collar, which, perversely, had her wanting to lick his tanned neck. "I even tried to get the guys down at the VFW hall to back me up."

"I take it from your scowl and the fact that you're not wearing cammies — which, by the way, wouldn't be any big deal around here, since just about every male wears them for hunting, fishing, and even mowing the lawn — they backed the parade committee instead."

"Got it in one."

He looked surly and hot. Kara reminded herself that she'd never been attracted to bad boys. But that didn't prevent the flutter behind her sternum.

"You're still the grand marshal," she reminded him. "The reason for the parade in the first place. So I'd imagine that if you decided to show up in a Hawaiian shirt and flip-flops, looking like an escapee from Margaritaville, no one would do anything about it."

"That's probably true enough."

He sighed heavily. Stretched out his long legs while spreading them in a way that drew her eyes to an impressive package she had no business checking out.

"So?" she asked through lips that had gone ridiculously dry. She was about to lick them, then realized, just in time, that he'd undoubtedly take it as a come-on. "If you've already got an excuse not to wear it, why, then, are you decked out in that Harm Rabb JAG uniform?"

"Did you not hear me when I said my mother wanted me to look like the Good Humor man?"

"Oh." The flutter behind her sternum warmed dangerously. "You're making the grand sacrifice for your mom. That's sweet."

He dragged both hands down his face. When she imagined those long, dark fingers cupping her breasts, playing with her nipples — which seemed to have taken on a mind of their own, pressing like pebbles against the front of her uniform — the warmth slid lower, into the pit of Kara's stomach.

"It is what it is," he muttered. Then he sighed heavily in a way that lifted his chest, which bore an impressive display of ribbons and medals.

"You've been busy since you left town," she said. Jared had earned his share of campaign ribbons and medals, but not nearly as many as these.

Sax glanced down at the colorful military fruit salad. "Yeah. I even won best of show." Humor burst like sunshine through the stormy irritation in his eyes.

She laughed, grateful for the change in mood while at the same time unsettled that she found him even more dangerous when he was smiling.

"They say," she said, feeling at ease with him again, in much the same way she had when Jared had essentially handed her over to him for safekeeping, "that a woman can

166

always tell how a man's going to treat his wife by watching how he treats his mother."

A dark brow arched as he looked at her, the intensity in his eyes not just due to their color, but frankly sexual interest. "You thinking about asking me to marry you?"

"Of course not." She felt the color burning in her cheeks. Which was ridiculous. The one thing she'd inherited from her mother was her absolute inability to blush. "It was merely a statement."

Channeling her cool-as-a-cucumber mother, she took off the dark glasses, leaned back in her chair, and crossed her legs. Even though he couldn't see them behind the desk, for some insane reason she was wishing she were wearing something other than these ugly khaki pants.

"So, since apparently you didn't come here this morning to bring me a Fudgsicle, I take it you're here about the discovery on your beach."

"It's a public beach," he reminded her. "But yeah." He reached into a pocket and pulled out a piece of paper. "Cait McKade's interested. And she figured that, rather than talk to me, then have me talk to you, then go back around again, it would be more efficient if you just called her directly. So here's her number."

He leaned forward, invading her space to hand it to her. When she took the paper, their fingers brushed, causing a spark of electricity that had her nearly pulling her hand away.

"Thanks. I really appreciate this." Had he noticed? Or had the reaction been solely on her part?

Sax had noticed. And damned if it hadn't felt like someone had touched a bare, hot wire to his fingers. The way her eyes had widened — just for a brief second, but long enough to give her away — Sax realized she felt it, too.

"No problem," he said. "I hear you're looking at some cold cases."

She angled her chin. Narrowed those expressive eyes. He wouldn't have guessed a cop would allow her feelings to show so easily. Then again, maybe he'd just gotten around her shields.

Sax liked that idea. A lot.

"And where did you hear I was looking into cold cases?"

"This morning, at the Grateful Bread, when I dropped in for breakfast." He shrugged. "It appears our pieces of skeleton are topic one on the gossip line. Even topping speculation that Brad Pitt and Angelina are going to be making themselves a movie here."

"And wouldn't that just make my day. I can't imagine what the security for such an event would involve . . .

"As for the cold case topic, John O'Roarke eats at the Grateful Bread every morning. But he wouldn't have said anything about it."

"When it came up, he neither confirmed nor denied."

"And Maude always brings yogurt from home. So it wasn't likely she'd be there."

"Wasn't this morning."

"So how did the word get out?"

"Then it's true?"

"Not really. Well, I intend to, since it's a logical thing to do, especially since Maude said my father was looking into cold cases before he died and —"

"He was?"

"Apparently. But his records are a mess. I tried wading through the box last night, but Trey was having a Friday-night sleepover, and between the manic, crazy blare of Wii Mario Kart racing and the constant need for refueling the players, who appeared to have developed tapeworms, I didn't get a chance to sort them all out."

She shrugged as she stood up. "Want

some coffee?"

"I wouldn't turn it down."

"Black?"

He nodded. Although she appeared to be a cop through and through, the sway of her hips as she crossed the room revealed a woman beneath that starched uniform. A woman with one hell of a nice ass. "No sugar."

"Besides," Kara said as she poured the coffee into one of the extra mugs, refilled her own, and stirred in two yellow packets, "it's not as if our John or Jane Doe hasn't been dead for a while. Another day probably won't make that much difference."

"Probably won't. Thanks." As he took the coffee she handed him, his eyes skimmed to the gun at her hip. "That's loaded, right?"

"This may be Mayberry on the bay, but I'm not Barney Fife. Of course it's loaded. Why?"

"I was just thinking about your dad. And how he died."

"What does that have to do with . . ." Her voice trailed off as his words sank in. "Surely you're not suggesting his shooting death might not have been an accident?"

"Lots of folks die in accidents," he said. "Lot of blue-on-blue friendly-fire fatalities in war taught me that better than most. And hey, maybe I'm overly paranoid after spending so many years focused on bad guys. But you've got to admit, it is a coincidence."

She put her mug down on her desk, sat down, and rubbed her temples. "If someone did murder my father, odds are it's an entirely different case from the one concerning our skull and bone."

He thought it telling that she'd put ownership on both of them. As if they were kind of an unofficial team. He liked the idea of their being partners. Gave him more opportunity to be with her. Not that he was going to have all that much free time, what with getting Bon Temps ready for Cole and Kelli's reception. But Kara Conway was definitely worth juggling some stuff around for.

"It was probably an accident," he said.

"That's more likely."

He could tell she wanted it to be. And he didn't blame her. He dreaded the day he might pick up the phone to hear that his dad had died. But murder? He wouldn't stop until he had the killer's balls nailed to Shelter Bay's jailhouse door.

"But any chance of a connection between Dad's looking through cold cases and those body parts is still worth pursuing," she said. Her jaw firmed. That cleft in the middle of her chin deepened.

"It's going to take Cait's guy some time to reconstruct that skull. Might as well dig around. See what turns up."

"That's what I'm going to do. While checking all the missing-persons records for the last ten years or so to see if I can find a dental records match."

"I might be able to give you a hand."

"What?"

"You know. Maybe help you sort through the files. It's not as if you have a lot of spare deputies," he pointed out, looking around her office, which was about the size of a broom closet. If she wanted to have a meeting with four other people, one of them would have to sit out in the hallway.

She took a long drink of coffee, then shot him a sharp "don't mess with me" cop look over the chipped rim of the white mug. "I realize it takes a while for the military mind-set to fade, but in case you haven't noticed, you're a civilian these days."

"You could always deputize me."

"I could also poke my eye out with a sharp and flaming stick. Yet, oddly, neither one is high on my must-do list."

She lowered the cup and folded her hands in front of her. He recognized the look. It was the same one her father had given him after he'd wrecked his Camaro drag racing one long, hot summer.

"Besides, you haven't been home for years. Any names in those files probably wouldn't mean a thing to you."

"Names around here never change. Most people stay. Or if they do leave, they generally come back. Like us." Another thing they had in common. If he was keeping score. "Plus," he pointed out, "we didn't exactly run in the same circles back then. I probably know a lot of people your mama wouldn't have wanted you associating with."

"Such as Shelter Bay's purveyor of porn," she muttered.

He flashed her his best grin. "Exactly."

"I heard you're planning to restore Bon Temps. Which, given the condition it's in, is going to take up a lot of your time."

"You heard right," he said. "Cole's fiancée has her heart set on having her reception there, and we're going to do our best to make sure that happens. But SEALs are born to multitask." Since she'd shown up at his house, Sax had also found himself making additional plans. Plans that involved the sexy cop who was looking at him like she might study a police mug shot.

"I'll think about it." She glanced down at her watch. "Meanwhile, I have to get to work. Providing security and traffic control for your parade."

"There's a total of three stoplights in this entire town," he said. "Which doesn't make for a lot of traffic to control. So why don't you ride along?"

"Me? Ride in the parade marshal's car? With you?"

"Well, you could run alongside, like those Secret Service agents do. But you'd probably be more comfortable inside the car."

"I'd also feel like a damn fool." Her eyes widened. "That's it, isn't it? You may have fought terrorism all over the world, you may have battled bad guys, but you're afraid of a simple parade."

*Bull's-eye.* "No." He folded his arms over his chest. "I'm not."

"Then why do you suddenly have that Bambi-in-the-headlights look in your eyes?"

"I'm *not* afraid. I just don't like being the center of attention. If you were in the car, you'd be taking some of the focus away from me."

"The way you look in those Navy whites, Brad Pitt wouldn't stand a chance of getting attention away from you." She stood up. "Don't worry. The entire street's only six blocks. It'll be over before you know it."

"Where have I heard that before?" Realizing there was truly no way out of this gig, Sax reluctantly pushed to his feet as well. "Oh, I know. That's what my SEAL battle buddy Zach Tremayne always used to say about firing squads."

# 15

Damned if it didn't appear that everyone in Shelter Bay had broken away from work and their usual schedules for what had, to Sax's horror, escalated into a daylong celebration.

Although it wasn't yet noon, a festival mood was definitely evident as partygoers, many wearing red, white, and blue, crowded up to tables groaning with local specialties: crab cakes, clam chowder, salmon burgers, scallops, oysters, and hand-cranked marion-berry ice cream. There were also dishes displaying the multiculturalism of the com-munity — Thai, Italian, Chinese, and, of course, representing the Cajuns, his parents' shrimp-and-crab gumbo.

If all that weren't enough, over by the yacht club dock, people waited, paper plates in hand, for the cornmeal-battered prawns and chips Jack Parrish, owner of The Fish House, was deep-frying in two fifty-five-gallon barrels over an open fire.

Booths draped in patriotic banners offered local arts and crafts made in the area — the common themes, he noted, being whales, dolphins, and puffins — and a brass band from the Shelter Bay High School livened things up from the bandstand, where Sax's parents had informed him they'd be performing this evening.

Although he'd been pleased for his mom and dad, he'd damn well not been psyched about having to stick around here until nightfall.

"A firing squad would probably be easier," he muttered to Kara. "And a lot quicker way to go." Since the parade was going to circle the town, beginning and ending at the town square, they'd walked across together from the sheriff's department.

"Sorry. It's such a nice day, I just can't get into the mood to shoot anyone." Kara frowned as they viewed the couple coming toward them. "On the other hand, I could be convinced otherwise."

Sherry Archer apparently was one of those women who, once they found a style that worked for them, stuck with it. Her bleached and teased Linda Evans *Dynasty* do appeared to have been sprayed to a helmet hardness, since it didn't so much as bounce an iota as she sashayed her way toward them on a pair of spindly skyscraper stilettos.

She'd poured her buffed, toned, and spray-tanned body into a stoplight red sundress that hit midthigh. Although he'd never claim to be an expert on women's fashions, especially having spent so many years in a part of the world where females were covered head to toe in body-concealing burkas, Sax suspected rhinestone straps were overkill for the daytime. Despite being made of some sort of stretchy material that clung like a surgical glove, it was so tight he wondered how she could possibly sit down in it. Her lips were the color of a cherry snow cone, her sunglasses as red as her impractical high heels and studded with more rhinestones.

"Well, don't you just look delicious enough to eat up with a spoon," she gushed as she threw her arms around Sax and enveloped him in a cloud of gardenia perfume. Remembering a time when he'd welcomed such displays of affection from the former cheerleader, although his mind wasn't engaged, Sax waited for his body to respond.

Nothing. Nada. Zip.

He glanced over Sherry's bare shoulder in time to see Kara roll her eyes. Winking back, he put his hands on the blonde's waist and, careful not to tip her over, moved her a bit away from him.

"Want some ice cream, little girl?"

She laughed, a bit too long and too loud, then playfully slapped his shoulder. "You are still *such* a bad boy. It's a good thing that Gerald's going to be in that car with us, or I wouldn't trust you not to make untoward advances." Her lacquered hair didn't budge as she tossed her head. "Or myself, either."

The gilded feminine invitation hung in the hot, humid air between them. Once again, Sax wasn't the least bit tempted. Which either had something to do with the fact that Kara was standing there watching him, or maybe Cole was right about its having been too long since he'd gotten laid.

*Damn.* What if that old "use it or lose it" bromide was true? Sax had always figured sex was like riding a bike: that you never really lost the ability, no matter how long it had been since you'd climbed on.

Deciding to think about that later, he focused on what she'd just said.

"You two are going to be in the car?"

"I'm mayor," Gerald Gardner said. He puffed out his chest, clad in what Sax figured was his official blue mayor suit.

"And I just happen to be Shelter Bay's

179

Miss Hospitality." Sherry flashed him a huge white beauty-queen smile that didn't cause a single wrinkle.

It occurred to him that, since she'd been married, it should technically be *Mrs.* Hospitality, but Sax didn't quibble the point.

"You've always been real hospitable," he said instead.

"Why, thank you, darlin'. I do try."

She patted his cheek and simpered like some heroine out of one of those costume movies he'd watched at Troy's Place, a rec center run by volunteers in Baghdad. Normally a romance wouldn't be his usual choice of entertainment, but back then he'd been passing a good time with a sexy brunette soldier who'd been into Jane Austen, and hell, even Chuck Norris blowing bad guys away got old after a while.

"Well." Kara entered the conversation. "I guess I'll get to work."

While he might not have felt anything when Sherry had smashed her paid-for breasts against his chest, Sax did find himself wishing that Sheriff Conway would be the one sitting in that parade vehicle with him.

She'd just turned to leave when a tow-headed boy who — *damn* — was a dead ringer for Jared Conway at that age came racing across the lawn toward them. "Hey, Mom," he shouted. "Look what I won pitching a football through a tire."

He was waving a plush gray whale over his head.

Back in the city, Kara probably would've been expected to remain professional at all times while in uniform. Proving yet again that small-town life was different, she crouched down and hugged him.

"Great job," she said.

"Your dad was one the best quarterbacks who ever played at Shelter Bay High," Sax volunteered. "Guess you got your arm from him."

The boy looked up at Sax. Seemingly unimpressed by the snazzy dress white uniform, he said, "My dad was a hero."

"Absolutely," Sax agreed.

The small chin, which, now that he studied the kid more closely, Sax could see was dented just like his mother's, came up. "If he was here, they'd be having this parade for *him*." Jared's son didn't tack on *and not you,* but it came through loud and clear all the same.

"You've no idea how I wish that were true," Sax said. "Both that he were here and that the parade were for him." And wasn't that the absolute truth? He held out a hand.

"I'm Sax Douchett. I was friends with your dad back in high school."

One small hand continued to clutch the toy whale. The other remained at his side. "He never talked about you."

Tough case. Sax decided that if *his* father had been killed when he was Trey Conway's age, he'd probably have grown up with an even bigger chip on his own shoulder than the one he'd already had.

"Guess he had more important things to talk about," he said easily. "And it was my brother Cole he was best friends with."

"Cole was a Marine. Like my dad."

"And like *our* dad." He winked at Kara. "All the men in my family were Marines, going back to Arcenaux Douchett, who fought with Andy Jackson in the Battle of New Orleans. I turned out to be the black sheep of the family by going into the Navy."

The kid remained unimpressed. Sax reminded himself that he'd been telling people for weeks that he was no hero. Apparently Kara's son was in full agreement.

"We need to get going, Douchett." Gerald shot an impatient glance at the snazzy gold Rolex that, like his hurry-up attitude, was definitely was more suited to some big-city mogul than a guy who'd inherited a small-town bank and car dealership on the Oregon coast.

"Folks seem to be having a good enough time," Sax countered. "I doubt if they'd mind waiting a bit longer." He glanced down at Kara's son. "How would you like to ride along?"

The small freckled brow furrowed. Kara had had freckles when she'd been Trey Conway's age. Sax wondered what had happened to them. Where they'd gone. When he considered checking the rest of her out, his hormones spiked. Which was reassuring. Apparently he wasn't dead yet.

"With you? Like, in the parade?"

"Sure. You can stand in for your father. Seems to me Jared Conway's the one due some serious recognition."

"Soldiers shot guns into the air at his funeral. He was a policeman when he got killed, but the guy from the Marines who came to our house said he'd still earned a military salute."

"Absolutely, it was well deserved. I wish I could've been there, but I was off fighting bad guys at the time."

"My dad fought bad guys in the war, too." The chip on that small, narrow shoulder was still there. But it was starting to splinter. Just a bit.

Trey looked up at Kara. "Mom?"

She, in turn, looked at Sax. Studied him, as if she were looking for the catch.

"If the situation had turned out different, Jared would make the same offer," he said quietly.

"Yes." Her lips curved a bit and her eyes softened at Sax's suggestion. "He undoubtedly would." She reached down and tousled her son's hair. "Have fun."

"Thanks!" His freckled face lit up like a full moon.

"Don't thank me," she said. "Thank Mr. Douchett."

He looked up at Sax, his expression turning serious again. "Thank you, sir."

"My pleasure." Sax put his hand on the shoulder clad in a navy blue T-shirt bearing the image of a snarling bulldog. Above the dog it read, MY DAD'S A U.S. MARINE. Below it: AND HE'S MY HERO.

He was headed toward the car when Kara caught hold of his arm. "Thank you," she said.

"It's no big deal. I meant what I said, Kara. This parade should be for Jared. But I'll do my best to stand in for him."

As he'd promised the man who'd become her husband he'd do when Jared and Cole had left town for boot camp. Something that

184

had proven more difficult than Sax ever could have expected.

## 16

"Nice car," Sax told Gerald as he took in the '59 Ford Fairlane convertible. He'd always believed in giving credit where credit was due, and besides, he was going to need this guy's approval for the loan to repair Bon Temps. "Looks as good as it probably did when the original owner drove it off the showroom floor."

The banker/car dealer/mortuary owner puffed up like a pigeon. "I restored it myself."

"And did a great job, too." The car had been waxed to a mirror sheen.

"Your name should be bigger," Trey said as he observed the small black-and-white WELCOME HOME, SERGEANT DOUCHET signs on the back door. In contrast, huge red-white-and-blue Gardner Ford dealership signs covered both front doors, with a third on the trunk.

"Gerald's got himself something to advertise," Sax said magnanimously. "I don't."

"The dealer banners were already made for other occasions," Gardner said stiffly. "The 'welcome home' signs came that way from the printer."

"And they're just dandy."

Sax decided there was nothing to be gained by pointing out the missing T on his last name. Especially since he suspected it hadn't exactly been an accident. The guy had always resented the fact that although his father may have supplied the uniforms for the Shelter Bay American Legion baseball team, Sax's father, the coach, had him riding the bench most of the season.

As Lucien had told both Gardner and his father, it wasn't personal. The truth was that Gerald couldn't bat worth beans. And worse, in Lucien's opinion, he threw "like a girl."

The Shelter Bay Pipe and Drum Corps led the parade, along with a high-stepping drum major with a tall hat and a trio of pretty high school girls in sparkly outfits tossing their batons up in the air.

Behind the car, uniformed veterans from the Korean, Vietnam, and Gulf wars showed they still possessed the right stuff as they marched in snappy cadence to the loud-speaker blaring Sousa marches from a flatbed truck carrying three surviving Greatest Generation veterans of the Second World War.

People had temporarily abandoned the festivities to line up alongside the road. Those who'd served snapped off salutes as he went by, which was more than a little weird, since, not having served in the officer ranks, Sax wasn't used to being saluted. Others, including the women, stood with hands over their hearts.

Children waved small flags, and people cheered and shouted out his name as the car drove by. Which was weirder than the salutes.

Gardner drove, while Sherry displayed her sweeping windshield-wiper pageant wave from the passenger seat. Not wanting people to think he didn't appreciate their coming out to welcome him back home, although he felt like a damn fool, Sax waved, too.

"My dad got a lot of medals, too," Kara's son said, looking at Sax's jacket display.

"Like you said, he was a hero, your dad. It's only right he was awarded medals for bein' brave."

"I'd rather have my dad than any medals."

"I'd feel the same way. My dad was in Vietnam when I was a boy. I missed him a lot. Worried a lot, too."

"But he came home."

"Yeah."

Silence. Then a long sigh.

Then, "I took them to school. The medals. In the special box that the grief counselor said Mom and I always have to look at together."

Sax suddenly felt as if he'd been dropped into the middle of a conversational minefield. One false move and he could blow everything to kingdom come.

"Did your mom know?" he asked with a great deal more casualness than he was feeling.

"Yeah. She worried about it, but Grandma drove me to school and gave the box to the teacher. Then she picked me up again, so I wouldn't lose them." He rolled his expressive eyes. "Like I'd do a dumb thing like that."

"Good to be careful, though."

"After I did the show-and-tell, my teacher got this idea that we'd all collect stuff for the troops and send a box to Iraq."

"That's a great idea."

"That's what Mom says. . . . She cries sometimes."

Okay. Make that a minefield in a damn pit of quicksand. "Does she?"

"Yeah. She's real quiet, 'cause I think she doesn't want me to know, but I hear her sometimes when I get up to go to the bathroom late at night."

The idea of Jared's wife crying herself to sleep in her pillow took a painful slice at Sax's heart. He rubbed his chest. Which didn't help.

Even if he had a single clue how to talk about something as serious and personal as this, and had known what to say, this sure as hell wasn't the place. So Sax decided to change the subject.

"So," he said as he switched to waving to the other side of the street, "you like whales?"

"They're cool. My dad took me to Sea World when we lived in California. There were killer whales there that did tricks. Which was way cool. But I felt bad about them not being free out in the ocean."

"Captivity's the pits." And didn't Sax know firsthand about that?

"Dad said that they're not named that because they kill people. And that they're not even really whales, but really big dolphins."

"Orcas," Sax said.

"Yeah. But though they got to eat fish and stuff, I still felt sorry for them. They're not

190

like the kind of animals who are supposed to live with people. Like dogs and cats. Dad promised we'd go to the pound and pick out a puppy the weekend after Sea World. Then he got shot." His eyes glistened in a way that ripped a few more pieces off Sax's heart. "I got really mad at him about that."

*Oh, Christ. Do not let me screw this up.*

"I haven't lost my dad. But I did lose friends in the war. And yeah, I think being angry is a pretty natural way to feel."

"That's what the grief counselor said." He hugged the plush whale to his chest, as if it were the puppy he'd been so cruelly cheated out of, and looked at Sax with wide blue eyes. "Do you think my dad knows that I didn't mean to be mad at him?"

"Absolutely." Having enough problems with his own ghosts, Sax couldn't imagine how it would feel being eight years old and being haunted by thoughts of what might have been. "I've got me a dog."

"Really?" Boyish interest seemed to burn away the sadness. "What kind?"

"I'm not sure." Damn, how did Sherry do it? SEALs were tough, but his forearm was starting to cramp from all the stupid waving. Good thing the town was only six blocks long or his hand might fall off his wrist before they got to the end of this dog-

and-pony show.

He changed sides again, switched hands. "I think she may be a cross between a wolfhound and a Hummer. But she sounds just like a seal when she barks. Not a Navy SEAL. The kind with flippers, that eat fish."

The small freckled brow furrowed in a way that was an echo of his mother's. "That's a joke. Right?"

"Wait till you see and hear her. You can decide for yourself."

"We had a lady come talk to us at school. About what it's like to be a veterinarian."

"That'd be Dr. Tiernan."

"Yeah. She runs a shelter, too. For dogs and cats who don't have homes. I wanted to go check it out, but Mom says that with her and Grandma working all the time, it wouldn't be fair to the animal."

He could hear Kara's crisp, no-nonsense, "mother knows best" tone in those words. For all that she'd always claimed to be the polar opposite of her mother, the two women had far more in common than he suspected either one realized.

"She's probably right about that. Moms are usually pretty much on the mark about most things. But there's enough of Velcro to share."

More brow furrowing. Small front teeth

— with a gap where one had fallen out — worried his bottom lip.

Then, "You call her Velcro 'cause she sticks to you, right?"

"Got it in one. You're one smart kid. Maybe you can help me train her. So far all she knows how to do is fetch. Though she doesn't always bring whatever I throw back. But she is a champion eater and sleeper."

"I don't know if Mom would let me."

"Your mom and I are old friends. Leave it to me and I think we can talk her into it."

"Cool!" Beaming again, he pumped a fist into the air. Then, as the loudspeaker began blasting out a deafening "Stars and Stripes Forever," Kara's son finally got into the spirit of the day and began waving wildly to the crowd.

Experiencing the same rush of cooling relief he might if he'd just escaped a potentially deadly firefight, Sax let out a long breath, pasted a returning hero's smile on his face, and reminded himself that as bad as this was, at least he'd made it home alive and in one piece.

Unlike his ghosts.

And Jared Conway.

## 17

Danny Sullivan, John's nephew, still resembled Donny Osmond. He had the same shaggy hair that flopped over his forehead, puppy-dog eyes, and dimples that creased his cheeks when he smiled.

Which he did, easily and often, as he left the booth where he'd been dutifully selling myrtle-wood sea animals, birds, and lighthouses carved by his uncle to join Kara and Faith.

"Dandy day," Danny greeted them both with his Osmond grin. "And, Kara, you did a super job keeping things under control."

"Thanks. But Shelter Bay's not exactly *Homicide: Life on the Street.* The worst problem John and I had to deal with was Ron Bonham and Jim Flynn getting into that fistfight. Which still wasn't very exciting, given that they'd been hitting the beer keg a few too many times and couldn't even manage to stand up."

"Uncle John said he took them in to sleep it off."

"For a while. He's going to let them out tonight after the fireworks, so long as their wives agree to drive them home."

"If I were Ron, after knocking over that dessert table, I'd be more afraid of my wife than I would you or John."

"Since Pamela's state-fair-blue-ribbon-winning blackberry heather pie ended upside down on the grass, I wouldn't want to be in the car for that family discussion," Kara agreed.

"So what were they arguing about?"

"They were a bit incoherent, but according to witnesses, they were in disagreement over the best Civil War game ever." The annual rivalry between the Oregon State and University of Oregon football teams dated back to 1894 and was one of the most anticipated aspects of the season. Every true fan had an opinion as to which trumped them all. One thing everyone could agree on was that there was no neutral ground in this Civil War — the Beavers' black and orange or the Ducks' green and yellow were the only available choices. Neither color option, to Kara's mind, flattered any woman forced to wear them on game day.

"Ron, being an Oregon fan, insisted it was

the 2008 game," she revealed.

"The Fog Bowl," Danny said. "Even the TV cameras couldn't follow the ball toward the end of the game. But the Ducks pulled it out."

"Apparently so. Jim, on the other hand, having gone to Oregon State, insisted it was 1962."

"OSU's punter booted a spiral that accidentally hit a Duck's leg and bounced into the arms of a Beaver. Quarterback Terry Baker threw a thirteen-yard pass, giving the Beavs the victory and a trip to the Liberty Bowl in Philadelphia. Got himself a Heisman trophy in the bargain."

"What is it about men that they can't remember to pick up bread at the grocery store, but they can remember every minute detail of a mere football game?"

"The Civil War is not a mere football game. It's a religion in these parts. And besides, I'm a history teacher." Dimples flashed appealingly. Unfortunately, they didn't strike a single chord with Kara. "We like looking back. In fact, I was remembering just this morning that dress you wore to the senior prom. You were sure a picture."

"It was a nightmare of purple tulle." Kara still couldn't decide what she'd been thinking, deciding to go with a vintage fifties look. The color had complemented her red-brown hair, but all those layers of ruffles had been a fright.

"I thought it was real pretty. Feminine . . . You know, I was thinking —"

"Hey, Mom!"

Saved by her son.

Kara's mind was scrambling to come up with some way to turn down whatever invitation John's nephew was about to offer, when Trey came running toward Kara, the grin on his face as wide as a slice of the moon that had begun to rise on the horizon. She tried to recall the last time she'd seen him so carefree and happy and came up blank.

He was also soaking wet. "What happened to you?"

"Nothing. But guess what?"

"What?"

"Sax said I could help him train Velcro."

"Mr. Douchett told you about his dog?"

"Yeah. But he told me to call him Sax. So, can I?"

"We'll see."

The moon grin disintegrated like coastal fog burned away by a summer sun. Small shoulders slumped. He was the picture of exaggerated eight-year-old dejection.

"Whenever you say that, it always means no."

"Not always," Faith, who'd joined the celebration after her early shift at the hospital, said. "Sometimes parents just have to take a little time to weigh matters."

He muttered something beneath his breath.

"Excuse me?" Kara asked.

"Nothin'."

She was tempted to look down and see if her cop oxfords had suddenly morphed into black boots with long, pointy toes. Because watching the pleasure drain from her son's face, Kara felt like the Wicked Witch of the West. *And your little dog, Toto, too.*

"I said I'd take it under consideration," she reminded him. "And you still haven't told me what happened."

"To your clothes," Faith supplied when Kara's question was met with a blank look.

"You're soaking wet," Kara said.

"Oh, that." He looked down at the drenched Marine bulldog shirt. "Me and Sax were having a water-blaster war. And I won!"

"Good for you. And it's 'Sax and I,' " Kara corrected absently.

She glanced around and, sure enough, saw Sax headed toward them, his oversize dog bounding along beside him.

Her first thought, when she viewed the water blasters he was carrying in each hand, was that she didn't want Trey playing war. G.I. Joe and all his other plastic superhero action figures were one thing. After all, Jared had bought those toys for their son over years of birthdays and Christmases. They were small and in no way resembled the real thing.

Of course, the yellow-and-green Super Soakers would never be mistaken for actual weapons, either. But, although she was a second-generation cop herself, the idea of Trey even pretending to shoot at anyone was discomfiting.

"They're just toys," Faith murmured as the boy went racing off toward man and dog. "You had an Annie Oakley toy pistol in a pink holster that you wore everywhere when you were his age."

"Times were different then. I don't recall any children shooting classmates at school when I was growing up."

"You can't keep him in a bubble. Besides, the other night, while you were out investigating that abuse-of-mailbox case, he created a rather inventive pistol out of LEGOs."

"You didn't mention that."

"You got home late. And I didn't feel it was a portent of some dire things to come. I have a photo of your father as a child wearing a Daniel Boone Halloween costume, complete with coonskin cap and toy rifle. You pretended you were Annie Oakley. And both of you turned out to be admirable individuals."

"I'll second that," Danny Sullivan, whom Kara had forgotten was standing there, said.

Realizing he was still awaiting an answer, she said, "I'm sorry. I'm not really into dating."

"Are you into eating?"

"Of course she is," Faith leaped in.

"I was thinking we could have dinner at The Fish House sometime next week. Maybe check out that blues club that opened up in Cannon Beach afterward."

"Oh, Danny." Kara managed, just barely, to stifle a sigh. "This just isn't a good time. I've got this new possible crime that's going to demand a lot of attention, and some cold cases I need to look back through; then there's Trey —"

"I'll be home with Trey," Faith volunteered way too eagerly.

"It's just dinner," Danny jumped in, apparently wanting her to know that he had no part in her mother's blatant matchmaking attempt. "You have to eat, right?"

"It'd have to be an early evening . . ." She wavered.

"I'll have you back home by ten."

She caught a glimpse of Sax getting nearer, while Trey was bounding around him with as much enthusiasm as his dog.

Her son wasn't the only one who'd gotten wet. The white T-shirt Sax had changed into after the parade clung to his chiseled abs in a way that caused an estrogen spike Danny Sullivan's dimples never would.

Heaven help her, maybe she *did* have a thing for bad boys after all!

"Tuesday," she caved. "I'll try to wrap up by six. We can meet at the station, if that's okay with you." Having him pick her up at her mother's house was definitely too high school.

"Six it is." His grin was quick and bright and utterly harmless. With that mission successfully accomplished, he walked back over to the woodcarving booth, passing Sax on the way.

"Well, isn't that interesting," Faith murmured as they watched the two men shoot each other looks. "Seems a competition is afoot."

"You're reading too much into that."

"Perhaps." Even as Sax kept walking

straight toward them, Danny gave in to impulse and shot an uncharacteristically hard parting glance back over his shoulder at the former SEAL. "Perhaps not . . . Of course, Sax Douchett is a totally inappropriate candidate. But it never hurts for a woman to have potential beaux vying for her attention." She smiled. "It keeps them on their toes."

"I don't know which is worse," Kara muttered, "hearing you use the word *beaux,* or the idea of having any."

"Sherry Archer can be annoying at times. And I'm admittedly relieved that you don't feel stifled by living at my house. But there's one thing she has right."

"And that would be?"

Her mother's gaze moved back and forth between the two men again. "That it's high time you moved on with your life." Her expression, which had always turned to New England granite whenever Sax Douchett's name had come up, softened ever so slightly as she observed the way her grandson was looking up at the former SEAL. "For yourself. And your son."

# 18

He was getting to her. The same way she'd always gotten to him. Sax had always known that Kara's heart belonged to Jared. He doubted, even during that one massive mistake of a kiss they'd shared, she'd ever thought of him in the way he too often had thought about her.

The night Jared, Cole, and he had gotten drunk down on the beach before the two went off to boot camp, when Jared — who, like Cole, was a year older than both Kara and Sax — had asked him to "take care of my girl for me," Sax found himself unable to refuse.

What he hadn't realized, his mind clouded by the six-packs they'd polished off, was that he was about to learn the meaning of the word *masochist.*

His senior year of high school would always go down in Sax's mind as both the best and worst year of his life. The best because, thanks to Jared's request, he'd had an excuse to pass time with Kara. To drive her to school, take her back home again, and, as corny as it sounded, carry her books.

When he'd first returned to Shelter Bay a couple weeks ago and climbed into the driver's seat of the Camaro his father had so faithfully kept running for him, although he knew it was physically impossible, Sax could have sworn that the strawberry shampoo she'd used in those days still lingered in the car.

Old memories he'd kept at bay for all the years she'd been married had come flooding back. And while dropping into the sheriff's office to visit an old friend would have been the most natural thing for him to do, he'd kept his distance.

But now, watching Danny Sullivan hit on her, Sax realized that giving the widow space might not be the most effective move. Especially since the ballplayer-turned-teacher was precisely the type of man Dr. Faith Blanchard would want for her daughter.

Sullivan was a nice enough guy: good-looking, respectable, and, being a teacher, he was undoubtedly good with kids. Having never gone to war, he probably didn't have any damned annoying ghosts haunting him.

He was also the wrong man for Kara Blanchard Conway.

Of course, just because Sullivan wasn't the right guy didn't mean that Sax was.

In fact, if you got right down to it, there was probably one thing he and Dr. Faith Blanchard were in full agreement on — he was undoubtedly the worst guy on the planet for Kara to get mixed up with right now.

Sax knew that.

She'd always been a forever-after kind of girl. And even if he'd been an until-death-do-we-part kind of guy, like Cole was turning out to be, Kara deserved better than getting involved with anyone who brought a damn team of mouthy SEAL ghosts to bed with him.

# 19

How was it, Kara asked herself as she sat on the blanket her mother had brought, watching the fireworks explode in the sky, that being with Sax could be both familiar and strangely unsettling at the same time?

She'd always thought of him as a friend. No. *Jared's* friend. From the day they'd first met on the playground, Jared Conway had always been at the center of all her relationships. He'd been the dazzlingly bright sun around which everyone who knew him revolved. Since Jared had never met a stranger, all of his many friends had been connected, in varying ways, because of their relationship to him.

She'd sensed that something had transpired between her fiancé and Sax the day Jared and Cole had climbed onto that Greyhound bus headed to the Marine boot camp at Parris Island.

Although she'd planned to drive Jared to

the diner that doubled as a bus depot, then go home alone after she'd waved him off with a brave smile and undoubtedly some tears, Sax had shown up at her house with Cole riding shotgun and Jared already in the backseat of the Camaro.

Thinking back on it, after giving that strange, one-armed gesture that passed for a guy hug, Sax had hung back on the periphery with his parents and grand-parents, leaving Jared and her to share as private a good-bye as you could possibly have when families of three other recruits were all there for the same reason.

She'd been braver than she'd thought herself capable of being. Somehow she'd managed to hold back the tears stinging her eyes, assuring Jared that she'd be fine and would write him every day. A promise she'd never failed to keep.

Afterward, when the bus had finally dis-appeared into mist caused by the rain that had been falling all morning, without a word Sax had ambled over to her in that lazy, loose-hipped stride that had nearly every girl in school swooning after him, taken her by the hand, and led her, as if she were a child, back to the car.

And then, instead of taking her back to her empty house, he'd started driving.

It could have been minutes, hours, or a lifetime as they traveled along the coast road, her face buried in her hands as she wept.

Once she'd finally cried herself out, he silently handed her a box of tissues from the glove compartment.

Then he drove back into town to the window at the DQ, where he ordered two hot-fudge sundaes and cherry Cokes.

He didn't say a word until they got to her house. Which, given that both her parents were working, was empty. Taking her hand again — and again, more as if she were a child needing guidance than some girl he might be interested in — he walked her to the front door. Since nobody in Shelter Bay had ever locked their doors back then, there was no reason to wait for her to pull out a key.

Instead, he placed his hands on her shoulders and, more serious than she'd ever seen him — then or now — he'd looked down into her swollen, blotchy, tearstained face and said, "It's going to be okay, Kara. *You're* going to be okay."

Now, all too aware of the former SEAL sitting on the other side of her son — who'd insisted he stay — she remembered that because it had been Sax, she'd actually believed him.

The fireworks had been synchronized to the music blaring from the flatbed speakers. When the K-Bay FM deejay coordinating the event had first stated his desire to use the antique cannon in the park, along with fifteen war reenactors firing off Civil War muskets for the finale, Kara had balked.

But like most radio personalities, he'd seemingly been born with a quick and ready tongue, and after he'd finished explaining why and how the display was going to work, she'd come to the conclusion that the staged gunfire wouldn't be any greater risk than the fireworks themselves could be. And they did, after all, have a fire department pumper truck standing by, just in case.

"The 1812 Overture was written to celebrate the Russians' victory over the French," she explained to her son as the night sky lit up with blinding color that had the crowd oohing and aahing in unison. "According to what James Thompson from the radio station told me, when half a million French troops invaded Russia, the people all were told to go to church and pray for a miracle to protect their homeland and keep them safe."

*Damn.* The moment she heard herself saying those words, Kara feared her son would point out that he'd prayed every night for his father, but no higher power had opted to send a miracle their way.

"Hear that?" Sax asked, deftly cutting off any chance for Trey to bring that difficult topic up. "That's 'La Marseillaise,' the French national anthem. The first part you heard were the cellos and violas, which are kinda sad instruments, which are supposed to tell you that the people are about to be in a world of hurt.

"Now, this back-and-forth battle between a Russian folk song and the French anthem is telling about the battle."

"The French song keeps getting louder," Trey said.

"Sure is. Damn if you aren't one smart kid," Sax said approvingly. "Because the French are gaining more and more victories. Pretty soon, it's looking like everyone in Russia's going to be eating frog legs and French fries."

"I like French fries."

"Never met anyone who didn't," Sax agreed. "So, hear that? Where the music changes?"

Trey tilted his head and concentrated. "Yeah."

"That's another Russian folk dance. This is where Tchaikovsky, the Russian composer who wrote the overture, is telling how the czar — that's like a president for life, but he's not elected — instructed all his people to save their Rodina, which is Russian for motherland. So all over the country, people from all the villages came running out of their houses and churches and raced toward Moscow.

"This part is where Moscow's burning, the French keep advancing, and it looks like, despite trying their best, the Russians are flat-out doomed."

"That's very impressive," Kara said, "that you know all that." Until tonight, her knowledge of Tchaikovsky had been limited to seeing *Swan Lake* with her mother in Portland, and performing as one of the snowflakes in Shelter Bay Elementary School's Christmas performance of *The Nutcracker* when she'd been in the sixth grade.

"I got myself a full scholarship to study music at UC Berkeley after graduating high school," he reminded her.

"But you dropped out." *Damn.* She could've bitten her tongue. "Sorry."

"Nothing to be sorry for. Believe it or not, I was doing really well there and enjoyed learning all the different kinds of music and the history and all, but then nine-eleven came along and, well, playing tunes just didn't seem like what I should be doing, so although my mama wasn't real happy with the idea of her baby boy going off to war, I turned the rudder and changed course for the Navy."

Yet another surprise. When Cole had shown up in Oceanside to help her bring Jared's body back home to Shelter Bay, he'd mentioned that Sax had left school to become a SEAL, but she'd guessed that he'd gotten bored in the staid confines of academia. Or more likely — and didn't this make her feel guilty for thinking so? — been expelled for bad behavior.

Which apparently hadn't been the case. It was obvious that he still loved music. And although she knew how much he hadn't wanted to go through with this celebration the town council had forced on him, by doing so, and inviting Trey to participate, he'd enriched the experience for her son. And for that she was hugely grateful.

"But it's too nice a night to be thinking about all that," he said over an earsplitting whistle as a rocket shot into the air. Watching him as carefully as she was, Kara saw Sax flinch, then stiffen as every atom in his body appeared to go on full alert. She'd seen that happen enough times with Jared to recognize it as a lingering reaction to war, when rockets weren't something meant to entertain, but to kill.

A second later, as sparkling white firework stars cascaded downward, she watched him relax again. But she could still sense a simmering discomfort just beneath the surface.

"So" — he doggedly continued the story of the overture — "just in the nick of time, God intervened, sending a winter freeze colder and deeper than any Russia had ever experienced. And let me tell you, I've been there, and that is one cold place."

"I hear the wind!" Trey began bouncing up and down with an enthusiasm Kara hadn't witnessed since Jared had first returned from Iraq. Before everything had gotten so tense and strained.

"I do, too," she said.

"Music, done right, can conjure up some pretty fierce images," Sax said. "Now those French guys try to retreat, but their guns got stuck in the ground. Which is when the Russian people grabbed them up and began to fight back. . . .

"In a minute you're going to hear all the church bells ringing and guns firing across the land as people thank God and celebrate being delivered from their enemy."

"Mr. Thompson told me that the composer originally planned for sixteen cannons to be shot during this part." Kara was pleased to be able to add something to the conversation. That had been the persuasive deejay's argument for shooting off the ancient cannon.

"He's right," Sax said. "Tchaikovsky designed an electric board with buttons to push for each cannon. It was really complicated. Too complicated for the time, so nobody ever let him try it."

Although she didn't like thinking of herself in that way, Kara would reluctantly admit that like all cops — hell, all people — she tended to stereotype. The world — and her job — was easier when things were more black-and-white, good guys, bad guys, and everyone wore labels like they used to put on you back in high school. Those "most likely to" tags she and Sax had talked about earlier.

But Sax Douchett had never fit tidily into a box. She knew that some people in Shelter Bay, including her mother, had seen only his bad-boy persona. But because of that deal he'd apparently made with Jared, she'd witnessed another, more tender, caring, even protective side.

Of course, both sides had been sexy as sin. Not that she'd ever allowed herself to think about that.

Except for that one night.

"That's too bad," Trey interrupted her turmoiled memories. She hadn't thought about that kiss for years. And now it kept replaying in a seemingly endless loop over and over again in her mind. "That he didn't get to use the cannons."

"Yeah." Sax reached over and ruffled her son's hair. "I always thought so, too."

An instant later, the town's single cannon boomed. Kara was relieved when it didn't take off anyone's hand. The muskets were all shot in impressive unison as the music soared in jubilation and the sky exploded in the finale — a dazzling display of red, white, and blue pyrotechnics.

The crowd, as if holding one collective breath, was silent. Then, as the last light twinkled out, they began to applaud.

As the old Jim Croce song pointed out, there were some things you just didn't do.

Such as spitting into the wind.

Tugging on Superman's cape.

Pulling the mask off the Lone Ranger.

And the one thing every law enforcement officer knew was that you damn well didn't tempt fate by making the mistake of saying — or even *thinking* — how quiet things were.

Nonetheless Kara was just congratulating herself on getting through the largest public event during her tenure as sheriff without a serious incident, when a scream shattered the still smoke-filled air.

# 20

It was bad. Not as bad as it could've been.

But not good, either.

Danny Sullivan, who, according to witnesses, had packed up his uncle's carvings and been sitting on a folding lawn chair during the fireworks, was lying facedown on the grass. His face, what she could see of it, was bloodied, and more blood was slowly oozing from a wound at the back of his head.

The good news, according to Kara's mother, who'd checked his airways and pulse and elevated his bloody head, was that he was breathing. The bad news was that he was unconscious. As she pulled on the gloves she'd gotten from her cruiser, Kara gently pushed away damp hair and — *damn* — viewed a bullet wound.

The flickering Victorian gaslights in the square, while charming, provided scant illumination. What she wouldn't give for bright-as-day klieg lights. The alternative had been to turn on the spotlight on her patrol car, which was casting eerie shadows over the park.

Reaction to the shooting was mixed. Several gawkers stood around, watching the action surrounding the victim as if it were merely an episode of *CSI Shelter Bay*.

Others, as word rippled through the crowd, quickly gathered up their blankets, coolers, and children and headed off for their cars, just in case a would-be killer was in their midst, targeting them as the next victims.

"He'll need to be airlifted to the trauma department in Portland," Faith said as she continued to examine him while his uncle took her place, holding Danny in his arms. "ASAP."

"I'm already on that," Kara said as she punched in the emergency number on her cell.

"Can't think of anyone who'd want to shoot Danny on purpose," John, obviously shaken, said. "Gotta be random. Some idiot shooting up in the air in a lame-brained attempt to celebrate."

"That's more than likely," Kara agreed as she stood up, took out the camera she'd brought along to take pictures of her son, and began snapping photographs. Needless to say, Shelter Bay's budget didn't allow for a police camera, let alone an official photographer.

"Do you have to do that?" John complained. As she'd want to do if it were Trey who'd been shot.

"Even if it *was* an accident, since it's still a crime to shoot a gun within city limits, that makes this a crime scene," she said gently.

If Danny Sullivan had been shot at close range, there'd likely be gray matter all over the booth. On the other hand, she'd once been called to the scene of a shooting on the beach at Oceanside on the Fourth of July. A seven-year-old girl building a sand castle had been hit in the arm by a bullet shot into the air nearly a mile away.

"When the hell are idiots going to realize that what goes up always comes down?" John muttered.

Not sure what her digital lens was able to pick up, she took a few shots of the crowd, just in the unlikely event she might get lucky and pick up the shooter. Sometimes bad guys enjoyed hanging around watching the drama they'd created. She had the feeling she was going to need all the luck she could get in this case.

Damn if she didn't have a logistics prob-lem. Unlike California, where by now a parade of black-and-whites would have already arrived on the scene, lights flashing, sirens blaring, her manpower was a joke.

She knew that if instructed, John would stay here, follow orders, and interview bystanders. But Danny was his family. And family belonged with their own at a time like this. No way was she going to keep her deputy from going to the hospital with his nephew.

But if *she* stayed here, that would mean John would be the one questioning Danny when he woke up. She couldn't allow herself to believe that the man who'd so charm-ingly asked her out earlier would not wake up.

It wasn't as if John O'Roarke wasn't a good cop. But she'd always been a control freak. And besides, John would be the first to admit that she was far more experienced.

Yet, with her mother going in the evac copter, if Kara flew to Portland, what would she do with her son? Who was currently be-ing kept away from the scene by Cole Douchett and his fiancée.

"I can take Trey home with me," Sax volunteered, making her wonder if he'd been able to view the internal conflict in her expression. Or, more unsettling, read her mind.

"It's already past his bedtime."

"No problem. He can sack out at the house."

Only two days ago there was no way she would've just handed her only child off to this man. Tonight she was grateful for the offer.

"I don't know how long I'm going to be."

"Don't worry about it." He shrugged. "Tomorrow's Sunday, which means no school. If he ends up having to spend the night, I'll just feed him breakfast and take him with me to the lumberyard to buy some Sheetrock and stuff for Bon Temps."

"He'd enjoy that."

Since they'd never owned an actual house that wasn't on base, Jared had never been much of a handyman, even when he was home. And her own skills were pretty much limited to changing a lightbulb. On the rare occasion she'd had need to wander into a Home Depot with her son, Trey had, like most boys, proven enthralled with power tools.

Sax nodded as if there'd never been a question of her refusing. "Then it's set."

Kara knew it was the logical answer. She also knew it was what Jared would tell her to do, if something like this had happened when he'd been deployed and unable to care for their son. But then again, when she was married, she'd never had the kind of thoughts she'd been having toward this man.

"I want to tell him myself," she said, throwing in the towel. "Let him know everything's going to be okay."

She'd no sooner said the words than Danny's eyelids fluttered open. "I know this is a cliché," he said. "But what the hell happened?"

"You don't remember anything?"

He frowned, obviously in pain. "I remember talking to you. And doing a piss-poor job of asking you out." Despite the seriousness of the situation, his lips quirked just a bit at that. "And the fireworks. Until the finale."

He shook his head, then flinched. No wonder, given that he had a hole in it. "After that it's a blank."

"Retrograde amnesia's perfectly understandable with a head wound," Faith assured him as she took his pulse for a third time.

"So, I'm okay?" he asked.

"Your pulse is thready," Kara's mother reported. "But you're not only holding your own — you're doing amazingly well for someone with a bullet wound in his skull."

"A bullet?"

"Probably an accident," John said. "Some yahoo shooting off a gun along with the fireworks."

*Damn.* Even as John had been reassuring him, Danny's eyes began to roll back in his head and he looked on the verge of passing out again.

Kara held her breath as her mother rechecked his signs. Then Faith turned toward her. "So far, so good. Go tend to Trey; then do whatever you have to do here at the crime scene. Then you can drive to Portland. Although I doubt he knows anything that would prove helpful to your case, you won't be able to talk to Daniel until he's out of surgery."

It wasn't the best solution, but it was the most logical. But it was also yet one more reason to be in Sax's debt.

"If you remember anything, however seemingly unimportant . . ." she began to tell Danny.

"I'll tell Uncle John," he assured her. "Don't worry about me." Even as his eyes glazed with pain, he managed a weak grin toward Faith. "I'm in great hands."

"I'm not going to argue with that," Kara said.

Leaving John and her mother with Danny, Kara wove her way through the crowd to where her son was eating an ice-cream cone.

"Your son," Cole Douchett said, "appears to have a hollow leg."

"Tell me about it." She forced a smile even as part of her mind was still fifty yards away at the crime scene.

Having already had one possible murder tossed into her lap with that bone and skull found at Sax's camp, Kara wasn't at all eager for another.

She had, after all, come home expecting to play Officer Friendly during safety talks at the school, hand out the occasional barking-dog warning, break up a few bar fights. Mailbox bashing and jaywalking were supposed to be major crimes in Shelter Bay.

It *had* to be an accident. A random shot fired by someone who might not have even had a clue what he'd done. And once he (and experience had taught her such shootings were usually done by males) learned what had happened, unless a witness had been present to testify against him, the odds of the shooter turning himself in weren't all that strong.

Which meant that, if Danny was worse off

224

than he appeared to be, and actually did die of that head wound, some citizen of Shelter Bay could get away with, at the very least, manslaughter.

When another thought hit home like a mallet to the back of her head — that her father had also died at the hand of an unknown shooter — Kara's blood turned cold.

# 21

"Is Mr. Sullivan going to die?" Trey asked as Sax drove across the bridge leading to the twisting coast road.

"Your grandmother's a super doctor," he said. "I'm sure she'll have him back on his feet in no time."

"I hope so. He's nice. He gave me this. For free." He dug into the pocket of his baggy shorts and pulled out a small wooden dolphin.

"That was real nice of him, all right."

"His uncle carves them."

"So I've heard."

"Did a bad guy try to kill Mr. Sullivan?"

"I suspect it was probably an accident."

"A bad guy tried to kill my mom."

"You mean your dad." It had been a long, exciting day. Made sense the kid would be confused.

"No. *That* bad guy *did* kill my dad. It was another bad guy who hurt my mom."

226

"Really." He wasn't going to pump Kara's son. That would be wrong on so many levels. But, damn, he was curious.

"That's why she moved us here. Because she was afraid I'd end up an orphan."

Talk about your conversational minefields. Sax suddenly found himself almost regretting the offer to take Kara's son off her hands for the night.

"Did she tell you that?" It didn't seem like the Kara he'd always known. Then again, he sure as hell wasn't the person he'd been back in high school, either.

"Nah. I overheard her talking to Grandma one night. The bad guy who hurt her got sent away to jail for a long, long time. But she told Grandma that there are always more where he came from. So we came here, where things are quieter and more peaceful."

And couldn't he hear Kara saying those words? "They're usually quiet, that's for sure. Except for fireworks."

"And shootings."

"Accidental shootings."

"Maybe." The small face illuminated by the dashboard lights frowned. "But sometimes bad things happen when you don't expect them. Like hurricanes and earthquakes. And floods and tsunamis."

"Now, those last two I know somethin' about," Sax said. "The dance hall I'm going to be rebuilding was hit by a couple storms that spun off a typhoon. Which is the West Coast version of a hurricane."

"I know about typhoons because I watched a show about them on the Discovery Channel. They have a lot of shows about natural disasters."

"You thinkin' about becoming a scientist when you grow up?"

"Not really. At least, I don't think so. I just want to be prepared, for whenever something bad happens."

Talk about your emotional IEDs. No way was he about to touch that one. But Sax did decide that he was also going to ask Kara if she knew her son was focused on such bad stuff. He didn't know much about kids — hell, he didn't know anything about them — but given her son's background, he wondered if Trey Conway could be having a bit of PTSD himself.

"There you go, dude, wading into stuff that's none of your business." Jake the Snake popped up from the backseat. Sax shot him a look in the rearview mirror.

"It *is* his business," Cowboy argued, "since he's hot for the kid's mama."

*I'm not hot for anyone.*

"You are such a freaking liar, Douchett," Randy said. "But it wouldn't matter. Because like it or not, you can't stop playing the hero."

If he'd been such a damn hero, the guys sprawled in the back of the Camaro wouldn't be dead. They'd be ragging him in real life.

"It wasn't your fault," Randy said.

They'd always been able to read one another's minds, which was why they'd made such a good team. But, damn, they'd gotten a lot better at it since they'd gotten killed by the Taliban in those Afghan mountains.

Apparently death gave you superpowers. Not that Sax wanted to find out for himself anytime soon.

*Don't you ladies have anything else to do up there? Like polish your halos? Or maybe play the sound track from* Apocalypse Now *on your harps?*

"I wasn't issued any harp," Jake said. "How about you guys?"

"Not me," Cowboy said.

"Me, neither," Randy responded. "But I sure as hell wouldn't turn down a Fender Stratocaster."

"I saw Merle Haggard playing at a roadhouse in Abilene," Cowboy said. "He had a

229

Martin acoustic. Which is what I'd want, because it pretty much sets the gold standard when you're talking country music."

"Country music is an oxymoron." Randy shook his head. "Only a shitkicker would want to spend eternity listening to somebody-done-somebody-wrong songs about dogs, liquor, and pickup trucks."

"A helluva lotta folks like dogs, liquor, and pickup trucks, son," Cowboy countered.

*You're all nuts.*

Or maybe it was *him* who'd gone crazy.

And wasn't that a fun thought?

# 22

Two hours after discovering Danny Sullivan lying beside his uncle's booth, Kara arrived at OHSU on the sprawling Marquam Hill campus.

She'd already learned on her drive from Shelter Bay that Danny had been transferred from trauma to surgery, so after flashing her badge at the guard, she found her way to the surgical floor, where she was informed by the nurse behind the counter that her mother, who'd once been on staff here, was still in surgery.

"He'll be okay," she assured John, who appeared determined to pace a path in the waiting room's checkerboard floor. "Mom's the best."

"You don't have to tell me that. But, damn, shouldn't we have heard something by now?"

"Maybe no news is good news?" Obviously encouragement wasn't her strength.

Even she cringed at the trite platitude.

He shot her a look, but she was thankful he didn't bother to respond and continued pacing.

"I don't suppose he remembered anything on the flight in?"

"No. But I've gotta admit that I didn't really pressure him. The EMT and your mother wanted him to stay calm."

"As he should. We'll have plenty of time to see if anything pertinent comes back later. I'm going to get some coffee. Would you like some?" Like the already wired-to-the-hilt guy needed any caffeine, but she felt she should ask.

"Yeah, though I'd prefer something a hell of a lot stronger, I'll take a cup," he said. "Black." He dug into his pocket for change.

Kara put a hand on his arm. "I've got it covered."

She was on her way back with the coffee when a team from the ER came rushing by with a loaded gurney. From what she overheard them tell the surgical unit RN, the patient had been stabbed during a domestic dispute.

Which had Kara flashing back to when she'd looked out the sidelight of the front door and seen those two officers — one she recognized as the department chaplain —

standing on her front step.

Wanting to put on the most positive face possible for John, she shook off the memory and was reassuring him yet again that all would be well when her mother, dressed in green scrubs, appeared in the doorway. She looked, as always, far cooler and more composed than either John or Kara.

"Your nephew is one hardheaded young man," she informed John.

"And here I thought he was always pretty easygoing."

"I meant physically. Amazing, the bullet didn't penetrate his skull, but shattered upon impact. It split into three separate pieces, with the fragments running beneath his skin. One exited through his right cheek, which explains some of the bleeding; another lodged behind his left ear.

"We were able to remove the one behind the ear, as well as the third piece lodged in the dura mater, which is the covering next to the skull." She held out a plastic bag toward Kara. "I thought you'd want them. For evidence."

"Thanks."

Finding it odd to be working on a case with her mother, Kara took the bag, noticing that it had already been labeled with Danny's name and the date. Then, for good measure, maintaining the chain of evidence, her mother had signed it.

"So he's okay?" John asked.

"He should be fine. But we'll want to keep him overnight up in neuro for observation. Why don't you sit down and let me draw you a picture, to explain things a little better?" she suggested.

Although Kara could practically feel the wound-up energy still radiating from John's every pore, he threw his body into the chair as instructed and folded his arms.

"The brain, as you know, is primarily protected by the skull, which acts as the first barrier of protection against assault." With a ballpoint pen, she sketched a cutaway picture of a head on a notepad. "As a barrier, it works very well, but it's also hard."

She smiled — with her lips and her eyes. More, Kara couldn't help noticing, like a woman than a doctor.

"As I said, in Daniel's case, harder than most. The thing is, because the skull's so hard, the brain needs cushioning. Otherwise, even the slightest impact to the head could cause the brain to bang against the inside of the skull, resulting in serious damage."

"Like shaken baby syndrome," Kara said. She'd caught a case of that tragedy her first month riding patrol.

"Exactly." This time the smile, which reminded Kara of the gold stars Trey's teacher put on his spelling tests, was aimed toward her. "The meninges form a system of protective coverings of the brain. The layer closest to the brain is called the pia mater. The one on top of it is the arachnoid mater." More sketching. "The one closest to the skull, and where the bullet fragment lodged in Daniel's brain, is the dura mater.

"Although their primary role is to protect the brain, the meninges also contain blood vessels. Some ruptured as a result of the impact, which is what mostly caused all that blood back at the park and took us so long to repair in surgery. I didn't want to leave him with any risk for a later rupture."

"You saved his life."

Her mother did not argue. "The team saved his life. I certainly didn't do it alone. He's in recovery now. And I know he's anxious to reassure you."

"That's Danny." The older man's voice sounded choked, as if he were having to push the words past a lump in his throat. "Always thinking of everyone else."

"He's a good man," Faith said. "Go see him so he won't worry. Then, since I doubt you'll be leaving —"

"Wild horses couldn't drive me away." His jaw jutted out. Stubbornly. Resolutely.

"I doubt any would dare try. However, speaking as a physician, I'm going to prescribe something besides coffee in your stomach." She gestured toward a woman in cheery daisy-print scrubs who appeared in the doorway. "Nurse McCarthy will show you to recovery. Then, after you're finished with your visit — and I wouldn't make it too long, because Daniel's been through a lot tonight — why don't you join me in the café on the third floor and we'll get you something to eat."

"I guess I could eat something," he allowed. Then, docile as an oversize lamb, he followed the nurse out of the room.

Kara's mother watched him leave. Then she turned toward Kara. "How about you? Feel like something to eat before you go back home?"

"You're staying here."

It was not a question, but Faith answered it anyway. "I didn't lie when I told John that Daniel's prognosis was good. But head injuries can be unpredictable on a good day. I'm sticking around. Just in case we have any surprises."

Kara would expect no less. "I guess I could eat something," she said, unconsciously echoing John. "Maybe some soup. Or half a sandwich." She wasn't really hungry after all the food at the welcome-home celebration, but coffee, mixed with nerves, had begun doing a number on her own stomach.

She ended up with a shrimp-and-pasta salad, while Faith went with a vegetarian wrap and garden salad with nonfat dressing on the side.

"Do you know what I used to do when you were younger and I'd get overwhelmed with my competing roles as mother, wife, and physician?" Faith asked as she dipped just the tip of a leaf of spinach into the dressing.

"Work harder?" Kara stabbed a piece of tortellini.

"Well, that, too. But I'd pretend that I was Donna Reed. Or Jane Wyatt's character, Margaret Anderson, the mother from *Father Knows Best*. In the sitcom I'd envision to be my alternative life, I was a stay-at-home mother whose only worry was what to fix for the bridge club luncheon."

"I didn't know you played bridge."

"I don't. Like golf, which most doctors seem addicted to, I never had the patience for it. But my point was that in my fantasy, I didn't have to worry about my patients because I didn't have to work. Your father's income was more than enough to pay for everything we needed."

"But you've never worked solely for the money," Kara argued. The truth was that if workaholic Dr. Faith Blanchard ever calculated her hourly wage, she'd probably rank below the guy currently mopping the cafeteria floor.

"Of course I didn't. This was my mental escape. Also, since there were no stranger dangers or whacked-out kids with guns in school allowed in my 1950s suburban paradise, I never had to worry about where you were, or what you were doing. Because you'd always be safe."

"I wouldn't mind that part of it. The not worrying."

"What mother wouldn't give anything to be free of that concern?"

"So what would you do all day? In this sitcom of your life?" Kara was fascinated to discover that her logical, no-nonsense mother had fantasized about anything, let alone living a life that Dr. Faith Blanchard undoubtedly, in reality, would have found stultifying.

"Well, to begin with, I'd breeze into the kitchen in a lovely starched housedress wearing a string of perfect pearls. I'd tie on my ruffled pink apron —"

"Those shows were black-and-white."

"True. But in my fantasy the apron was always pink. Not that obnoxious Barbie pink, but a soft pastel. Like that shrimp." She pointed a fork at Kara's salad. "I'd get the percolator going and start the bacon sizzling in the pan and put Wonder bread in the toaster. Just as I'm putting the bacon and fried eggs —"

"Which you only ever let Dad and me have on our birthdays. Or Father's Day."

"Cholesterol is a killer," Faith said mildly. "Fortunately, people didn't know to worry about it back then. So, just as I'm putting the artery-clogging breakfast on the table, you and your father come downstairs. Your father is dressed in a gray flannel suit."

"Funny uniform for a small-town sheriff."

"True. But he's not a sheriff. That's too edgy. Police work can be dangerous.

"No, in my fantasy Ben would work in an office downtown. I'm not quite sure what he does, but it's a job that requires he wear a suit and tie and carry a briefcase, but doesn't stress him out so much that he has a heart attack at his desk and leaves me a widowed mother with a young child to support."

She winced at that, and reached out and

239

put her hand on Kara's. "I'm sorry. That was thoughtless."

Kara shrugged. "Fantasies aren't supposed to be politically correct. If they were, they'd be boring. So." She took another bite of salad. "I'm in need of a little fantasy R and R myself, so continue on."

"Well, while I've been bustling around the kitchen, without a single argument over why you can't go out looking as if you stepped out of a Madonna video, instead you've dressed yourself in a charming little angora sweater and poodle skirt and put your hair in a perfect, perky ponytail."

"It wasn't Madonna." Her mother's taste had always tended toward the classics: Bach, Beethoven, Mozart. And Tchaikovsky. Which had Kara thinking how strange it was that her mother and Sax would have anything in common. "It was Cyndi Lauper," she corrected. "Girls having fun sounded like, well, fun."

The phase had lasted all of two weeks her sophomore year. Then, realizing she wasn't the Cyndi Lauper fun-girl type, she'd gone back to her boring old lack of style.

"Easy for you to say. You didn't have to try to keep your daughter from leaving the house looking like she was about to audition for a porn movie. Thank heavens

Shelter Bay Elementary had taken a page from the Catholic school handbook in those days and required uniforms, which kept you looking decent on school days."

Since they were getting along so well, Kara decided against mentioning that a *decent* uniform of plaid skirt, white blouse, and knee socks was a popular porn film staple.

"You greet me with, 'Good morning, Mother, darling.' I respond, 'Good morning, my beautiful pet.' "

"Okay. You're coming really, really close to my gag reflex with that one."

"We all smile benevolently at one another as we sit down for a lovely, leisurely breakfast. Of course, your father will be reading the paper, but you and I discuss your plans for your sleepover. I promise there will be fresh-baked cookies and cupcakes, which makes you smile. I hand you your lunch box —"

"Annie Oakley," Kara remembered.

"That's a bit of reality that's allowed to stay in," Faith agreed. "I kiss you good-bye and watch as you skip out the door and down the sidewalk to school. Then I hand Ben his briefcase, kiss him on the cheek as well, and stand in the doorway, watching as he walks out to the car and drives away. I wave across the street to my neighbor

Janice, who's doing exactly the same thing. Because, of course, our lives all mirror one another's."

"Spookily like Stepford wives."

"That's not a problem because the book hasn't been written yet. Since no one has told us we're supposed to be unhappy, we believe all the glossy magazines that reinforce our comfortable domestic bliss."

"So, in this fantasy, you've all drunk the fifties happy-housewife Kool-Aid."

"True." Her mother sighed. "But it's such damn tasty Kool-Aid."

"God, I hate to admit this," Kara said, dragging a hand through her hair. "But it's coming in a close second place to my own fantasy of Gerard Butler showing up at my door with a can of whipped cream."

"Ah, the ubiquitous whipped cream." Faith sighed. "I used to have a similar one about Robert Redford."

"No way."

"Way." Her mother looked just like a cat that'd been lapping at top cream. "And Paul Newman. He and Robert and I are in Brazil, where it's very hot and very, very steamy."

The idea of her mother fantasizing a threesome with Butch Cassidy and the Sundance Kid was mind-boggling.

"I believe we've just entered the TMI zone," Kara said, trying to scrub the unwanted erotic image from her brain. "Can we get back to the fifties, when women's lust revolved around the perfect Jell-O mold?"

"That's probably safer," Faith agreed. "So, while I'm watching you skip down the sidewalk, and your father drive down the tree-lined street, although I know it's petty, I allow myself to think how you are prettier than Janice's child, and how my husband is handsomer than hers.

"I quickly tidy the house while humming happily to myself. Something theatrical. Perhaps from *South Pacific.* Then Janice and Helen, from next door, drop in for our morning kaffeeklatsch. Helen has brought her frosted pecan cinnamon coffee cake."

"Because carbs and calories don't exist."

"Of course not. After they leave, I'm not sure exactly what I do, because it was never shown. Perhaps read some thought-provoking novel."

"Like *War and Peace.*"

"That works. Though *Anna Karenina* was actually a better book. Anyway, the day just breezes by and you come home from school and we both sit down to a plate of brownies —"

"Which you baked after whizzing through *War and Peace*."

"Exactly. Then, after valuable mother-daughter bonding time, you obediently run upstairs to do your homework while I cook dinner."

"Meat and potatoes."

"Well, I certainly wouldn't feed Ben take-out pizza. Pot roast is his favorite. With Parker House rolls and a fresh green salad. As I hand him his martini, he tells me how good dinner smells. I love it when he compliments me."

This time her mother's smile was spookily reminiscent of Donna Reed's.

"I put the dinner on the table, take off my apron, light the candles, and we all sit down to dinner to discuss one another's days."

"Not that you'd have all that much to add to the conversation," Kara pointed out. "Except for perhaps a book report."

"True. But that doesn't matter. Because just being together, the three of us, ending our day in my homey kitchen, makes me feel complete. And satisfied with my lovely, perfect life. And my lovely, perfect family."

Faith sighed again.

Kara echoed the sigh. Then she said, "I honestly don't know what's scarier: that the outdated, antifeminist scenario is, at this moment, immensely appealing, or that you thought it up."

"I didn't. All those TV writers, who were undoubtedly males, did. And while it's admittedly horribly chauvinistic, as I said, it got me through some tough times when I found myself juggling too many balls." She took a sip of water and eyed Kara over the rim of the plastic glass. "But I never faced anything as difficult as you've had to go through."

Was that actually a compliment?

"I'm doing okay."

"I'd never expect less. Because you come from tough stock. What's even more admirable is how you've managed to keep Jared's death from having a devastating effect on your son. I'm not sure that, at your age, I could have done as well."

The fork that had been on the way to Kara's mouth dropped to the table. No mistake about it, that had *definitely* been a compliment.

"You've no idea how much that means to me." She'd never uttered a more truthful statement. "To hear you say that."

"You've no idea how bad it makes me feel to hear that you needed so to hear me say it." Faith pinched the bridge of her nose. "Watching you with Trey, I'm beginning to suspect I wasn't a very good mother."

"Don't be silly. You were great. Okay, maybe you weren't Donna Reed or Margaret Anderson, which, quite honestly, would've weirded me out, but you were definitely a role model."

"Yet you became a sheriff. Not a doctor."

"Ah." Kara lifted a finger. "But you showed me a woman could be anything she wanted to be. Including a sheriff."

Faith's expression softened. "Well, that's something, I suppose." She glanced up. "John's here."

Faith followed her gaze to the man weaving his way between the tables, which were surprisingly crowded for this time of night.

"He's got a crush on you, you know," she told her mother.

"I know. Ben knew, too. He told me . . ."

"Told you what?" Kara asked when Faith's voice drifted off.

"That if anything ever happened to him, I ought to consider marrying John O'Roarke. He felt he'd take good care of me."

"Oh, God. That's just too weird." It had been a long, exhausting day.

"You find it strange that your father would be thinking of my welfare?"

"No. What's strange is that that's exactly the same thing Jared did when he went off

246

to the Marines. He essentially handed me over to Sax for safekeeping."

Her mother arched a brow. "I never knew that."

"Sax was always a sore topic with you, so I never shared my suspicions back then. But he admitted it the other day."

"And here I always thought he was trying to make time with his friend's girl."

"He never tried anything."

Which was true. *She'd* been the one to initiate that kiss. Which had started out as a kiss of gratitude. Then it had turned into something else. Something that could have turned out dangerous, if Sax had let it. Which he hadn't.

At the time she'd been embarrassed. But grateful. Now she realized that despite his devil-may-care attitude, even then he'd possessed a steely self-discipline and sense of honor that must have served him well during his years as a SEAL.

"Well." Her mother blew out a breath, touched her napkin to her lips, then put it on the table as she stood to greet the man who'd nearly reached them. "Perhaps I misjudged him on that issue. But he's just back from war. And he doesn't, from what I can tell, even have a job. Daniel Sullivan would still be far better husband material."

"I'm not in the market for a husband."
Which was definitely true.

But with all her attention directed toward Kara's deputy, Faith didn't hear the denial. Or more likely chose not to.

# 23

This was getting to be a habit Sax could get used to: sitting out on his covered porch, strumming his Gibson Kristofferson SJ to the accompaniment of the night rain on the roof, watching Kara Conway coming up his driveway.

He was thinking that a gentleman would go racing out to the car with an umbrella. Unfortunately, while no one had ever referred to him as a gentleman, it was a moot point, since he didn't own an umbrella.

Neither, apparently, did she. Or else she was in too much of a hurry to bother with it, because after opening the cruiser's door she dashed across the drive and up his steps.

"I'm sorry." She swiped her damp bangs off her forehead. "I didn't expect it to be so late."

"Don't worry about it." He put the guitar aside. "It's not like I had anything real important to do, anyway."

She glanced past him into the dimly lit cabin. "Is Trey asleep?"

"He was out like a light before we got here. I put him to bed in the upstairs guest room, and checked him a couple times, but he's still sawing some serious Zs."

"It was a busy day for him," she said. "The parade, all the food, the fireworks, then Danny's shooting . . . And it's not that I don't trust you, but would you mind if I checked him myself?"

"Of course not. I guess you remember the way?"

Although she'd never been one to blush, a tinge of color lit her cheeks. "I suppose I can find him," she said mildly.

With that, she disappeared into the house, leaving him wanting to bang his head through the white siding.

*Hell.* Could he be any stupider? Letting her know that *he* knew this was where she and Jared had sneaked away once back when they were in high school. His grandparents had been down in Louisiana, visiting relatives. Having promised to look after the house for them, Cole had given his best friend the key so they could have themselves a romantic evening.

Sax wondered what she'd say if she found out he also knew that this was where she and Jared had given their virginity to each other. Although Jared had never been one to kiss and tell, it hadn't taken a genius to recognize the signs the next morning when they'd all gone out surf fishing for stripers together. The kid couldn't stop grinning like a damn fool, even after he'd lost his rod and reel to a shark who'd snapped up his bait and swum away with it.

Although Sax had already been enjoying the pleasures of local girls for some time, he'd never felt the way Jared Conway had looked. Not then. Not since.

"Forbidden fruit is what you've got here, son." Cowboy, who was leaning against one of the porch pillars, repeated what Sax had already considered. "Gotta definitely be the most succulent, sweetest flesh."

"But she's not forbidden anymore," Randy pointed out. " 'Cause her Marine husband took himself a bullet."

"Which was a crying shame," Jake allowed with uncharacteristic sympathy. "But if she's been celibate all this time, the lady's definitely gotta be ready for blastoff."

And wasn't this just what he needed? "If you guys aren't going to go back to wherever you came from, would you just shut the fuck up?"

"You think we like hanging around here,

watching you look like a pussy-whipped fool?" Cowboy retorted.

"Just do her," Jake said. "So we can all get on with the damn mission."

"Which would be?" Sax tried yet again to get one of them to say why they seemed determined to haunt him. It would be one thing if they seemed pissed that he was alive and they were dead.

He could get that.

Hell, he'd probably feel that way himself, if their situations were reversed.

The problem was, they were acting just like they used to, when they'd hang around shooting the bull and talking about women.

"Did you say something?" Kara asked from the doorway.

"Just talkin' to myself, I guess." Sax blew out a breath. "How's the kid?"

"You nailed it. He's out like a rock. I think a typhoon could hit the coast and he'd sleep right through it."

Without waiting for an invitation, she sat down on the chair next to him and rubbed the back of her neck. "I was worried that all the talk of heroes, not to mention what happened to Danny, might have had him thinking about his father. He didn't sleep for weeks after the shooting."

"He talked about Jared," Sax said. "About

him being a hero and all. He talked about you, too."

The words were out before he could call them back. *Damn.* What was it about this woman that always had him acting on impulse?

"Oh?" The slender lady hand that he was still having trouble imagining holding that nine-millimeter she wore on her hip stilled. Her shoulders tensed. "What did he say?"

"Nothin' much." He shrugged. "Other than giving away all your deep, dark secrets."

"Nice try, Douchett." She relaxed again. Slightly. "But I don't have any deep, dark secrets."

*Nice try back atcha, sugar.*

She was good. He suspected she'd developed that ability to prevaricate while interviewing bad guys in the box at her police station. But his own time in the military had taught him to spot a lie. Because when you were dealing with an enemy who didn't wear a uniform, your life might depend on your instincts.

"How's Danny?" he asked, deciding not to call her on it. There was time to find out what happened to her down in Oceanside. And there was always Google, though he'd rather just have her tell him herself. "And John?"

"John's a basket case. Danny should go right out and buy himself a lottery ticket, because tonight, anyway, he's the luckiest guy on the planet."

She told him about the bullet. And the pieces.

"You still looking at it as an accident?"

"I don't know. It's the logical answer. But . . ."

"You're thinking it's a bit of a coincidence. Two accidental shootings in a town that hasn't had one for the past six years."

"How would you know that?"

"Not much you can't find online these days. The monthly county police report — going back years — is archived on the news-paper's Internet site."

"There's still no connection. And unless someone gets a guilty conscience and decides to come forward, my father's case is pretty much closed." She rubbed the back of her neck again. "Then there's your body to deal with."

"Feel free to deal with it any way you'd like."

She paused. Opened her mouth. Shut it. He could almost hear her processing the double entendre she'd probably been so exhausted she hadn't even realized she'd said.

Sax could have let it go.

Probably should have.

Hell, any woman who had a lick of sense would probably choose the easygoing Danny Sullivan over a former SEAL haunted by dead battle buddies.

If he had a sister, Sullivan would sure as hell be the guy Sax would want her to hook up with.

"I didn't mean it in any sexual way," she said.

"I know." He smiled. "I just figured it was too good an opportunity to pass up."

"That's odd."

"What?"

"That you'd mention passing up an opportunity."

So they'd both been thinking about that kiss. Which, if her thoughts had gone anywhere along the lines of his, gave him an advantage over Sullivan. Which only had Sax feeling even guiltier than he had been since surviving that shoot-out in the Kush, since even thinking about moving in on a guy who was lying in a hospital bed after getting shot in the head was just lower than a rattlesnake in a rut.

"My mother and I were talking about you

tonight."

So much for the perceived advantage. Dr. Faith Blanchard had always considered him the Antichrist. "Well, that couldn't have been good."

"Actually, it was." She rolled her shoulders. Rubbed her neck again. Despite her looking dead on her feet, the lady's nerves were stretched so tight, he wouldn't have been surprised if she snapped like an over-tightened guitar string.

"Hell, I'm being a lousy host. How would you like a drink?"

"I'm beat. And I'm driving. Throwing alcohol into the mix would be asking for trouble."

"My mom brought over some sweet tea this afternoon."

"That sounds perfect."

He stood up and went into the house to retrieve the drinks, determinedly ignoring the ragging coming from his ghostly teammates for having girlie tea in his fridge.

## 24

When Sax returned to the porch, the guys were blessedly gone and Kara was talking on her cell phone.

"That was your friend," she said when she snapped the phone shut. "The former FBI agent."

"Cait." He handed her the glass.

"Yeah." She took a sip and sighed as if she'd just taken a taste of magic nectar. "I'd forgotten how much I love your mother's sweet tea. Needless to say my mother doesn't allow it in the house."

"Your mama always did run a tight ship."

"Tell me about it." She took another, longer drink. "She's coming by the office tomorrow."

"Not your mother." He took a pull from the bottle of beer he'd brought out with the tea.

"No, Cait McKade. She says her forensics friend is interested in the skull. Seems he likes puzzles, too."

"Which that sure as hell is."

"True. I also told her about what happened tonight at the park." She frowned at that. "I'm still not exactly sure how it came up."

"Cait was a homicide cop before she was FBI. She was also supposedly one of the best interrogators in the business. Which means she's probably pretty good at getting people to volunteer information."

"As a cop I should know better, but it sure worked on me. And guess what?"

"What?"

"She says that she might be able to get some prints off the bullet pieces."

"Really? After they've been inside someone's head?"

"The slug never actually entered the brain, which was the lucky part. But yeah. Something to do with the acid in perspiration etching fingerprints into the metal that can survive weather and all sorts of other stuff."

"Interesting." He took another drink. Pondered that. "Course, if the shooter was wearing gloves, the tests wouldn't work."

"It was a warm day. If the shooter was wearing gloves, not only would someone undoubtedly have noticed, but we can probably rule out its being an accident."

"Good point." He lifted his bottle in a salute. "Guess that's why you're the sheriff and I'm the out-of-work vet."

"You fought a war. Were held prisoner in what had to have been horrific circumstances. I'd say that entitles you to some time off." She glanced over at the mahogany guitar. "That's funny."

"What?"

"It never occurred to me before, but that's the wrong instrument. With your name, you'd think you'd play a saxophone."

"That's what my folks were hoping," Sax revealed. "Lots of people just assume it's for Saxton, but Dad's a sax player himself, so he was hoping it'd rub off on me if he started me out right from the beginning."

"Which was pretty much guaranteeing you'd refuse to go along with the plan."

"Rebel without a clue," he laughingly agreed. "I do play a little tenor sax. From time to time. But I've always felt more at home with the guitar. Back to when Dad and Mom would let me sit in at Bon Temps."

"So, are you going to play at Cole's wedding reception?"

"Mom and Dad are going to sing. So, since it's a family gig, I'll probably sit in for a set or two."

"That's nice." She sipped the tea and considered the idea. "One of the problems with eloping is that I missed out on a reception."

"You'll have to come to this one with me. Drink some champagne and pass yourself a good time. I'll bet your dance card would fill up fast enough."

"I can't remember the last time I danced." She thought about that. "Jared wasn't a dancer." She shook her head. "So, God, it must've been the night of the prom."

"Which is one of my fonder memories of this town."

"It was just one dance. And since you were playing your guitar in the band that night, I'll bet the only reason you danced with me at all was because Jared probably asked you to. As part of that watching-out-for-me deal the two of you had going."

"Yeah. He did." *Make sure my girl has a good time, Douchett. We can't have her sitting around like a wallflower, feeling sorry for herself.* "And believe me, it was the hardest thing I ever did."

Lines furrowed between her expressive eyes. And damned if law-and-order sheriff Kara Conway didn't appear to be pouting. "Well, that's certainly complimentary."

260

"It's the God's honest truth." He raised his right hand to emphasize the statement. "Just swaying to the music, feeling your body against mine, and wanting to touch you, all over, was the closest thing to torture I'd ever known."

Up until that time, anyway. Later, while he'd been held prisoner, he'd discovered the real meaning of the word.

"There were about three layers of starched petticoats between us," she pointed out. "And I had no idea you ever thought of me that way."

"You weren't supposed to know. And for the record, if I'd had a clue I was going to end up feeling that way about you, I would've figured out how to get out of the deal when Jared brought it up. But then you started to grow on me."

"Be still, my heart." She patted her breast. "Another compliment like that and you'll risk my melting into a little puddle of girl-ish need at your feet."

"Never happen. Your son's proof that you're one tough cookie. You've done real well where he's concerned, Kara."

"Okay." Although the fog was beginning to rise, Sax thought he saw a mist of moisture in her eyes. "Now you've hit my soft spot."

"That's probably the way it should be between a mother and son. . . . I know you said your personal life isn't any of my business, but I guess you know about those TV shows he's been watching?"

"All those damn disaster programs?" She leaned her head against the back of the rocker and closed her eyes. "Yes. I know about them."

For a long, silent time there was only the sound of the surf crashing against the cliff, and white, paper-winged moths flinging themselves against the glass of the porch light.

"The therapist we were both seeing back in California assured me that it's natural behavior for kids of his age. That after the death of a parent, or someone else close to them, they can develop an interest in the various causes of death."

"Like natural disasters."

"Exactly. For very young children, death is too remote a possibility. It's just something they read about in fairy tales, or see on a Disney video. Or even when they see a dead animal on the side of the road. There's no immediate connection. But children the age Trey was when Jared was killed begin to personalize death. Which is why they can obsess over disasters or worries about bad guys or bogeymen hiding in the closet or under the bed."

"Okay." Sax blew out a breath. This entire relationship with Kara and her son was turning out to be one conversational mine-field after another. "I wasn't going to bring this up, but I think this is where I need to tell you that along with that whacked-out guy killing Jared, Trey said something about a bad guy trying to kill you, too."

"What?" She was obviously shocked by that revelation. "Trey couldn't possibly know that."

"So it's true?"

"Unfortunately, yes. But there's no way he could know about that. I was always careful to keep it from him."

"My mom used to have a saying about little pitchers having big ears."

"My mother used to say that to my father, too. Whenever she'd catch me eavesdrop-ping."

"Which is what kids do. Apparently Trey overheard you and your mom talking about the bad guy who hurt you being sent off to jail, and you being afraid he could end up an orphan."

"Damn." She shook her head. He saw the muscles tighten in her shoulders. "That's why I came back here: so that, short of mailbox bashers, he wouldn't have to worry about any more bad guys."

She dug in the pocket of her trousers. Pulled out a Kleenex and dabbed at her eyes. *Hell.* Although he'd never considered himself a coward, Sax would rather face an entire village of armed jihadists than a woman's tears.

"You don't have to tell me about it if you don't want."

She shrugged. "Despite my apparently failed attempt to keep it from Trey, it's not any big secret. I screwed up a traffic stop. They're usually routine, but they can also be dangerous, because you never know if you're pulling over a mom late picking a kid up from soccer practice or someone with felony warrants out on them.

"It was night and I saw this guy with a broken taillight who wandered across the centerline. Which sometimes I might have given a pass, but it was a slow night, so I ran a check on the license plate and the car didn't show up stolen. We later found out that was only because it had been taken from a shopping center and the owner hadn't discovered it missing yet.

"So I flipped on my overheads, pulled him over, and called in my location to dispatch. So far, so good."

Sax felt his gut clench. He knew how it felt when you were about to put yourself in harm's way. It was really weird thinking that he and Kara would grow up to have that in common.

"After I called in my location, I turned on the front-facing floodlights. Then I got out of the cruiser as quickly as possible, because one of the things they teach you in the academy is that your car is your coffin."

"And isn't that an encouraging thought?" He'd been in some Hummers in the Kush where he'd felt exactly the same way, but he hated the idea of Kara being in the same situation.

"Admittedly it sounds extreme, but it's true. The one thing you don't want to do is get trapped in your patrol car by taking too much time to release the seat belt, or retrieve your citation book and give anyone inside the car a chance to jump out and attack you.

"Looking back on the situation, which I had to do during the IA investigation, and again in the courtroom when I was called to testify, because the guy actually pleaded not guilty, claiming he believed his life was in danger from a rogue cop —"

"Which was bullshit."

The corners of her lips lifted in a hint of a

smile. "Thanks for the vote of support."

"I've seen guys go rogue. It's one of the dangers of spending too much time in a war zone. But anyone who knows you would know there's not a rogue bone in your body. You were probably the most by-the-book cop on the force."

"Anyway, I *did* do everything by the book that night. A lot of what happened during the confrontation is a blur, but I clearly remember lifting up a little on the trunk as I went by, just as I'd been taught, to make sure no one was hiding in there.

"I'd just gotten up to the driver's-side door when, the next thing I knew, I was on the ground, fighting to keep my weapon from this hopped-up meth dealer — who, from the way he'd freaked, apparently had a liking for his own product.

"I got beaten up pretty bad, but I managed to call in on my radio mike. And the dashboard camera showed that while we were grappling for my gun, I managed to shoot him in the thigh. He got back in the car and took off, but they caught up with him a few miles down the highway, and, like Trey said, after a jury found him guilty, he's doing time."

She drew in a long breath. Let it out. "You know how, during high-stress situations, time seems to slow down?"

"Yeah." He was all too familiar with that concept.

"Well, while the altercation seemed to last a lifetime as it was happening, my cruiser's dashboard camera and dispatch records show that a pair of patrol cars managed to arrive within two minutes of my call."

"Thank God." Never, in his worst nightmares, could Sax have pictured the smart, shy girl he'd gotten his first — and only — crush on in such a life-or-death situation.

"I've gone over it again and again, and I don't think I made a mistake, but it's possible that I lost concentration for just that all-important second as I approached the driver's-side door. It would have been Jared's and my anniversary, and my mind kept jumping back and forth between that day in Tijuana when we got married to the day his lieutenant and the police chaplain arrived to break the news of his death."

"That had to have been tough."

"It was. And oddly, a lot tougher than coming close to dying myself. You know how they say the first stage is denial?"

"Yeah."

"Well, I fell headfirst right into it. The minute I saw the unmarked police vehicle drive up the day Jared died, I suddenly felt

267

cold all over. Because if he'd just been taken to the hospital, I would've gotten a call. Their faces, when they got out of the car, told me he was dead.

"So, as crazy as it probably sounds, I figured that if I bolted the door, if I refused to answer it, if I didn't let them give me that 'We regret to inform you' spiel, Jared wouldn't really be dead."

A tear rolled down her cheek.

"They rang the bell. Knocked on the door. Of course they knew I was in there, because my car was parked outside on the street. So, although it sounds ridiculously dramatic, I dropped down to the floor and crawled into the back bedroom, then climbed out the window. And began running.

"The lieutenant saw me cut across the lawn and took off after me. He tackled me halfway across a neighborhood park. Which definitely captured everyone's attention. And probably horrified him as we rolled around on the grass, with me screaming like a banshee."

Except for that one night, she'd always been as cool as a cucumber. Sax couldn't imagine the pain she must've been experiencing to behave so out of character.

"I'm sorry. That you had to go through that."

She drew in a deep breath. Although there'd been only that one tear, she scrubbed at her face with her hands. "You know what they say — about what doesn't kill you makes you stronger."

The words were no sooner out of her mouth than she closed her eyes again and shook her head. "Damn. Of course you know that."

"We're not talking about me," he said. "What happened up in the Kush was a risk of the job. I knew that going in and each and every time we went out on a mission. You, on the other hand, were blindsided."

"I was a military wife. A cop's wife. A cop myself, dammit. I knew the risks. And accepted them."

"Knowing in the abstract isn't anything like actually expecting anything to happen. Look, one minute you were living a fairly ordinary life, probably worrying about how to pay bills like everyone else, making grocery lists, thinking about some school play your kid might be in; then suddenly, without warning, your world turned upside down and inside out. And yours and Jared's and your son's lives changed forever."

"You nailed it." She glanced up at him.

"How did you know?"

"Because I've made a few of those calls myself. Fortunately not the announcement ones, but I've visited homes of team members I lost over the years. The parents are hard enough to take, but the wives . . ."

It was his turn to take a deep breath. He dragged his hands through his hair as he thought back on Cowboy's pregnant wife. Randy's fiancée. Jake's wife and mother of his twin toddler daughters who'd been too young to grasp the enormity of their loss.

"You were just a kid, about the same age as Trey, when you fell in love with Jared. You were still a kid when you married him, when you sent him off to war, and sure, you knew that death occurs in the military. And on the police force.

"But that doesn't mean that anyone — troops or spouses — ever expects it to hit home. You're too young for widowhood to have been in your plans. It had to have jolted all sense of stability. And security."

"I'm not sure it has that much to do with age. I doubt my mother was expecting to lose a husband either."

"Probably not. But the fact is that both Jared and your dad died too damn young."

"It was my fault." Her words, barely more than a whisper, were easily heard in the still of the night. "Jared's death."

"And how, exactly, do you figure that?"

"I encouraged him to go to work for the force when he got back that last time from downrange. He seemed at loose ends, and since police forces are all based on a para-military system, I thought it might help make the transition to civilian life easier."

"Did it?"

"I guess. Maybe. Hell, I don't know." Her tortured, confused expression broke a heart Sax had forgotten he possessed. "Maybe it would've been worse if he'd gone to work selling shoes, or insurance, or working construction, like he considered doing when he first got out. He seemed to like being a cop well enough. Especially the helping-people part. He was always good at con-necting with civilians."

"Well, then. There you go."

"But his temper definitely became shorter after each tour, and although he denied it, I think he was having flashbacks. There'd be moments when he seemed to zone out. But he kept insisting nothing was wrong."

"That's not unusual." Sax sure as hell hadn't told anyone about his ghosts. Not even when Cole had given him the perfect opening. "He wanted you to see him as a manly man. The guy everyone in town knew you worshiped from day one. Not as some vet with a messed-up head."

"But it didn't change the way I felt. To me he'd always be the man I loved. And if his head was messed-up, well, we could fix it. The same way we did all our other problems."

Like her pregnancy, Sax thought. Her father probably would've been supportive, even though he also would've undoubtedly wanted to kick Jared's bony ass for messing with Ben's baby girl. But Sax imagined Kara's mother would have been less than thrilled about her valedictorian daughter getting knocked up and running off to get married to a guy on the verge of deployment.

"But he wouldn't listen," Sax guessed.

Jared Conway had been a great guy. But that same toughness that had probably made him a gung-ho Marine had also contributed to him being one of the most hardheaded individuals Sax had ever known. And given that Sax had spent more than a decade with SEALs, that was really saying something.

"No. We argued about it. A lot. Including the morning he left for work." She rubbed her temples, looking so weary and oddly frail that Sax had to fight the urge to take her into his arms.

Damn if it wasn't déjà vu all over again. They'd been here before. *Done* this — her crying, him trying to make her feel better — before. That night he'd managed to stop before things had gotten out of hand. Tonight, when every atom in his body was aching for her, he wasn't sure he could.

"He called me from the station. Before going out on patrol. He apologized, said he'd been a damn fool to risk losing Trey and me —"

"You wouldn't have left." The two of them had always been so emotionally entwined it had been impossible to imagine one without the other.

"Never." She paused. "Unless Trey became at risk."

"Which Jared never would've allowed to happen. So I guess you made up."

"As much as is possible in a quick, rushed phone call. He promised he'd call the VA and arrange for some help as soon as he finished the shift."

Her voice became choked as she pushed those last words past the obvious lump in her throat. Damned if he didn't have one of his own.

She didn't say what they were both thinking: that Jared had never had a chance to make that call because some damn cretin had had anger-management problems of his own.

"If he hadn't been thinking about our argument, if he weren't probably going over what he was going to say to the vet counselor —"

"No." About this Sax was perfectly clear. He took both her hands in his. Held them against his chest and looked her straight in the eye. "Jared was a professional. I've never been a cop, but like you said, there're a lot of similarities between the police and the military. He knew how to compartmentalize. He also knew what even us noncops know: that domestic calls can be the most unpredictable and dangerous. So he would've stayed focused on the mission. It wasn't his fault he died. And it definitely, absofuckinglutely wasn't your fault."

The tears she'd been holding back began to fall. *Shit.*

Even as he knew he was taking a huge risk, Sax drew her close. His hand, which had been able to hold a sniper rifle steady for hours, felt unreasonably huge and clumsy as he stroked her back.

"My head knows you're probably right." She snuffled against the front of his shirt. "But my heart . . ." She lifted her gaze to his. "Maybe it's having grown up Catholic, but once the guilt gets inside —"

"It's like a goddamn virus in your bloodstream," Sax said. And didn't he know firsthand about that?

"Exactly." She thought about that for a moment. "Remember that song the class had voted the prom theme song? The Faith Hill one you danced with me?"

"The one from the movie *Pearl Harbor*." At the time Sax had thought it was a damn stupid choice, because, hey, nothing said teenage love like reminiscing about one of America's greatest tragedies.

"That's the one. 'There You'll Be.' I voted against it because I thought it was the wrong choice back then." She unknowingly echoed his thoughts. "But now, those lines about 'all the ways you were right there for me' and 'the strength you gave to me' ring so true. I don't know what I would've done if you hadn't been there for me after that home pregnancy test turned out to be positive."

On the day of the prom. Her eyes had already been red rimmed when he'd picked her up at her parents' house. He'd figured at the time she'd been weeping because Jared hadn't been there to take her to the dance. Leaving her stuck with him.

"Which I guess turned out to have been a good thing," he said. "You having Jared's son."

"Yes." Despite her eyes being still wet, she smiled at that. "Trey's a blessing." She sighed, but this time the soft breath didn't sound as sad. "This is getting to be a bad habit. Me crying all over you."

"Hey, a couple tears aren't exactly bawling your head off."

"True. But we've both been ignoring the huge elephant in the room. Or on the porch."

"What elephant would that be?" he asked, knowing all too well.

"That pity kiss we shared the night of the prom."

"You needed comforting. When a guy's eighteen, he pretty much goes on instinct. Since I had no real good advice to give you, I went with the first thing that popped into my mind."

"I never told Jared."

He'd been wondering about that. "Wasn't all that much to tell."

"I guess not." Did she sound a little disappointed by his claim — which was totally a lie — that the kiss hadn't rocked his teenage world? "But here's my idea," she continued. "Maybe it's time I was there for you."

"I'm doing okay."

"I'm not questioning that or I wouldn't have let Trey come home with you. But maybe we can act like each other's support system. Like those sponsors they have in twelve-step programs . . .

"If I start feeling too guilty, I'll call you. And you can talk me off the ledge. The way you did that night. And surprisingly, it's a relief to have someone to talk with about Trey. About how and why he feels the way he does. If my mother ever knew all the details of what happened to me . . ."

Her voice trailed off again.

"Mothers worry," he said, even as he suspected Dr. Faith Blanchard would've called the Oceanside hospital and gotten hold of her daughter's medical records. Which meant she knew exactly what had happened.

"Tell me about it."

They sat there, side by side, neither one saying anything.

Sax was just thinking how comfortable it was to be with Kara this way, in this place, when finally she broke the silence.

"So, my idea is, if you ever start having problems readjusting to civilian life, or dealing with everyone making you out to be the town hero, which has got to be a burden —

especially given that, from what I've heard, you were the sole survivor of that last mission — you can call me and I'll do the same for you. Not that you'd need talking off a ledge," she said quickly. Too quickly. "But just in case you need a sounding board. Someone to vent to."

"SEALs don't vent. That's for girlie men." He smiled when he said it, which drew a welcome smile in return.

"Of course they don't. But everyone needs someone. And with Cole all caught up in getting married, you probably wouldn't want to go dumping personal stuff on him. So I'm just saying that if you should need someone, well, I'm available."

Sax understood her reasoning. But dammit, he didn't want to be Kara's sponsor, like they were in some damn twelve-step program. Sure, he'd do anything in his power to help her dump the guilt he knew all too well, guilt he also knew Jared would not want her to be feeling. But the problem was, there were a lot more things he'd rather be doing with her. Hot, wet, carnal stuff.

Stuff he had no business thinking of. Not as messed-up as he was right now. But sometimes the little head refused to listen to the big head.

She said she was available. Probably, with

a little bit of effort, he'd be able to move things beyond what she was suggesting. The trouble with that idea was that the last thing he wanted was for her to regret being with him.

Which she probably should. Because, if he were to be honest with himself, while he might not be as bad off as it sounded as if Jared had been, he also doubted he'd be in any shape for a serious relationship until he managed to exorcise those ghosts rattling around in his brain.

As Quinn McKade's sniper spotter, it hadn't been anything for him to take an entire day to move the length of a couple football fields. What a lot of people didn't realize was that while ten percent of his and Quinn's job had been to act as surgeons with bullets (neutralizing the enemy), ninety percent of the time they were moving forward of the team, gathering intel, lying in wait for hours. Or even days.

So even as he felt the painful ache of desire, although it sure wasn't his first choice, Sax was willing to help Kara find her way off this dead-end road that had led her to an undeserved guilt trip.

He was going to stay patient and do this for her. Not for Jared, who — thank you, Jesus! — hadn't shown up to warn Sax away from his wife.

At least, not yet.

## 25

What was it about Sax Douchett that had always had her telling him things that she'd never shared with anyone else? All right, obviously she wouldn't have been able to keep her unplanned pregnancy a secret for long. But still, Sax had been the first to know. Even before she'd broken the news to Jared.

She'd never really had anyone to share such confidences with. Not that she hadn't had girlfriends. She had. But they'd been casual, occasional slumber-party type friends. Certainly not anyone who knew all your secret hopes and desires and would sigh, giggle, and moan with you over your latest crush.

Because Jared had always been not only her latest and only crush, but her best friend. These days he'd have been her BFF. Unfortunately, as she'd discovered the hard way, *forever* could be a relative term.

During her senior year, after Jared had enlisted, Sax had done his best to fill that huge gaping hole in her life, and only now was Kara beginning to fully understand the sacrifices he'd made in order to always be there for her.

He'd also been hot. Not that she'd been the least bit tempted to stray while Jared was away. But she had, after all, been a normal teenage girl with normal teenage hormones, and there'd been something wickedly sexy about Sax. He'd been Johnny Depp in torn blue jeans.

So, needless to say, she'd looked.

And that one unforgettable night, she had done more than look.

Not that their shared kiss would have gone anywhere. Even if Sax hadn't pulled away. Because if there was anything worse than a pity kiss, it would have to be pity sex, and fortunately he'd saved her from having to suffer that!

At least, that was what Kara had always told herself, on those rare occasions she allowed herself to think about it.

She could tell he was interested. That if she suddenly jumped him now, right here on his wraparound porch, he probably wouldn't push her away. And if it weren't for Trey, she might actually allow herself to just go for it.

She was, after all, a grown woman, with a woman's needs, and considering that Jared's PTSD — if that was what it, indeed, had been — had made him uninterested in sex from the time he'd returned from Iraq, then factoring in his deployment, she realized it had been a very long time since she'd had an orgasm that hadn't been of the do-it-herself variety.

The truth was, celibacy was making her feel old. Older, even, than her own mother, who'd definitely had a speculative gleam in her eye as John O'Roarke had headed toward them across that cafeteria floor.

The problem was, Kara wasn't solely a widow. She was also a mother of a son who'd already lost one person he'd adored. If she became emotionally involved with someone, it followed that Trey, too, would be affected. And if any hypothetical affair she might be considering went south, he'd only be hurt again. Something she couldn't allow.

"We're just talking friendship," she said. "Not the kind with benefits."

"You just lost me."

"I mean, we can't have sex," she decided.

Sax rubbed that shadowed chin. Slowly. Thoughtfully. As if thinking her words over.

"Okay. Though I don't recall suggesting it."

"You hadn't. *Yet.*"

*Damn.* She hadn't meant to say that out loud. But now that she had, perhaps it was a good thing just to get the subject out into the open.

"But I thought it was only fair to let you know, in case you ever might want to consider it — not that I'm saying there aren't a lot of women in town who'd love to go to bed with you, because you're even hotter than you were back in school, but . . . And, oh, God, now I'm babbling, which I never, ever do, so would you please just tell me to shut up before I make an even bigger fool of myself?"

"I'm a male." He told her something that was all too obvious. The man radiated what were undoubtedly lethal amounts of testosterone without even trying. No doubt about it — Sax Douchett should come with a bright red warning label attached. "No way am I going to think a woman foolish, or tell her to shut up, when she's telling me I'm hot."

"Now you're laughing at me." She could hear it in his voice.

"Not at you. Maybe at the situation," he allowed. "And the timing, which, between us, always seems to suck."

And couldn't she agree with that? "It's nothing against you, personally."

"Glad to hear that."

"It's Trey. I don't want him hurt."

Every bit of humor left his eyes. His mouth, which had been quirked at the corners, hardened into a harsh line. "No way would I ever do anything to hurt your son, Kara."

"You wouldn't mean to." *Damn.*

Why didn't someone just throw her a shovel so she could dig this hole she'd gotten herself into a little deeper? Like to China?

"But if we were to get involved and become a couple, since you've already invited him to ride in the car at the parade with you, and play with your dog, well, he'd become even more involved with you."

"And the harm in that would be?"

"When we broke up, either you'd be out of his life —"

"Interesting that you're already looking ahead to the breakup before we've gotten to first base," he said mildly. "So, who, exactly, do you see doing the dumping?"

"I've no idea." Weren't there earthquakes in this part of the country? Couldn't the ground just open up and swallow her? Now? And put her out of her misery? "It could be mutual."

"Amiable, then."

"This isn't high school, when sex is a forbidden, guilty pleasure and breakups are earth-shattering. We're both adults. We were once close friends, so there's no reason to think we couldn't have sex —"

"Or a longer-term sexual relationship."

"Or that," she agreed. The idea was so damn tempting. "But Trey's a child. He doesn't understand that affairs don't necessarily last. So he'd get his hopes up. Maybe even start thinking of the possibility of you becoming his stepfather. Then his heart would be shattered again. And I can't risk that."

He remained quiet for a while, looking out over the ocean, where the whitecaps were gilded with silver moonlight. Somewhere in the distance, a buoy clanged. Why couldn't there be buoys in life? Kara wondered. To warn a person away from dangerous shoals?

"And you think I'd risk that?" he asked finally.

"You wouldn't mean to, but it could still happen."

"A meteorite could hit this porch while we're sitting here, too."

"I know you think I'm being foolish —"

"No. I think you're being a protective mother. The way good mothers are supposed to be."

"Okay." She blew out a quick breath, relieved that not only had they come to an understanding, but it looked as if she might even be able to escape this too-personal conversation with a modicum of dignity intact. "Then we agree?"

"That you're a supermom? Absolutely."

"I was referring to our being friends."

"I've always been your friend, sugar. Your having a son hasn't changed that. Hell, if you'd come back home with Jared, we'd still be friends."

Kara wasn't sure that would have been possible. But since it was a moot point, she wasn't going to argue it. "*Just* friends." She wanted to get this clear. For both of them.

Another silence. Which lasted longer than the others. "I can live with that."

"Really?"

It was what she'd wanted. So why did she suddenly feel disappointed he'd agreed so easily? If he were seriously interested in her, in a sexual way, shouldn't he at least try to stake a claim?

Which was even more ridiculous, since no way would she want a man who even thought along those lines.

He laughed, a deep, rough sound that got beneath her skin and made her tingle in places she'd forgotten she *could* tingle. "I suspect this is one of those cases where I'm damned if I do, and damned if I don't. There's no right answer. . . .

"Tell you what. Trey and I, we'll be guy buddies. You and I will be friends. Kinda like we were back in our senior year. You want to take things to the next level, you're going to have to be the one to make the call. How's that?"

"Entirely reasonable."

Kara told herself that a prudent, sensible woman would be relieved to have gotten her point across so well. And she'd always been both prudent and sensible. So why was she feeling let down?

"You're dead on your feet," he said, unknowingly giving her an excuse for her uncharacteristic ambivalence. "Maybe I ought to carry the kid out to the car and give you a ride home."

"Don't be ridiculous." A burst of welcome annoyance burned away the odd lingering confusion. "I'm a cop. I've worked double shifts lots of times. I'll just go in and get him and —"

"Why don't you leave him here?"

"Because he has a perfectly good home

with my mother and me."

"Your mother's in Portland with John and Danny," he reminded her. "And you're meeting with Cait tomorrow morning. It's Sunday. I'll feed him breakfast, take him with me to the lumberyard to pick up some building materials for Bon Temps. Maybe let him hammer a few nails, get him some lunch, then drop him back at your mom's house around suppertime."

"That's very generous of you, but —"

He put a finger against her lips, cutting off her planned protest. And Kara knew she was in deep, deep trouble when that simple touch had her toes curling in her shoes — those ugly black oxfords that suddenly had her wishing she were wearing something sexy, like Sherry's high, rhinestone-strapped sandals.

"It's what friends do," he said. "Truth is, I'm looking forward to it. And, since you're the one who mentioned the boy living with two women, having him spend the day with Cole and me learning manly construction skills isn't such a bad thing."

"It's a good thing." And something Jared had always been looking forward to doing once he got out of the Marines and settled into normal family life. "May I ask you a question?"

"Sure."

"Does anyone ever say no to you?"

"You would have. That night. Even if I'd begged."

The look he was giving her was even warmer than that brief touch had been, creating sparks from embers she'd thought had long cooled.

*You have two, maybe even three crimes to solve,* she scolded herself firmly. *You don't have time to even be thinking about sex.*

"I have a hard time imagining you begging for anything." She stood up. "I want to check Trey one more time. Then I really do need to go."

After ensuring that her son was still fine — better than fine, if the way he was sleeping with his arm flung around Velcro's huge neck was any indication — Kara decided that Sax's suggestion really did make the most sense.

While he might not have gotten off the porch when she'd arrived, he walked her to the cruiser. She'd just reached for the door when he caught her hand.

"What?" she asked as he turned her toward him.

"We forgot something."

His eyes, in the spreading circle of light from the porch, turned from their usual electric blue to the color of a storm-tossed sea.

"What?" she asked again.

He cupped the fingers of his free hand under her chin. "This."

Before she could utter a single word of protest, he'd pulled her into his arms.

Kara reeled from the raw hunger of Sax's lips as he crushed his mouth to hers. Despite last night's hot dream, where he'd kissed her exactly like this, again and again, all over, she couldn't have imagined the tempest that suddenly swirled around them in the moist, salt-tinged air.

Unlike on that long-ago night, he wasn't gentle. But as he fed her hard, passionate, openmouthed kisses, Kara didn't want gentleness. There was an aggression in his kiss, a harshness that might have frightened her had her own needs not been equally as powerful. And as urgent.

If sin had a taste, oh, God, it would taste exactly like Sax Douchett! Hot, hungry, and dangerously male. The man tasted so good she could eat him up even as he devoured her. She twined her arms around his neck and kissed him back, hard, tongues tangling, matching his greed.

She was sandwiched between the hard metal door of her cruiser and the wall of his body. Her breasts, crushed against his chest, ached. Wanting, needing more, she wrapped her left leg around his, pressing her hips against his erection.

His strong hands grabbed her butt, not gently, lifting her up, grinding his pelvis against hers. One of them — it could have been either him or her, or maybe both — moaned.

Just when she feared they were on the verge of combustion, the same way he'd done so many years ago, he suddenly backed away, breaking the exquisitely painful contact and leaving her reeling.

She sagged a little against the cruiser. Stared up at him.

"For the record," he said roughly, "unlike the first one, that wasn't any damn pity kiss."

That said, he opened the door of the black-and-white and waited while she unclipped her keys from her utility belt, climbed into the driver's seat, and struggled to make her numbed fingers fasten the seat belt.

"Drive safely."

"I'm a cop. I've taken tactical and high-speed driving courses. I know how to operate a vehicle."

"Not saying you don't." He stood up

again, shoved his hands into the back pockets of his jeans. "I'll bet you're a dynamo behind the wheel. But the roads out here are narrow, winding, without any shoulders, and accidents can happen to the best of us. And since friends care about friends, I care about you."

That was perfectly reasonable, Kara told herself as she drove back into town to her mother's home.

But was it enough?

Deciding that she'd worry about what to do about Sax later, when she had time to absorb this new twist to her life, she turned her mind instead to a more immediate problem — the need to talk with her son about what had happened that day she'd almost lost her life.

She now realized she'd made a mistake by trying to keep it from him. Because, as bad as what had happened might be, she feared his imagination was making it worse.

When he'd been younger, he'd loved the children's classic *Where the Wild Things Are,* begging her to read it again and again every night before bed. And just last fall she'd taken him to see the movie about the little boy who, after a fight with his mother, ran away to the land of wild things, who proclaimed him their king.

Unfortunately, he'd learned at too young an age that in real life, wild things could be just as unpredictable, but far more dangerous than their fictional counterparts.

# 26

Faith was tired. Not just the usual long-day-topped-off-by-emergency-surgery tired. But fatigued with a weariness that went all the way to the bone.

She'd been feeling this way for months, even before Ben had been killed, which was why she couldn't merely blame her depression on having been widowed.

Realizing that the old adage about a lawyer representing himself was applicable to doctors, as well, she'd also had a full physical with her own internist, who'd ruled out clinical depression, and any physical reasons for what she could only describe as malaise.

And, although she hated to admit it, dammit, boredom.

It wasn't that she didn't love her work. She did. And just when cutting open a brain might seem to have become routine, she'd catch a rare case like Danny Sullivan's, and that old adrenaline burst she'd first experienced as an intern on neurological rotation would kick in.

But like all adrenaline bursts, while exciting at the time, it only left her feeling even more drained.

She'd also discovered that she disliked the paperwork involved with serving as the hospital's administrator. Soon after Shelter Bay Memorial Hospital had been bought by a health provider with several other medical facilities under its corporate umbrella, she'd been surprised to be offered the job by the company's CEO.

She had, of course, gone home and discussed the offer with Ben. Although, until his dying day, he continued to believe he'd done the right thing for his family by moving from Portland to the slower-paced existence of Shelter Bay, and while she hadn't hesitated when he'd suggested the idea, there'd been times over the years when he'd expressed regrets about the professional sacrifice she'd been forced to make.

Despite having always assured him, whenever the subject came up, that she was perfectly happy with how her life had turned out, Faith secretly missed the excitement working in a city hospital provided. So she'd accepted the job, hoping that it would provide a career challenge she'd been missing.

Instead, she'd found herself drowning in meetings and reports, many of which seemed unnecessary, others downright trivial.

Not that her job was trivial. Just the opposite. After all, the majority of U.S. health care was provided by small community hospitals like Shelter Bay's, rather than large, academically affiliated tertiary-care centers such as OHSU.

But while all medical care facilities faced the same difficulties with financial pressures, increasing regulation, public reporting, and increasingly complicated health care for an aging population, the impact of those problems was magnified in smaller hospitals. The same way waves were more likely to capsize rowboats than ocean freighters.

She'd gone into medicine to fix people. To make them better. Which she liked to believe she'd done way more often than not. And those times when a patient would show up with brain cancer or an inoperable tumor, she liked to believe she'd helped make their inevitable passing a little easier.

Although she'd never adopted the God complex so many of her peers seemed to wear like a second skin, having worked with a range of administrators over the years — some good, some bad, and some downright ugly — she'd possessed what she now realized was an admittedly exaggerated Superwoman vision of what type of administrator she'd be if she ever received the opportunity to be in that position.

She would be understanding. Kind. Honest, forthright, and ethical. Her obligation would be to both the hospital staff and patients, and most of all, she'd be fair to all.

It had taken her less than one week to discover that in this new position, her true work would no longer revolve around patient care. That she'd be single-handedly responsible for ensuring there was enough operating capital for proper health care, equipment, and employee payroll.

She'd once spent several weeks on an OB/GYN internship in a Sister of Mercy hospital, and when she'd complained about how much time was being wasted diligently documenting every billable item down to the last aspirin, the nun who was CEO of the hospital had succinctly explained, "No money, no mission."

What Faith hadn't understood was that as much as she might try to play the role of a benevolent leader, issues of loyalty and fairness came up on an almost daily basis. An act of generosity to one was, especially in this self-centered culture, inevitably seen as depriving someone else. Even a proposed solution to modernize and streamline the cafeteria kitchen had been met with union opposition because it risked putting some employees out of work.

Faith understood that the need to protect one's own situation was merely human nature, but over the past few months she'd come to the conclusion that even Wonder Woman — were she to ever find herself in Faith's position — would become discouraged.

There were times when she felt that if she heard, "It's not fair," one more time, she'd scream. Then throw herself off the top of the Shelter Bay Bridge.

"What's wrong?"

The male voice shattered her introspection and she glanced over to see John, looking about as haggard and exhausted as she felt, standing in the doorway leading to his hotel suite bedroom.

He'd argued that he wanted to spend the night in the ICU with Danny, which hadn't been allowed. Faith could have possibly found an empty room for him to bunk out in for a few hours, but she'd felt he needed time and space to decompress and unwind. Which was why she'd talked him into letting her book them a two-bedroom suite at the hotel closest to the hospital campus.

He had, naturally, insisted on paying not just his share, but the entire amount. Understanding male pride, and also realizing that he wanted, in some personal way, to pay her back for taking care of her nephew, she hadn't argued.

Nor had she protested when he'd stopped in the lobby store on the way to the elevator and bought a bottle of wine and a corkscrew. She figured they could both use a drink after what they'd been through.

"Nothing." She managed a smile. "I was just talking to myself."

"I thought maybe you had a call from the hospital."

"We've only been gone ten minutes."

"Yeah. But stuff happens."

Indeed.

"If I didn't think Daniel would be fine, I wouldn't have dragged you away," she assured him. Then she picked up her purse and gestured toward the bottle of Cloudline pinot noir still on the table. "Why don't you open that while I go freshen up?"

Each bedroom had its own bathroom, and Faith had to bite back a groan as she looked at her reflection in the mirror. Although she'd loved her husband beyond description, when John had been walking toward her across the hospital cafeteria, for a fleeting moment her heart had taken a little leap and she'd felt exactly like a teenage girl again.

Unfortunately, the makeup she'd applied before going to work had long ago melted away. She also had flat surgical-cap hair, and the dark shadows beneath her eyes betrayed both age and exhaustion.

She dabbed concealer over the bruiselike shadows, a bit of peach blush to add some much-needed color to her cheeks, touched up the shine on her nose, and brightened her lips with a subtle, nude-tone lipstick that hopefully wouldn't have John realizing that she'd spiffed up solely for him.

"And once again the teenage girl rears her insecure head," she muttered, trying to finger-fluff some body back into her hair.

He'd opened the wine and had poured two glasses when she'd returned to the living room.

"Thank you," she said as politely as if she'd been having tea with the queen of England. Or the First Lady.

Would he think she wanted him to sit next to her if she sat on the sofa? Or if she chose the chair, would he feel she was seeking distance to warn him away? Uncharacteristically indecisive, after accepting the glass he held out to her she wandered over to the window.

"We lucked out with the view. Last time I stayed here, my room looked down on the highway."

And wasn't that sparkling opening repartee? *Next you can dazzle him with an update on tomorrow's weather forecast.*

"Yeah." He came over to stand beside her. "It is nice."

She'd never noticed before how large he was. Not fat. He was remarkably fit for a man of his age, and as a physician, she'd seen a lot of men. But unlike Ben, who'd been tall and lanky, John O'Roarke was tall, and well . . . substantial. He towered over her in a way that could have been intimidating, had he not possessed such a kind and gentle soul.

They stood there in a silence that managed to be charged, yet still oddly comfortable at the same time, sipping their wine, looking out at the river.

After a while, he slanted her a sideways glance. "You look tired."

So much for the hoped-for cosmetic fix. "It's been a long day. I'm not as young as I used to be. I guess I don't bounce back as fast as I used to."

*Smooth move. Point out that he's in a hotel room with an old, haggard broad.*

"I didn't mean that the way it sounded." That he'd picked up on that feminine pique she'd been appalled to hear in her voice reminded Faith that he was, after all, a trained investigator. And expert at catching nuances and listening as much to what people *didn't* say as what they *did.*

He touched his palm to the side of her face, turning her head toward him. Then skimmed a calloused finger beneath her eye. Although she knew it was physically impossible, she felt as if he'd touched one of those sparklers the kids had been waving around at the park during the fireworks to her skin.

"You look tired," he repeated. "But beautiful. You've never looked anything but beautiful to me."

"I've never been as dramatic-looking as Gloria." His wife had been a striking brunette who'd always made Faith feel washed-out by comparison.

"Glory was dramatic. Both in looks and temperament." He smiled, as if to himself, at some memory. "See this?" He touched the finger that had created such warmth to a thin white line at his temple.

"It's a scar."

"From a coffee cup she threw at me our first year of marriage." The smile reached eyes that were as tired-looking as her own. "Woman had a temper that could blow like Mount Saint Helens. And a pitching arm like Sandy Koufax. But she was just as quick to make up."

When those dark eyes softened, Faith realized he was thinking about makeup sex. With his wife. And wasn't that yet another waste of expensive department-store lipstick? Another less-than-brilliant idea — not only bringing up his beloved wife, who'd died too young, but inviting comparison.

"You miss her." *Duh.*

"Sure. The same way you miss Ben." He frowned. "I miss him, too. And I'll always feel guilty I didn't get the guy who killed him."

"It was an accident."

"Probably." Was the hint of doubt she thought she detected in his tone merely her imagination? "But if I'd only known he was checking back on cold cases, maybe I could've uncovered something. . . ."

"What?" Faith's blood, which had been nicely warmed by the wine and the proximity to a very appealing man, turned to ice. "Surely you're not suggesting Ben's death might not have been accidental?"

"Hell, Faith, I don't know." He shrugged wide shoulders she knew, from watching the way he'd taken such devoted care of Gloria in her final months, were capable of carrying heavy burdens. "But Kara's got this expert coming in tomorrow" — he glanced down at his wide-banded stainless-steel watch — "today," he corrected. "Cait McKade's a former FBI special agent who supposedly knows about a way to get prints off slugs. All we've got is a shell casing, but just maybe she can do something with that."

Faith was reeling. And not from a single glass of wine.

"Kara's bringing in a former federal agent to investigate her father's death?" And had never mentioned a word about it?

"Not exactly. Sax Douchett suggested the woman because apparently they're friends and she knows a forensic pathologist who might be able to do something with that skull found in the cave on the beach. The thing is, we don't have any unexplained deaths in Shelter Bay. Never have. So Kara's going to give Sax's friend the casing and just see if something shows up."

"Well." Faith was floored that her daughter could have kept such important and personal information from her.

"She undoubtedly didn't want to worry you unnecessarily," John suggested reassuringly. "Since it probably won't turn out to be anything."

Although she'd always prided herself on her ability to multitask, Faith was stunned when she was suddenly struck with three disparate emotions simultaneously.

The first was shock at the unsavory possibility that her husband had been murdered.

Second, if that was the case, she wanted the killer apprehended. And despite having always voted for the most liberal candidate on the ballot, she decided there was something to be said for an eye-for-an-eye concept of justice.

But at the same time she was considering the gut-level appeal of bringing the death penalty back to Oregon, as she gazed up into the warmth of caring in John's patient eyes, Faith experienced a wistful longing that had her going up onto her toes.

He paused. Just long enough to give her time to accept what she was doing. To change her mind.

Which she had no intention of doing.

There was a question in his eyes. Without words, she answered it.

He exhaled a breath. Tossed back his wine,

as if wishing it were something stronger, then took her own half-empty glass from her hands and walked a few feet away to place them both, side by side, on an end table.

Feeling as if her shoes had been nailed to the carpet, Faith remained where she was.

And waited.

And then he was back. With his eyes on hers, he took her face in his hands, cupping her cheeks in his wide palms. The pads of his fingers were heavily calloused from his woodworking, but his touch was as light as dandelion fluff. As reverent as a prayer.

Although they'd both gone still as stones, inside, her heart was hammering against her ribs. A liquid warmth was flowing through her veins.

*Please.*

Faith had no idea whether she'd said the word out loud, or whether he'd simply read the plea in her mind. But whichever, he responded, lowering his head to close that small breath of space between them.

As the softness of his mouth touched hers, she breathed in the scent of him — the lingering antiseptic of the hospital, the soap he'd used to wash his military-short hair, the decidedly male musk she hadn't even realized she'd been missing that she was inhaling like a woman who'd been crawling on her hands and knees across the Sahara and had suddenly come across an icy spring.

Her hands came up around his neck as he kissed her with tenderness. With heat. And with a need she could feel pressed against her belly.

"Do you have any idea how much I want you?" His voice was rough. Pained.

Her heart hammered more fiercely. "Tell me."

After kissing her so deeply he stole her breath, he placed his hot mouth to her ear and proceeded to do exactly that, sharing all the hot, sexy things he wanted to do to her. With her.

The same things she wanted him to do to her. Was desperate to do with him.

She dragged his mouth back to hers.

The tenderness was gone, burned away by a fiery need. As flames licked through her own blood, Faith said yes. Yes. And yes again. To everything.

# 27

Having originally planned to be career military, and not wanting to subject a family to constantly having him go wheels-up at a moment's notice, which was pretty much the way SEALs lived, Sax had never given much thought to having kids.

But as he pushed the flat cart through the aisles of Lombard's Lumberyard, he was getting one hell of a kick out of Kara's son, who was nearly bouncing off the walls with excitement.

"What color are you going to paint the walls?" Trey asked as they stood side by side in front of the racks of chips. They'd already arranged to have the Sheetrock, shingles, electrical, hardware, and plumbing supplies, along with some heavy-duty mops and buckets, delivered to the job site and were now down to the fun stuff.

"Hadn't really given it all that much thought," Sax admitted. "What looks good to you?"

"I wanted to paint my room at Grandma's red. But she said it would make me too excited to get to sleep."

"Don't want people sleeping at Bon Temps. But if they got too excited, maybe they might start getting into fights."

"Mom and Dad hated when they got called out to bar fights on the job."

Since he doubted that was information they would have shared with their child, Sax decided this was yet another case of eavesdropping. Which belatedly made him wonder what, if anything, the kid might have overheard of the conversation he and Kara had had last night, when Trey was supposed to be sleeping.

"So maybe we'll choose something else." He looked at the rows and rows of green shades. "Celery. Sage. Basil. Dill. Key lime. Mint. Who thinks up all these colors?"

"They're all named for food," Trey pointed out. "Which might be good if you're going to be serving meals."

"Can't pass a good time without food. Problem is, green makes me think of bein' back in the military, where they seemed to buy it by the barrelful."

"Grandma says blue is relaxing. That's why she painted her bedroom blue. Sorta that color." He pointed at one of the darker chips in the next row.

Sax shook his head. "I'd be laughed out of town if anyone ever heard I'd bought myself a can of paint called Teeny Bikini."

"Yeah." Trey pulled a face. "It is a girlie name."

"Sure is. Besides, while we don't want folks to get overexcited, we also don't want them falling asleep during the *fais do-do* 'cause they're so relaxed, either."

"What's a fay-doe-doe?" Trey pronounced it carefully, phonetically, but came pretty damn close.

"Technically, it translates to going to sleep, from when mamas would put their children down to bed in a little side room of the dance hall, so the babies could sleep while the grown-ups partied. Over the years, it just came to mean a dance party."

They went back to perusing colors, making their way back to the beginning of the display.

"Are you going to be cooking Cajun food?"

"Sure. That and a bunch of seafood, probably." Sax was beginning to realize there was a lot more to opening up a place than just getting rid of spiders and fixing up Sheetrock.

"Cajun food uses a lot of pepper sauce, right?" Trey asked after they'd dismissed a bunch more shades.

"We like our food spicy, that's for sure."

And their women, too. Which Kara had definitely proven herself to be with that kiss last night.

"Then maybe you ought to go with that one."

Sax plucked the chip Kara's son was pointing to out of the rack. " 'Cajun Red,' " he read. "Good call, and near exactly the color of boiled crab shells."

"That's what I was thinking. And it looks like Tabasco sauce, too."

Sax tilted his head and studied the small, serious face. "Smart head and a good eye. That's a pretty awesome combination."

"I just notice things," Trey said with a shrug.

Kara was right: The kid needed some male influence in his life. You expected to hear compliments from moms and grandmas. That was their job. His own mom had certainly always been overly generous with her praise. But a single positive word from their dad could have Sax, Cole, and J.T. beaming inside for days.

"I was thinking about something else," Trey said. The enthusiasm in his voice validated Sax's thoughts about the effect of male approval. "Bon Temps is all about having fun, right?"

"The name means 'good times.' No point in going to all the trouble to fix it up if people don't pass themselves a good time."

"When we lived on the base in California, they used to hold this Mardi Gras celebration every year, like they do in New Orleans, which was a lot of fun. So maybe you oughta hang up a bunch of those beads they throw from floats, and masks and stuff."

Sax rubbed his chin as he pictured Bon Temps with gold, purple, and green Mardi Gras masks on the Tabasco-colored walls, and beads strung from light fixtures. "My mom and dad had it done up more like an old Cajun cabin," he said. "Rough wood tables, benches, butcher paper on the tables for shelling the crawfish, that sorta thing. But you know, *cher,* your idea sounds real festive."

"And bright colors would be exciting. But in a good way. So people would want to hang around and spend a lot of money," Trey suggested.

"Now you're talking." Sax put his hand on the boy's shoulder. "Let's go buy us some brushes and tarps and stuff while Mr.

Lombard mixes us up a mess of Cajun Red."

"All right." Trey pumped a small, triumphant fist in the air.

At first it had seemed a little strange, taking over what should've been Jared Conway's job. But as they debated the merits of rolling over spraying, Sax realized that somewhere during the shopping trip, it had begun to feel pretty damn right.

# 28

Kara hadn't exactly known what to expect from Cait McKade. The magnolia-drenched voice on the phone suggested the wife of Sax's former SEAL teammate might be a Southern-belle type, but her previous careers as a homicide cop and FBI Special Agent didn't mesh with the idea of big hair and sparkly earrings.

Which had left Kara admittedly curious.

One thing she never would have expected was the attractive redhead in the black sleeveless top and slacks to be so hugely pregnant that Kara was afraid she might go into labor at any moment.

Cait turned down the offer of anything to drink. "I pee all the time these days," she said as she slowly, laboriously lowered herself into the chair on the visitor's side of Kara's desk. "No point in making it worse."

"I appreciate your coming all the way here. But is it safe for you to fly this late in your pregnancy?"

She laughed at that, a rich amusement tinged with irony. "Fortunately, Phoenix Team has a private jet. Plus, believe it or not, I'm only at twenty-four weeks."

"Wow." Surprised that the other woman was so large at only six months, Kara had spoken without thinking. "I'm sorry. I didn't mean —"

"Don't worry about it." Cait held up a hand to ward off any prolonged apology. "I know I look like a damn water buffalo. But I'm carrying twins. Both of whom, if the gymnastics inside me are any indication, are destined to be Olympic pole-jumping champions, or play linebacker for the Carolina Panthers. Which is undoubtedly more likely, since their father is six-foot-five and built like Mount Rushmore."

"Ouch." Kara unconsciously covered her own stomach with her hand, inwardly cringing as she thought about the prospect of giving birth to twins. Let alone such large ones.

"Ouch, indeed. I've already informed my OB that if she doesn't come through with every drug in the hospital meds cabinet, I'll have no choice but to drag out my old FBI Glock and shoot her."

"Sounds totally reasonable to me," Kara

said sympathetically.

"So." The other woman stretched out her legs, frowned at her obviously swollen ankles, and said, "Why don't you show me what you've got?"

"I've no way of actually knowing if the cases are connected," Kara said as she got up and went over to the closet.

"What does your spidey sense tell you?"

"That I've three unsolved cases in a town that isn't supposed to experience real crimes."

"Three?" An auburn brow arched. "You mentioned the bones you found out at Sax's place. And the bullet fragments from yesterday's shooting. That's two."

"Sax seems to believe there may be another." Kara took down the Baggie containing the spent shell casing found near her father's body. "No one ever found the bullet that killed my father last fall. But we do have this. Not that it'd probably be that much use to you."

"Actually, like I told you when I called, there's a new technique for retrieving fingerprints from bullet casings and bomb fragments after they have been fired or detonated. It relies on the subtle corrosion of metal surfaces."

"My father was shot six months ago."

"Doesn't matter. The patterns of corrosion remain on the metal surface long after any finger residue is gone. And what's really cool is that scientists have shown that even if the metal's cleaned, heated to as high as a thousand degrees, or even painted over, fingerprints remain."

"I never heard about that."

"It's not that well-known. Yet. The Brits are using it more than police in this country. But Phoenix Team likes to stay on top of things. I'm no scientist, but it has something to do with chloride ions from the salt in sweat, which produces lines of corrosion along the ridges of the fingerprint."

"Unless killing was your business, you'd probably sweat a bit while loading a gun," Kara said.

"That'd be my thought. The cool thing is that when metal's heated —"

"Which is what would happen when a gun's fired."

"Exactly." Cait nodded. "When it's fired, the chemical reaction speeds up and actually makes the corrosion more pronounced. The only way to get rid of it is to abrasively scrape the surface layer of the metal off." She studied the cartridge shell. "Which wasn't done here. Another thing working in our favor is that different metals corrode differently. One of the ones the test succeeds best on is brass."

Which was what gun cartridge casings happened to be made of.

"Bingo," Kara said.

"Bingo, indeed. Whoever loaded the gun that killed your father or shot that guy in the park yesterday would've used their thumbs to push the shell and bullets in. That's who you want. The people who loaded those guns."

"I'm impressed." And encouraged.

The other woman shrugged. "It's my job." Cait turned the bag over and over in her hands, studying it thoughtfully. "You said Sax feels there's a connection?"

"There's nothing to point to that, but —"

"Quinn has always said that he never worked with a spotter who possessed even an iota of Sax Douchett's instincts. So, if I were you, I sure wouldn't discount them now."

"I'm not." Kara retrieved the box with the skull and bone.

"Oh, wow." Cait was gazing down at the contents of the box with the same expression Kara figured had probably been on her own face. "This is way cool."

It was odd thinking there was another woman on the planet who thought the same way she did. "And probably old."

"Looks that way to me," Cait agreed. "Though I've seen from all my years working the cop shop in the Low-country how water can do a real number on human remains. But the forensic guy I know is really, really good, so we'll see what he can do."

She closed the box again, took a seal from her bag, stuck it on the lid, and signed and dated it as Kara's mother had the bullet fragments from Danny's skull, continuing the chain of evidence that could prove so important later in court.

"I really appreciate this," Kara said. Then she asked the question she'd been holding back since the other woman's arrival. "I guess your husband and Sax are close friends?"

"Although Quinn doesn't like to talk about those days much, from what he's said, they were closer than a lot of blood brothers. SEALs get their job done by not being noticed. Which means they're a close-mouthed lot at the best of times. But when two guys are out there in front, crawling through God knows what for hours on end, their entire world narrowed down to what they can see through a rifle scope, I suspect they get pretty damn good at reading each other's minds."

"I imagine so." Kara considered how good Sax seemed to be at sensing *her* thoughts and wondered if it was a skill SEALs developed in training. Or perhaps it was the other way around: that men who already possessed such talent were more inclined to go into Special Operations.

"I suspect a bit of both," Cait replied when she shared that thought.

"So," Kara asked carefully, wanting to know more about Sax, but not wanting to appear to be digging for information — which, of course, she was, "I guess, since he made it back home, they weren't together on Sax's last mission. The one where Sax was captured."

"No. Quinn had, thank heavens, already left the Navy by then. But they were together on another mission in Afghanistan that got dicey, and since Quinn had already decided that he'd rather write than fight —"

"Wait a minute." Kara held up a hand. "Your husband is Quinn McKade? Who wrote *Kill Zone, Dead Center, American Sniper,* and *Shadow Team*?"

"That's him. I guess you've heard of him."

"He's been a must-buy for me since his first book. And I just made the connection. . . . Wow. You're Cait from the dedications."

"That would be me."

"Well, other than a minor character on a sitcom I pulled over for speeding one time on the Pacific Coast Highway, you're my only other brush with fame."

Cait laughed at that. Then immediately sobered. "Anyway, as I said, Quinn left the SEALs, but Sax stayed in and became a sniper for another team. Needless to say it was a tough time on all of us when he got captured."

"I can imagine. He certainly seems to have come through the experience well. Considering."

"You think so?"

"My late husband was a Marine who came home with PTSD problems. Problems I don't see in Sax."

"Maybe that's because spec-op guys tend to be really good liars. Quinn tells me it's because since they don't go into a mission guns blazing, like the Marines and infantry, they often have to fit into their environment. Which requires the ability to lie their asses off when necessary. Now, as he puts it, by writing novels, he's lying for a living.

"But just because Sax seems to not have any problems, I'd have a hard time believing that's true. Especially since . . ."

Her voice trailed off. She frowned. "Damn. I don't know what's wrong with me these days. I think it must be pregnancy brain fog. I'm talking too much." Her breasts rose and fell like twin peaks as she sighed heavily. "I think the reason I feel comfortable discussing Sax at all with you is because he told me what good friends you are. And how far back you go."

"To high school." Kara wondered what, exactly, he'd told the former FBI agent.

"Yeah. That's what he said." Cait tilted her head and studied her with what Kara recognized as a cop look. "And you can tell me it's none of my business, but it's not like him to ask favors. So I'm guessing you were very close?"

"Sax's older brother, Cole, was my husband's best friend. When Cole and Jared went off to Marine basic training, Sax watched out for me."

"Sounds like that hasn't changed."

"I guess not." It was true. So far as it went. In other ways, everything had changed.

"Since you don't appear to be blind, and I'm guessing that, since you were married and Sax mentioned a kid, odds are you're not a lesbian, you've undoubtedly noticed that the guy's really, really hot."

Kara folded her arms. "Are you asking as an investigator? Or as Sax's friend's wife?"

"Actually, I'm asking as a woman who's eating for three, hasn't had anything since breakfast, and is long overdue for a lunch where I can talk about girl things like men and sex and date flicks for a change instead of bodies and bullets. And, if you happen to want to talk about a certain hot former SEAL, I'm up for that, too."

It wasn't what she'd planned. Then again, Sax was keeping Trey until suppertime. With her mother still in Portland, since it was technically her day off and she hadn't had a real girls' lunch since moving back home, there wasn't anything to keep her from taking Cait up on her suggestion.

Plus, the idea of learning more about Sax's life while he'd been away from Shelter Bay was more than a little appealing.

"The Sea Mist has tables overlooking the water where you can watch the whales. And the smoked clam chowder and crab cakes are to die for."

Cait pushed herself to her feet. "Let me stop by the john to pee. Then you're on."

# 29

Faith woke to a gray sky. A slanting rain was hitting the window, streaming down the glass, obscuring the world outside.

Some people might find such a scene gloomy. To her it was like being wrapped inside a cocoon.

Beside her, John lay on his back, one arm over his head, the other flung over her bare breasts. When she reached down to tug the sheet up to cover herself, he mumbled a complaint in his sleep, and drew her closer.

She could have pulled away, but it felt so good to wake up in a man's arms again. When he'd kissed her, not the light, soft brushing of lips, but that deep, soul-stealing kiss she'd felt all the way to her toes, Faith had assured herself that it was only sex. It was no big deal. People, after all, hooked up all the time. Although they might not have used the same term when she'd been in college and med school, one-night stands had pretty much been the norm. Except for her. She'd had two affairs before meeting Ben.

But each time they'd been serious relationships she'd mistakenly thought would become permanent.

The first had been her freshman year at Duke, just as the Woman's College and Trinity College had merged into the coeducational Trinity College of Arts and Sciences, which added to the sense of change as thick as the scent of magnolia blossoms in the humid North Carolina air.

The boy she'd given both her heart and virginity to had been the son of a fisherman, a scholarship student from the Outer Banks whom she'd met her first day of freshman orientation.

His eyes had been as blue as Paul Newman's, his body young and hard and virile, and his Southern drawl, so different from the Mid-Atlantic Main Line Philadelphia accent she'd grown up with, had turned even her name into poetry.

He'd been an art major, the most bohemian person she'd ever met, who wore torn jeans, white T-shirts, and actually went to class without shoes. Which was when Faith had discovered that male feet could be extraordinarily sexy.

He'd smoked dope, drunk cheap wine by

the gallon, and, his sophomore year, grown a goatee that often rubbed her skin painfully raw in places she'd never imagined any man's mouth touching.

Her parents, needless to say, had been shocked when she'd brought him home that first Thanksgiving. Which, looking back on it now, Faith realized, had been part of his appeal.

She'd loved him with all the fire and passion and, yes, wide-eyed, naive foolishness of a first grand love. After having her heart shattered when he unceremoniously dumped her for a model he met in his life drawing class, Faith swore off men and turned her full attention and devotion to getting into medical school.

No nun had ever embraced celibacy with the fervor and dedication she had. Until her internship, when a surgical resident — who wore his God complex like a second skin — had slid under her defenses by letting her scrub in on a trigeminal neuralgia radiosurgery using the then experimental Gamma knife technique.

He, too, had turned out to lack a monogamy gene, but she never resented discovering that he routinely slept with both attractive female interns and nurses, because during that life-altering surgery she'd found her medical calling. He'd gone on to have a brilliant medical career, only to ironically die of a brain tumor a few years ago.

Meanwhile, the artist, too, had done well; she'd recently read that his last painting had sold for half a million dollars, and he and his fifth wife — a wealthy society gallery owner who handled his paintings — had a Park Avenue apartment and homes in Florence, Italy, and Paris.

Ben, on the other hand, had been neither brilliant nor rich. What he'd been was a good man. The type of man who truly lived the "protect and serve" motto of police work. She'd known he was well-thought-of in Shelter Bay — after all, the people continued to elect him, and the last three campaigns no one had even bothered to run against him — but she'd had no idea how many lives he'd touched. It seemed everyone in town had a story to tell about some act of generosity they'd experienced from him.

John was much the same. Salt of the earth, a one-woman man, faithful to Gloria O'Roarke to the end, caring and compassionate. He was also more laid-back than Ben had been, which she might have considered a negative when she'd been younger. But now, feeling more than a little beleaguered by responsibilities, she found that trait appealing.

As if he'd sensed her studying him, he opened his eyes. And grinned sheepishly. "Sorry," he said. "I think you wore me out." There was an appealing twinkle in his eyes as he skimmed an appreciative glance over her. "I'm kind of out of practice."

"If that's how you make love to a woman when you're out of practice, I'm really looking forward to watching you get your groove back, so to speak."

"I've never had any complaints." It wasn't said as boasting, merely a fact, of which she had no doubt. "Then again, I've only ever been with one other woman."

"Only one?"

"Glory and I lost our virginity together our senior year of high school, parked out on the cliff overlooking the coast. That was pretty much it for me. Never felt a need to look any further."

"I met Ben later in my life. So I was with two men before him. But, like you, I was never tempted after him."

She'd been trying to tug the sheet up, now that he was awake, but he took her hand, lifted it to his lips, and smiled again over the top of their linked hands.

"Guess we both missed out on the sexual revolution," he said with easy humor.

"I suppose so." How could just his lips brushing over her knuckles make her want to jump his manly bones? "Though I don't think we missed much. One-night stands and hookups were never my thing."

"Mine either, obviously." His expression sobered. "*This* was no one-night stand."

It wasn't a question, but Faith answered it anyway. "No." They'd been headed toward last night for a while. John's nephew getting shot had just given them both the extra shove they needed. "I don't know where we're going —"

"Sometimes the best journeys aren't planned down to the nth degree."

She'd heard that. But had never been able to embrace the concept. She was a neurosurgeon. Being a perfectionistic, detail-oriented individual went with the territory.

"I'm not very good at going with the flow."

"No problem. I am. So I'll teach you."

She lifted her chin. "I've always been an independent woman."

He laughed at that. A huge, rumbling laugh that burst forth from deep in his chest. She could actually feel it against her breasts. "Why don't you tell me something I don't know?" he suggested.

Then, still holding her hand, he ran his free one down her hair, which, she feared, must look an absolute fright. But from the way he was looking at her, either he didn't notice or didn't care.

"Can we talk about this later?" he asked. "Because after all that time in the hospital yesterday, I'd really like a shower." The broad hand that had stroked her hair moved down to smooth over her shoulder, his fingertips brushing against the crests of her breasts. "And I don't want to take it alone."

To Faith's shock, the suggestion made her blush like a love-struck teenager. She could feel the heat rising in her face, so bright it would have been impossible for him to miss.

The last time she'd gone with the flow was when she'd let Ben pick her up that night they'd first met, when she'd attended a riverfront festival in Portland with friends. And, Faith reminded herself, look how well that had turned out.

They'd just gotten beneath the steaming-hot water when her BlackBerry rang from where she'd left it on the suite's table.

Years of medicine left her unable to ignore it. Especially when she had a postsurgery patient in the hospital.

"I'm sorry." She went up on her toes, gave John a quick, hard kiss, grabbed a towel from the rack on the wall, wrapped it around herself, and ran back into living room, leaving wet footprints on the carpet.

The call was, as she'd feared, from the hospital. She kept the conversation brief, aware of John now standing in the doorway, a towel draped low on his hips.

"What's wrong with Danny?" he asked.

"I'm sure it's nothing," she said in her most reassuring physician's tone.

"Faith." He crossed the room and took hold of her shoulders. "You don't need to treat me with kid gloves. I'm a cop. I've also spent hours in hospitals with Glory. So just give it to me straight; then we can deal with it."

"Okay." She blew out a breath. "But first you need to understand that medical terms don't necessarily mean a prognosis, and —"

"Faith," he repeated, cutting her off. Although his voice was strong, his face had gone ashen. "Just say it."

This was not the first time she'd ever said the words to a patient's family member. But never had they been so personal.

"I'm so sorry, John." She placed a comforting hand on his arm. "Daniel's in a coma."

# 30

Trey hadn't wanted to like Sax Douchett. First of all, he was a SEAL. And his dad had always said that SEALs were the hotshot cowboys of the military. When he'd been a little kid, he'd thought that being a cowboy would be a cool thing. Until his dad explained that it meant they lacked discipline.

Which Marines, his dad always said, had in spades.

Wanting to grow up to be a Marine, just like his dad — one of the few, the brave, the proud — Trey had worked really, really hard on his own discipline.

Sometimes he messed up, like when he left his bike in the driveway and his grandmother almost ran over it when she came home from the hospital late one night, but all his teachers, here and in California, were always telling him that he was the best kid in his class.

So when he saw his mom smiling up at that cowboy SEAL, he'd gotten mad. That was the special look she'd sometimes given his dad. She wasn't supposed to look at other guys like that.

But then the SEAL had invited him to ride in the parade. And better yet, had let him play fetch with Velcro. Even if the dog didn't always bring the stick back, it was fun to toss it.

The lumberyard had been neat, too. Especially when Sax had bought him his own toolbox filled with stuff so he could help fix up Bon Temps. He even showed him how to hold the hammer. Not at the head, which was the way he'd been doing. But at the very end of the wooden handle.

"Let the tool do the work," he'd said. And although in the beginning he bent as many nails as he got straight, he'd just begun to get the hang of it when Sax had said they should go get lunch.

And *that* was when things turned from cool to awesome.

The inside of the VFW hall was the most *guy* place Trey had ever been. The walls were paneled with boards that had big knots in them, the top of the bar was carved with initials and symbols of different units, and the most awesome of all was the stuffed animals. Not stuffed toy ones like the whale he'd won at Sax's welcome-home party.

But *real* ones.

The kind that used to be alive.

And were now dead.

Though a lot of them looked as if they could come to life again at any second.

"Is that a grizzly bear?" he asked, staring up at the huge, snarling animal standing next to the jukebox.

"Sure enough is," the bartender, who'd told him to call him Pete, said. "Bagged him myself in Alaska, on some R and R after a mission in Panama."

"On Operation Just Cause?" Trey asked.

"Got it in one." Pete glanced over at Sax, who was seated on the stool beside Trey. "Kid knows his military history."

"My dad was a Marine," Trey announced.

"Yeah, I got that from your shirt," the bartender said.

"Jared Conway was a hero," Sax said.

"That Conway's kid?" a voice called out from the pool tables.

A man ambled over, a mug of beer in his hand. His hair was the color of a carrot, tied back in a ponytail with a leather string, which Trey figured his dad would consider a lack of discipline, but if the guy was in this place, then he must have been a veteran, so Trey straightened his back in the respect he'd been taught.

"Yes, sir," he said. "Jared Conway was my dad."

"Hell of a thing happened to him," the man said. "Name's O'Riley. Tim. Served in the sandbox about the same time as your dad. I was Airborne, so our paths never crossed over there. But he was a couple years ahead of me in school, and I remember him being a straight-up guy. And a real ROTC star."

"I'm going into ROTC. When I'm old enough." Trey decided not to mention that that was another one of those things his mom said they'd talk about when the time came. Which wasn't encouraging. But he'd already made up his mind.

It was Tim O'Riley's turn to shoot a look at Sax. "Apple didn't fall far from the tree with this one," he observed.

"Seems not," Sax agreed.

Trey liked talking about his dad, which he couldn't do much with his mom because he was afraid he'd make her cry. And whenever his dad's name came up in front of his grandmother, she'd get a sort of pinched look to her face that gave him the idea that his father hadn't been her favorite person.

As if they knew just how he was feeling,

other veterans got up from tables and came over to the bar and began telling stories about his dad. Stories neither of his parents had ever talked about. Like how he'd been an Eagle Scout, and the time he'd rescued a little kid, younger than Trey, who'd gotten caught in a riptide on the coast, and his dad had gotten a medal from the fire department for bravery.

"Your dad was a bona fide all-American hero," one guy wearing a black leather vest with all sorts of patches on it said. His gray hair was pulled back in another one of those ponytails. "Semper Fi, kid."

"Semper Fi," Trey repeated along with the other Marines in the room.

And he suddenly realized, as he looked over at the snarling grizzly bear, and the mountain-lion head glaring down from the wall, and the rattlesnake coiled on the shelf holding the bottles behind the bar, that right now, here, in this very special place of warriors, he wasn't afraid of those dangerous-looking animals.

Or of volcanoes, or typhoons, or tsunamis, or any other of the disasters that could kill innocent people that he'd seen on TV.

Because every man in the room seemed to agree with Tim O'Riley and Sax: that the apple hadn't fallen far from the tree.

*Semper Fi, Dad.*

Proudly lifting his glass of root beer, Trey Conway joined in the toast to his all-American hero father.

# 31

Since Cait McKade had, like Kara, been a cop, what had started out as a planned girls' lunch turned into the two of them sharing former cases.

It was only when a diner at a nearby table gasped in shock as Cait shared the story of the Flamemaster, a serial arsonist who'd terrorized the Low-country city of Sommersett, South Carolina, a few years ago, that they realized the entire restaurant had gone unnaturally quiet as everyone avidly eavesdropped.

They'd laughed afterward out on the sidewalk, so hard that Cait had sworn she was in danger of wetting her pants. After stopping back at the sheriff's office so she could take care of that problem, Kara had driven out to the small airfield with her, and been impressed by the gleaming white jet waiting on the tarmac.

"The guy who created Phoenix Team has

deep pockets," Cait divulged. "And doesn't mind spending it. Although I've met him only once, I've got to admit that if I weren't madly in love with my husband, I might've been tempted to try to get past his shields."

"He's former military?" Kara wondered how anyone in the service could acquire such wealth.

"I'm not sure. He's a mystery man who doesn't give anything personal away. I don't think even my old partner, who runs the day-to-day operation, knows that much about him. He is one magnificent hottie, though. Dark, silent, and brooding, like an Irish Heathcliff."

"Dark, silent, and brooding guys tend to be high-maintenance." Kara had watched military wives who'd married the type and usually learned to regret it.

"Probably are. But you can't deny they have a certain appeal."

Kara was still thinking about that after Cait had taken off, headed back east with the box of bones, bullet fragments, and the casing from the shell that had killed her father. She'd sensed that Sax hadn't survived his years at war totally unscathed, yet although he'd played at being the rebel back in high school, deep down he'd been a warm and caring person. And always, with her and now with Trey, unrelentingly good-natured.

It also occurred to Kara as she hit the clicker to open the house's three-car garage that, were she to get to know him, Kara's mother might realize how much Sax had in common with her father.

Her mother's car wasn't in its slot. Which was odd. When Kara hadn't heard any further updates on Danny's condition, she had assumed all would be well. Which meant that her mother and John should have been home by now.

She entered the kitchen door, pulled out her phone, and had just dialed her mother's number when she was tackled from behind and thrown facedown onto the hardwood floor.

As strong hands began to pound her from above, causing a feeling of déjà vu to flood over her, Kara began to fight.

For her life.

## 32

"Okay," Faith told John as they drove the rental car the short distance to the hospital, "the first thing you have to understand is that a coma is not an automatic synonym for a persistent vegetative state."

"No offense, Faith," he said through clenched teeth, "but I wish you wouldn't even use those words in regard to Danny."

"I strongly doubt we'll have to. As I said, he came through the surgery with flying colors. He's a young, healthy male in peak condition. Although I hate to make a prognosis without examining him, since you and I are closer than the usual doctor-patient family relationship —"

"Now, there's an understatement," he muttered. But she thought she detected just a hint of his usual humor in the tone.

"— I suspect we're merely dealing with brain swelling from the trauma of first the gunshot wound, followed by the surgery."

"*Merely?* That sounds damn serious to me."

"It's not that uncommon. And I'll get to it in a minute. But first, the word *coma* itself simply means a loss of consciousness. Medically, it's a sleeplike state from which people can't be aroused, even if stimulated."

"I know you're trying to be encouraging, sweetheart. But that's not exactly helping."

"I'm sorry. But you wanted me to be straight with you, and that's what I'm trying to do. It's not uncommon, in the case of brain trauma, for a person to drift in and out of consciousness for minutes, hours, or even days."

"Well, now I'm really relieved."

She shot him a look. "Do you want the prettied-up version? Or the facts?"

He winced a little at her sharp tone. "Just the facts, ma'am," he said. "And I just realized something."

"What?"

"I think we're having our first fight."

She couldn't help herself: Despite the seriousness of their situation, a laugh escaped. That was something else she and John had in common, Faith realized: Cops and doctors both shared a dark sense of humor. Sometimes it was the only way to get past the tough things they witnessed.

"Getting back on point," she said, dodging any discussion of their personal relationship, which she needed time to sort out, "I sincerely doubt that we're looking at days, because the duration usually relates to the severity of the injury to the brain. And Daniel's injury was, as I told you, remarkably light, given the circumstances.

"Some doctors set the time at six hours. Loss of consciousness for less than that is limited to a concussion. The long-term outcome for those patients is excellent. Longer than six hours, there's a broad spectrum of consciousness."

"How broad?" he asked as she pulled up to the valet parking.

"Let's just jump off that bridge when we come to it?" she suggested.

They made their way up to the intensive-care unit. Outside the door, Faith paused, holding his arm. "Before we go in there, you need to know that even when people are unconscious, their senses can still be intact. They can still hear, feel, smell, taste."

"I've read that. Also that hearing's the last to go."

"It's true. The brain is a miraculous thing. Studies have proven that people in a coma who are spoken or sung to have more brain-wave activity."

She decided against mentioning that a person could be clinically dead and still able to hear what was being said around him.

"So it's important that you talk to Daniel. Encourage him to wake up, but keep your tone casual. Maybe talk about the parade, the fireworks, conversational things."

"We were going fishing next weekend," he said. "On Cole Douchett's boat."

"Perfect. And you still could well make that trip. Besides, planning for the future is a good thing. A positive thing."

While John talked nonstop to his unconscious nephew, Faith ordered a new CT scan, which showed what she'd suspected — that trauma had caused Daniel Sullivan's brain tissue to swell against the inflexible bone.

In some cases, she might have relieved the pressure inside his skull by placing a ventriculostomy drain to remove cerebrospinal fluid. Had the swelling been massive, she might have removed a piece of his skull, giving his brain room to expand while placing a small pressure valve inside to measure pressure on a moment-by-moment basis, then later reimplanted the bone after the swelling retreated.

But given that Daniel's case didn't appear to be all that severe, Faith opted for nonsurgical management.

"We'll keep him in the ICU to prevent further injury," she told John, who appeared to have aged a decade in the two hours since she'd received the call from the hospital. "There's no miracle drug to immediately improve brain function, but we can use medication to modify his blood pressure and optimize the delivery of oxygen to the brain tissue. Which should prevent further swelling.

"Plus, the fact that he's withdrawing from painful stimuli, and showing pupillary response to light, neither of which was occurring when the resident first called me, is a very good sign."

"Then he's coming out of it?"

She was a doctor. Trained to compartmentalize. But the naked hope in his husky voice was painful.

"It's still too soon to tell." She would not, *could* not lie. "But if I were a betting woman, I'd definitely bet the farm on Daniel."

It was only a white lie. And the relief that flooded over his haggard, yet still handsome face made the small prevarication worthwhile.

Her phone, which she'd switched to vibrate when she'd entered the hospital, buzzed from her jacket pocket.

Normally she didn't take personal calls when she was on duty, but since the caller ID showed Kara's phone, she took the call.

Only to hear the most frightening sound any mother could ever hear: her child's shouts as she sounded as if she were being savagely attacked.

"I'm sorry," she told John, who caught her upper arms as she swayed. "I need . . . I . . . Oh, God."

After lowering her to a chair, he plucked the phone from her icy hand, appraised the situation, and quickly placed calls to the state police and the Shelter Bay sheriff's office.

"Trey," she managed, as the initial shock subsided and the clouds began to lift from her brain.

"I'm already on it," he said. "Hey, Sax," he said as the voice on the other end of that call answered. "We've got ourselves one effing serious problem."

# 33

Kara had been trained in hand-to-hand combat and various martial arts, which should have given her an advantage. But her mind had been on other things and she certainly hadn't been prepared to be ambushed in her own house.

"I'm a cop, dammit," she shouted as she went for his eyes, which was the only part of his face she could see, given that he was wearing a black hood, like some damn video-game ninja. Even as flashbacks to that violent attack in California came flooding back, although she missed his eyes when he turned his head, she continued to land punches wherever she could — his face, his shoulders, his chest.

*Fight.* Since flight wasn't an option, even if she had wanted to choose it, training, instincts, survival all kicked in with a huge adrenaline rush. But he was larger. Stronger. As they rolled across the kitchen, limbs tangled, arms flailing, a full-powered impact of his fist exploded against her jaw and caused the back of her head to slam against the granite-topped island, making her see stars.

Another blow, between her ribs, sucked the wind from her lungs. But that didn't stop her from kicking out. She managed to knee him in the groin, but although he roared in pain, it didn't disable him the way it always had her opponents in training.

*Trey.*

Even as she fought for her life, even as sweat stung her eyes and blurred her vision, her son's name sounded over and over again in her head like a mantra, keeping her focused on her goal.

Which was to stay alive. Because no way was she going to allow this cretin to make her baby boy an orphan.

*Trey.*

At least, unlike on the side of that California highway, there was no chance of his getting her gun, since she'd locked it inside its box, in the cruiser's trunk, as she always did before coming home, to keep it out of her son's hands.

And, if he had a weapon of his own, wouldn't he have used it?

So logic told her that he was unarmed.

There was, fortunately, another thing in her favor, she thought as they wrestled for superiority. While he might be stronger and outweighed her by at least forty pounds, he wasn't as fit as she was. He was already panting, obviously winded.

*Trey.*

Taking advantage of his weakness, relying on her police academy training, she slammed the side of her hand against his windpipe. Wheezing, he struggled to his feet. Holding on to the back of a chair, he still managed to kick her in the head before lumbering out of the kitchen and into the garage.

Her phone had skittered beneath the table. Moaning, the coppery taste of blood filling her mouth, Kara crawled toward it. She'd just managed to curl her fingers around it when her roiling stomach threw back the clam chowder and crab cakes she'd eaten with Cait McKade.

Then everything went black.

# 34

Having finished up lunch at the VFW, Sax was back at Bon Temps. He and Cole began ripping filthy Sheetrock from the inner walls with crowbars and hammers while Trey kept Velcro from eating pieces of whatever she could scoop up from the floor by taking her outside and attempting to teach her how to do a high five.

Though the good-natured mutt was attempting to be a fair student, her attention span wasn't exactly stellar, and from what Sax could tell, most of the time she wanted to lick the boy's face and chase sticks.

Once again, watching the carefree kid and joyful dog, it crossed his mind that Kara had definitely done the right thing in bringing her son back to Shelter Bay. Cities offered a lot of pluses, sure enough. But there was nothing as heady as the freedom a small, safe community offered growing up. Even something as simple as a burger at the

VFW had proven a big deal; as all the guys who'd known his father shared their stories, Trey Conway's face had brightened up like a kid who'd just received a thousand Christmas mornings. All at once.

Sax wished he'd had a camera, so Kara could've seen it. He was just hoping that there'd be more such moments when Brooks and Dunn began belting out "Little Miss Honky-Tonk" from his cell phone.

He dug it out of the front pocket of his jeans and, not recognizing the number, flipped it open. "Douchett."

"Hey, Sax," John O'Roarke said. From the strain in his tone, the deputy was not calling with good news. "We've got ourselves one effing serious problem."

Sullivan might be competition. But Sax had hoped to live to a ripe old age without ever hearing those words again. "How's Danny?" he asked, even as he braced for the worst.

"He's in a coma, though Faith says signs are good for a full recovery. But I'm calling about Kara. She's in trouble, Sax."

Sax heard the stress. Panic surged through his bloodstream as the man on the other end of the phone choked up. Making sure Trey was still outside, Sax pressed the speaker option, so Cole, who'd stopped work, could hear the conversation.

"She'd just called her mother when someone attacked her in the house. I called OSP and the local cops, but I think you'd better get over there." Another, briefer pause. "And if you've got a gun, I'd take it."

Sax felt the blood draining from his face as he got slapped with a cold, metallic panic he could actually taste. It was the same way he'd felt up in those mountains, when he'd thought for sure he was going to die.

Unlike a lot of former military guys he knew, he'd gotten rid of his weapons when he'd left the military. During those seemingly endless visits to the families of his fallen teammates, Jack Daniel's had become his best friend. It was, for a time, the only way he'd found to numb the pain. And the guilt.

Then, his duty done, he'd come home to this westernmost part of the country, where he'd liberated his dog, started hanging out with his family again, and things had begun getting a little better. Which hadn't stopped him from getting into a knock-down, dragout fistfight with Cole, who'd driven out to the cliff house and given him the bigbrother lecture about his drinking.

Which, at the time, being three sheets to the wind, Sax hadn't been all that amenable to hearing.

Afterward, as they'd lain out on the sea grass that served as a front lawn, panting, faces bruised, knuckles swollen, Sax had begun to laugh. And laugh.

Until he cried. Like a damn baby.

Then he'd set about straightening out his life. Which he mostly had. Except for his ghosts, who'd left him alone today.

"I've got what I need." His fingers curled around the wooden handle of the oversize, twenty-eight-ounce framing hammer. "Tell Faith that I'm on my way."

"I'll take Trey over to Mom and Dad's," Cole said after Sax closed the phone. "The mutt, too."

"Thanks . . . Shit." Sax skimmed a hand over his hair. "What the hell do I tell the kid?"

"Nothing for now, because you don't know anything. Just say you've got an errand to run, and I'll take it from there."

"Thanks." Gratitude nearly weakened Sax's knees. What the hell did guys who didn't have brothers do?

"You'd do the same for me," Cole said. "And if you're even thinking of hugging me, little bro, you can just put that out of your mind and get the hell out of here."

Which, after what he felt was a calm and

collected, yet hugely sanitized explanation to Kara's son, was exactly what Sax did.

# 35

Kara was shaken. Embarrassed at being caught so off guard. But most of all, she was majorly pissed off.

Whoever had attacked her had more than beaten her up. (Though she'd definitely gotten some licks in herself.) He'd invaded her home, dammit! If her son had been there, instead of at Bon Temps with Sax . . .

Every mother-bear instinct rose, burning away the pain as the paramedics who'd come screaming into the driveway, sirens blaring and lights flashing — good luck keeping this under wraps — fussed over her.

Apparently, the one lucky thing about this debacle was that since she was calling her mother when the bad guy jumped her, John, able to hear the fight, had placed the necessary calls to authorities. The unlucky thing was that she couldn't imagine how horrible it must have been for her mother to listen to her daughter being attacked.

"I don't need to go to the hospital," she insisted yet again.

What she needed was to call Sax so she could warn him not to bring Trey home while the ambulance was here. Kyle Murphy, her young deputy, appeared totally over his head. Although he was eager and smart enough, being just out of community college he was green as spring grass. Kara suspected mailbox bashing would be over his head.

Meanwhile, after taking her statement, two OSP detectives were busy dusting for prints. And, wow, wouldn't her mother love coming home to this mess? At least Kara had refused to sit on the couch. No way was she going to risk getting her mother's milk-white upholstery bloody.

"You were unconscious," the EMT said.

"Only for a second. If that. Probably a nanosecond. At most."

*Note to self: Call a cleaning service to take care of fingerprint dust.* Meanwhile, couldn't all these people just leave? Or least give her back her damn phone?

"Your nose looks broken," one of the medics pointed out.

It felt like hell; she'd give him that. She gingerly lifted her finger and slid it beneath the cold pack he'd taped to her face. Her nose, which had already slanted a little to the left before the attack, currently felt about the size of a Muppet's nose.

"As a medical care professional, you should know that it's often impossible to diagnose a broken nose until the swelling goes down," she countered. "Look, I'll take some Tylenol. Besides, my mother's a doctor. If it does turn out to be broken, she can handle it."

"Your mother's a neurologist."

"Exactly, so if I *do* have a concussion, she can take care of that, too." It had, the deputy had told her, been John O'Roarke who'd sent out the SOS after they'd overheard the altercation on Kara's phone.

"I'll be fine. Really. And if I drop dead of a head injury, I promise not to sue."

He opened his mouth to argue yet again. Then all action stopped at the earsplitting squeal of car brakes.

Looking out the bay window, Kara watched as a familiar white muscle car with orange hood stripes pulled up in front of the house. Sax Douchett exited the Camaro like a shot, and, despite the circumstances, Kara couldn't deny that the sight of him racing across her mother's emerald green lawn was a hugely welcome sight.

Prayers he'd thought he'd forgotten had

reverberated through Sax's mind as he'd floored the Camaro all the way from Bon Temps to Faith Blanchard's house. Back during those illegal races on the beach, the beast had been clocked at zero-to-sixty in four seconds, and the quarter-mile drag distance at thirteen-point-eight seconds. He wouldn't have been surprised to learn that he'd beaten that record by the time he pulled up in front of the house with a screech of brakes.

"Are you all right?" They hadn't strapped her onto the gurney yet, but she was sitting on the floor of the living room.

Sax had thought he couldn't feel more panicky. He'd thought wrong. His already unsteady heart plummeted to his feet when he saw the front of her torn shirt stained with blood.

He shoved past the medical workers and the cop who didn't look old enough to drive that cruiser parked in the driveway and crouched down in front of her.

"I'm fine. . . . Well, okay, maybe not exactly fine," she admitted when he lifted a brow. "But as I keep telling these guys, I don't need to go to the damn hospital."

He liked that she had her temper up. It showed that although she looked like hell, her injuries weren't all that serious. Having watched SEAL team medic Lucas Chaffee triage guys on battlefields, Sax figured she would've earned the lesser green tag for "walking wounded." Though he did notice that she'd flinched when nodding toward the medical crew.

"Where's Trey?" she asked. Impossibly, she went even whiter beneath the ugly bruises as she glanced out the window toward the car. What, did she actually think he'd bring her kid along with him to something like this?

"Cole took him over to my folks' house."

"You didn't say anything about this, did you?"

"First of all, I wouldn't have known what to say, since I still don't know what happened. And of course I wouldn't. I just told him I had to run an errand."

Her breath hitched. "Thanks." Relief flooded into her remarkable amber eyes. She was going to have one hell of a shiner tomorrow.

"How did you know to come?"

"John called me from the hospital. After he called all these guys."

"My mother must've been thrilled about that."

"It was her idea."

"Okay," Kara said. "I'd better run by St.

360

Andrews and drop some bucks in the poor box, because obviously a miracle has just occurred."

Along with her flash of temper, Sax found the dry humor encouraging.

"There'll be time for that later." He wanted to touch her. Not sexually. But to soothe. He had a strong urge to stroke her hair, her face, to take her into his arms. But he didn't dare for fear of hurting her more. "After we spring you from the hospital."

"Not you, too?" She folded her arms across the front of her torn khaki shirt. "I thought you were supposed to be my friend."

"I am. And friends take care of one another. Which is why you have a choice: You can either climb up on that gurney yourself, or I'm going to pick you up and put you on it."

She managed a glare. The flash of spirit was another good sign. "Bully."

"Sticks and stones." He folded his own arms and gave her his best "don't fuck with the big, bad SEAL" look. "Well?"

She blew out a frustrated breath between unnaturally swollen lips. Looking at her, Sax struggled to stay on mission, which was first to get her proper medical care, then get her to bed. Alone. Then figure out what to do with Trey.

Finally, once everything had settled down, he was going to find the bastard who did this to her and beat the guy slowly, painfully, into a bloody pulp.

"Bully," she muttered again, as she nevertheless pushed herself to her feet. Sax immediately caught one arm, the EMT the other. She might talk a tough game, but she was definitely swaying like a drunk.

They got her onto the gurney and strapped her in.

"I'm coming with her," Sax said.

"Sorry, Mr. Douchett," the paramedic said, sounding as if he really meant it. "But only family's allowed in the ambulance."

Sax was tempted to play the hero card, which might get him a seat. But knowing how crowded ambulance space was, and not wanting to get in the way if some so-far undiagnosed problem suddenly arose, he didn't press the issue.

"I'll be there before you get out of the CT scan," he promised.

She tilted her head, narrowing her eyes a bit, revealing that even that small gesture hurt. *Yep.* She was definitely suffering the mother of all headaches.

"The hospital is all of ten minutes away," she pointed out. "Since I doubt you're going back to work at Bon Temps, you're hanging around here to talk to the state cops, aren't you?"

He could foresee the argument now. If he said no, she'd accuse him of lying. If he told the truth, she'd remind him that she was the law around these parts and he didn't have any authority to go sticking his nose in where it didn't belong.

"Yeah."

"You have no official role here, Sax."

"Maybe it's not official," he conceded. "But someone beat the hell out of you, Kara. On purpose. Now, you can get up on your feminist high horse and call me a Neanderthal if you want, but that pisses me off. So, yeah, I'm going to indulge my inner caveman long enough to find out what clues those hotshot big-city detectives making a mess in your mother's kitchen might have found. Then, if they don't find the guy, I will."

"You're talking vigilantism."

"And your point is?"

She briefly closed her eyes — from pain or an attempt to garner calm, he couldn't tell. "I have many points. Which we'll discuss later."

She opened those pain-filled eyes again and looked straight up into his.

"Right now I just want to get this circus over with so I can reassure my mother, figure out what to tell my son, get back to work, and apprehend the guy myself. And if you so much as interfere in any way in this case, Douchett, I will personally lock you up for obstruction of justice and throw away the key."

She didn't mean it. And they both knew it. Kara Blanchard Conway had gotten a lot tougher during these intervening years, which made sense, given all she'd been through. Like the old saying went, the only thing tougher than a soldier — or in her case, a Marine — was a Marine's wife.

But the thing was, bruises and scrapes aside, the new self-confidence she wore like a second skin looked damn good on her.

# 36

Kara hated hospitals. The last time she'd been in one had been to give birth to Trey. Although Jared hadn't been there, being deployed overseas, it had still been a happy occasion.

This was not. After having her clothing taken away from her, she was poked and prodded, then moved from cubicle to cubicle, where she was left alone to stare up at the ceiling, try to figure out who had attacked her and why, and worry about her son as she waited for what seemed an interminable time for a wearying series of tests.

Meanwhile, borrowing a cell phone from a nurse, since OSP had kept hers, she called her mother in Portland and reassured her that she was all right.

"I know," Faith said, her voice sounding atypically shaken. "Sax called as soon as the ambulance left the house to give me an update."

"Did he mention the state police guys are making one hell of a mess?"

"That's not important." Okay, that statement alone showed how upset her mother — aka Ms. Clean — was. "Houses can always be tidied up. The only thing that's important is that you're safe. And that Trey wasn't with you when you were attacked."

"I've been trying not to consider that possibility," Kara admitted.

"It's a blessing he was with Sax," Faith agreed. Yet another uncharacteristic statement. "Sax also told me that his brother had taken Trey over to his parents' house. I just talked with Maureen Douchett, and she says he can stay as long as necessary."

"That's kind of her. But he's a smart kid and I'm afraid he'll start to worry. Especially after having to spend last night at Sax's house because of Danny being shot. I was planning to sit down and talk with him about that tonight, in case he was having any flashbacks to Jared being shot."

"Sax said you're not exactly looking your best."

"I've got some bruises. And my nose may or may not be broken, but I can explain that away by saying I was in an accident."

Kara hated the idea of lying to her son.

But until she could capture her assailant, and assure Trey that she'd be safe, she didn't want him worrying about her being at risk. Especially after what Sax had told her about his having overheard her talking with her mother about that prior attack in California. Which was something else she'd intended to discuss.

"That's probably wise," Faith said again. "But you can't take him home with police tape all around the house."

"Good point." And something that should have occurred to her. And undoubtedly would have if it hadn't been for the maniacs pounding away with jackhammers inside her skull.

"Obviously a hotel's out of the question, since he'd only ask more questions." Faith paused. "I think the only solution is for the two of you to spend the night at Sax's house."

*O-kay.* Kara was seriously tempted to pinch herself to make sure she wasn't suddenly having a hallucination. Maybe she really had suffered a head injury.

"You can't be serious."

"It's the only logical solution. Sax suggested it."

"He did?" Without so much as discussing it with her?

"Yes. And we both agreed it's the best thing to do under the circumstances."

"I now know how Alice felt when she fell down that rabbit hole." Next thing she knew, the Mad Hatter would be inviting her to a tea party.

"Sarcasm is good," Faith said. "It shows your mind's still alert. And I believe it was you who told me that Sax may not be the incorrigible young man I remember him having been. People are, after all, capable of change, and his time in the military seems to have matured him."

That amazing statement had Kara thinking that the next call she made should be to the *Shelter Bay Bugle,* to tell them to stop the presses, because Dr. Faith Blanchard had just said a positive thing about former bad boy turned Navy SEAL Sax Douchett.

"It would have been nice if someone had thought to ask me," Kara said a bit crankily.

"Decisions had to be made and you weren't available. Besides, it's not as if you're not an independent woman. You're perfectly capable of refusing Sax's offer. If you have a better solution."

Which, dammit, Kara didn't. And her mother well knew it.

"How's Danny?" she asked, wanting to change the subject.

"He's regained consciousness, which is a good sign. John's going to stay here with him while I come home to take care of you."

"I'm fine," Kara said. "Well, not exactly fine," she allowed when she sensed her mother, who'd undoubtedly already spoken with the ER doctor, preparing to argue. "But they're not even going to keep me here overnight for observation."

"And why do I suspect that has something to do with your refusing to stay?"

"I'm fine," she repeated. "Even coming here was a waste of everyone's time, and I'd feel guilty about your leaving Portland with Danny still unstable."

"I'm certainly not the only neurosurgeon in Oregon."

"True. But you're the best. And I'd never forgive myself if Danny crashed while you were here putting ice packs on my stupid bruises."

Kara was accustomed to her mother having missed a great many events in her life — spelling bees, debate tournaments, and the sixth-grade science fair, even though Faith had been the one to help Kara make that papier-mâché model of a brain.

She'd also missed Kara's wedding — which, in truth, hadn't been her fault, since Kara and Jared had eloped to Mexico —

and the birth of her grandson.

She and Kara's father *had* dropped everything to rush to California during that roadside attack. But since mothering skills weren't her strong suit, and Kara admittedly made a lousy patient, the situation between them had felt even more strained than ever. Meanwhile, her usually easygoing father had practically lived down at the police station, determined to make sure Kara's colleagues and the DA didn't botch the prosecution of his daughter's attacker.

Unsurprisingly, both parents had also pushed for her to return home to Oregon so they could "take care" of her and Trey.

Which, with Kara still determined to stand on her own two feet, and uneasy about uprooting her son after all he'd been through, had not been something she'd been prepared to do. Yet.

"This isn't like California," she assured her mother. "I'm really fine. More embarrassed that I let some cretin jump me in my own house than physically hurt. All I need are some ice packs, aspirin, and a good night's sleep.

"So there's really nothing you could do for me. Besides, even if you could hand Danny off to another doctor, John needs you. After all he went through with Gloria, being back at a hospital has to be hard on him."

"He's like your father in that he doesn't share his feelings easily. But I suspect you're right."

"Well, then. It's settled."

"If you're sure," Faith said, continuing to sound uncharacteristically uncertain.

"Positive. Would you do me one favor?"

"Of course. You're my daughter."

"Would you call the Douchetts and tell Trey that I'm going to be delayed, but we're going to be spending the night with Sax?"

"Certainly. I was going to call Trey to tell him good night, anyway. As I did last night. From how excited he sounded about Sax's dog and plans to go to the lumberyard, I'm sure he'll be thrilled at the idea of a sleep-over."

Her mother had called Trey at Sax's? Yet another surprise.

"Thanks."

"It's no problem. And, Kara?"

"Yes?"

"You've no idea how terrified I was to hear you in danger. If I'd lost you . . ." Her mother's voice dropped off, but not before Kara had heard the sob in her tone. "I wouldn't want to live."

Kara knew the feeling. All too well.

"I'm fine," she assured her mother.

"You're far better than fine, darling. And I love and admire you more than you could ever imagine."

Kara had always known that both her parents loved her, but just hearing the words out loud caused a lump to rise in her throat.

Her voice wanted to crack. She refused to let it. "I love you, too, Mom."

After the call ended, as Kara continued to stare up at the ceiling, it dawned on her that just as she couldn't remember her mother ever saying those words to her, neither could she recall her ever saying them to her mother.

Which meant that, in at least one way, the attack that had landed her in the hospital just might actually prove an unexpected benefit.

# 37

Sax's mom and dad's home was nothing like his grandmother's. As soon as Trey walked into the house, Mrs. Douchett gathered him into her arms for a huge hug. Then she asked him if he was hungry.

Which, although he'd had a cheeseburger and fries at the VFW, Trey realized he was.

"I don't want to be any bother," he said politely, as he'd been taught.

"Don't you go talking foolishness." Mrs. Douchett ruffled his hair.

Although she must be really old if she was Sax and Cole's mother, she was, except for his mom, the prettiest woman Trey had ever seen. Pretty enough to be on TV. Or in the movies. Thinking about it, he realized she reminded him a lot of Snow White, who he'd had his picture taken with when his mom and dad had taken him up to Disneyland. Even though he'd only been a little pre-K kid, he'd understood the lady dressed up in the costume wasn't the *real* Snow White. But he'd still felt really, really special when she'd bent down and kissed his cheek. Mrs. Douchett made him sorta feel the same way.

"Nothing I love more than feeding a man," Sax's mother said. "Good thing, too, since I've been living with a bunch of them since I married my Lucien." She turned toward the tall man standing across the room and threw him a kiss.

For some reason, watching them like that caused tears to well up in Trey's eyes.

"Poor *cher.*" Mrs. Douchett looked about to hug him again. Which he wouldn't have minded, even though he was embarrassed to be caught almost crying, but instead she put a bowl in front of him. "You've had a rough couple days, what with that accident happening to Danny Sullivan, and now your mama having to take care of an emergency. Fortunately, God never threw us a problem that a good spicy crawfish gumbo couldn't make better."

Trey had never had gumbo. And it sure looked different from anything he'd ever eaten before, but his dad had taught him all about discipline and his mom had taught him manners, so no way was he going hurt this beautiful woman's feelings.

The gumbo, which was sorta soup with rice, hit his tongue with a burst of fire. He reached for the glass of water Mrs. Douchett held out to him. "It's a little hot," she said. "But you look like a boy capable of handling some real Cajun Tabasco."

Wanting to be the kind of boy she'd approve of, gathering up his nerve, he took another spoonful. This time, with Trey being more prepared, it didn't burn quite as much. He took a third taste, and all the flavors came together in a way that made him think this might just be the best bowl of soup he'd ever eaten.

"This is really good," he said between slurps. Definitely better than the canned soup he was used to.

"A young man of discerning culinary tastes," Mrs. Douchett told her husband as she put a big hunk of bread on a plate next to the white bowl. "You'll be wanting this to scoop up the last bits with. Then how would you like some bread pudding?"

"That sounds great." Trey had never had bread pudding either, but right now he was willing to trust Sax's mom with anything she wanted to feed him.

"Nobody makes bread pudding like my wife," Mr. Douchett said. "It'll make an entire chorus of angels sing."

Mr. Douchett was right. By the time Trey finished the dessert, he decided that angels would be lucky to get even a bite of Mrs. Douchett's bread pudding.

After being given a tour of the Douchetts' bait shop, which smelled like, well, bait, he was getting beaten in a game of checkers with a really old bearded man who turned out to be Sax's grandfather, when the old-fashioned phone on the wall rang. Mrs. Douchett exchanged a look with Cole and her husband as she picked it up.

She turned away. The conversation was short. And for the first time since he'd walked into the house, Trey sensed tension.

He'd gotten pretty good at picking up on grown-ups' moods after his dad had come back from his last deployment. His mom had assured him that his dad was just still stressed out from being away for so long, and they had to be patient and give him time to adjust to not fighting a war anymore. But he'd overheard a lot of yelling, which had left him feeling scared. A lot of his friends' parents had gotten divorced after their moms or dads had returned home from war. Even though his mom kept telling him everything would be okay, and that his dad loved them both very much, he'd worried that his parents would break up, too.

Then his dad had gotten killed, and as terrible as he'd felt about that, and as sad as he'd felt when he heard his mom crying at night when she thought he was sleeping, there were times when Trey felt guilty for feeling a little relieved that he didn't have to always worry about doing something that would set his dad off.

So for a long time he'd just pretended that his dad wasn't really dead at all. That he'd just gone away on deployment again.

"That was Sax," Mrs. Douchett told him after she'd hung up the phone that was as red as the crawfish she'd put in the gumbo. The same color he and Sax had picked out for the walls of Bon Temps this morning. She was smiling, but her voice sounded a lot like his mom's had sounded after one of those fights. Sorta tight and sad.

"He says he's going to be tied up a little bit longer. And your mom's still busy on her case. So he's hoping you won't mind staying here for a while more."

"Sure," Trey said, trying to read the look she'd just shot Cole.

"Hey, sport," Cole said with what even Trey realized was fake enthusiasm. He was sounding exactly like Trey's dad used to sound when he'd try to pretend everything was okay. Even when it wasn't. "I was thinking about taking the *Kelli* out for a while to check some fishing sites. How'd you like to come with me?"

Sax had told him that Cole was a fisherman. So Trey guessed that the *Kelli* must be his boat. Still trying to figure out what was going on, he didn't answer right away.

"I'll come with you two," Sax's dad said. "Nothing like passin' a good time with a sunset boat ride."

"Might as well come along," the old man said, pushing himself out of the rocking chair. "Been a coon's age since I've been out on the water."

Okay. Now everyone was starting to act weird.

Trey looked over at Mrs. Douchett, who seemed to be able to read his mind, because she gave him another of those hugs and whispered in his ear, "Don't worry, *cher.* Everything's going to be just fine. I promise."

She might not be *his* mom. But she was a mom. And not just any mom, but Sax's mom.

Which was why, since the idea of going out on one of those boats he was always looking at in the harbor sounded like fun,

378

Trey decided to trust her.

"Will we see any whales?" he asked.

Cole grinned, looking a lot like Sax. "I guarantee it," he promised.

Which was good enough for Trey.

# 38

The air in the emergency room waiting area was rife with the aromas of disinfectant, pain, fear, and despair.

"Where's Kara Conway?" Sax demanded of the clerk on duty, raising his voice to be heard over the robotic announcement over the loudspeakers announcing the ETA of yet another incoming ambulance.

An elderly woman — whose badge pinned to the blue-and-white smock pronounced her to be a volunteer — looked up at him over the half lenses of her reading glasses.

"Are you referring to Sheriff Conway?"

"Have they brought in any other Conways today?" Sarcasm sharpened his already frustrated tone. "She also happens to be the daughter of Dr. Blanchard, the administrator of this place." There were times to pull rank. This was definitely one of them.

"You needn't get huffy, young man." She began leafing through a stack of pink, white, and yellow forms, nodding when she apparently found the one she was looking for. "And you would be?"

"Sax Douchett," he ground out between gritted teeth.

"Really."

She took off the glasses and studied him for what seemed forever, taking in his raggedy jeans coated with sawdust, sweat-soaked T-shirt, and face he figured was probably smudged with dirt. What did she think? That he went around in full dress uniform with medals pinned to his chest like he'd worn in that damn parade?

He was about to reach across the counter and snatch those papers out of her hand, when she said, "That would make you the war hero."

"Yeah. That's me." It was the first time he'd claimed the title. But he'd do whatever it took to get to Kara.

"Well, then." She nodded, apparently satisfied. "Thank you for your service. My late husband fought in Korea. At the battle of Heartbreak Ridge."

"Tough place."

What it had been was a monthlong fiasco with several hundred of America's best dying on the ridgeline. He felt for her husband, but wished she'd just cut to the damn chase and tell him where the hell they were hiding Kara.

"So I've heard. Though he always refused to talk about it." She waved toward a set of swinging doors. "The sheriff is doing as fine as can be expected," she said. "Girl comes from tough stock. You'll find her in there. Second cubicle to the left."

Sax found Kara sitting on a gurney in the curtained-off cubicle, dressed in a pair of blue scrubs that replaced her bloody uniform. Although he'd already seen her at the house, one glance at her bruised and swollen face caused a white-hot rage to flare inside him.

Sax had killed before. But only in the line of duty. And, although watching a target for a very long time through a sniper scope gave him an up-close-and-personal view of a guy he was about to blow to kingdom come, it had never actually *been* personal except when blasting away at those terrorists who'd killed his teammates up there in the Kush.

These feelings were even more intense than those had been. For the first time in his life Sax understood how a reasonably sane person could commit cold-blooded murder. His hands ached. Sax glanced down and saw that they'd tightened into painful fists.

"So, what's the verdict?" he asked with a great deal more calm than he was feeling as he flexed his fingers.

She was holding a new cold pack to her right cheek, which appeared to have suffered the most damage. A white butterfly bandage marred her left check; another had been placed at her right temple.

"I have a minor concussion, which isn't even worth their keeping me overnight for. Some bruised, luckily not broken ribs. And, as you can see from my face, I'm not going to be a candidate for Miss Shelter Bay anytime soon."

"You could be. Maybe not now," he amended when she opened her mouth to argue. "But once those dings heal. I'd always thought my mom was the prettiest female in Shelter Bay. Until you showed up on my porch."

Color bloomed beneath her bruised cheeks. "You're just trying to make me feel better."

"Absolutely." His voice was as raw and rough as his still-ragged emotions. Sax struggled for calm. He wanted to curse. To rant. To rave. He wanted to go down to the VFW, get a gun from one of the guys, and go hunting whoever had done this to her.

As a hot rage simmered inside him again,

Sax struggled, for Kara's sake, to tamp it down. She'd already been through too much today. She wouldn't want — or need — him to go off like some crazed, half-cocked he-man. Especially after what she'd told him about Jared's problems with PTSD. What Kara needed now was tenderness. And care.

"Is it working?"

"Surprisingly, I think it might be. Because I'm not even pissed off at you for conspiring with my mother. Which, by the way, was nearly as shocking as having that bastard jump me."

"She surprised me for a minute, too. Then I think we both realized we have something in common."

"Which would be?"

Her hair, caked with dried blood as it was, was sticking out in spikes. He gently smoothed it down. "You."

Tears suddenly shimmered in her eyes. "I'm not going to cry."

"Might be a good thing if you did," he suggested. "And I've got a pretty wide shoulder if you feel inclined."

"Maybe later. After the guy's behind bars," she said. "Right now I can't risk falling apart, because I'm the sheriff, dammit. With an assault charge I have a personal

384

reason for needing to solve. If I was this guy's target, I want to get him. If I was a random victim — and I *hate* thinking of myself that way — and there's a predator roaming the streets of Shelter Bay, I need to stop him before he preys on another woman. Besides, equally important, I need to stay strong for Trey's sake."

Sax figured she'd probably been doing exactly that for her son's entire life. "I'd tell you that you're the strongest woman I've ever met," he said, which was true. "But since compliments seem to be making you feel even worse, I'll save that for later, too."

"They cut off my ring." She unfolded her hand, showing him the familiar gold band. "My knuckles are all swollen from punching the guy, so they sawed it in half."

Her voice trembled, another sign of her struggle to fight off the tears she was entitled to.

"I imagine a jeweler could repair it." He wondered, despite what she'd said about having gotten past all the official phases of grief, if she planned to wear it the rest of her life.

"I guess." She was turning it over and over again in her palm.

Seeing the pain in her eyes, he lifted her bruised and swollen knuckles to his lips.

Then, before she could pull away, he said, "Let's get you settled into the house. Then I'll go back to Mom and Dad's and pick up Trey."

She took the hand and slid off the gurney. "Maybe we should get him first."

"He's out on Cole's boat. Plus, I thought you might want to clean up beforehand."

She wrinkled her nose, taking in the medicinal odors of the hospital and the acrid smell of dried blood. "Good idea." And one he knew she normally would have thought of. Yet more proof that she was more shaken than she was letting on.

"I wanted to stick with the accident story and wait until we caught the guy who did this. But I'm going to have to tell him, aren't I?"

"If you don't, he'll probably hear it at school."

"Since half the neighbors were out in the street when they wheeled me out to that ambulance, and the sheriff being attacked is probably the biggest story the *Shelter Bay Bugle* has had to report on since that beached whale a few years ago, it's going to be impossible to keep it a secret."

"We had a mission code," Sax volunteered. "KISS."

"Keep It Simple, Stupid. Cops have the

same thing."

"Yeah. That's it. Just tell him that you walked in on a burglary in progress, that yeah, the guy got a few licks in, but so did you. And that you chased him away, he won't be back, and you expect to apprehend him real soon."

"That sounds like a press briefing."

"Short of taking him out of school and keeping him away from the TV, that's the best you can do."

"I know. But it's hard."

"I know."

Actually, Sax figured that was the understatement of the century. Especially after what the kid had already experienced in his young life.

They went through the seemingly interminable checking-out process. Then, although she'd protested that she didn't want them, that she needed to stay alert for her son, he insisted on taking the time to fill the prescription she'd been given for pain pills. SEALs might swear by "vitamin M" — Motrin — but he had a feeling that once she got into bed, she'd be grateful for the good stuff.

Finally they were in the car, headed toward the coast.

Sax remained silent, figuring that if she

wanted to talk, she would.

"I don't want to talk about it." She confirmed his thoughts as they crossed the iron bridge. "Not now."

"Not now," he agreed. Along with discipline, the Navy had taught him patience.

The sun was lowering into the sea as they reached the house, turning the sky a brilliant rainbow of oranges and purples. Instructing her to stay put, he went around the front of the car and opened the passenger door. Fortunately, it wasn't raining. If he was going to stay here, and it appeared he was, he was definitely going to have to clean out that garage his pack-rat grandfather had filled to the rafters.

"I think I could live here a hundred years and never get tired of that view," he said.

"I don't blame you." She paused after he'd helped her out of the low-slung car. "It's stunning." She lifted a hand and shielded her eyes against the dazzle of jewel-toned sky as she spotted the rising spray of whale spouts just beyond the breakers. "Especially the whales."

"Yeah. They're cool. Trey was jazzed when he saw them."

"I don't know how to thank you for all you've done to help with him," she said.

"He's a cool kid. I've enjoyed every moment." From the halting way she was climbing the steps to the porch, Sax suspected her ribs must hurt more than she'd let on at the hospital. Having had his share of injuries, he knew how even bruised ribs could make every breath difficult. She'd hurt like the devil in the morning. But at least she'd know she was alive.

Since Trey would be sleeping in the extra bedroom again, and the second guest room was still filled with yet more stuff his grandfather had left behind, Sax helped her up the stairs and led her to his own room. "The bathroom's right in there." He pointed toward the door on the far side of the room. "Bath or shower?"

"A bath sounds heavenly," she admitted. "But getting in and out of the tub might be more than I'm up to right now."

"I'd be happy to help."

The touch of sexual suggestion he'd allowed to slip into his tone made her laugh, as he'd intended. Unfortunately, he realized it had been a mistake when she pressed a hand against her chest, right beneath her breasts.

"Sorry," he said.

"No." She managed another of those valiant smiles that broke his heart. "I appreciate your not treating me like some weak-ass invalid."

"For the record, your ass is terrific, and *weak* is never a word I'd use in regard to you, sugar. As for that invalid deal, as much as I understand and respect your independence, it really wouldn't hurt to let someone take care of you once in a while."

Apparent surprise steamrollered over the pain that had been glazing her eyes. She looked up at him, then shifted her gaze out the window, where a giant ball of sun was sinking beneath the sea, gilding the water a shimmering gold and bronze.

"Now, there's a concept," she murmured. Then she looked back up at him. Strain showed in her eyes and the brackets on either side of her mouth. "I'm not sure I know how to do that."

He wondered if she realized how much she'd revealed with that single statement. He and his younger brother, J.T., might've given their mother fits over the years (while Eagle Scout Cole had always been Mr. Firstborn Perfect). But Maureen Douchett had never been stingy about showing her love.

He could remember her rubbing calamine lotion over his body after he'd gotten into a mess of poison oak when he was about the age Trey was now. Remembered numerous times she — and his father — had taken turns staying up all night to put cool cloths against his fevered forehead. And those times when he'd gotten the flu and she'd never uttered a single word of complaint about changing the sheets he'd hurled all over.

Sax reminded himself to tell his mom how much he appreciated her maternal comforting the first chance he got. Although he knew for a fact that Kara's mother loved her — hadn't she sounded uncharacteristically near panic earlier today on the phone? — apparently she had saved all her TLC for her patients.

Or perhaps, he considered, they just emotionally drained her so much that when she got home from the hospital, she had nothing left for her own daughter.

"It's always good to learn a new skill set," he said. "Meanwhile, why don't you start with a shower?" He went over to the myrtlewood chest he'd helped his grandfather make more than two decades ago and pulled out a black T-shirt. "I don't have any pants that'll fit you," he said apologetically.

*Damn.* He should've at least dropped by her house on the way over here. Which showed he hadn't been thinking clearly either. "But I'll pick up some things for you and Trey on my way over to my folks' house."

"Thanks." As she took the shirt from his hands, their fingers briefly touched, creating a spark that shot through him like a lightning bolt. He knew, from the way her eyes widened, that she'd felt it, too.

"Well." They stood there, inches apart. She looking up at him, he looking down at her.

Feeling a pull of desire as strong as the tides pounding away at the cliff outside the house, Sax shoved his hands, which were practically itching with the need to touch her, into the back pockets of his jeans to keep them out of trouble.

"Take your shower," he said. "I'll fix you something to drink."

"I probably shouldn't. Not after that pill you forced down my throat back at the hospital."

"I was talking about a cup of hot tea."

"Tea?" She looked up at him, clearly surprised. "You make tea?"

"Well, in the interest of full disclosure, it's probably not what anyone would serve to the queen. But my mother stocked the kitchen before I came home, and put in a box of Earl Grey I haven't opened. So, while I may be no expert, I figure it can't be that hard to put a bag in a cup and nuke it."

"That pretty much makes us even on cooking skills," she admitted. "And tea sounds heavenly."

With that she turned on her heel and, holding the shirt against her bruised ribs, walked into the bathroom with more energy than he would've thought she could've mustered under the circumstances and shut the door behind her.

God help him, it was happening all over again, just as it had that long-ago night on the beach. It was madness to want any woman the way he wanted Kara. Insanity to *need* any woman the way he needed her.

But that didn't stop his mind from conjuring up an image of the two of them engulfed in clouds of steam, the heat lamp overhead casting a ruby glow over their wet bodies as he picked up a bar of soap, rubbed it between his palms to create a lather, then spread the fragrant bubbles over her slick, slender body.

He imagined the shuddering, gasping sounds of her breathing as his touch lingered at her breast, circled taut nipples. Then he'd continue down, slowly, erotically, lower and lower, the feel of his hands splayed across her stomach making her moan. And reach for him.

But he'd evade her touch, continuing his erotic journey, drawing out the sensations until she was begging him to take her. Now.

"Damn." Hot and bothered, he readjusted his jeans to make room for the mother of all hard-ons, and left the bedroom before he gave in to impulse and joined her in that shower.

## 39

Faith and John were back in the hotel room. While the swelling in Danny's brain had begun to recede, there was no way she was risking taking him out of the ICU and back home to Shelter Bay yet. But he was well enough for her to take a break and try to gather up her emotions that had been shattered while she'd been forced to listen to Kara being attacked by that monster.

"Damn," John said, as he threw his body down onto the sofa in the suite's living room. "This has been one hell of a couple days."

"Tell me about it." She sank down beside him. "At least Daniel seems to have turned the corner."

"And Kara's okay."

"She's always been incredibly strong. And she sounds as well as one can be after such a nightmare." Faith dragged her hands through her hair, appalled to notice they were still trembling. She'd always had the steadiest hands of anyone she knew. It was a necessity in her business. "I'm so proud of what she's made of her life — her career, what a wonderful mother she is — but there are times I honestly wish she'd chosen any other line of work. The idea that a child of mine could be attacked, not once, but twice, is abhorrent."

"It's tough, but so is she."

"She's only twenty-eight. Which is so young to have so much responsibility."

"In years maybe. But don't forget, she spent most of her childhood hanging around the sheriff's office. Not only was she essentially a single mom holding down the home front while Jared was off fighting terrorism, but she has a degree in criminal justice, and spent several years as a cop in a city.

"She's really good at her job, Faith. In time, she'll probably be as good as Ben. Besides, there are other sheriffs around the country even younger than her. And normally, when you're dealing with a population of under a thousand people, there's not all that much danger of having to worry about serious crime."

"Her father and I wanted her to come home after California. Where she'd be safe."

Faith felt tears stinging at the back of her lids and resolutely blinked them away. "And now this happened."

"I promise you, sweetheart, this isn't going to end up like Ben's shooting. We'll get that bastard who did this to her. And make him pay."

Faith never cried, because her parents had drilled into her that showing emotions demonstrated a lack of control. Later, during her medical training, she'd learned to lock any feelings away, because they could interfere with her work. Plus, what good would it do for the parents of a seven-year-old whose brain she was going to be cutting into to know that sometimes she was as nervous about the procedure as they were?

Everyone who'd ever worked with Faith, her patients and their families, or even those who knew her socially, were always describing her as being cool as a cucumber. *Grace under pressure,* one resident had written in his evaluation during her internship.

She also knew there were those who'd accused her of being too cool during that terrible time after her husband's death. Although she'd pretended to ignore them, there'd even been the occasional whisper that anyone who wasn't more shaken could possibly have been involved in what had officially been declared an accidental death.

Knowing the truth, that her heart had been shattered when John had shown up at the hospital to break the news about the shooting, Faith had mostly been able to keep those accusations from getting under her skin.

But even watching herself, as if from a distance, imagining how others must have seen her, she realized that her behavior must seem unnaturally unfeeling. The problem was, in the beginning, she'd been shocked to the point of numbness. How could the strong, honest, wonderful man she'd fully expected to spend the rest of her life with be snatched away in the amount of time it took a bullet to escape the barrel of a gun?

She was, admittedly, a control freak — a necessary personality trait for any surgeon, especially one who went spelunking around in people's brains.

Then later, whenever those banked emotions would attempt to break free, she resorted to her lifelong behavior pattern of cranking the screws down even further.

But now, exhausted, physically and emotionally drained, she felt like a pane of glass with a thousand cracks in it, on the verge of shattering.

"I'm sorry." Appalled when tears began to

overflow her eyes and stream down her face, she dashed at them with the backs of her hands. "I'm afraid I'm on the verge of falling apart."

"Nothing wrong with that." John put his large arm around her and pulled her close. It made her feel small and vulnerable. But safe. "There were times I drove out to the cliff all alone and bawled like a baby during the two years of Glory's cancer battle. You've been through a rough patch these past few months, Faith. Seems you're entitled to let go for once in your life."

And that was exactly what she did as she buried her face in the front of his shirt and let the tears she'd been holding back too long break free.

# 40

Sax was waiting on the dock as the blue fishing boat came chugging into the brightly lit harbor. He could see Trey, wearing a bright orange life jacket, standing at the bow of the *Kelli,* Velcro right beside him. Sax's grandfather stood behind Kara's son, one hand on the boy's shoulder, a fond gesture Sax remembered well. Cole manned the wheel while their dad worked the lines.

It was a damn pretty boat. Cole had loved the sea all his life. And now he loved the woman he'd named the boat after. The same woman he was about to pledge to spend the rest of his life with. Strangely, that didn't seem as weird to Sax as it did just a couple days ago.

The boy's smile immediately disappeared when he spotted Sax standing alone on the dock.

"Where's Mom?" he asked as he jumped off the boat onto the floating wooden dock before anyone could catch him. Velcro was on his heels.

"She had herself an accident," he said, as the dog barked with joy and danced around him. Sax decided obedience training was definitely going to have to be added to his already packed agenda. "Got herself banged up some, but she's going to be just fine. She's out at my house waiting for you."

"Your house?" Those lines that were carbon copies of Kara's furrowed his freckled brow. "Why not Grandma's?"

"Because your mom's got herself some bruised ribs, so walking up and down those stairs by herself while your grandma's in Portland could be kinda hard." That part was the absolute truth. "Besides, no place better to recuperate than on the coast, drinking in all that fresh salt air."

"We've got salt air at Grandma's, too," Trey pointed out.

"True enough," Sax said as he waved good-bye to his grandfather, father, and brother, and began walking with the boy and dog to the car. "And if you really want, we can go pick her up and take her back to your grandmother Blanchard's —"

"No." The bluff worked, as Sax had hoped it would. Because he hadn't really had a plan B if Trey had balked. "That's okay. I like being at your house." Then came the question he'd been hoping he could avoid. "What kind of accident?"

"She fell down." True again. Sort of, anyway.

"Mom never falls down." Sax could feel the suspicion radiating from the kid, who was obviously sensing something more was going on. But he felt he owed it to Kara to let her tell the story in her own way.

"Everyone falls down occasionally. She tripped over a kitchen chair." He was on a roll. Given the overturned chair he'd seen lying on the hardwood floor when he'd come barreling into the house, that was yet another accurate statement. "So, after checking her out at the hospital —"

"Mom went to the hospital?"

Panic had the young voice going high enough to crack crystal. "Just to be checked out," he repeated. "To make sure the ribs weren't cracked. But although your mom likes to think of herself as Wonder Woman, she looked to me like someone who could use a little TLC. So, since your grandmother's still in Portland, I figured, as her friend, I'd let her stay at my place, pick you up, bring home some pizza and a movie or two."

"She likes mushy love stories."

They'd reached the car. Velcro leaped into the backseat; Trey climbed into the passenger seat. "It's been my experience that most women do."

"I like comic books about superheroes," Trey said while buckling up his seat belt. "But Mom says most of the movies about them are just too violent for a boy my age."

And couldn't he just hear Kara's voice laying down that law?

"What does she let you watch?"

"Movies about animals. Which is okay, because I like those a lot."

"I imagine Surfside Video should have plenty of those. So," he said as he got behind the wheel and turned the key, causing the oversize engine to start up with a mighty roar. "What are we getting on the pizza?"

"I like 'em loaded. Even with anchovies. Mom says they're disgusting and always takes them off her pieces."

Sax laughed for the first time since getting the call from John O'Roarke. "Definitely a case of the apple not falling far from the tree. Your dad was the exact same way."

"Really?"

"Absolutely. Everyone always bitched whenever he'd win the coin toss to choose the ingredients. Cole always said it was like chowing down on bait."

The small face, which had been wrinkled with worry, lit up from within as if Trey had swallowed the Shelter Bay lighthouse. "It's cool Dad and I both like them," he said.

"Cool indeed," Sax agreed.

The air inside the car suddenly chilled. *Damn.* Wasn't this just what he needed to top off a suckfest day?

Sax looked up at the rearview mirror. Sure enough, the guys were sitting back there with Velcro. He couldn't shoot them the finger, or even a glare, just in case the kid would choose that moment to glance over at him.

But as it turned out, he needn't have worried. Because Cowboy merely grinned and gave him two thumbs-up; then they all faded away, as they always did, into the mist.

# 41

It was the sound of the wind, moaning like the spirits of all those sailors lost at sea, and the rain pelting against the window that woke Kara.

She forced open her eyes, which felt as if they'd been weighed down with stones. The unfamiliar room was dark. Disoriented, she struggled to sit up, then wished she hadn't done so when the gingerly executed movement caused rocks to tumble around in her head.

So she lay back against the pillow, trying to get her bearings.

A flashback of the attack hit like a jolt from a Taser. She instinctively flailed out, hitting at nothing but air.

Her heart pounding against ribs that felt as if they'd been hit by a baseball bat, she closed her eyes and concentrated.

It was okay. She was at Sax's house on the cliff. In his room. And his bed. Thanks to that pill he'd forced on her back at the hospital, and the crash that was inevitable after such a wild adrenaline rush, she'd dropped like a stone into sleep.

He'd brought her here after helping her escape the hospital, had given her his T-shirt, made her tea in a heavy mug with the eagle-trident-and-anchor SEAL symbol printed on it, then helped her into bed.

Which had felt really strange. And not just because her head had begun spinning from the painkiller. But because she could not, in her memory, recall ever being taken care of.

Oh, her parents had certainly clothed and fed her. And her father had always been her biggest booster. But while he'd fed her confidence, he'd never been one to believe in pampering. Nor had her mother, perhaps because when she spent her days with patients with serious problems, a skinned knee or head cold just didn't seem all that life-threatening. Which they weren't. But still . . .

Jared had loved her. She'd never had a moment's doubt about that, even during those last difficult days. But he'd been a Marine at heart. He'd always said that if cut, he'd bleed the Marine battle colors of scarlet and gold. While it was a valiant thought, the only color staining the front of the blue police uniform on the day of his death had been red.

Even so, just as he wasn't given to grand gestures, neither had he been one to coddle anyone. Not Trey. Nor her. It wasn't because he hadn't cared; it just wasn't in his nature. Perhaps, she thought now, if he had understood that sometimes it was okay not to always be tough, he might have gotten help earlier.

Sometime during childhood, she'd taken on the role of the family caretaker: making sandwiches and heating up soup for her father's and her dinner when her mother couldn't get home from the hospital, struggling to ease her husband's stress, which oddly always seemed worse when he was back home than when he was deployed. She'd learned, in counseling, that for military personnel, often "real life" was more difficult because it was more untidy. Less regulated.

So she'd tried to create a home schedule that didn't allow for surprises, even going so far as to make a chart she kept on the refrigerator door. Her efforts had seemed to work. Until . . .

*No.* She wouldn't think about that. Not now. Her eyes stung. Kara blinked furiously. Her son was just on the other side of that wooden door. She had to be strong for him.

She reached out to turn on the bedside light, but nothing happened. Groped around and felt the flashlight lying on the table. Turned it on, saw the broken gold ring glinting in the narrow yellow beam, and felt a pang of loss.

Sax was right: She could have a jeweler repair her wedding band. But another part of her wondered if maybe Sherry might actually have a point about it being time to move on with her life.

She'd told Sax she'd been through all the stages of grieving. Which was true. But the ring had been one thing, along with the box of medals and memories that were fading every day, that had kept her connected with Jared. It had also left her in a sort of limbo, which had been okay, since, as she'd also told Sax, she was dealing with a lot of things right now. Deciding to think about it later, when her body wasn't feeling as if it had been run over by a bulldozer and her head wasn't pounding, she managed, with no small effort, to climb out of bed. Wincing at the pain in her bruised ribs, she hobbled across the plank wooden floor to the window.

The fog surrounded the house like a thick gray blanket. Every so often the eerily wailing wind would part the fog, allowing her to catch a glimpse of turbulent surf and the steady flash of the Shelter Bay lighthouse, warning any ships that might be caught at sea during the storm away from the rocky shoals.

She moved the flashlight around the room until its beam found her overnight bag lying on a chair. Sax had chosen well, though she couldn't help but be a little embarrassed at the idea of him going through her underwear drawer. And not because of its being underwear, but because except for two steel gray cotton sports bras she wore while running, it was all unrelentingly white. Unrelentingly boring.

She'd once owned enough lace and satin lingerie to outfit a harem. Jared had bought her the first scarlet-as-sin nightgown at the San Diego Nordstrom right before they'd taken the trolley across the border into Tijuana to get married. At the time she'd been relieved that he still considered her sexy even though she was pregnant.

Later, she'd spent weeks before he arrived home from deployment shopping for the sexiest outfits she could find. Which had occasionally been embarrassing, since his taste had tended more toward the more outrageous Frederick's of Hollywood than Victoria's Secret, but she'd loved making him look at her as if she were the hottest woman on the planet.

Toward the end, she'd gone even further, dressing up in a sexy, skintight nurse's uniform, a see-through harem costume, even a too-short-to-be-legal French maid's outfit. But nothing had worked. Their lovemaking, which had once been so joyful, had become as arid as that Iraqi desert he'd spent too much time in.

So, after his death, she'd gathered up all the seductive lingerie, stuffed it into a black plastic bag, and late one night tossed it into a Dumpster two blocks from their town house.

Bygones, she told herself now, as she took out a pair of panties and the thick terry-cloth robe that would hopefully hide the fact that she'd decided the one thing she didn't need was a bra digging into her bruised ribs.

Going back in the bathroom, she flicked on the light switch, only to find it didn't work either. Deciding the storm had knocked out the power, she tentatively ran the flashlight beam over her body, which was scraped raw in places and badly bruised. Afraid of what she'd see, she then studied her face in the mirror. Although thanks to the earlier shower she was clean, she still looked like a shipwreck victim who'd been dragged in from the sea.

Her eye was turning out to have a hell of a shiner; her bruises, like the ones covering her body, were already starting to turn purple; and beneath the bruises, her complexion was still nearly as white as the butterfly bandages on her cheek and temple.

One look at her and Trey would probably freak.

Hoping that the rest of the house was as dark as this, she drew in a breath that, despite the medication, hurt like hell, squared her shoulders, then left the bathroom to face her son.

# 42

Sax's back was to the doorway, but he knew the moment Kara entered the room. And not just because her kid's eyes widened to saucers, but from the way the air stirred, the way it always did whenever she came near.

He turned around. Although her body was engulfed in folds of black terry cloth, her feet were bare, the polish on her toenails gleaming like pink seashells on the beach. Desire hit. Hard.

"Mom!" Trey practically tipped the chair over as he jumped up and ran across to her, flinging his arms around her waist. Sax watched her flinch, but wasn't the least bit surprised when she didn't so much as whimper at what had to have been major pain. "Are you okay?"

"I'm fine." She hugged him back, then put her hands on his upper arms and moved him a bit away. "Just banged up a little."

"Sax said you fell down in the kitchen. That you tripped over a chair."

"He's right. As stupid as it sounds, I did."

"Wow." He was studying her with not a little skepticism. "You must've fallen on your face."

"That's pretty much it."

Sax could tell Kara hated being dishonest with her son, but understood the reason. Though the kid was smart as a whip, which meant they wouldn't get away with keeping the truth from him for long.

"Your son has the appetite of a shark," Sax said, deciding to help her out by changing the subject. Obviously she needed time to work up to what had actually happened.

"I had a cheeseburger at the VFW club," Trey informed his mother. "And French fries. Then Sax's mom made some gumbo. And bread pudding. It was really good."

"Mrs. Douchett has always been a wonderful cook."

"Yeah. That's what Sax's dad said. Then we went out on the boat. Then Sax and me —"

"Sax and I," Kara murmured as she gingerly made her way over to the table.

Although he ached to give her a hand, not wanting to set off any more alarms with her son, Sax merely pulled out a chair. Shooting him a grateful glance, she sat down.

"Sax and I got a pizza. Loaded. Sax said Dad liked anchovies. Just like me."

"He certainly did." She smiled at that. Though she looked a little sad, too.

"I figured pizza might be a bit much for you to handle," Sax said.

"You figured right."

"So how would you like some minestrone?"

On cue, her stomach rumbled.

"Obviously, it sounds wonderful." She glanced over at the pot he had sitting atop a camp stove. "Did you make it?"

"No. I cheated this time and picked it up with the pizza at The Gondolier." He spooned the thick soup into a white bowl. "Mrs. Mancuso's nearly as good a cook as Mom."

"I know. I'm totally hooked on her clam linguini. I could probably eat it every day, if I let myself."

"I'm partial to her scallops Florentine."

"I've been tempted to try that, but I always fall back on the linguini."

He put the bowl on the table in front of her, along with a spoon and, since he'd run out of the paper napkins his mother had stocked his kitchen with, a piece of paper towel. "We'll go there for dinner and I'll share mine."

Okay, so he was pushing, bringing up that date thing again with her kid in the room, which pretty much prevented her from refusing. But Sax was encouraged when she paused, seemed to consider, and finally said, "I'd enjoy that."

She glanced around the room at the candles he'd lit.

"This is nice."

"The power goes out here a lot. I keep the stove for cooking and the candles for light."

"We got some movies, too. But Sax didn't want to turn on the generator because he didn't want to wake you up," Trey volunteered.

"I'm not sure a freight train could've woken me up. What movies did you get?" she asked as she took a tentative sip of her minestrone. Sax told himself that he was watching only because he worried that eating even soup might hurt her lips. Not because he was fascinated by her mouth.

*Liar.*

"*Ice Age* and *Air Bud,*" Trey said. "*Air Bud's* about a dog that can play all kinds of different sports. We got the one where he plays football on Josh's — that's the boy who rescued him — junior high football team."

"Interesting you should choose that one,"

Kara murmured.

"I like football."

"So you keep telling me," Kara said, exchanging a look with Sax, who knew they were both thinking about his offer to help the kid learn some football plays.

"Anyway," Trey said, practically jumping up and down in his chair, "these two Russian dognappers kidnap Buddy because they want him to be in this Russian circus."

"So it's an adventure story, along with a football story."

"Yeah. But that's when the power went off. So I haven't found out how Josh gets Buddy back."

"Well, I'm sure he will."

"Yeah. Because there are a lot of other *Air Bud* movies after that. He plays baseball and soccer, and even volleyball on the beach."

He looked over at the dog, who, now that the pizza box was empty, which meant no more treats would be forthcoming, was lying on her back, long legs up in the air, happily snoring.

"Maybe I could teach Velcro some more tricks besides fetch," he suggested to Sax.

"Sounds good to me. Why don't we start with a Frisbee? I can pick one up in town tomorrow; then, if your mom gives the go-ahead, we'll take her down on the beach after you get out of school."

"Wow. Sweet!" That actually got him out of his chair and running over to her side. "Can we, Mom?"

"Shouldn't you be working on Bon Temps?" she asked Sax.

"I will be. But since I'm the project boss, I figure I can give myself a little time off. Besides, all the guys were friends with Jared. They're not going to have any problem with my taking his boy out to toss a Frisbee around for a while."

The comment about having a hamburger at the VFW had flown over her head in the vast litany of other meals her son had managed to consume in a single day. But now the relevance sank in. Obviously the other vets, who'd known Jared, had shared stories with Trey. Stories that helped keep his father alive for him. Something she admittedly hadn't been doing. And with Jared's parents having moved to Nevada, the responsibility had fallen on her.

In the beginning, it had been just too hard and he'd been too young. Later, she'd worried she'd only bring up memories of that day their lives had changed so horribly. Now she realized that she'd been remiss. If even *her* memories were fading after all those years together, how must it be for Trey,

417

struggling to keep an emotional connection with his father?

She turned from Sax to Trey.

"So you met some of your father's friends?"

"Yeah, and it was really great, Mom," he said, confirming her thoughts. "Did you know Dad was an Eagle Scout?"

"I did."

"And that he saved a little kid from drowning?"

"I remember that well." And she should have shared it with her son. But, given that they lived near the beach in California, while she'd taught him about the dangers of riptides, and going out into the surf without an adult present, she also hadn't wanted to make him overly afraid of the water. One of the problems with being a single mother, even during her married years, was concern that she would, as her father would have so bluntly put it, "sissify" her son.

"And that he was in ROTC? Just like I wanna be when I get to high school?"

Kara decided this was no time to remind him that was a topic they'd tabled for later. "He looked very handsome in his uniform," she said instead.

"This one guy told me that apples don't

418

fall far from the tree. Which means I'm just like Dad."

"You are." She bit her lip, then realized her mistake as it hurt like hell. "I have some pictures of your father when he was your age. And I think one of him in his Boy Scout and ROTC uniforms. I'll have to get them out. Maybe we can put them in an album together."

"Okay. Guess what else I did?"

"Go hunting sharks?"

"Nah. Though I did go out on the *Kelli.* That's Cole's really cool fishing boat. And me and Sax went to the lumber store and I helped pick out the paint color. We chose Cajun Red."

"That sounds perfect for a Cajun restaurant."

"Yeah." He nodded vigorously. "That's what Sax said. Then I came up with the idea of decorating it with beads and stuff, you know, like at the Mardi Gras celebration we went to back in California?"

He had, for the longest time, called it "back *home* in California." Kara was pleased that he apparently was now thinking of Shelter Bay as home.

"I do."

"Sax said it wasn't like his parents used to have it, but that it was a perfect idea. And *I* thought of it. All by myself."

"It's brilliant," Sax said. "Gonna really make people want to pass themselves a good time."

"That's what Bon Temps means," Trey said. "Good times."

"I always had a great time there," Kara said. "Everyone in town did. It'll be nice to have it back up and running."

"Yeah. We're in a hurry because Cole's getting married soon, and Kelli — the lady the boat's named after? — really wants to have her party there. It's a real mess, but Sax and the guys are going to get it done in time, huh, Sax?"

"Wouldn't want to let a lady down on her wedding day."

"She's having cupcakes. Sax's grandmother brought some back from the store, so we took some out on the boat with us. I had red velvet. It was really good."

"It sounds like it. I'll have to stop in to the store and try one out."

"That's a good idea. We could buy a whole box so Grandma could have some, too. Sax's grandma said they have lots of different flavors, so we could get, like, a selection. Like we used to do when we went to Dunkin' Donuts to get a box to go meet Dad whenever he'd come home."

"Sounds like a plan." The pain and fatigue were coming back. She could hear it in her voice and hoped Trey hadn't.

Apparently he had. Trey tilted his head and studied her. "You must have really tripped hard over that chair."

"It was a nasty fall," she allowed. She looked over at Sax, viewed the encouragement in his eyes, and decided just to go for it. "Actually, I was sort of knocked down."

Sticking to the story of the burglar, Kara made the incident sound as benign as she could, unable to tell if his silence the entire time was a good sign. Or bad.

"But as you can see," she said with forced enthusiasm, "I'm doing okay. It's not nearly as painful as when you fell off your bike and broke your wrist."

"I was just a little kid," Trey informed Sax. "In first grade. But I didn't hardly cry, did I, Mom?"

"No." She ruffled the corn-silk hair. "You were very brave."

He puffed up his thin chest. "Like Dad."

"Exactly." If her father had been alive, he could have filled in for Jared, teaching Trey about manly things, and giving him someone to talk about guy stuff with. Then again, if her father were alive, she and Trey would probably still be in California.

Perhaps she should have returned home to Shelter Bay right after Jared's death. But she hadn't wanted to take Trey away from friends and out of a school where he was doing so well. Then there was the disconnect she'd always felt with her mother. The fact was that she'd always felt as if she'd never quite lived up to Faith Blanchard's high standards, so it had been easier just to avoid the situation entirely.

"The burglar got away?" Trey broke into her thoughts.

"Just for now. The state police have a lot of clues. We'll get him." She could tell that he still wasn't quite buying into that probability. Then an idea occurred to her. "Sax volunteered to help."

That was all it took. "Hooyah. The guy's toast," Trey said as he flashed a thumbs-up at Sax. Who flashed one back. "We got a movie for you, too," he said, appearing ready to move on now that he knew SEAL Sax Douchett was in their corner.

"Did you?"

"Yeah. *Casablanca*. Sax says it's kinda a war movie, but there aren't any bombs or anything in it. That it's mostly a love story."

"It is." She looked at Sax, who was sitting across from her, elbows braced on the heavy wooden table, chin resting on the back of his hands, looking at her in a way that caused her once romantic heart, which had been locked away for so long, to stutter. "That was very thoughtful."

"Trey said you liked romantic movies," Sax told her. "Plus, a reunion plot seemed appropriate. Under the circumstances." He lifted his own mug, which held coffee. " 'Here's looking at you, kid.' "

Maybe it was the drugs still in her system. Maybe it was the hot, sweetened tea, Mrs. Mancuso's comforting minestrone, and the flickering candlelight, but for some reason, despite all she'd been through today, the classic line made her chuckle.

Then laugh.

And laugh.

It had been so long since Kara had had anything to laugh about, she couldn't seem to stop. Tears began flowing from her eyes even as she doubled over from the pain.

"Mom?" Trey went from laughing along with her at the joke he couldn't possibly understand, since she didn't even herself, to near-panicked concern.

"It's okay." Sax stood up and put a comforting hand on the boy's shoulder. "The doc at the hospital gave your mom some happy pills. Guess they just kicked in.

"Let's get you back to bed." Sax lifted her

up from the chair as if she were as light as thistledown. Then, with seemingly not a bit of effort, he scooped her off her feet and into his arms.

"Storm's let up," he said to Trey. "About time Velcro took care of business. How about you do me a favor and take her outside? But stay on the porch while she runs around, okay?"

Worried eyes went from Sax to Kara, then back to Sax again. Kara could see the wheels turning in his young head as concern for her battled with boyish trust for the man who, like his father, was a bona fide hero. With medals to prove it.

"Okay," he said. "Come on, Velcro."

The dog rolled over. Stood up and stretched. Then looked up at Sax, as if questioning whose authority she was supposed to obey.

"Go on," Sax said with a wave.

Claws clicked on the hardwood floor as she followed Trey out the door.

# 43

"He trusts you," Kara said as he carried her effortlessly into the bedroom.

The myrtle-wood furniture was simple, almost Shaker style. The walls had been painted a soft white with framed oil scenes of the beach and Shelter Bay she knew had been painted by Sax's grandmother hanging on the walls. She suspected the gauzy curtains hadn't been his personal choice, but had been left behind when his grandparents had moved into town.

"Like I said, he's a good kid. And he seemed to have a great day."

"Like Disneyland, Sea World, and the San Diego Zoo all rolled into one," she said. "I owe you."

"Since you're on mind-altering drugs, I'm going to ignore that ridiculous statement."

"But —"

"You don't owe me a damn thing." He laid her on the bed.

"Because we're friends." Hadn't she been the one to suggest watching out for each other?

"I've decided that deal isn't going to work for me."

"Oh?" Fortunately, that single syllable didn't reveal the snap of nerves his statement caused.

"Here's the deal." The mattress sagged, just a bit, as he sat on the edge. "You and I aren't teenagers anymore. We're adults. Single, unattached adults who've shared the experience of being put through one hell of a crucible, and neither of us came out totally unscathed. But the thing is, we're both stronger for the experience."

When she opened her mouth to comment on that, he put his finger against her lips. "Can we at least agree on that?"

Since it was exactly what she'd been about to do, Kara nodded.

"When I kissed you? Out on the beach? The night of the prom?"

"The pity kiss." Even with all that had happened, the memories had kept slipping back, like a thief from the mist, ever since she'd been called out here.

"Okay, there's one thing we need to get straight. Sure, that pregnancy test coming up with the little pink plus sign put a hitch in your plans. And you had all the reasons in the world to be scared and worried, and I felt like hell about that.

"So, was I sorry for you? Sure. But it never was a damn pity kiss. It may have started out as an impulse to make you feel better, but I wanted you, Kara. I wanted you then, and I want you now. Before you were off-limits, because you belonged to Jared."

She thought about telling him that she hadn't *belonged* to anyone. But it would be a lie. There were times she couldn't even recognize that love-struck girl she'd been back then.

"But now he's gone, and I'm goddamn sorry about that; really I am. But there's nothing either one of us can do about it. And the way I look at it, nine years is a hell of a long time to wonder about how things could be between us."

"You've been thinking about me for nine years?"

"Not really."

"Well, that's brutally honest."

"You were off-limits," he reminded her again. "The problem with carrying a torch is after a while it burns down and scorches your fingers. So, yeah, sure, I wished you a happy life with Conway and moved on. But now you're back home, and I'm back, and there's nothing in my way, so I intend to have you."

She angled her chin. "You think it would be that easy?"

"Hell, sugar, nothing about you has *ever* been easy."

"I feel the need to point out that your attitude is unattractively sexist."

"I'll cop to that. You can also throw in primitive and chauvinistic while you're at it. But it's also real. . . .

"There's this SEAL philosophy we all memorize in BUD/S training: 'I will never quit. I persevere and thrive on adversity. If knocked down, I will get back up, every time. I am *never* out of the fight.' "

"I wasn't aware we were *in* a fight." She rubbed her forehead, where the cut skin beneath the butterfly bandage was already starting to pull.

"Do you have anything on under that robe?" he asked.

He couldn't be thinking about having sex. Now?

"Your T-shirt. Why?"

"Because I thought I'd help you out of it so you can take another pill and go back to sleep."

"I don't want another pill."

"Tough. Your body heals better when it's

not having to fight pain."

"You can't let me oversleep. I have to take Trey to school in the morning."

"Leave that to me. You need a day off."

"I'm the sheriff."

"Who has three deputies."

"Two are green as spring grass. And John —"

"Is coming home tonight. I talked with him earlier," he tacked on at her sharp look. "If a major crime wave hits town, I'll let you know."

"Excuse me for considering Danny being shot in the head and my being attacked sort of a crime wave for Shelter Bay."

"All the more reason for you to be in full fighting form when you go back to work. So, here's the deal . . . You're staying here if I have to tie you to the bedposts."

"You wouldn't dare."

"You're right." His grin was quick and wicked and managed to cause that now familiar sexual tug that, just for a moment, overcame the pain. "But I gotta admit it's an intriguing scenario."

It was so simple for him. So easy. He'd always been a wizard with flirtation. She'd watched as he'd flash that sexy smile that lit up his neon eyes, causing females from eight to eighty to fall under his spell. She'd also watched as he'd moved from girl to girl, yet he'd somehow always managed to stay friendly with his former girlfriends.

Her senior year, there were also those girls who'd formed various popular cliques who'd never have given a shy bookworm like her the time of day suddenly wanting to befriend her. Having spent three years being ignored by those very same girls, Kara didn't need her four-point-six GPA to realize they saw her as a way to Sax.

"I can't think about this now."

"You're right again. You've had a crappy day and my timing, as usual with you, sucks."

His hands moved to her waist and untied the sash; then he boosted her into a sitting position while he helped her out of it. Although the oversize T-shirt covered her to midthigh, she felt uncomfortably exposed.

He pulled the sheet over her, then went into the bathroom. She heard the water run, a pill being shaken out of the plastic bottle. Then he returned with the glass of water, which he held out to her with the white oval tablet.

"I hate this," she muttered, nevertheless swallowing the pill.

"And I hate this for you."

He bent toward her. Surely he wasn't going to kiss her? Not when she looked like the Bride of Frankenstein? When her son might come bursting in at any moment?

"Get some rest." His lips brushed the lobe of her ear. Which was just about the only part of her that didn't hurt. "You know what they say about things always looking better in the morning."

Although she knew firsthand that wasn't always true, Kara found herself comforted — not just by his words, but by his strong and steady presence.

"Could you do me a favor?" she asked.

"Anything," he responded promptly.

"Could you stop by the house in the morning, after taking Trey to school, and see if the box of cold cases I picked up from John is still in the closet of my bedroom? It's upstairs at the end of the hall."

"You're thinking whoever was in the house was looking for it?"

"It didn't occur to me earlier," she admitted. "But yeah. It makes sense."

"Especially if one of those cases has anything to do with that skull and bone."

"Exactly."

This time his smile was slow and warmed her all over. "You always were one smart cookie. Want some help looking through them?"

"No. You really need to work on getting Bon Temps ready for Cole's wedding reception. Trey and I have already taken up too much of your time."

"Since it's possible that pill's starting to kick in, I'm going to assume it's clouding your thinking and not tell you how ridiculous that statement is. But don't worry. I hung out with the state cops for a while before catching up with you at the hospital, and there didn't seem to be any sign the guy had gone upstairs. I think you surprised him by coming home when you did."

"Well, that's a silver lining."

"Yeah. So I'll retrieve the box and bring it back here."

"Thanks."

"No problem. Now get some sleep." He took hold of her hand and gave it a gentle, comforting squeeze. The meds the doctor had given her were really, really good, because she was already beginning to float as he left the room.

There were two of him now, blurring in and out as he stopped in the doorway, looked back over his shoulder, and said, "You'll dream of me."

Was that a threat?

Or a promise?

Whichever, she considered through the

mist clouding her mind, he was probably right.

"Remind Trey it's lights-out at nine thirty. And even if the power does come back on, there's no TV watching the last thirty wind-down minutes, though he is allowed to read."

"Lights out. No TV. Reading allowed." Sax snapped a salute. "Got it."

"And don't forget to make him brush his teeth before going to bed. He's been cavity-free. I'd like to keep it that way."

"Want me to stand over him while he flosses, too?"

"I may be drugged," she said, "but I can recognize sarcasm when I hear it."

Sax's only response to that was a laugh.

Then he blew her a kiss and left the room.

It was only after he'd closed the wood plank door that she reached up, caught the air kiss in her hand, and touched it to her lips, which, although it was undoubtedly just her imagination, aided by prescription drugs, seemed to warm.

Kara didn't know how long she'd been sleeping when she woke again, needing to get rid of all the tea and soup Sax had pushed down her earlier. Although a quick check of the lamp showed the power was still out, the storm had passed, leaving behind a full moon that lit the room nearly as bright as day.

She went into the bathroom, took care of business; then, checking her watch that was lying on the bedside table next to her broken wedding band, she saw that there were still five minutes left to say good night to Trey before lights-out.

She walked across the hall and, just in case he'd actually fallen asleep early from his own busy day, quietly cracked opened the door, and what she saw made her heart turn over in her chest.

He was sitting up in bed, wearing his Batman pajamas, Velcro sprawled at his feet. His stuffed bulldog, Chesty, which Sax had thoughtfully retrieved from the house, was propped up beside him; on the other side was Sax, his arm looking ever so natural around her son's shoulders, while Trey read out loud from *Captain Underpants and the Big, Bad Battle of the Bionic Booger Boy.*

While he'd gotten hooked on the series about an elementary teacher turned into a superhero by two troublemaking boys with their 3-D hypno-ring, Kara had the feeling that part of the appeal of the books for Trey was that the irreverent tone and occasional bad word included in the stories slightly scandalized his grandmother.

Not wanting to disturb them, and not even sure she could speak without breaking down, she crept back to her bed. Sax's bed.

But as she lay there, listening to the rain on the roof and watching the flash of the Shelter Bay lighthouse on the bedroom walls, Kara realized that somehow, when she hadn't been looking, Sax Douchett had managed to infiltrate his way into her lonely heart.

# 44

"I don't see why I have to go to school," Trey complained the next morning.

"So you don't become a third-grade dropout and end up living in a refrigerator box under the Shelter Bay Bridge," Sax countered as he fried up some bacon to go with the biscuits and eggs the kid had settled for after being informed that no, Sax didn't have any Pop-Tarts.

"I've never seen anyone living under the bridge."

"That's probably because every kid in town stayed in school and became a productive member of society." Sax put the plate in front of him. "I don't think your mom would be real happy about you being the first person in your family not to finish elementary school."

Trey poured nearly half the jar of honey onto one of the biscuits, downed it in two bites, then scooped up a forkful of eggs. "I wasn't going to drop out," he said around a mouthful of scrambled eggs. "I was only talking about skipping today. To stay home with Mom in case she needs anything."

"Your mom assured me she'll be fine for a few hours. If I didn't believe that, I wouldn't leave her alone."

"There's only another week of school before summer vacation, anyway." Trey tried a different tack. "Since we already finished our end-of-school tests, I could probably miss the whole next week and no one would care."

"I'll bet your mother would. And if it were up to me, I might let you off the hook today."

"You could write an excuse to my teacher."

"And get my tail chewed off by your mother and grandmother?" Sax leaned against the counter and crunched a piece of bacon. "Sorry, pal. Not even for you would I put my butt on the line that way."

"You can't be afraid of girls. You're a hero. And you're going to find the burglar who broke into Grandma's house and hurt my mom."

"Your mom's going to find the burglar," Sax said. "With John O'Roarke's help, because he's her chief deputy."

"But you're a SEAL."

"I *was* a SEAL. But your mom's the sheriff. And she's smart. And good at her job. So, like you said last night, the guy's toast. As for being afraid of girls, believe me, when you get older, you'll realize that facing down two angry females can be a lot more dangerous than a whole horde of Taliban."

"I could help you with Bon Temps," he wheedled.

"I have every intention of taking you up on that offer this afternoon. *After* you finish your homework. Which you can do at Bon Temps while us guys hang the new Sheetrock that's being delivered." He refilled his coffee mug. "Meanwhile, I have to go to the bank this morning to get some money to fix the place up. And believe me, that's not going to be any fun."

"Mr. Gardner's bank?"

"It's the only one in town."

"He asked Mom out when we first got back to town. Before he married that rich lady from Portland."

The biscuits, eggs, and nearly a quarter pound of bacon had almost disappeared, which brought back a memory of Sax's mother swearing that every time that Jared Conway spent the night, he ate up the entire

438

day's profits. The more time he spent with Jared and Kara's boy, the more of both parents he saw in him.

"Did he?"

"Yeah. She turned him down."

"Your mother has always had great taste."

"That's what Grandma said when she told her about it."

Sax took the now empty plate off the table and put it into the dishwasher. His grandmother had always insisted that newfangled appliances just made a person lazy. Deciding that was definitely a generation gap of major proportions, Sax had had one installed shortly after moving into the house.

If you'd asked him just twenty-four hours ago, Sax would've said that there wasn't a man on the planet Faith Blanchard would have considered good enough for her daughter. After yesterday's phone conversation, he was thinking that maybe Kara's mother was mellowing toward him. Just a bit.

"Smart lady, your grandmother," he said. He scooped up the backpack and handed it to Trey. "Ready to go?"

"Yeah. I guess." Trey looked toward the doorway leading to the hallway.

"She was still sleeping when I checked in on her a few minutes ago. But she'll be fine," Sax assured him. "I'll see to it."

"You promise?"

"On my word as a former Navy SEAL."

Although it wasn't a Semper Fi pledge, it seemed to satisfy. "Okay," Trey said.

They were halfway to town when Trey asked, "Are you going to ask my mom out?"

"That's the plan." Sax slid him a sideways glance. "Do you have a problem with that?"

"Nah. You're nothing like that jerk banker."

"I appreciate the vote of confidence."

"Are you going to kiss her? And do all that mushy stuff?"

"Yeah. I intend to. And believe it or not, when you're older, you'll get so you like that mushy stuff."

"Mary Lou Long kissed me on the playground last week." He rubbed the back of his hand against his mouth, as if he could still taste the girl's lips. "It was gross."

"Give it time," Sax advised. "One of these days you may look up and decide that Mary Lou is suddenly a lot more appealing than you thought."

"Some of the boys at school get crushes on girls."

"Do they?" Sax desperately hoped they weren't going to get into one of those birds-and-bees conversations.

"Yeah. But I don't, because crushes are

like the flu. They make you lovesick. Besides, girls always end up dumping boys anyway. And pretty girls, like Mary Lou, are the worst. Because they just like to collect boys. Like comic books.

"They're also a lot of work because you have to always keep your hair combed and behave yourself around them. Barry Johnson had a crush on Madison Palmer and he even quit eating sugar so he wouldn't be too hyper around her."

"That's one heck of a sacrifice."

"Yeah. I'd rather have a chocolate-chip cookie than a stupid girlfriend." There was a long pause as they came off the bridge and turned onto Harbor Drive leading toward the school. "Johnny Jones says girls like football players." His voice went up a little at the end of the comment, turning it into a question.

Sax wondered if perhaps, despite the kid's claims of not liking the opposite sex, the desire to sign up for Pop Warner this fall had anything to do with the supposedly high-maintenance Mary Lou Long.

"I guess some do. Though it's been my experience that most girls worth having as girlfriends are the ones who like a guy for who he is."

Trey gave him a look that came just short

of rolling his eyes. "I guess when you get old you forget a lot about being in third grade."

Sax laughed. "You know, pal, I think you may be right."

# 45

"I could get used to this," Faith said as she lay on her back beside John in bed and stretched with feminine satisfaction. Despite the cool-as-a-cucumber attitude she'd worked all her life to achieve, one place she'd always allowed herself to let loose was in bed.

She and Ben had experienced some spectacular sex during their marriage, but what she'd mostly found herself missing after his death was the intimacy that came in the quiet moments of afterglow. When it felt as if you were the only two people in the world.

"That's the idea," John said, sounding as satiated as she felt.

She turned toward him and trailed her fingers down his still-damp chest. The silver hairs sprinkled with the darker ones reminded Faith that however young she might feel while making love with this man, they didn't have all the time in the world.

Not that they were old. To her mind, they were merely in their prime.

"Do you ever wonder," she asked, "about roads not taken?"

He covered her hand with his larger one. "Not really."

"There's never anything else you wanted to do with your life? Surely, when you were a child, you didn't imagine yourself being a deputy sheriff?"

"When I was Trey's age, I wanted to be a cowboy. When I was in high school, I thought maybe I'd play wide receiver for the Dallas Cowboys. But they still haven't called." He shrugged. "So I decided law enforcement wasn't such a bad backup occupation."

"No. Though it's dangerous."

"Life's dangerous. I could walk out of the house in the morning and get hit by a bolt of lightning. Or drop dead playing tennis."

"You don't play tennis."

"See. There's one risk averted."

"I'm serious."

He tilted his head and studied her. She recognized the look. It was a cop look. One that delved deep. "I can see that." His still-hard chest rose and fell beneath her hand as he sighed heavily. "Would you do me a favor?"

"What kind of favor?"

"Would you put something on? Because I'm trying to pay attention, and while I may not be a hormone-driven sixteen-year-old anymore, the sight of a sexy woman's tits are still damned distracting."

Although his tone was as gruff as a bear just waking from hibernation, she decided to take his statement as a backhanded compliment.

She rose from the bed, glad she'd taken the time for the three-times-a-week Pilates workout that had kept her body pretty damn good for a woman of her age as she felt his gaze on her ass.

She slipped into the hotel robe. Then, not wanting to risk getting distracted, instead of getting back into the bed, she sat down in the striped upholstered wing chair by the window.

"I enjoy my work," she began slowly, choosing her words with the same care she'd select a scalpel from a steel surgical tray.

"Makes sense. Since you're damn good at it." Sighing heavily, as if sensing this wasn't going to be quick, he hitched himself up in bed, still naked as the day he came into this world.

"Would you do *me* a favor?"

"You know I would."

"Would you pull the sheet up? Because you're not the only one who can be distracted."

He chuckled at that. One thing Ben and John had in common was that neither could keep a decent brood going more than a few minutes.

He did as she'd asked, but unfortunately the white sheet draped over his lower body proved even more distracting, as it outlined his masculine quadriceps.

And was that a . . . yes, it was. She didn't need a medical degree to know what that tenting of the sheet below his waist meant.

"See something you like?" His voice was still rough, but this time wickedly so.

"You know I do." She felt a warm, stirring response to his arousal and tried to assure herself it was only physical. Even as she knew it was much, much more than that. Which was why this conversation was necessary.

She'd been questioning her life before Ben had died. Even more afterward. But then Kara and Trey had come to live with her, and she'd settled back into a routine. A pleasant, comfortable routine that nevertheless hadn't quite stilled the restlessness inside her.

"But this is important."

"Okay." He held up a hand. "Just give me a minute." He closed his eyes. As she watched, the erection deflated. Not entirely. But it was still an admirable display of self-control.

"How did you do that?"

"Easy. I thought about baseball."

"Baseball?"

"Yeah. I go through the entire lineup of the 1963 Chicago White Sox. Dad grew up a South Sider, so even after we moved here when I was sixteen, I kept up the tradition of being a fan. Usually by the time I get to Sammy Esposito, I've pretty much got things under control."

"Maybe the government should hire you to make a sex-education PSA," she suggested dryly.

"At least you can still make a joke. That's maybe a good sign you're not going to tell me that while you've had fun rolling around in the hay with me, it's not going to happen again, but hey, at least we'll always have Portland."

"No." She was surprised at what sounded like insecurity. "That's not what I want to discuss at all. And despite the possibly tragic circumstances that got us into that bed, *fun* doesn't begin to cover it. *Remarkable* might come closer. . . . But, getting back on track, I was always happy married to Ben."

"Even a blind guy could've seen that."

"I fell in love the moment I saw him."

"Which must've been terrifying. Since it would've been totally uncharacteristically out of control for you."

"True." She wasn't as surprised as she might have been just days ago at how well he knew her. "All my plans flew out the window at that moment."

"You finished your residency," he remembered.

"Yes. But getting married and having a child certainly weren't in my plans. Well, maybe they were," she amended. "But not at that time, because I'd seriously started thinking about using my training to make a difference in the world. I'd even sent in applications to both Doctors Without Borders and the Peace Corps two days before that weekend I met Ben."

"Timing, they say, is everything."

"Isn't it? And I'll never regret our years together, not just because I loved my husband to distraction, but also because I was blessed with, first, a wonderful daughter. Then my grandson."

"Kara's always been in a class by herself," John said. "Just like her mother. And Trey's

448

one dynamite kid."

"He is, isn't he?"

Faith often regretted her initial reaction to Kara's pregnancy, which had been less than enthusiastic. In fact, afraid her teenage daughter had been about to ruin her life, Faith had even gone so far as to suggest an abortion. Not only had Kara flatly refused to even consider the idea, but it had caused a serious rift between them that had begun to heal only during these past six months.

"So. Even though Ben's death was a tragedy that left me reeling —"

"You didn't show it." He rubbed a stubbled chin that had felt like the finest grade of sandpaper as his clever mouth had sampled every bit of her body. "Which, I guess, was the point."

"I'm a doctor. If I crumble, patients will lose confidence in me. Plus, after Kara and Trey came to stay, I worried that if I allowed myself to mourn outwardly, I'd have them reliving their own tragedy."

"You should have told me. I was a wreck when I lost Glory. I would've understood, Faith. And given you a shoulder to cry on."

"And haven't you already done that?" she murmured.

"When are you leaving?" he asked, seemingly out of the blue.

449

She glanced around the room. "Leaving here?"

"No. Your work at the hospital. And Shelter Bay." He waved a hand in the direction of the coast. "To head off and save the world."

"I'm not sure the world can be saved," she admitted. "But it'll probably always need more help assuaging hunger and disease."

"You've thought about this a lot."

"I told you, since my twenties."

"Well." He rubbed the back of his neck. Looked up at the ceiling for what seemed like a lifetime but, if she'd set a stopwatch, was probably less than twenty seconds. "So, when and where are we going?"

# 46

When he'd come by the house to pack clothes for both Kara and her son yesterday, in a hurry to pick up Trey and get back to the coast house, Sax hadn't taken time to check out her bedroom.

Today, telling himself that a few extra moments wouldn't make any difference, he allowed himself to linger. In direct contrast to the professional law enforcement image Kara showed to the world, her room was pretty and feminine and smelled of flowers. It was the kind of room a man would feel comfortable in only if invited.

Which, Sax reminded himself, Jared had been.

Then he wondered what kind of guy he'd become that he could feel any jealousy toward a dead friend.

A pair of fat white candles and a dish of dried rose petals shared the top of the dresser with framed photos of friends and family.

There were the inevitable photos of Jared, looking like a recruiting poster in his snazzy blue Marine uniform. Another, obviously an inexpensive studio shot, like the kind you got at Walmart — of a beaming Kara holding a toddler Trey, while the proud father stood behind them in front of an obviously fake backdrop of autumn-colored trees.

Going back in time even farther was a faded Polaroid of all of them — Cole and Kelli, Jared and Kara, himself with some pretty blonde whose name he couldn't even remember, and J.T., who, being the youngest brother, had always insisted on tagging along — laughing around a campfire on the beach.

Sax couldn't remember who'd taken the photo. Nor could he remember the day. Because there'd been so many of them. All of which had always seemed absolutely perfect, back when they'd been impossibly young, foolishly optimistic, and the big, wide, wonderful world had been theirs for the taking. When unexpected pregnancy, heartaches, wars, even the early death of one of them would have been impossible to imagine.

"Glory days," he murmured, trailing a

finger down the front of the photo.

Then, reminding himself that he hadn't come here to reminisce about the past, he went into her closet and found the box right where she said she'd left it: on an upper shelf next to a stack of shoe boxes.

As he carried it out to the car, something Kara had mentioned that Cait told her hovered in mind. Close enough to almost grasp. But not quite.

As he drove back toward the coast, Sax concentrated on remembering. Because over the years as a sniper spotter, then a sniper himself, he'd learned to trust his instincts. And every instinct he possessed was telling him that whatever it was he couldn't quite grab hold of, it just might help provide the answer to Ben Blanchard's death.

# 47

Kara had always had a low boredom threshold. Which was why, after she'd awakened to an empty house shortly before noon, she decided that she'd pampered herself long enough. She went into the bathroom, took a long, hot shower, and washed her hair. Then she put on a pair of jeans and a T-shirt and sneakers, and went into the kitchen to make some coffee.

Her mother called again while the coffee was dripping through the machine. After assuring her one more time that truly, she was doing fine, Kara was relieved to discover that Danny appeared to be out of the woods and the three of them would be heading home from Portland later this afternoon.

When she warned her mother again about the mess the state police had made, Faith blithely told her not to worry and that Sax had arranged for a company from Salem who cleaned up crime scenes to take care of the damage.

"Well, he certainly seems to have everything under control," Kara said dryly.

"Doesn't he?" Was that a chirp?

"How's John?" Kara asked.

"Absolutely fabulous." Definitely a chirp. Or at least the closest thing she'd ever heard to one coming out of her mother's mouth. "We need to talk," Faith said, turning serious again. "When I get home."

"Sure." Kara guessed this was going to be where her mother was going to explain that she and John had become an item.

Which, Kara thought, meant that, as much as she disliked the idea, she'd better give Sherry a call and start her looking for a new place. Because while the house certainly had more than enough room for three adults and one small child, at this stage of a budding relationship, her mother and John O'Roarke definitely didn't need a pair of chaperones living under the roof with them.

Insisting yet again that she truly was feeling much better, she cut off the call. Then, after downing two Motrin she found in Sax's medicine cabinet, she called the office.

"You're supposed to be resting," Maude said.

"I am. As a matter of fact, I'm sitting on

the Douchett porch, watching a pod of whales."

"Good. Stay there."

"I'm the sheriff."

"Good thing you reminded me. Else I might've forgotten that little fact."

"Look." Kara let out a long breath. "John's in Portland with Danny, who is, by the way, apparently on the road to recovery."

"I know. John called in three hours ago."

And didn't that make her feel like a slacker?

"He also told me it'd be okay to have Kyle go ahead and talk to that anchorwoman from KEZI in Eugene," Maude revealed.

"Our Kyle?" The green-as-grass recruit?

"You know any other?" Maude asked. "You're the one who hired him, after all."

"As a deputy. Not a news spokesperson."

"From what I hear, you're not exactly in any physical shape to appear on television. John's out of town; your other deputy, Marcus, who's nearly as green as Kyle, checked himself off the duty roster because his wife went to the hospital in labor an hour ago. You know I'm too damn blunt not to say what I think about the yahoo who shot Daniel Sullivan, which probably wouldn't be the best PR move for the department. Which leaves you two choices: Ashley, aka Dispatcher Barbie, or Kyle. Since the anchor-person's a woman, and Kyle's real pretty, I'd say John chose the best candidate."

"Have the reporter do a phone interview," she decided. "With me."

"Well, here's the thing," Maude said. "She's already in town and has met Kyle. And she wants to put him on the air. I think she's going for the female audience."

"I could order him not to talk to the press," Kara said, thinking out loud. She was, after all, the boss, even if Maude mostly seemed to forget that crucial fact.

"You could. But then she'd just go talk to the state cops who've been going door to door, trying to find a witness who saw the guy break into your mother's house."

"They're still on the case?"

"They might not have gotten excited about your bleached-out old skull. But yeah, even they're taking the attack of a fellow police officer seriously. Of course, they also have a real tendency to hog the camera. And maybe spin the story to make it look like you're not up to protecting your own town."

It was, Kara thought, a distinct possibility. Local and state cops, who were on the same side when it came to fighting the bad guys, also had a built-in distrust of one another. And she knew small-town law enforcement officers, such as herself, were often per-ceived to be inferior.

"And even if you could get them not to hold a press conference, which John already told them not to do, by the way — and backed it up with a call to their boss, some guy he and Ben used to go steelhead fishing with every year — that reporter would have no choice but to go around town sticking her microphone in front of folks on the street to get their takes on what happened. Hard to control your message that way."

*Damn.* Once again the dispatcher had a point.

"We'll split the difference," Kara said. "I'll do a phone interview with her. And Kyle can show her the crime scene. Since I don't want our conversation to go out over the police band, I'm going to call him as soon as I hang up and let him know that in no way is he allowed to make any supposi-tions."

"I told him, since it's not as if you have a lot of clues, other than those bullet frag-ments your mother dug out of Daniel's skull, just to ask for anyone who knows anything about the incident to come for-ward," Maude advised her. "Then shut his pretty mouth." She paused. "But it's a good compromise," she allowed. "And one your dad would have thought of."

The compliment, coming from a woman who'd yet to give her one in the six months she'd been sitting behind her father's desk, shouldn't mean so much.

But, dammit, Kara thought, as she dialed Kyle Murphy's cell phone, it did.

# 48

Shelter Bay First Coastal Bank was situated at the highest point in town, in a huge red-brick building faced with four white pillars, which, to Sax's mind, had always looked ridiculous hovering over the small community of brightly painted coastal cottages. It had been founded by Joshua Gardner, Gerald's great-great-grandfather, who'd seeded the family fortune during the Great Depression by foreclosing on fishing boats, businesses, homes, lumber companies (including acres of timber), sawmills, and all the land they sat on up and down the coast.

If it had been up to future generations of Gardners, the entire coastline would be nothing but glass-front condos and pricey vacation rentals, but fortunately locals had always been adamant about overdevelopment, often forgoing easy profits to protect one of the most pristine environments in the country.

"Old Joshua was definitely overcompensating for something," Sax decided as he parked the car in front of a bronze statue of the bank's founder gazing out to sea, as if, having run out of things to buy up in coastal Oregon, he was looking for new opportunities overseas.

The inside of the bank was just as ostentatious, the marble walls covered with gilt-framed paintings. Some were of local scenery, but the majority were portraits of various Gardner males, including the one Sax had come here to see today, striking leaders-of-capitalism poses.

He was not the least bit surprised when Gerald kept him waiting thirty minutes past their scheduled appointment time. When his secretary — an Angelina Jolie look-alike whose collagen-enhanced lips made her appear to have stumbled into a nest of Africanized bees and come out the worse for the encounter — finally ushered him into the office, the banker didn't even bother to look up from the papers he was studying.

Sax waded across the plush red carpet and sat down in the seat across from the wide ebony desk. A nearly empty desk, making him wonder exactly how much work went on in here.

Knowing that he was being played, but refusing to rise to the bait, Sax just sat there, looking out the window at the expansive view of the town, the bay, and the iron bridge leading toward the coast.

Finally, after another five minutes of silence, during which time Sax wasn't offered so much as a glass of water, Gerald Gardner looked up.

"Douchett," he said.

"Gardner," Sax responded as the guy gave him one of those up-and-down appraising looks.

Sax had dressed for the meeting in a pair of ironed jeans, a blue, open-necked dress shirt with the sleeves rolled up halfway to his elbows, and a pair of classic, black-and-white Converse All Star Chucks.

He'd been planning to spit-polish his single pair of black dress shoes, but Cole, who knew more about getting loans because of his fishing charter business, had insisted the trick to getting money was not to go in looking as if you needed it.

Gerald, on the other hand, was wearing another one of those high-priced suits and silk ties, which made him look ridiculous in a town where people tended more toward jeans, T-shirts, Gore-Tex vests, and rain slickers.

Another silence ensued.

Again, utilizing his vast store of patience, Sax waited. And stared right back at him.

The banker was the first to look away, glancing back down at the papers in the manila folder. "What can I do for you?"

"It's all in there." Sax gestured toward the folder he'd dropped by the other day after lunch with Trey at the VFW.

"You want to refurbish Bon Temps."

"That's right."

"And your collateral is your grandparents' house?"

"The house and the oceanfront land. Which I bought from them when I came home." Admittedly for far less than they could have gotten by selling it to a developer.

The cliff house had originally belonged to the elderly widow of a timber baron for whom his grandmother had worked as a housekeeper/cook. Sax's fisherman grandfather had also moonlighted as the widow's gardener and handyman. Having no children of her own, their employer had willed the home to them, which was how they'd ended up with such a pricey bit of real estate. His grandfather had wanted to just sign the deed over to him, but Sax had insisted on buying.

Gerald studied the papers again. Yet more gamesmanship, which had Sax wondering why the hell he'd bothered to come here in the first place. He just should've gone to Eugene, or Corvallis, or Salem. The only problem was, judging from the banks he'd called, credit appeared to be tighter than a tick. He'd hoped perhaps small-town connections might prove more helpful.

He'd already realized, while forced to cool his heels out in the waiting room, that he'd been dead wrong.

"Then you also paid for that home and business for your parents."

"Not much to spend your pay on in Iraq or Afghanistan. I had enough saved to handle things."

"Yet the purchases left you without all that many accessible funds."

"The house and the land it's sitting on are damn valuable. Even in today's economy." Hadn't he been approached by half a dozen real estate speculators hoping to flip it and turn a pretty profit once the market picked up again?

"And you're willing to risk losing it? For a dance hall?"

He made it sound like a brothel. Sax had realized, when he'd first seen those signs on that parade car, that Gardner still held a

464

grudge over Lucien Douchett's keeping him on the bench. And now that Trey had revealed that the banker had asked Kara out, only to be turned down, the obvious fact that Sax and Kara were still close must have grated.

But even that probably hadn't rankled as much as the fact that, whether Sax wanted to claim the designation or not, he was a hero. While Gardner was a banker. Not exactly the most popular occupation in the country these days.

"If I considered it a risk, I wouldn't be putting the land up as collateral," he said mildly.

"Yet you've never been to college."

"Actually, I was studying music at Berkeley when I left to fight for my country after nine-eleven."

"Music." He didn't bother to conceal his scorn. "Did you happen to take any business courses?"

"Nope. Not a one."

Gardner shot his cuffs, exposing diamond studs set in what looked like platinum. "Yet you expect First Coastal Bank to give money to someone with your lack of cash reserves. And no experience?"

"I've never expected anyone to give me anything." Sax wanted to punch the guy's supercilious face. "That application is for a loan. Which I intend to repay. On time. With interest.

"As for experience, I grew up over Bon Temps. I was washing dishes there when I was six, standing on a stool to reach the shelves. I was busing tables at twelve, and cooking at fifteen. I learned math helping my parents balance receipts at the end of the day.

"So yeah, maybe I don't have a framed diploma in Latin from some fancy business college, but I'm definitely not without experience."

"Working for a restaurant is a great deal different from actually running one," Gerald said. "I'm sorry." He closed the folder. "First Coastal just doesn't consider you a viable risk."

He'd seen it coming. But pride — and a Cajun stubbornness that went all the way to the bone — had him seeing it through.

He stood up. Plucked the folder holding the balance sheet he'd spent most of the night working on from the glossy top of the desk. "First Coastal," he said with his most winning smile, "can eat my shorts."

"Way to go, Sax Man," Randy said as he walked out of the bronze door of the bank. "That's telling the fat douche bag."

"It was a stupid, sophomoric thing to say," Sax muttered.

"But you enjoyed the hell out of it," Cowboy drawled.

"You bet," Sax agreed.

"So where are we going now?" Randy asked as they all climbed into the Camaro.

Sax knew better by now than to suggest his teammates stay behind.

He headed down the hill toward Harbor Street.

"I'm suddenly having myself a craving for cupcakes."

# 49

An hour later, Sax's blood turned to ice when he returned to the house and found Kara missing. He also came as close to panic as he'd ever been when he viewed her purse, which she'd insisted on dragging from her mother's house to the hospital with her, on the kitchen table.

*Damn!* He should've thought of taking a couple guys off working on Bon Temps to come out here and guard her while he'd been taking care of business.

"You've lost your edge," he muttered as he grabbed a set of binoculars and ran out onto the porch.

And breathed an enormous sigh of relief when he saw her down on the beach, engulfed in one of his old parkas, walking in the rain.

He forced himself to walk when he wanted to run down the steep stone path.

"Nice day," he said as he caught up with

her as she paused to study a pebbly starfish in a tide pool.

Kara had come down to the beach in a rotten mood. Partly because she'd been forced to do that damn interview. And partly because she'd found herself wondering what the hell was keeping Sax. Even though she'd tried to tell herself her growing impatience was solely because she wanted to dive into that box of cold cases, the truth was that she missed him.

"I like the rain," she said, refusing to look up at him.

"Good thing. Since we get our share of it. Though I've got to admit I can think of a lot better ways to spend a rainy day."

She could hear the good-natured leer in his tone. "I'll just bet you can. Then again, you seem to have sex on the brain."

"I've got *you* on the brain," he corrected. His deep, suggestive tone, which had her envisioning making love in front of a warm, crackling fire, did nothing to calm her tangled nerves.

When he went to take hold of her arm, to lead her around a stack of driftwood nearly as high as her head, Kara shook off his touch, moved away, and stood on the beach staring out at the fog-draped sea stacks.

"Did you find the box?" she asked.

"Yeah. It was right where you told me it'd be."

"Well, that's something."

As she watched the sea lions on the rocks of the sea stacks beyond the tide line, Kara was grateful for the gloomy day. It was, in some small measure, a counterbalance to the fierce and heated storms Sax was capable of stirring up inside her. With a single touch. A mere look.

"You might want to come back in and check the files out," he suggested.

"They're called *cold* cases for a reason. A few more minutes aren't going to make that much of a difference."

She began walking again.

Seeming undeterred by her lousy mood, Sax walked along beside her, weaving around seaweed and shimmering jellyfish the size of marbles that had been stranded by the surf. "Something happen while I was gone?"

"How about the fact that you appear to be trying to take over my life?"

"And how, exactly, would I be doing that?"

"You called a company to clean my mother's house."

"I'm sorry. I wasn't aware you intended to clean it up yourself."

Frustrated because he was right, she

turned on him. "I would've found someone to do it."

"I'm sure you would have. But you were, understandably, knocked out when Trey and I left. So, since I know a former SEAL who's set himself up a business cleaning up crime scenes in Salem, I thought you might appreciate my giving him a call."

"I do." That was true. But, frustrated by this situation, and not at all looking forward to an interview where she was afraid she'd come off looking like a victim instead of a cop, what he viewed as being helpful — and she saw as controlling — didn't help her rotten mood. "So, thanks," she said with a decided lack of enthusiasm.

"You're welcome," he replied easily.

She began walking again. Although it wasn't doing her bruised ribs any good, in the past exercise had always elevated her mood. Not today.

"Don't you want to know how I found out?"

"I'm assuming your mother told you."

"Bingo. Give the big bad SEAL a Kewpie doll," Kara ground out as she came to a sudden halt where churning water thundered against the cliff. "Dammit! It's a dead end."

"Too bad. Guess we'll have to turn back.

Go up to the house and dry off."

Her last nerve snapped. "Don't you dare be calm when I'm not!"

"Okay. I'll get on board. You want me to be mad, since I haven't had the best morning of my life, I can do that. But first why don't you tell me what we're pissed off about?"

"My mother suddenly seems to have fallen into the camp of your female admirers. She actually likes you. Why, I've no idea."

"Wow. You're right. That is a biggie. You know, if it weren't for you, I might mistakenly think it was because she finally caught on that, despite my admitted teenage-rebellion phase when she couldn't stand my guts, I'm actually a fairly decent human being."

"You are, dammit!" The coastal wind practically whipped the words from her mouth. "You're a kind, decent, considerate, caring, sexy man."

"I must also be stupid. Because I'm still not getting what the problem is."

"I don't either. Not really," she admitted. "It's just that I hadn't planned for any of this."

"We both know that the old cliché about life happening while you're making plans is all too true."

She'd never met a man with more patience. Which, conversely, was only making her more impatient.

"I don't want to get involved with you."

"I think it's too late for that."

"And I don't want to have sex with you." *Liar, liar, pants on fire.*

"That's not it." He cupped her chin in his hand, lifting her frustrated gaze to his. "Maybe the deal is that you're trying to convince yourself that you don't *want* to want to have sex with me. And losing the argument."

Damn him. He'd nailed it. "If it were just the two of us —"

"If that's our only problem, you don't have to worry. I've never been into threesomes."

"That's my point. Not the ménage part. But we're still talking about three people." She exhaled a weary breath. "Whatever happens, Trey's involved. He adores you, Sax. In two days you've managed to do what I've been trying to do for months: You've brought optimism back into his life."

"And that's a bad thing how?"

Because it was impossible to think clearly with his hands on her, Kara backed away. "I told you. If things don't work out between us, if something goes wrong —"

"Look," he said. "Any relationship between the two of us is going to involve Trey. There's no way around that. And you know, I'm glad, because I really like your kid, Kara."

"I can tell that. But —"

"No buts about it. Here's the deal. I'd feel the same way about your son even if you weren't his mother. If we take this thing to the next level, and for some reason it doesn't work out, like let's say you discover I'm a dud in the sack —"

"I have a strong feeling that's not going to be a problem."

He flashed his trademark Sax Douchett grin. "I'm going to do my best to make damn sure it isn't." Then he immediately sobered. "But we've been through too much together not to remain friends. And no way am I not going to stay friends with your son if we stop sleeping together."

She didn't smile back, as Sax had hoped. "That's another thing you need to know," she said.

"What's that?"

"I don't take sex lightly." Her glorious amber eyes were wide and as sober as he'd ever seen them. "I wish I could. . . . But I can't."

"Believe me, Kara, I don't take *anything*

about you lightly. I've been thinking about you and me a lot since the other night, and it seems to me that the best relationships, the ones that last, are frequently the ones that are rooted in friendship. One day you look at someone and it's like a light has been switched on. And the person who was just a friend is suddenly the only person you could ever imagine yourself with."

"Good try, Douchett. But I happen to have seen that episode of *The X Files*."

"Busted." So much for the idea of cribbing from the pros. "But just because someone wrote those lines for a TV show doesn't mean they're not true." He drew her into his arms and ever so tenderly skimmed his tongue across the tightly set seam of her lips.

Although the wind and rain had grown cold, her lips warmed as his tongue sought hers.

Her hands lifted to his shoulders, holding on as desire swirled through her blood, hot and insistent.

Then he swore softly as a wave hit the boulder they were standing on, drenching them both in a cold saltwater spray.

"Do you think we could continue this conversation somewhere a little warmer?" he asked.

"Like a steaming-hot shower?"

He kissed the wet tip of her nose. "You're still the smartest girl in Shelter Bay."

# 50

As much as he wanted Kara, as much as Sax knew she wanted him, he couldn't help being concerned that he was going to hurt her. Not emotionally. No way would he allow that to happen. But physically.

"Maybe I ought to take a rain check," he suggested as he hung both their wet parkas on the peg by the front door.

She put her hands on her hips. "Change your mind already?"

"Hell, no. What I'm trying to say is that you've been through a lot. You could've been beaten to death yesterday."

Instead of looking traumatized, she scowled at the memory. "I held my own."

"I'm not saying you didn't. But you're bruised —"

"So we'll shower in the dark. Or maybe light a candle. Then you won't have to look at the marks."

"That's not my point, dammit. What I'm

trying to say, obviously very badly, is that as much as I want you, I'm thinking it might be better if I practiced restraint."

"Restraint." She angled her head. Studied him.

"For now. Until you're fully healed." He could do this, Sax assured himself. He could somehow wait a little longer. Of course, he might go insane, but it was a price he was willing to pay. For her.

"Don't look now, Sax, but it's a little late in life for you to decide to become a Boy Scout."

His laugh sounded as rough and edgy as he felt. "Believe me, sugar, I'm about the farthest thing you'll ever find from a Boy Scout."

She moistened lips he could still taste. Her smile was slow and willing. "Believe me, *sugar*. A Boy Scout is the last thing I want right now."

"What *do* you want?"

*You,* he waited for her to say.

"I believe you said something about a shower?"

"That was the original plan."

"But now you'd rather wait to share it with me until you get a permission slip from my doctor?"

"I'm trying to be a gentleman here, Kara."

"I'm not exactly looking for a gentleman either."

He hadn't remembered her being into torturing a guy. Not on purpose, anyway. But apparently she'd picked up a few tricks over the years, because she chewed idly on a fingernail as she gave him a slow, definitely smoldering look from the top of his head down to his rain- and surf-soaked Chucks.

"You do realize that the majority of home accidents occur in the bathroom?" she asked silkily.

"I've heard that," he said as she went up on her toes and brushed her lips against his. Then retreated.

"Which makes the bathroom the most dangerous room in the house."

"And your point is?"

"If you're really serious about taking care of me, perhaps you shouldn't let me shower alone. Just in case I have a relapse, or pass out or something." Damned if she wasn't laughing at him. With her eyes, and her mouth.

Deciding that trying to figure out the female mind was like trying to unlock the secrets of the universe, and taking care not to jar her sore ribs, he scooped her into his arms and carried her down the hall.

"We're both wearing too many clothes,"

she complained as he reached into the shower stall and turned on the water.

"I can take care of that."

He placed the condom he'd been carrying in his jeans pocket, just in case, atop the stacked towels on the vanity. Then his fingers got busy with the buttons on the white cotton blouse he'd packed for her instead of a T-shirt, thinking it would be easier for her to put on. Which it might have been. But as his fingers uncharacteristically morphed into ten thumbs, he was deciding it was a hell of a lot more difficult to take off.

Finally, they were standing together under a hot spray of water. "I should've asked," she said as he soaped her slick body, struggling to tamp down the renewed fury as he tried to be gentle while smoothing his hands over the huge purple bruise on her hip. "How did it go with Gardner?"

"How about we talk about it later?" He spread the bubbles over her breasts and her heart picked up its beat beneath his fingertips.

"Later," she agreed with a soft moan as his other hand slipped slickly between her legs. "Much, much later."

As badly as he wanted her, *ached* for her, Sax found himself hesitating yet again. She looked so wounded. So fragile.

"Tell me if I hurt you," he said.

"You could never hurt me."

As if deciding to take matters into her own hands, Kara put his face between her palms and pulled it down to her breast.

Not being a total idiot, he took the rosy tip of her breast between his teeth, drawing a soft moan of surrender. After giving the other breast equal treatment, he moved on, scattering kisses over her stomach, including the narrow white lines that were evidence of her having carried her son all those months.

From the way she murmured a faint protest, he suspected she might be self-conscious about those stretch marks, yet he knew she'd never regret how she'd gotten them.

Sax found them, like everything else about her, perfect.

He continued his journey — to the inside of her thighs, the back of her knees, her ankles, then back up again.

This time her stomach muscles quivered when his tongue glided back over them, revealing that she was every bit as seduced as he.

"Sax." Just as it had been in his fantasy yesterday, water was streaming over her.

Over him. Her hands reached between them, searching . . . causing the breath to clog in his lungs. "Please."

"Not yet." If she touched him, really touched him, *there,* he'd be a goner.

Her body arched up as his mouth found her. She clutched at his shoulders, but before she could recover from that first, quick climax, he speared his tongue inside her, causing her to cry out in what sounded like astonished pleasure.

He caught her as she went limp, not allowing her to fall as she lost herself to the spiraling pleasure.

"Lord, you're magnificent," he murmured.

He grabbed the packet, tore it open, and hoped she wouldn't notice that his hands actually shook as he rolled it over his erection. Then his mouth found hers again and drank deeply.

Trying to control the hunger that was tearing away at him, he lifted her up, joining their bodies, hot, slick flesh to hot, slick flesh.

She rocked, matching his frenzied rhythm, as the air clouded with steam and they took each other.

*Not yet.*

Only after her body went taut again, only

after she'd convulsed around him did Sax
allow himself to fall.

# 51

Sax was sitting on the edge of his bed, watching her dress.

Kara should have felt uncomfortable moving around the room naked, with his eyes watching her every move. But he'd already touched her everywhere. Tasted her everywhere. So, deciding it was a little late for modesty, she opted instead to savor the pleasure of back-to-back orgasms in the shower.

Then that third one once they'd made it to the bedroom.

"I told you to tell me if I was hurting you."

Since her back was to him as she retrieved a pair of the white panties she swore she was going to replace with something colorful the first chance she got from her suitcase, Kara didn't see the shadows darkening his eyes like an impending storm.

"You didn't."

"You've got new bruises."

She followed his gaze to the marks on each hip. And amazingly, considering what they'd just shared, she felt a stirring of renewed desire.

"I didn't notice," she said mildly. "I suppose I was just too busy screaming my head off with multiple orgasms from your ravishment." She glanced out the window at the whitecapped waves. "Good thing you live out here all alone. Or your neighbors would be calling Maude saying they were sure that Douchett boy was over here committing murder."

"It's not funny, dammit. I hurt you."

"You made me feel fabulous. Fantastic. No, neither of those is enough of a superlative. Fantabulous." She nodded. "That's closer. But still doesn't cover it."

He smiled, as she'd meant him to. "Maybe we should fight more often."

"Maybe we should just skip the fighting part." Returning to the side of the bed, she bent down and gave him a long, deep kiss, wondering why it was that when his mouth was on hers, she couldn't even feel her swollen lips. "And next time go directly to the makeup sex."

That drew a laugh. "I always knew you were one smart female."

"Strangely, since you so thoroughly ravished me," she said after they'd dressed and gone downstairs to the kitchen, "I'm feeling no pain. If we could only figure out how to bottle whatever magical sexual healing powers you possess, we could make a fortune."

"If you're truly not feeling any pain, it's probably from leftover endorphins."

"Spoilsport." He'd brought home more soup from his trip into town, this time a delicious crab egg-drop soup from the Jade Garden. She pointed her spoon at him. "I'd rather believe in magic." She took another sip. "So, what happened with Gerald?"

"Turned me down flat. And enjoyed every moment."

"I'm so sorry." She wondered what that would mean for Cole's wedding. And since she couldn't envision Sax going to work with his brother, if he wouldn't be able to fix up Bon Temps, would he leave town?

"Doesn't matter." He placed a glass of his mother's sweet tea on the table for her. "I found other financing."

"In Shelter Bay?" There was, unfortunately, only one bank in town. And while she'd been impatient with how long Sax had seemed to be gone, he certainly hadn't had time to go to Eugene or Portland. "Where?"

"Take the Cake."

"Excuse me?" She stared up at him.

"What did you do? Offer the baker gigolo services in place of paying interest?"

"No. But I'll take it as a compliment that you think any woman would pay for me to, well, service her."

"Believe me, Sax, if you decided to turn pro you could make a fortune right here in Shelter Bay. But how —"

"Cole told me the owner used to be an accountant. I thought maybe she might be looking for some freelance work."

"I heard she's so booked up, she's looking for an assistant."

"So she said. Good news for her. Not so good for me. Initially. But she did hook me up with a money guy she knew in Salem. Seems he's a jazz buff who used to come over to the coast for blues nights at Bon Temps. Figured it was a good investment, so he's in. In a lot better deal than I could've ever gotten from Gardner, even if he weren't still pissed about my father benching him."

"He always held grudges."

Kara remembered a time when Susi Markham, whose Goth style disguised a straight-A average, turned Gerald down when he'd asked her to the junior class Valentine's dance. Although it was never proven who'd written, *Want a BJ? Call Susi Markham,* with her phone number on every

487

stall in every boys' restroom in school, rumor had it that it had been Gerald's way of getting revenge.

Susi had merely laughed it off, gone on to graduate in theater from the University of Portland, and, last Kara heard, was touring the country with the road company of *Wicked.*

"Maybe the town will get lucky and one night the feds will descend on the bank and close it down. Meanwhile, he's not worth thinking about."

Kara could definitely agree with that.

As Sax put the dishes in the dishwasher, she began going through the cold-case files he'd brought with him. There were a handful of break-ins, two cases of arson — a restaurant and a lumber mill. Although the militant environmental group CHAOS had been the prime suspects, the district attorney, who'd been planning a run for governor, had refused to prosecute for fear of losing the cases, which would have lowered his conviction rate. From the scrawled notes, her father had been furious about what he'd viewed as a dereliction of duty.

There was a purse snatching, and — wow, call in the FBI — someone had walked away with a pair of silver salt-and-pepper shakers from the *Bay Princess*, a tourist dinner cruise ship that operated out of town during the summer months.

Nothing certainly that could have caused anyone to want to kill her father for.

"Find anything interesting?"

"Not unless you consider six incidences of someone stealing women's underwear from the Suds City Laundromat back in 1994 a crime wave."

She sighed and opened yet another folder. There was only a handful more to go.

"Sax?"

"Yeah?"

"Do you remember Celia Vernon?"

"Sure. She lived with her mother and stepfather out in that trailer park by the county line. We hooked up a few times the summer after our junior year."

Celia, Kara remembered, had been one of the wilder girls in school. Tamping down the little green twinge of jealousy, and refusing to wonder whether or not Celia had ever been in the backseat of Sax's Camaro, she continued reading all the notations written in the margin of the report.

"Do you recall what happened to her?"

"She was talking about taking off with some cowboy from Pendleton she met waiting tables down at The Cracked Crab. When she stood me up one night, then wasn't around the next day, I figured she went through with the plan."

"Apparently not." She turned the file toward him. "Her mother reported her missing."

"That's not so surprising. Not that her mother reported her, but that she took off. She hated her stepfather. Said he was always coming on to her. And I remember her mother being not a great prize, either. Which was one of the reasons she was thinking of taking off."

"It's the timing that may prove problematic."

"Why?"

"Because this missing-persons report was filed the summer between our junior and senior years. And, apparently, according to my dad's notes, Celia never made it to Pendleton."

# 52

Sax felt the hair rise on his neck. Never a good sign. "Did your dad have a suspect in mind?"

She skimmed over the report, turned the page. "No. But he didn't believe she'd just decided to leave on her own, because she'd left too much personal stuff behind."

"Maybe she wanted to start over."

"Perhaps." She read some more. "He was going to go interview her mother again."

The woman had been a piece of work back then. Unless a miracle had taken place between that summer and now, which Sax strongly doubted, the old bag could've only gotten worse. "Did he? Talk with her?"

"It doesn't say. But I'm going to check it out." She took out her cell phone and called information, only to learn that there was no listing for an Eve Vernon — not in Shelter Bay, nor in any of the other nearby coastal towns.

"I guess that leaves going out to her last known address," she mused.

"Not alone, you're not."

"I believe we've already discussed the fact that I'm not wild about your tendency to try to take over my life."

"I'm not going to apologize for wanting to keep you alive."

"In case you've forgotten, the Shelter Bay sheriff's office has three deputies on the payroll."

"Believe me, folks out there hate cops. No one's going to be greeting you at the entrance with a wicker welcome-wagon basket, and you — and John, or that fresh-faced kid —"

"Kyle Murphy."

"You and John or Murphy could end up getting blown away by some drug dealer who thinks you've shown up with a warrant to take him in. And speaking of getting shot, Celia told me her stepfather was doing a pretty brisk business selling guns out of the trailer."

"You never turned him in?"

"I was seventeen. He was a drunk with a mean temper and an arsenal he wouldn't have hesitated to use on anyone who got in his way. What do you think?"

"I think I'm glad you stayed out of it."

"That was then. This is now. And it'd be better if I come with you, Kara. Especially since Celia's mom had kinda taken a shine to me." The woman Celia had claimed bought her drugs by hooking had also offered him a freebie, but Sax didn't feel that was relevant to the subject.

"Name me a woman in this town who hasn't. And let me point out yet again that you're not a police officer."

"Thank God. But I am a guy who cares about you. Who doesn't want to see you hurt again, and damn well would never forgive himself if you put yourself in a situation that could end up with Trey being without either parent."

"That's a low blow."

"If you knew anything about SEALs, you'd know that we're more than willing to fight dirty. If necessary. Besides, I've got a vested interest in this case."

"Because you knew Celia?"

"Yeah. But mostly because, if it turns out she never made it out of town, then I could end up a suspect in a murder investigation."

"That's ridiculous. You'd never kill anyone."

"Want to bet?" Remembering how he felt when he'd first seen her at the hospital yesterday, Sax wasn't so sure about that.

"War's an entirely different situation." Misinterpreting his comment, she waved it away. "You're incapable of cold-blooded murder. Especially not of some girl you were" — she paused, as if seeking an appropriate word — "close to."

Actually, though he and Celia had screwed like bunnies that summer, he'd never been serious about her. Not just because she wasn't the type of girl a guy got serious about. But also because she'd made it clear from the beginning that he wasn't her only summer fling.

"I wasn't the only guy she was seeing that summer."

"Oh?" She perked up at that. "Do you remember who else she was with?"

"I didn't know. It could also have been more than one guy. Celia was generous with her favors."

"Girls who push the limits that way end up dead a lot in the city," Kara mused. "But it'd be more difficult to get away with murder in a small town, where everyone knows everyone else. And everyone's business."

"How many times do serial killers turn out to be the town Cub Scout leader, or general good neighbor?" Sax pointed out.

She rubbed the vertical line between her

brows. "Good point." She skimmed a broken fingernail over the front of the manila folder. "And okay, if her mother's still living there, you can come out there with me. But" — she held up a warning finger — "you can't say a word. This is still my investigation."

"I'll promise to be on my best behavior."

"Good. Though I have to admit that I've decided I like your bad behavior. A lot."

"I try."

"Though it does occur to me that you spent a very long time driving me crazy." She got up from the table and skimmed her hand down his chest. "If we're going to be partners, even unofficial ones, it only seems fair that I should get equal time."

"You're right." He took her hand, led her back upstairs to the bedroom, then flopped down on the mattress, his arms stretched out in a position of surrender.

"Feel free to have your way with me, sugar. I'm all yours."

# 53

It did not take a great deal of convincing on Sax's part for Kara to agree to spend another night at the cliff house. Later that evening, after she'd called her mother to let her know, Faith showed up at the house, surprisingly with Kyle Murphy, who was driving Kara's cruiser.

"I thought you'd want your own car to take to work tomorrow," she explained. "So your deputy agreed to drive it out here; then I'm taking him back to the station."

"That's a good idea."

"It was Sax's." Faith smiled at the former SEAL who'd once been the bane of her existence. Who smiled back.

Weird.

Her mother skimmed her fingertips over Kara's face, which was now turning into a rainbow of colors. None of them pretty.

"It's not as bad as I'd feared," she said, studying Kara more like a physician than a mother. "And I brought you some makeup to help cover the bruises until they fade. Let's go into the bedroom and I'll examine you." She glanced over at Sax again. Then at Trey and Kyle. "Surely you all can find something to do."

"Tide's going out," Sax said. "We'll go look for stranded baby sharks."

"Perfect." The chirp was back. Kara's mother didn't exactly clap her hands in that oddly cute way Paula Abdul had back when she'd been judging *American Idol,* but she came perilously close.

"That wasn't necessary. Because I'm fine," Kara protested as Sax, Trey, and her deputy obediently left the house.

"Gracious," Faith said. "I hadn't realized you'd received a medical degree during the short time John and I have been in Portland."

"And I don't recall you being so sarcastic."

Faith grinned — not her trademark cool smile, but a quick, bold flash of perfectly straight white teeth.

"I've turned over a new leaf." She made a scooting motion with her hand toward the hallway. "Let's get this over with. Because I have news."

Since she'd already confirmed that they'd brought Danny back with them, and that he was fine and currently staying with his uncle, Kara guessed her mother's news didn't concern him. But from that oddly uncharacteristic smile and what appeared to be an actual twinkle in her eyes, whatever it was appeared to be good.

She stripped down to her underwear, feeling a bit uncomfortable being examined by her mother in the room that she feared still smelled of sex. But if Faith noticed that, or the rumpled sheets, she didn't comment. Instead she briskly and professionally worked her way from the butterfly bandage on Kara's temple to the swollen bruise on her ankle, which she'd slammed against the iron leg of the chair while kicking out at her attacker.

"This appears new." Faith's fingers skimmed over a mark on Kara's neck.

Terrific. Was there anything that could make you feel more like a teenager again than having your mother notice a hickey? "Curling iron," she mumbled.

"Isn't that odd?" Faith continued to study it. "Given that a curling iron leaves a burn. Yet this is most definitely a bruise."

Kara caved. "I should know better than to try to fool a doctor."

"You should know better than to try to fool your mother," Faith said mildly. Her expression sobered. "John said that your attacker might have had something to do with a cold case your father was working on."

"That's a possibility." John wasn't one to gossip about police business. But this was different — because it not only involved his lover's daughter, but perhaps Faith Blanchard's husband, as well.

"He also said that you believe your father's death might not have been an accident."

"I honestly don't know, Mom. I suppose he told you about Sax's friend's wife. The former F.B.I. agent."

"Yes."

"I'm working the case from the files. She's got people working on the shell casing. If we get a match, or I find a connection, I promise you'll be the first to know."

Her mother, who'd always been composure personified, shivered. "I hate the idea of anyone murdering Ben."

"You're not alone there. But if someone did, I promise, John and I will get him."

"I have not a single doubt about that." Something shadowed Faith's already sober eyes. "Now, get dressed. Then we really need to talk."

"If it's about Sax —"

"It's not. At least, not directly," Faith amended. "Get dressed. Then I'll explain everything."

"Oh, super. Because I'd really love to know the true story behind Bigfoot. And black holes. And if Scully and Mulder have managed to unearth the truth yet."

The mood, which had turned serious during the discussion about her father, lightened, as Kara had hoped. Her mother flashed one of those grins again. One that made her look at least ten years younger. "Brat."

"I do have one more question."

"Which would be?"

"Who are you? And what have you done with my mother?"

Faith laughed.

Then left the room, leaving Kara staring after her.

## 54

"I can't believe it," Kara said, still stunned three hours later.

Her mother had left to return home. Trey was in bed with Chesty, Velcro, and a stuffed bear wearing a hospital gown and carrying crutches Faith had bought him at the hospital gift shop.

She and Sax were sitting outside, watching the moon float across an amazingly clear, star-studded sky.

"What can't you believe?" His arm was around her shoulder, her head on his. Sax figured he could easily spend the rest of his life here, just like this. With Kara on the porch, and Trey asleep inside.

As good as the mutt seemed to be for the kid, Sax knew the value of brothers. Maybe he and Kara could talk about that later. Once she got used to the idea that he was really in this relationship for the long haul.

"That your mother and John are in love?"

he asked. "Or that they're leaving Shelter Bay to have themselves a grand adventure?"

"Neither one is young anymore. And if they want to be together, which I honestly think is great and I'm happy for them, why can't they be together here? They could get themselves killed going off to some godforsaken third-world war zone."

"They could also do the world some good. There's this guy, Shane Garrett, an Army SOAR helicopter pilot, who was on the team with Quinn and me. He married a former relief doctor. Which is what your mother told you she'd wanted to do back in her twenties, then deferred the dream for a family after falling in love with your father."

"She also said that she never regretted a moment of that decision."

"And you believe that?"

"Absolutely."

"So do I. But your father's gone and you're a grown woman. Would you prefer her to stay here, stick to the status quo in a job she's clearly less than thrilled with, and spend the rest of her life wondering *what if?*"

"Of course not. I guess, along with worrying about her, I'm also upset about John."

"Why? He and your mom have been friends for years. They seem a great match."

"I know. They've both suffered the loss of someone they loved, someone they expected to live the rest of their lives with, so I'm honestly happy to see them have this second chance at happiness.

"And John did agree to stay on until I can find someone to replace him. But although he insists he didn't want to be sheriff, he's been like a rock to me. I honestly don't think he can be replaced."

"He's a special guy, all right. But you'll find someone. And you know what? From what I can tell, you're pretty much a rock yourself. You'll be fine."

"If I didn't think I could do the job, I wouldn't have taken it." She sighed. "I guess I'm just not that wild about change."

"Few people are."

"Do you miss it?" she asked.

"Miss what?" he asked idly, as he ran his free hand up her jeans-clad thigh.

"Having grand adventures all over the world. Going, what do you call it, 'wheels-up' at any minute?"

"Yeah, that's what we called it. And no, I don't miss it."

She turned toward him, her expression earnest. "It seems, after all you've done, running a dance hall and restaurant in a town with a population of less than a thousand might seem a little stale."

"When I was younger, I got off on the extreme stuff," he admitted. "And there's probably nothing like the adrenaline rush you get in a battle. But I'm not like some of those guys who defined themselves by their military role. And who get withdrawal when they're away from the action."

Like it sounded as if Jared had been. Kara's soft sigh told him that her mind was running along the same lines.

"I was drifting when I came back here. I knew I was through with the Navy, but I didn't have a clue what I wanted to do next. I watched Cole running his fishing business, caught up in tasting cupcakes and talking about bachelorette parties, looking at travel brochures for his honeymoon and trading in his truck for that kiwi hybrid, and thought maybe he was making a mistake.

"But now I realize he's the luckiest son of a bitch on the planet. And if you tell him I said that, as much as I love you, sugar, I'll call you a damn liar."

He felt her tense. "You said the L-word."

"Yeah. I guess I did. It just slipped out. So?"

"It's too soon."

"Nine years ago would've been too soon. Our personal roads were taking us in opposite directions. Besides, even if Jared hadn't been in the picture, we weren't ready for each other back then.

"We are now. But don't worry; I'm not going to turn crazy stalker on you or anything. Like I said, I'm a patient man. I'm willing to give you time to realize that you're so in love with me you can't think straight."

"Some men's egos are not to be believed," she huffed. Since things were getting a little more emotional than she might be able to handle right now, he'd decided that would draw a rise out of her. "Awful sure of yourself, aren't you, Douchett?"

"No." He touched his smiling mouth to her frowning one. "I'm awful sure of you." He kissed her a second time. The third time he felt her lips curve beneath his. "Of us."

He wanted to take her. Here. Now. With the crashing surf below, and the white galleon moon and stars whirling above.

If it hadn't been for her son sleeping just inside . . .

But without Trey, Kara wouldn't be the woman she was.

She pressed her fingers against her temple. "It's my fault."

"What?"

"I told you I don't take sex lightly. So now that we've gone and done it —"

"Several times. And hopefully it was as good for you as it was for me."

"It was amazing. But just because we shared amazing sex doesn't mean you need to feel obliged to tell me you love me."

Okay, so that bit about it being as good for her as it had been for him admittedly hadn't been that great a joke. Still, he'd meant it as one. But damned if she hadn't taken it seriously. As she'd always done with so many other things in her life.

Sax decided it was past time for Kara to loosen up — as she had in the shower, then later in bed — and start having herself some fun.

"Wow." He shook his head. "That accusation definitely came out of left field."

"Cait told me that SEALs don't go into battle guns blazing."

"As a rule, if guns are blazing, we haven't done our job right," he agreed, wondering exactly where and how this conversation had gone so badly offtrack.

"So you need to fit into your environment."

"True again. Sounds as if Quinn's shared some stuff with her."

"It appears so. Including the fact that SEALs are really, really good liars."

Okay. That hurt.

"Is that what you think?" The warm, fuzzy feeling he'd been experiencing just moments ago was getting burned away by a flash of temper he'd inherited from his mother. He'd thought the Navy had trained it out of him, since, contrary to Hollywood's often skewed portrayal of war, cool heads usually trumped hot in battle. Apparently, as he'd been discovering the past few days, he'd thought wrong. "That I'd actually lie to you to justify doing what we both wanted?"

"I wasn't calling you a liar." Her eyes glistened suspiciously, and damned if her lips hadn't begun to tremble. Just a little.

Now he'd upset her. *Smooth move, Douchett.* He glanced up and viewed the guys shaking their heads, looking thoroughly disgusted. Bad enough he was screwing this up. The last thing he needed was an audience.

"I was merely trying to explain that just because we slept together, you needn't feel obliged —"

"Fuck."

Her eyes widened at the word, which, especially being a cop, she'd heard before. But not from him. He might have been a SEAL, but having his dad wash out his mouth with a bar of Ivory soap for cussing at his mother when he'd been ten had taught him there was just some behavior, and some words, you saved for the guys.

"There's something you need to know, while you're making up your mind." He could win her over. In a heartbeat. But it was important that she come to the realization on her own. "I've known a lot of women. Been with a lot of women."

"Now that's a surprise."

She'd sure been a lot easier back in high school. "And I've been known to toss around a few compliments. Because I like women, so I enjoy making them feel good."

"Again, I'm shocked."

She wasn't going to ever make it easy on him. Maybe he was perverse, but that was one of the things Sax really loved about her.

"But here's the deal. I've always been real careful, even in the heat of, well, you know —"

"Amazing sex," she helped him out.

"Yeah. Even then. I've never, not once, ever told any woman I loved her." Because he didn't want her to think he was taking advantage of this confession, trying to get some more of that amazing sex, he pressed his lips against her forehead instead of taking her smart mouth. "Until you."

She shook her head. "Cait's right about

another thing."

"What's that?"

"You SEALs fight dirty."

He grinned. "You know what they say."

This time he kissed her on the mouth, a slow, deep kiss that had her kissing him right back.

Oh, yeah, and hooyah, the woman was crazy about him. "All's fair in love and war."

# 55

Displaying a sensitivity Kara wouldn't have guessed she possessed, Maude didn't say a word about the bruises that the concealing cream and liquid foundation her mother had shown up with last night couldn't quite hide.

Instead, she merely shoved a cup into Kara's hands and said gruffly, "Good to have you back."

"It's good to be back." Kara glanced around the office, seeing it with new eyes. Okay, so maybe it wasn't San Diego. Or Oceanside. Or even Salem. Maybe she did have only three deputies, two dispatchers, only two jail cells, and a broom closet that served as an evidence locker.

But this was *her* sheriff's office. *Her* town. And although she'd originally thought of this as an interim job, filling in temporarily for her father while the town council found a replacement, there was nowhere else on earth she'd rather be.

The aroma wafting from her mug, which bore a scenic photo of Shelter Bay's coastline, surpassed even Maude's usual stellar efforts. She took a sip.

"I'm tasting wild blueberries."

"Thought today called for something a little special," Maude said. "I drove down and got it from that Big Mountain coffee place in Depoe Bay."

"Well, it's delicious. Thank you."

"No problem. You've got a lot of messages piled up on your desk. Most are just people wishing you well. But there's a call there you might want to return first. A woman who didn't give her name, but she said it was really important that she talk to you. About a police matter."

As she carried the coffee into her office and shut the door, Kara wondered if the call could possibly be about Danny's shooting. "Maybe doing that TV interview wasn't such a bad idea, after all," she murmured as she sat down at her desk.

She'd just picked up the phone to call the number on the top of the stack of pink message slips Maude had left on her desk, when the dispatcher opened her door a crack.

"Sorry to bother you, Sheriff," she said. It was the first time Kara could remember the

511

dispatcher ever calling her by her title. "But Daniel Sullivan's here, and I didn't think you'd want me to keep him waiting."

"No, of course not — send him in." Kara stood up and walked around her desk just as Danny entered. He was wearing a baseball cap to cover the bald patches her mother had shaved on his head, but she decided of the two of them, he looked in better shape.

"Well, don't we make a pair?" He greeted her with a hug.

"We've both definitely had a couple rough days," she agreed.

"You look a lot better than I thought you would, from Uncle John's description of what happened."

"It probably sounded worse than it actually was."

"Yeah. I figured you'd say that." He glanced over at the chair. "Could I sit down a minute? I'm doing a lot better, thanks to your mom, but I still get a little dizzy, and I'm not sure there's room in here for me to fall down."

She was not surprised that he hadn't lost his natural good humor. Instead of sitting down behind her desk again, she took the chair next to his, turning it so they were looking at each other.

"You realize you scared us to death," she said.

"Yeah. Which is the pits, because it's kind of hard to impress a woman when you're unconscious."

*Please*, she prayed to whatever gods or fates might be listening, *don't let him have come here to ask me out again.*

"Speaking of which," he said, "although a lot of what happened during Douchett's welcome-home celebration is sort of a blur, I do seem to recall asking you to dinner."

"You did." Kara's mind was scrambling for some way to turn down someone who, only two days ago, had been in a coma.

"Well, here's the deal." He suddenly looked as uncomfortable as she felt. "I was wondering, since you didn't seem all that wild about the suggestion in the first place, if you'd mind if we sort of dropped the idea."

Relief flooded over her. "Not at all."

"Good." Again they seemed to be sharing the same feelings. "Because I met someone, and I think she might be the one."

"You met someone?" Kara felt her jaw drop. "Danny, you were in a coma!"

"Not all the time. There was this ICU nurse who was taking care of me. Since there wasn't much I could do except lie around and wait for more tests, she'd come in and talk to me whenever Uncle John wasn't there. In fact, hers was the first face I saw when I came out of the coma." His Donny Osmond grin had his eyes crinkling appealingly. "First I thought I'd died and she was an angel."

"Well, that's romantic."

"Yeah. She thought I was making it up when I told her. But I convinced her I meant it. Anyway, like I said, we clicked. Her parents are both teachers, so we have that in common. And she's got a two-year-old daughter from a marriage that went south. I always wanted kids, but it turned out my ex didn't."

"Sounds like a package deal," Kara said, wondering if someone had put something in Shelter Bay's drinking water. First her mother and John. Then her and Sax. And now Danny and some nurse he'd just met.

"I was thinking the same thing. Sara — that's her name — has some vacation time saved up, and since school's just about out, I'm not going back to the classroom until the fall. So we decided she and her little girl, Grace, could come spend a couple weeks here in Shelter Bay at Whale Song." It was a local B and B that, like Sax's house, had a stunning view of the sea and the resident whale pod. "And I can spend some time visiting them in Portland. See how things work out."

"I think that's lovely."

"Yeah." When he grinned again, Kara thought how fortunate it was that her mother had been there to possibly save his life. A life that just might include the wife and child John had told him Danny was now ready for. "Who would've thought getting a bullet in the head would've turned out to be a good thing?"

"It's a little dramatic," she said. "But whatever works."

"I saw the interview you did. The Portland station picked it up."

"I'm hoping it'll help find whoever shot you," she said.

His brow furrowed. "You still think it's an accident, though, right?"

"That's my take on it." Because she couldn't imagine anyone in town wanting to harm this genuinely sweet man. It'd be like shooting Bambi. "But I promise to keep you up-to-date on developments."

"Great. I'd appreciate that."

She walked him out and, just as he was about to leave, he said, "I know a lot of people thought Douchett was wild back in high school. But he's one of the good guys."

515

"I know."

"Yeah. I figured you did. But just in case he needs a reference, there was this time, back when we were freshmen, that this bully upperclassman decided I'd make a good punching bag.

"Sax didn't know me that well, but he came across the guy pounding the stuffing out of me in the locker room after soccer practice."

"What happened?"

"What do you think?" Danny winked. "Sax cleaned his clock. And the bully never bothered me again. Like I said, he's a good guy. And, not to sound like a high school yearbook comment, but I think the two of you make a real neat couple."

Kara was still laughing about that when she went back to work, dialing the number of the woman whose call Maude had suggested she return first.

## 56

When her call went into voice mail, earning her a cheery announcement that she'd reached the Fletchers, who'd get back to her as soon as possible, so please leave a message at the beep, Kara skimmed through the messages, finding that as usual, Maude was right about the others all being calls of condolence. Except for the automated one from the cable company, wondering if she'd like to change her phone service.

She was about to run a check and see if Celia Vernon's mother was still living at the address in the police report, when Maude opened the door again.

"You've got a lawyer, a weeping woman, and a guy who looks like death warmed over out there," she announced. "I'm hoping you'll take them off my hands."

"Absolutely."

The lawyer had Kara staying behind her desk this time. But she did stand up as the trio entered.

"Sheriff." The silver-haired man held out his hand. He was wearing jeans, a plaid shirt, and hiking boots. And carrying a well-used briefcase. "James Bradford, attorney-at-law with Bradford and Yongst down in Newport. I'm sorry to show up so casually, but I received the call from my clients while hiking up to Rainbow Falls and didn't want to take the time to change."

"Sounds important," Kara said as she shook the attorney's proffered hand.

She turned toward the couple, who were hanging on to each other as if they expected the ground to come out from beneath their feet at any moment. "And your clients would be?"

"Harlan Fletcher," the younger man choked out. "And this is my wife."

"Janice," she managed as she pulled a tissue from her purse.

Kara sat down again. "Well, Mr. Bradford, Mr. and Mrs. Fletcher. What can I do for you?"

"It's more what we can do for you, Sheriff," Bradford said. "My client, Mr. Fletcher, may have information regarding your mystery shooting."

"I didn't mean to do it," Harlan burst out. "I was just fooling around, joining in the celebration for the local hero."

"Now, Harlan," the attorney broke in. "Why don't you let me explain —"

"It sounds as if your clients are capable of speaking for themselves," Kara cut him off. "But first, Mr. Fletcher, I'm afraid I'm going to have to read you your rights."

"Seen that on TV," Harlan said. "Go right ahead, ma'am."

Everyone, including James Bradford, attorney-at-law, remained silent while she Mirandized the husband, who agreed that he understood his rights as she'd read them.

"Okay." Kara turned on the tape recorder. They'd had a video camera in Oceanside, but Shelter Bay's budget didn't provide for such extras. Not that one had ever been needed during her six-month tenure. Until today. "Now that we've dotted the legal Is and crossed our Ts, why don't you continue telling me what happened?"

"We couldn't get to the parade or the park ourselves," Janice Fletcher said. She paused to blow her nose. Opened the purse again. "Because our little girl has the chicken pox and we didn't dare leave her alone."

"How old is your daughter?" Kara asked.

The couple looked a little surprised by the seemingly irrelevant question, but the wife answered anyway. "S-s-s-seven."

"My son's eight. What's her name?"

"Harley." She sniffled as she looked over at her husband. Clicked the purse closed. "Since she's our fourth daughter —"

"And last baby," Harlan said.

"Definitely the last," his wife agreed. She clicked the purse open again. "We decided, since we weren't going to have a son, to name her after her daddy. Since we couldn't go with Harlan, Harley seemed close enough."

"I had a friend in California named Harley. I always thought it was a great name."

Having made the personal connection she'd learned could often be helpful in interrogations, Kara said, "So you were home when the fireworks went off?"

"We could see them from our rental house," Janice said. *Click.* "We brought the kids out on the roof for a b-b-better view." Tears began streaming down her face again. "We were having so much fun. I'd even made some popcorn."

"Then I got carried away," Harlan said. *Oh, hell.* Now he was crying, too. And Kara could see exactly what was coming. It was going to turn out to be what she and John had suspected all along. "And shot my twenty-two in the air when the fireworks went off. You know, to make some noise

520

ourselves."

"I've told you I don't approve of guns in the house with children," his wife said, showing a bit more spine than she had thus far.

"Man's gotta protect his property," he argued.

"Protecting property and shooting guns in front of your babies are not the same thing," Janice shot back. *Click.*

"I'm going to have to agree with your wife on that one." Kara weighed in on the domestic argument. "But that's a matter you two will have to work out yourselves. Meanwhile, you said it was a twenty-two?"

"A Smith and Wesson American Pride," he said. Despite the circumstances, he actually did show a little pride of ownership. Which caused Kara's sympathy meter to drop several degrees.

"The bullet Mr. Sullivan was shot with was a twenty-two-caliber." She repeated what she'd said during the telephone interview. "We'll need your weapon, Mr. Fletcher, for testing."

"I have it here," the lawyer said. He opened the briefcase and put it on her desk. "Don't worry. It's not loaded."

"Where have I heard that before?" Kara murmured, pushing it a bit aside with the eraser end of a pencil from the tin can pen-and-pencil holder covered with clothespins that Trey had made her for Mother's Day.

"All right. Here's what's going to happen, Mr. Fletcher." She folded her hands on the desktop, momentarily distracted by the absence of the ring she'd worn for so many years. "I'm going to be putting you under arrest for reckless endangerment. Which, as your attorney has undoubtedly explained to you both, is defined as wrongful, reckless, or wanton conduct likely to produce death or grievous bodily harm to another person."

"It was an accident," Harlan repeated doggedly. A little color had come back into his cheeks.

"I believe you. But while I don't have a law degree, I can tell you that to be guilty of this crime, you needn't have intentionally caused harm. You don't even have to know whether your conduct is certain to cause that result. The ultimate question, as the courts have determined, and Mr. Bradford can attest, is whether your conduct was of a heedless nature that made it actually or imminently dangerous to the rights or safety of others."

Unfortunately, she'd arrested enough people on this charge over the years that

Kara had the definition down pat. "As yours did."

Harlan Fletcher fell silent.

"Mr. Bradford said that what Harlan did could be a misdemeanor," Janice Fletcher said hopefully.

"That's true." She glanced over at the attorney and decided, from his expression, that he'd told them the other side, too. "It can also be determined to be a felony."

And didn't that get the waterworks flowing again?

"That's not my call. Meanwhile, Mr. Fletcher, I'm going to book you into the jail."

"You're putting me in jail?" The color drained from Harlan's face again.

"We discussed this," the attorney reminded his client. "The sheriff will take the case to the district attorney, who'll decide whether to prosecute."

"Which I believe you can count on," Kara said. "Then you'll have a court date. Which, given that Shelter Bay isn't exactly a crime hot spot, so there's not a backlog of cases, shouldn't be any later than tomorrow morning. At which time the judge will take your plea and either set bail —"

"How much?" Janice asked. "I lost my job washing dishes at The Fish House six months ago. First Coastal foreclosed on our home, and it's been a struggle to keep up with the rent on the house we're in now because construction has been slow, so Harlan hasn't been working regular, and —"

"Mrs. Fletcher," Bradford began to warn his client's wife.

"It's all right," Kara said. "I understand things are difficult these days. How long have you lived in Shelter Bay?"

"We moved here from Tillamook nine years ago," Harlan said. "Both of us have worked steady until this past year."

"Again, I can't speak for the court, but I suspect the judge won't find you a flight risk and will probably release you on a personal-recognizance bond."

"So we won't have to come up with any money?"

Kara wondered exactly how much time Bradford had actually spent with this couple.

"We came straight here," he answered her unspoken question. "Although I cautioned taking more time to prepare for this interview, the Fletchers were understandably upset. So we didn't have time to work out all the details."

"Well, the way it works," she explained,

thinking she should get a cut of the lawyer's fee for doing his job for him, "is that a dollar amount of the bond is set. However, if this turns out to be the case, Mr. Fletcher only has to sign the bond promising to appear on the future court date."

"He'll be there," Mrs. Fletcher said.

"Good. Meanwhile, Mr. Bradford will take care of the paperwork getting you pre-approved through the court."

She could tell he wasn't all that pleased at spending his hiking day filling out papers for the bond commissioner.

Nor was Harlan happy at the prospect of spending the night behind bars.

Kara thought about Danny, lying there in a pool of his own blood, with a potentially deadly head wound. Thought about Fletcher's own children, who might someday shoot themselves or a friend with that pistol.

Having grown up in hunting country, Kara was all for the Second Amendment — within limits, since, as a city cop, she'd also seen what happened when the bad guys were better armed than the police.

But as a sobbing Mrs. Fletcher left her office with the lawyer, Kara decided that if anyone ever put her in charge of the world, some people would just have to protect what was theirs the old-fashioned way. With fists, sticks, and stones.

# 57

Unfortunately, Eve Vernon had left Shelter Bay. Fortunately, she hadn't left Oregon, but moved to a town about an hour and a half's drive inland, where, according to the local sheriff, she'd been busted several times for soliciting at truck stops along I-5.

Although it wasn't her jurisdiction, after Kara assured the sheriff that she wasn't operating in an official capacity, he didn't have any problem with her and Sax going there to interview Celia's mother.

Since the sheriff's offer to accompany them was halfhearted at best, they decided, for the same reason Sax had talked Kara into letting him come with him in the first place — that Eve and her neighbors probably weren't that fond of cops — to talk to her by themselves.

She'd always looked rough. During the years since Sax had last seen her, she'd gone even further downhill. When they showed up at her rusted trailer propped up on blocks, a wasted, skinny-as-a-rail woman dressed in a halter top and miniskirt that showed off a dizzying array of ink opened the door with a beer in her hand and a cigarette dangling from her mouth.

It was definitely not her first brew of the day. After learning that they hadn't come here to pay to play, she got in a mood, not wanting to talk about her daughter, who, she claimed, was a selfish little bitch who'd just taken off so she wouldn't have to share the money she was going to be getting with her family.

"Money?"

"She got herself knocked up. Which is the oldest trick in the book for getting a man." She gave Kara an up-and-down look. "Something you figured out yourself."

"Excuse me?" Kara asked.

"Celia was working the cosmetic counter down at the CVS in Newport that day you came in and bought that home pregnancy kit. When you got married right after graduation, we had a good laugh together about little Miss High-and-mighty not being so pure after all."

Kara could feel Sax stiffen beside her. And although he remained silent, she knew the accusation was probably more difficult for him to hear than it was for her. She had, after all, had people say a lot worse things to her during her years as a cop.

"You filed a missing-persons report," Kara said, returning to her original questioning. No way was she going to discuss Jared and Trey with this horrid woman. "So you must have been concerned about her."

"I couldn't find the damn kid." The woman lit another Marlboro from the end of the one she'd just finished. "She said she'd landed in clover. So I figured the sheriff could get her back so I could get my share. Kids owe their mothers that much, right? It's not like I *had* to give birth to the little bitch. I could've gotten rid of her when I found out I was pregnant."

The interview went downhill from there.

"It's amazing," Kara murmured as they drove out of the place that looked like it could've been the set for *Deliverance II.* "Sometimes stereotypes really do exist."

"I told you we weren't exactly talking the Cleavers," he reminded her.

"Jared's folks live in a trailer park outside Las Vegas."

"Yeah, Cole mentioned something about that." They'd left town after scattering their son's ashes at sea, as he'd requested.

Partly, Cole had reported, because they

wanted to move somewhere hot and sunny. But mostly because they'd found it too painful staying where everywhere they turned around, everywhere they went in Shelter Bay, reminded them of their murdered son.

"Trey and I visited them a few times. It's a really pretty place," Kara said. "With flowers around all the mailboxes. And everyone's really friendly."

"They're probably friendly because they don't have Eve Vernon and her pals living in their park," he suggested.

Celia's mother's neighbors had looked as if they'd been seriously considering shooting the interlopers and taking Sax's Camaro to the local chop shop.

"Good point." She turned back toward Shelter Bay. "Can you imagine a mother treating her own daughter that way? As if she were nothing more than a commodity?"

"Unfortunately, I can."

"Yeah." She sighed. "Me, too. I saw things like that in California. But I don't think I'll ever get used to that kind of behavior."

"Probably wouldn't want to," he suggested.

"Good point. It's too bad she didn't remember anything about the cowboy from Pendleton."

"Sugar, that woman's brain was fried a long time ago. I doubt if she remembers what she ate for breakfast."

"Sure she does," Kara said.

"Beer," they said together.

"Celia wasn't like that," Sax felt obliged to say. "Yeah, she was a little wild, and I'll admit, at seventeen, I wasn't going to turn down what she was offering, but she hadn't had all the humanity knocked out of her yet."

He remembered a time when they'd found a lost kitten by the side of the road. Celia had named it Spooky, for its orange-and-black Halloween coloring, and taken it home, where she'd hidden it in her room. Whenever they'd go park out on the cliff or in the woods, she'd bring the cat along.

Then one day she hadn't. When he asked about it, she'd burst into tears and told him her stepfather had found it. Not wanting to know details, Sax hadn't asked. But now that he thought back on it, she'd gotten even more reckless after that incident.

"She wrote poetry," he remembered.

"Really?" Kara glanced over at him, clearly surprised.

"Yeah. They were mostly typical teenage stuff about car crashes, dying too young, broken hearts, suicide. But a lot were pretty good. I wrote some music for them, because she was talking about maybe getting a singing gig at some cowboy bar once she got to Pendleton."

"That's something that occurred to me when her mother mentioned her landing in clover. Granted, wealth is relative, but I've never met a rich cowboy."

"Could've been a rancher. Or a rancher's kid."

"True. Not that they're all rich, either. But she never said anything to you about his having money?"

"Not a word."

"You mentioned suicide. Maybe the cowboy or whoever the father of her child was refused to marry her. Do you think she could've gotten depressed and killed herself?"

For not the first time in the past few days, Sax found it ironic that he'd returned home to escape violence and death, and it just kept following him around. Like that black cloud over the head of that old cartoon character who used to be in the Sunday comics.

"Anything's possible," he supposed. "But if she'd committed suicide, someone would've found her."

"Maybe Velcro did."

"Maybe so. But again, given that she couldn't exactly bury herself, it seems the tide would've washed her up years ago."

"True . . . Her mother didn't exactly look like someone who'd take her child in for regular dental checkups," Kara mused. "Which means there probably aren't dental records."

"She probably didn't have checkups, but Celia had great teeth. Like I said, she had these dreams of becoming a singer. Or maybe even a movie star. So she used to bleach them. And once, when she broke one—"

"Or had it broken for her," Kara suggested.

"Yeah. That possibility never occurred to me back then," he said as they came around a tight bend in the road and approached a scenic lookout. "But I loaned her the money to get it capped."

"Did she pay you back?"

"No. But it didn't matter. I never expected her to when I made the offer."

"Pull over," she said suddenly.

Thinking she must have thought of something pertinent to the case, Sax jerked the wheel, turning into the parking lot of the lookout.

"What?"

"This." She unfastened her seat belt, leaned over the gearshift, and gave him a quick, hard kiss.

"What was that for?" he asked.

"Danny's right."

"About what?"

"You *are* one of the good guys."

"I seem to remember telling you that."

"And you know what else he's right about?"

"What would that be?"

She kissed him again. Long and deep.

"That we make a really neat couple," she said when they finally came up for air.

Sax laughed as he felt the dark cloud lift. "Told you that, too."

# 58

Over the next two weeks, Kara discovered that she did, indeed, enjoy change, even as, in many ways, her and Sax's lives fell into a predictable routine.

Her mother had moved into John's house to help him get it ready to sell. Together they'd joined Worldwide Medical Relief, the international relief group Sax's helicopter pilot friend's wife had once worked for.

Although John lacked a medical degree, his years in police work had left him with valuable people skills. In addition, like many men in Shelter Bay who'd grown up working construction part-time, he was handy with tools, which was definitely a bonus when it came to building emergency medical and refugee camps.

Kara closed her shooting case when the bullet fragments Faith had taken from Danny's head did indeed prove to have come from Harlan Fletcher's .22.

Deciding that he didn't represent a flight risk, and being aware of the family situation, the judge had sentenced him to six weekends in jail and a year's probation. And, once again showing the more personal relationships of a small town, the judge had gotten both Fletchers jobs at his cousin's cannery.

Her days fell back into comfortable small-town police mode, with the occasional petty problems from the tourists who flocked to the coast every summer and a missing kid — who was thankfully found safe — at a Rainbow Lake camp adding just enough variety to keep work interesting.

Frustratingly, she had no luck tracking down her unsub. But the fact that no similar attacks occurred in Shelter Bay or any of the other coastal cities pointed to the fact that her attack had been personal. She also spent time sifting through her dad's cold-case files, specifically the one regarding the missing Celia Vernon. Unfortunately, she couldn't find any man in town who'd admit to having spent any time with the girl that summer. Which wasn't surprising, given her reputation and the fact that most of the possible suspects were now family men.

Thanks to Sax, she did manage to track down the dentist who'd capped Celia's broken tooth. Although he'd retired five years ago, fortunately he'd shared her father's pack-rat tendencies, and after a day spent digging through boxes in his attic, she'd unearthed the dental records, which she sent on to Cait McKade's forensic guy. She also included Celia's yearbook photo, hoping the reconstructionist would find some similarities between the photo and the skull.

Unfortunately, as Cait explained, such work was tedious, requiring patience.

On a positive note, Cait did hope to have the tests back on the shell casing from the shot that had killed Kara's father within the next couple of weeks.

Now that he was out of school for the summer, Trey spent most days at Bon Temps. Every evening over dinner — most times cooked by Sax — he'd regale Kara with tales of how he'd painted a wall, sanded woodwork, or helped the men lay the wooden floor. After a trip with Sax to Corvallis to pick out plumbing fixtures for the kitchen and restrooms, he returned as excited as if they'd spent the day at Disney World.

Although they hadn't quite officially moved in together yet, they each kept clothes at each other's places, and even as her son bloomed before her eyes, Kara could feel herself opening up as well as Sax began to teach her the pleasures of "passing a good time."

On a day trip to Lincoln Beach with Sax and Trey, she blew her own glass fishing net float, which now sat in a place of honor in the cliff house. They took a night tour of the Shelter Bay lighthouse, and while the ninety-four-foot climb up the spiral stairs made her a little light-headed, Sax was there to steady her, and, as Trey pointed out, the "way cool" view of the town lights from so high up was definitely worth a little dizziness.

They dug for razor clams on the beach, rode bikes and ate chewy saltwater taffy on Seaside's famous promenade, took Cole's boat out for a day on the water, and visited the aquarium in Newport, where the walk through acrylic tunnels surrounded by several feet of seawater was like taking a stroll in the open ocean, a sensation enhanced by the waves surging against the tunnels.

As much as Trey enjoyed coming face-to-face with sharks, rockfish, and bat rays swimming above and below them, the "coolest" things, in his opinion, were the enormous suspended whale skeleton and the shipwreck at the bottom of the aquarium, which immediately had him declaring that he wanted to be an undersea explorer when he grew up.

Even when Sax wasn't dragging them out on coastal field trips, every day proved an adventure. Kara and Sax, by necessity, became experts at the five-minute quickie, which Kara found one of the most fun ways to pass a good time.

As each day went by, they grew closer as a unit, and Kara realized that they'd become a family when, wanting to keep flying his kite on the beach instead of coming in for dinner, Trey actually talked back to Sax, instead of treating him like a walking, talking superhero.

One night, after Kara's mother and John had taken Trey up to John's fishing cabin at Rainbow Lake for the weekend, Sax finally told Kara about his last mission, the one that had earned him those medals and the hero designation he hadn't ever wanted to claim.

They were sitting out on the porch at the cliff house, and it was as if a dam had broken inside him. The words flooded out: about the initial ambush, how each of his teammates had continued to fight while gravely wounded, of the days spent alone in the mountains, wounded himself, sometimes delirious, not sure whether he was dead or alive.

He told her about his capture, his imprisonment, being locked in a windowless room with a dirt floor. The degradation. Blessedly, he skimmed over the details of his torture, but the scars she'd discovered on his body while making love bore silent witness to all he'd suffered.

Even as horrible as all that had been, most heart-wrenching was how he'd spent the months after being released from the naval hospital, visiting his dead teammates' families, telling the story over and over again, making sure each person knew that their son or husband or fiancé had died bravely. Honorably. Fighting for his country. And that *they* were the true heroes.

Which finally led to him admitting to the painful, deep-seated guilt he'd originally denied. And his ghosts. Who, he realized as he told her about them, hadn't been showing up lately.

She remained silent as he'd talked for hours, the sky changing from black to deep purple to a silvery tint as the last of the stars faded and the sun prepared to make its appearance.

By the time he finished, dawn had painted

the sky a brilliant rose, and, as if from a trance, he'd looked around, seeming stunned to discover he'd talked all night.

Having already taken a personal day off work with plans for a romantic weekend just for two, Kara took him to bed — not for sex, but to comfort him; she wrapped her arms around him, spooning against his hard frame.

For the first time, he seemed free of the nightmares that had caused him to sweat, twist and turn, mumble, once even shout in his sleep. When she'd brought it up after the first night, he'd shrugged it off.

"Hell," he'd said, "who doesn't have nightmares from time to time?"

Understanding that healing had to come in its own time, she hadn't pressured him, willing to wait until he was ready to open up.

It was early afternoon when they finally woke.

"I'm sorry," he said. "I didn't mean to dump all that on you."

"I'm glad you did." She framed his face between her palms. "Because I love you, Sax. And what hurts you, hurts me." She touched her lips to his roughened cheek, his forehead, skimmed them over his mouth. "And hopefully it helped you to get it out."

It had. "Do you have any idea how re-markable you are?" he asked.

"I'm in love with you," she said simply, repeating those amazing words he'd never thought he'd ever hear. Never thought he'd deserve to hear. "Is there anything else you'd like to get off your chest?"

"Nothing important."

"Well, then, sailor, hold on to your hat. Because you are about to get very, very lucky."

Rolling over on top of him, Kara spent a long love- and laughter-filled afternoon showing Sax exactly how remarkable she could be. How remarkable they could be together.

## 59

Five days before Cole and Kelli's wedding, Sax showed up at her office, looking outrageously hot in faded jeans, a T-shirt, well-worn boots, and a tool belt. As sexy as she'd always found a man in uniform, Kara was discovering that there was definitely a lot to be said about a hot guy wearing a tool belt.

"There's been something bugging me about your dad's shooting," he announced.

"Well, that makes two of us." So far Cait's lab still hadn't come up with any prints from the spent cartridge.

"No. I mean it's been one of those things where this thought's been hovering right on the edge of my mind, but I haven't been able to grab hold of it."

"And now you have?"

"Yeah. I had this dream last night about being back in the Kush with McKade."

"Another nightmare?" How could she not have noticed?

"No. Thanks to you, those are gone," he assured her.

"You were ready to move on. I was just there."

"Ah, but I wouldn't have been *ready* to move on if you hadn't been there," he countered. "But getting back to why I'm here . . . This was just a dream, sort of like I was watching a movie, but not emotionally involved, you know?"

"I've had those."

"Okay, so McKade and I were in our ghillie suits —"

"Wait." She held up a hand. "I'm trying to picture this, but I don't know what that is."

"They're these suits SEALs wear to help us blend into the surroundings. If you're in a jungle, you'll put leaves and other nature-type junk on them. McKade and I made ours by tearing up some clothes we found in an abandoned village. They were those white shirts and pants the locals wear, so we blended in with the snow."

"I've always thought of Afghanistan as a dusty, barren place."

"It is. But those mountains are really high, and we were in near whiteout conditions fighting our way up the mountain into Pakistan."

The idea was chilling: both the thought of fighting a battle in a blizzard, and imagining the two men out there all on their own, undoubtedly outnumbered by the entrenched forces trying to kill them.

But she had to ask. "Wasn't that illegal?"

"Yeah, technically it was against the rules of engagement at the time. But we'd been in this copter crash, and that team pilot I told you about needed medical care. It's a long story, and we've all moved on, and don't worry. I'm not dwelling on it. Which is, in a way, too bad. Because if I *had* been thinking more about it, the idea would've clicked sooner."

"What idea?"

"John never found the bullet that killed your father, right?"

"No. Just the casing."

"Maybe because he wasn't looking in the right place."

"He was there," she argued. "Where my father's body was found. Where else would it be? Unless the shooter picked it up and took it with him." Which would definitely point to murder. "The coroner's report showed that the bullet exited the body," Kara said thoughtfully. Which made not being able to find it all the more frustrating.

"That's why we couldn't recover it for forensics."

"Okay, here's how it works. Although I'm trained as a sniper, on that team McKade was the sniper, and I was his spotter. What a spotter does is exactly what it sounds like: You detect, observe, assign targets, and afterwards, watch for the result of the shot."

"To make sure the bad guy's been hit."

"Right. You also have a spotting scope, which you use to read the wind. There're a lot of formulas for that, but basically you're making calculations for distance, slant range —"

"You just lost me again."

"That's the angle of the shot. You correct for atmospheric conditions, like weather, wind, and even mirages from the heat on the ground. Then you figure out the lead for any moving targets."

At first she was wondering why Sax was going into so much detail, as impressive as it was. Then comprehension dawned.

"Which means, if there's anyone who knows where a bullet's going, or has gone, it's a sniper spotter."

He knuckle-bumped her. "Got it in one."

"Following that train of thought, if you know what the weather was that day, and where the shooter was standing — which, by the way, we suspect we do from the way the ground was tamped down — and where my father's body was found —"

"There's an outside chance I might be able to figure out where the bullet ended up."

"Wow. I have no words for how impressed I am by your awesomeness."

"Why don't you wait until we try it out?" he suggested.

She was already out of her chair.

"I assume you brought your spotter stuff with you?"

"Roger that."

"Well, then." She took her pistol from her desk drawer, deciding she could go online and do an Internet search for the weather on that tragic day from her phone on the way out to the woods where her father had been killed.

"Let's go."

Kara had known Sax was smart. But she hadn't realized exactly how intelligent he was until she'd spent an hour with him tramping through the woods, watching him shooting spots with his scope, skimming through the pages of his spiral-bound olive drab sniper journal, which he'd told her was one of the few things he'd kept from his

SEAL days.

The journal, he explained, had plotting pages for cold bore (the first shot out of the rifle, before the barrel had heated up), range cards, data on stationary and moving targets, rifle data, elevation tables, wind correction tables, yet more tables for determining what a bullet would do under various atmospheric conditions, and records of not just every shot he'd ever fired on missions, but on the practice field as well.

"Police snipers keep journals," she said. "But I've never seen any this detailed." He was like the Einstein of snipers.

"Police snipers don't, as a rule, have to worry about being killed if they miss a shot," he pointed out as he scribbled some numbers onto one of the blank pages, then looked through the scope again.

"If I wanted to make sure I really hammered a guy with a deer rifle, which is what we've got to assume the shooter was using, since he wouldn't want to stand out if he ran into anyone arriving or leaving the scene, I'd go with a two-hundred-and-twenty-grain bullet because it'd do more damage, tear through more organs, and penetrate the target deeper and farther."

She couldn't help the sound of distress that escaped her lips.

He glanced up from the scope. And looked miserable. "Hell, I'm sorry, Kara. I got so caught up in the logistics, I forgot for a minute it's your dad we're talking about."

She took a deep breath. Cleared her head and willed her stomach not to toss up the bagel she'd picked up that morning from the Grateful Bread.

"I'm okay. Really," she said when he studied her with continued concern. "Just help me catch his damn killer."

"You went a little pale. Like during the lighthouse climb. You sure you don't want to go back and wait in the cruiser?"

"Not on your life."

"Okay, then. The downside of two-twenties in a thirty-aught-six is the bullet drop. At three hundred yards, which is the distance the shooter seemed to be from your dad — which, by the way, indicates we're not looking for a pro — you're going to be dealing with six or seven inches of drop."

He did some more figuring. Climbed the three hundred yards up the hill again. Looked through the scope. Then he finally nodded his head, appearing satisfied.

Kara watched, with building anticipation, as he came back down the hill for the umpteenth time to where her father's body was found.

Looking as confident as she'd ever seen him, he pulled on a pair of gloves, went over to a towering Douglas fir tree that looked to be several centuries old, unclipped a knife from his belt, and, as she watched with fascination, dug into the bark.

"Bingo."

He turned toward her, a silver-tipped Winchester two-twenty bullet in the palm of his glove.

"Oh, wow. I know you hate hearing it, Sax, but I've really got to say it."

"Oh, God, please don't."

"Sorry." She placed her crossed hands over her heart and said in the same breathless, feminine, adoring way Lois Lane might have said to Superman, "My hero."

# 60

In a last-ditch rush, Sax and Cole and many of the vets Kara had come to know had put the final table in place before the rehearsal dinner, which was also taking place at Bon Temps. Kara was not at all surprised when Cole and Kelli asked all the workers to join them for the dinner.

When they left the final Mardi Gras mask for Trey to hang on the wall, Kara didn't think she'd ever seen her son so excited. Or proud.

"Thank you," she said to Sax as celebratory high fives were exchanged all around.

"Thank *you*," he said back. Then he kissed her, at which point Trey dramatically covered his eyes, which had all the vets roaring with laughter.

Kara found it odd that she'd grown up in this town and had been sheriff for almost seven months, but this was the first time that she'd actually felt a true part of it.

She also found the occasion a little bitter-sweet, since she'd just hired a retired detective from Corvallis to fill John's shoes — not that she believed that would ever be entirely possible. This was the last occasion in possibly a long time that she, Trey, Sax, and her mother would be together again.

"I'm going to miss you," she told her mother as they stood together out on the patio beneath the purple-green-and-gold neon BON TEMPS sign.

"I'm going to miss you, too." She put her arm around Kara's waist and drew her closer as they looked out at the lights of the Shelter Bay Bridge. "It took us a while, but I think we've made it."

"Like a sitcom mother and daughter. But better."

"Much, much better," Faith agreed. "Actually, my life right now is so much better than any fantasy."

"You and John are good together."

"We are." Faith paused. "You don't think it's too soon? After your father's death?"

"Who's to say what too soon is?" Kara thought back on the conversation she'd had with Sax about her mother and John leaving on their shared adventure. "You were a wonderful wife. You were lucky to have Dad and he was fortunate to have you. But life moves on, and I couldn't be happier for you. Even though I do wish you two could've found an adventure closer to home."

They'd been assigned to Mali, in Africa, as part of a worldwide malaria relief effort.

"We'll visit often," Faith assured her. "No way would I miss watching my grandson grow up. Or your wedding."

"I don't remember saying anything about getting married."

"It's obvious you and Sax love each other. Marriage is the next logical step." Another pause. "John and I were thinking of having a Christmas wedding ourselves. Or maybe on New Year's Eve. We'll already be back here, all together, and celebrating it would add to the season's festivities."

"That's a great idea."

"I was also thinking that just perhaps . . . we might make it a double wedding."

Kara and Sax hadn't talked about marriage. But that didn't mean that Kara hadn't been thinking about it.

"Unless you wouldn't want to share the day," her mother said when she didn't immediately respond.

"It sounds lovely." Her mother hadn't been there for her first marriage. The idea of sharing the occasion with her the second time around was surprisingly appealing.

"Maybe just a bit premature."

"You've had a lot on your plate," Faith said understandingly. "You're right to take your time. And fortunately, thanks to Sax's restoring Bon Temps, you don't have to worry about a venue."

"There is that."

"There's something I want you to know," Faith said. She turned toward Kara, her expression as serious as Kara had ever seen it. Even more than when they were discussing the possibility of Kara's father being murdered. "I won't deny that your having Sax in your life, and in Trey's life, makes my leaving a little easier. But" — she held up a hand as if expecting Kara to argue — "that's only because I know he makes you happy. I also know that you're perfectly capable of taking care of yourself and my grandson. Because you are, honestly, the strongest woman I know."

*Okay.* That did it. Kara felt her eyes misting up. "Thank you. That means a lot. Especially coming from the strongest woman *I* know."

"Well, then." Her mother smiled. "Now that we've expressed our mutual admiration, what would you say to taking our magic bracelets inside and finding our men?"

After an embrace that, for the first time Kara could remember, didn't feel the least bit awkward, Kara said, "Sounds like a plan."

## 61

"Do I have to wear a tie?" Trey asked, coming close to a whine.

"If I can wear a neck strangler, you can put up with it for few hours," Sax told him without pity. "Here. Come into the bathroom and let me show you how to tie it."

"Don't see why I need to learn. Only person in this town who ever wears one is stupid Mr. Gardner." Who, needless to say, had not been invited to the wedding.

"There's a big wide world outside Shelter Bay," Sax pointed out. "Some places folks actually think ties are a big deal. And if you become a Marine, like your dad, you'll definitely have to know how to tie a squared-away knot."

"Okay," Kara's son said on a long, drawn-out sigh of surrender.

Sax put Trey in front of the mirror, stood behind him, and looped around his neck the piece of polyester printed with whales that Trey had picked out for himself on yesterday's shopping expedition.

"We'll do a four-in-hand. Because that's the easiest to start with." Sax put his hands over Trey's so they could tie it together. "You start with the wide part, here. Where the orca is." He began crossing it over the shorter, narrower part of the tie.

"Now turn it back underneath."

Trey's teeth were worrying his bottom lip as he concentrated. "Like this?"

"Perfect." Sax grinned up at Kara. "Kid's as good at this as he is pounding a nail. . . . Now, bring that orca back around the front again."

A few steps later, her son was standing there in the proper slacks and dress shoes he'd also objected to her buying, his corn-silk cowlicks slicked down, and in his face, so like his father's, Kara saw the man he would become.

"You look so handsome," she said, sniffling a little. "So grown-up."

"Geez, Mom." Trey looked over at Sax. "She's gonna cry."

"Women get emotional on wedding days."

"But Mom's not getting married."

"Doesn't matter. That's the way they're wired."

"I'm glad I'm a guy."

Sax ruffled the hair Kara had so carefully combed only minutes earlier. "Me, too."

As if Mother Nature were smiling on the happy couple, the day of Cole and Kelli's wedding had dawned bright and sunny.

The ceremony, limited to family and close friends, was held in the intimate parlor of the Shelter Bay lighthouse keeper's cottage, which had been restored with antiques replicating how the keeper's family would have lived during the 1870s.

Cole introduced a black-haired stranger with unsettling steel gray eyes as Gabriel St. James, a former Marine war photojournalist and friend, who Kara couldn't help noticing didn't speak more than a dozen words the entire day. And he certainly didn't appear to be in a very celebratory mood.

The bride was beautiful, as all brides should be. The food — all but the cupcakes, which were presented in a cake-shaped display and proved as delicious as they'd been billed — had been prepared by the groom's mother, and it was the best Kara had ever eaten. And the music, performed by the groom's family, was definitely enjoyed by all.

Watching the man she loved, jacket off now, tie loosened, hips swiveling, strumming that sexy red electric guitar, sent Kara's thoughts spinning back to the night of the prom, when he'd wowed all the girls, undoubtedly made more than a few boys jealous as hell, and for a fleeting second she'd actually forgotten until now, had had her thinking, *Mine.*

And now he was.

As if reading her thoughts, he looked straight at her, winked, and just as he'd done the night of the prom, he handed his guitar off to another band member so he could dance with her.

"Did I tell you how sexy you look in that dress?" he asked as they swayed to a slow ballad. His lips brushed her temple, which had healed without leaving any scar. His warm breath feathered her hair.

"About a dozen times." It was a flowered silk sundress with thin straps, a low back, and a short, flirty skirt that showed off her legs. With it she was wearing a pair of ripe peach–colored skyscraper sandals. She leaned against his solid strength and inhaled the seductive male scent not due to any expensive aftershave or cologne, but his alone. "But I wouldn't mind hearing it again."

"How about this?" He pulled her against an erection he made no attempt to conceal. "As much as I'm enjoying dancing with you,

I'm really looking forward to getting you home and taking that dress off you."

Her sexual senses, as they so often were with this man, were vividly alive.

"I'll help you," she promised.

Then, because they were getting close to making vertical love in public, she put a little space between them. "That was a huge surprise, seeing Trey playing the guitar onstage."

"It was an old Martin I used to drag around with me because it's smaller than the average model," he said against her lips. "I figured it'd be a good fit for him. He's been practicing in secret for weeks. To surprise you."

"Well, he certainly did that." She reached up and traced his lips with a fingernail she'd painted for the occasion in a peach that matched her new shoes. "I can't begin to tell you —"

She saw the sudden, hard alertness steamroller over the building lust in Sax's eyes an instant before someone cleared his throat behind her. She turned and came face-to-face with Kyle, his expression as serious as she'd ever seen it. He looked, she thought, like an actual cop.

"Sorry to interrupt, Sheriff," he said in a brusque tone that even sounded like a cop's.

"But a call came into the station I think you really need to handle."

She'd turned her phone off before leaving for the lighthouse, telling everyone that she was off the clock today. For Kyle to come here, the call had to be very serious.

"I'll be right back," she told Sax.

"I'll come with you."

The three of them made their way through the celebrating throng to the outside *gallerie,* which, Trey had informed her, was Cajun for *porch.*

She dialed the long-distance number on the piece of paper Kyle handed her.

Cait McKade answered on the first ring. "We've got a match," she said without preamble. "Thanks to Sax's finding that bullet, I can finally tell you who killed your father."

# 62

"Gerald Gardner killed Ben?" Faith asked, clearly stunned. "Surely there's some mistake. He's admittedly a very unpleasant man. But a murderer?"

Not wanting to disrupt the reception, after asking his parents to watch Trey, Sax joined Faith, John, Kyle, and Kara in the office of Bon Temps.

"Yeah, I'm having a hard time with it, too," Kara said. "But Cait McKade says the prints on the bullet Sax dug out of that tree match the ones of Gardner on file with IAFIS."

"That's the FBI's Integrated Automated Fingerprint Identification System, maintained to be the largest biometric database in the world," John explained to Faith.

"We lucked out that, since he's in a fiduciary business, his prints got put into the system in the first place," Kara said.

"Lucky," Faith said flatly in a tone that

suggested her husband certainly hadn't been lucky.

"We can't bring Ben back." John took hold of her hand, linked their fingers together, and brought their joined hands to his chest, against his heart. "But I promise you, Faith, we'll put the bastard who killed him behind bars."

"For the rest of his life," Kara agreed. Although the cop in her had found Sax's initial supposition about her father being murdered intriguing, she'd honestly thought all along that her father's death had been caused by an accident. The same way Harlan Fletcher had shot Danny.

"But why?" Faith asked. "What would his motive be? The only connection I can think of to Gerald Gardner is when Ben bought a patrol car at the GM dealership in Newport, instead of at Gardner Ford. But losing a customer is no reason to shoot someone."

"It's partly a hunch, but Dad was looking through old cold cases and the only one I can find he'd made recent notes on had to do with Celia Vernon's case."

"The Vernon girl," Faith asked. "Was that the girl who went to high school with you? The one Ben picked up — more than once — for underage drinking?"

"That's her." Celia's file had been extensive, but mostly minor busts — alcohol, marijuana, breaking curfew. Unlike the missing girl's mother and stepfather, both of whom had thick police jackets.

Kara filled her in on what Sax had told her. Along with their visit to Mrs. Vernon.

"That poor girl," Faith murmured.

"She didn't get many breaks, that's for sure," Kara agreed. The contrast between her life and Celia's had her feeling a bit guilty for ever complaining about her own mother.

"*A Place in the Sun*," Faith murmured.

"What?"

"It's an old fifties movie, based on Theodore Dreiser's *An American Tragedy*. Montgomery Clift gets this girl — Shelley Winters — who works at his uncle's factory, pregnant. But he's also involved with Elizabeth Taylor, who plays a socialite and represents the wealthy, privileged life Clift's character aspires to. So he kills Winters by throwing her overboard while they're out on a lake. In the end, he's convicted of murder.

"If Gerald was the father of Celia Vernon's child, since she's not the type of girl a boy from his family would be expected to marry, that would provide a motive for him to have killed her. And later kill your father if he discovered Ben was looking into the case."

"*If* Celia actually was pregnant," Kara said. Eve Vernon wouldn't exactly make the most credible witness on the stand. "But I haven't bought into the idea of the cowboy as the father from the beginning."

"That means it could have been Gerald in your house that day," John said. "Trying to retrieve the file."

"My thinking exactly," Kara said.

"I sure as hell wouldn't put it past the guy," Sax agreed.

Only minutes ago she'd been floating on air after a perfect day. Now, although she was grateful for Cait's help, the revelations left Kara feeling numb and angry at the same time.

"I need you to take Trey home," she told her mother. "But don't mention any of this."

"Of course I won't," Faith said. She put her hand on Kara's arm. "You'll be careful."

"You bet." Kara turned to Kyle. "I want to go home and change into my uniform. Then you and John and I can pay a little visit to Gerald."

"I'm coming along," Sax said.

Kara realized she should've seen this coming. She folded her arms across the front of the flowered dress. "While I appreciate all your help regarding Celia, and finding that bullet that filled in the final piece of the puzzle of Dad's death, you *are* a civilian."

"We have civilian ride-alongs," John pointed out.

Terrific. Now they were ganging up on her.

"Not for arrests."

"If I have to, I'll go out there myself," Sax said. "But you're not going to keep me away."

The warrior was back. In spades. Kara also knew he was right. Sax might respect her ability to do her job. But there was also no way she was going to be able to keep him away from this.

"It's not because I don't think you can handle it," he said, demonstrating that ability to seemingly read her mind yet again. "But I've got a hell of a lot invested in this. Celia was a friend. Gerald not only killed the father of the woman I love — he probably also beat the hell out of you. Which makes this extremely personal."

"That's my concern." She was aware of everyone watching the debate. "That you'll make this personal, go vigilante on me, and screw up my arrest. If Gerald is my unsub, and we've no proof he is, I want him behind bars. Forever."

"I'll stay out of your way." Heaving a sigh, he took her arm and pulled her a little aside, away from their audience, and lowered his voice. "Look, Kara. I understand you need a clean arrest. But you've got to understand how I feel. Now, I'm asking you to trust me on this. But if you don't let me come with you, I am going to come. One of the things I fought for was a free country. Which means you can't prevent a civilian from driving down a street."

"No fair playing the SEAL hero card," she muttered.

"I care for you. I care about your son, who could have lost his mother that day in your house if you weren't such a strong fighter. I cared about Celia, and I even liked your dad, though I suspect I sure as hell wasn't his favorite person. And I spent enough time as a SEAL to know teamwork. I'll admit I'd love to beat the guy to a bloody pulp. But despite having a few PTSD problems, I'm not out of control. I'll stay out of your way," he repeated.

They were wasting time arguing. And Kara did trust him.

She nodded. Then turned to the others. "Let's roll."

# 63

Unfortunately, like so much of police work, the arrest didn't go according to plan.

When they arrived at the Gardner home, his wife informed them that her husband wasn't home.

"Is he working late at the bank, ma'am?" Kara asked in her most collected cop tone, which was totally at odds with the turmoil churning inside her.

"That's what he said." Kara thought she detected the scent of liquor on Mrs. Gardner's breath. "That's what he *always* says."

"But?" Kara asked, even as she guessed the answer.

"He's with his slut, of course."

"I'm sorry. But would you happen to know who, exactly, your husband is seeing?"

"Seeing." The woman's laugh was a little too loud for the circumstances. Yep, she'd definitely been drinking. "Isn't that a lovely euphemism? The woman he's been *fucking*

568

is that slut Realtor."

"Sherry Archer?" Kara exchanged a quick look with Sax, who was standing nearby, silent, as he'd promised, but didn't appear nearly as surprised as she was by that piece of information.

"Do you know another slut Realtor in Shelter Bay?"

Kara wasn't about to touch that line. "Thank you, ma'am. I'm going to request that you not contact your husband."

"Are you going to arrest him for something?"

"We'd like to speak with him," John said.

"Ah." Mrs. Gardner nodded. "So now he's a person of interest."

That statement had Kara deciding that Edna Lawton wasn't the only person in town who watched too many TV shows.

"We just need to question him," she said.

"Well, do me a favor."

"And what would that be?"

"If Gerald gives you any excuse to shoot him, aim for his goddamn balls."

Sherry Archer's Tudor was, unsurprisingly, in the same gated subdivision. The mountaintop location provided a spectacular view of the town, the bay, and the ocean beyond. Unfortunately, it also allowed Gerald Gardner, who — in a bit of unlucky timing for them — had just left the house, to see the two patrol cars headed up the hill.

If he'd had a lick of sense, or ever watched *Cops,* Gardner would have known that the odds of a civilian escaping in a car chase were, well, pretty much zilch. Apparently he neither watched the reality show or had no sense, because he leaped into the Lincoln parked in front of Sherry's house, gunned the engine, then rabbited past them back down the hill.

In order to keep as much of the natural woods as possible, the roads zigzagged through the subdivision.

Grateful for her cop drivers' training, Kara downshifted as she approached another twist in the road, then, although cornering in a cruiser going at least fifty miles per hour wasn't for the faint of heart, punched the gas.

Although Gerald had a head start, and they'd had to make a U-turn, she caught up with him. John was close on their tail, lights flashing, sirens screaming.

"Since we don't have anyone to throw down a spike strip to shred his tires, I'm going to try to stop him," she decided. "Because if he gets into town, this could get dangerous."

"Guy's an idiot," Sax said. "He's got to know he's not going to get away."

"Bad guys panic," she said. "I've had them bolt on me before. It doesn't make any sense, but hey, if they thought like the rest of us, they wouldn't be bad guys."

"Roger that."

Continuing to rely on training, Kara slowed enough to bump the Lincoln's bumper. Once. Twice. A third time.

At that point, the banker should have caught a clue and stopped.

But apparently he was as clueless as he was heartless, because he sped up, veered wildly, and took the next turn on two wheels.

"That should do it," Sax said.

Just as predicted, the wheels went off the pavement, scattering gravel before settling into a shallow ditch on the side of the shoulderless road.

Kara slammed to a halt beside the Lincoln, jumped from the cruiser, and pulled the banker out from beneath the deflating air bag, which had exploded upon impact. Sax was right behind her.

"Gerald Gardner, you're under arrest. For homicide." Probably more than one, if he turned out to have murdered Celia Vernon. "And resisting arrest."

Kara took some pleasure in the fact that the air bag had broken his nose. And didn't she know just how that felt? "As well as reckless driving." She felt another little zing as she snapped the metal cuffs onto his wrists. "And I'm sure, by the time we get to the station, I'll be able to think up some other charges."

"I want my attorney," he said, interrupting her Miranda reading. Amazingly, despite the blood streaming down his face onto the front of his white shirt and a bump the size of an acorn on his forehead, he'd still managed to find some bluster.

"Fine," John said gruffly. "You can call him when we get to the station." He turned to Kara. "You had all the fun of the chase. Ben was my friend. Let my last official duty be to lock his killer up."

"He's all yours."

Kara watched as the two deputies put him into the back of their patrol. They did not, she noted, warn Gardner about lowering his head so he wouldn't bump it on the roof. Which he proceeded to do. Yet another clue he'd never watched *Cops.*

After the cruiser headed toward town, Sax took Kara in his arms. "You're shaking."

The red taillights disappeared over the hill as Kara clung to him. Tightly. "So are you."

It began to rain. As they stood there, drawing strength and comfort from each other, neither Sax nor Kara noticed.

# 64

*Two months later*

Summer was drawing to a close. The tourists had returned to their cities, and a touch of fall was in the air.

After years living in southern California, Kara had rediscovered how special having four seasons again could be. And while autumn was, hands down, her favorite season, this year it was proving even more special — because of Sax being in her and Trey's lives.

Despite her advanced pregnancy, Cait McKade had returned to Shelter Bay — this time with her husband, who hovered over her like an overprotective guard dog — to testify at Gerald Gardner's trial. The crowded courtroom burst into applause when the jury foreman declared him guilty of one count of manslaughter in Celia Vernon's case, one count of first-degree murder for Ben Blanchard's death, and assault and battery with intent to kill in Kara's attack.

The same lawyer the Fletchers had hired managed a plea bargain to kick the first murder charge down to manslaughter, claiming that Gardner had accidently killed Celia during an argument in the cave on the beach after he'd told her he wasn't going to marry her.

According to his story, which Kara didn't believe for a moment, the pregnant girl had lunged at him in a temper. He'd dodged her attack and she'd hit her head on the cliff. Panicked, the eighteen-year-old Gardner had buried her body beneath the sand and piled driftwood and boulders on top of it.

Kara wasn't happy about the plea bargain, since she knew, in her gut, that it was predicated on a lie. And she hated that Gardner had gotten away with the crime for so many years. But she did manage to achieve both closure and satisfaction as she watched the van take him off to the Oregon State Penitentiary in Salem.

"Are you two going to get married?" Trey asked one day after they'd come home from a shopping trip for school supplies.

"Well, I was going to talk to you about that," Sax said. "See if you had any advice for me, since popping the question to your mom is a pretty big deal."

"She likes flowers," he said. "And you're going to have to get her a ring. But she doesn't like diamonds."

"*She* just happens to be in the room," Kara pointed out. "And, for the record, I don't know a woman who doesn't like diamonds. I just don't think they fit my lifestyle."

"How about this?"

Kara drew in a quick, stunned breath as Sax pulled a small black velvet box from his pocket and handed it to her.

The ring lay on a bed of white satin. Three stones had been set into a woven, white gold band. "I had it made by that Celtic jeweler up in Cannon Beach," he told Kara. "Where we bought those earrings."

She touched the Celtic circles in question. "She makes beautiful things."

"I told her I wanted three stones to represent each of us, and she came up with these.

"The tigereye represents the dawn, that silver hematite is the dusk, and this obsidian" — he pointed at the heart-shaped stone in the middle — "is supposed to be midnight. I figured that also covers all the hours in the day that I love you."

She took the ring from the box and slipped

it on her finger. "It's lovely." The thought that had gone into it was even more so.

"She told me they're called sky stones," he explained carefully, as if hoping he'd made the right choice. "Apparently they were used by early druids for divination and to predict the future."

She held the ring up, admiring how it gleamed so warmly in the ruby sunset light streaming in through the window. "I believe it's already working."

"Really, Mom?" Trey asked.

"Really. Because I predict a wonderful and long future together."

She lifted her smiling face to Sax's and rewarded him with a long, loving kiss.

"A future of mushy stuff," Trey muttered.

"Get used to it, kid," Sax said. "Because you're going to be stuck with us for at least fifty years."

Trey grinned at that, but Kara thought she detected just a bit of sadness in his eyes.

Later that night, after he and Sax had finished reading the latest in the Captain Underpants saga, she slipped into her son's room and sat down on the edge of the bed.

"Are you okay with Sax and me getting married?"

"Sure. I was hoping you would from the beginning. Well, almost the beginning," he admitted. "I didn't want to like him. Because of Dad."

"I know."

"Do you think Dad's okay with this?"

"Absolutely." She skimmed a hand over his hair. He'd had it cut short like Sax's, and while she understood the need to emulate his role model, she missed the corn-silk strands. The style also made him look older than his almost nine years, which were already racing by too fast.

"You know what I really feel bad about?"

"What?"

"I never got to tell him good-bye. Or that I love him and I'm sorry about getting mad at him for getting shot."

"He understands that."

"That's what Sax said. Back when I first told him."

At first Kara hadn't wanted to get involved with Sax because of Trey. Later, she'd been surprised to discover that although she loved being with him, loved *loving* him, she'd been afraid to commit to forever. Because having already lost one man she'd loved, she'd been afraid to entirely risk her heart again.

"I had an idea the other day," she said carefully, "while we were out flying kites on the beach."

"What's that?"

"It's past your bedtime. Let's talk about this in the morning, okay?"

"Okay." He rolled over and hugged Chesty against him. "I'm really happy," he said into his pillow.

"Me, too," Kara murmured.

Then she slipped out of the room and went out on the porch to discuss her plan with Sax.

## 65

It was, Sax thought, as they made their way down to the beach below the cliff house, a perfect day. The robin's-egg blue sky overhead appeared endless, and the breeze coming off the ocean could not have been better for flying kites.

Sax was carrying the colorful dragon kite he'd bought for Trey at the beginning of the summer. Trey — wearing a new T-shirt he'd asked Sax to help him buy that read, MY MOM'S THE SHERIFF AND SHE'S MY HERO — was holding tight to a note he'd written to his dad that morning after breakfast on a piece of his new back-to-school filler paper.

When Sax had awakened in the middle of the night and found Kara missing from their bed, he'd known she was in the kitchen, writing her own note to Jared.

Sax understood that a part of Kara would always love Jared. They'd talked about that, and he'd assured her that he'd accepted it.

Because all her feelings for him, her marriage, her having a son with Jared Conway, had made her the woman she was. The woman he loved.

So he was okay with Jared Conway being Kara's first husband. Just so Sax got to be her last.

After getting the kite airborne, Sax showed Trey how to cut a slit in the paper, fold it, then send it skimming up the kite string.

"Wow," he breathed. "It's up there really, really high."

"Highest I've ever seen one fly," Sax said.

Kara was next. As she folded her note, Sax noticed that she'd tied something onto the paper: the ring she hadn't worn since they'd cut it off at the hospital. Although she'd taken down the photos from her dresser, Sax had known she'd kept the ring in the bedside table drawer. Seeing it now told him exactly how committed she was to beginning their new life together.

The note skimmed up the string, a little slower than Trey's due to the extra weight. Mother and son were holding on to the string.

"When you're ready," she told Trey.

He gave it one last serious look. His eyes were shiny.

His weren't the only ones.

"You hit the jackpot, Sax Man," a familiar voice said as Kara and Trey released the string, setting the kite free.

The guys had made themselves scarce the last few months. Sax walked over to them. "Roger that," he said.

"It's about time. This is an okay place," Cowboy drawled, looking around the beach. "But now that we've got you straightened out, it's time for us to move on."

Comprehension finally sank in. "That was the mission, wasn't it? To get me past the guilt trip and hook me up with Kara."

"The lady sheriff was a bonus," Randy said. "That was all your doing. But yeah, SEALs don't leave men behind. And as long as you were stuck back in the Kush, well, we weren't going anywhere."

"And now you can?" The kite was flying higher and higher, becoming a bright dot in the cloudless sky.

"Hooyah," they said in unison, just like they had during BUD/S. The same way they had on so many shared missions.

"Hooyah," Sax repeated softly as, still together, they faded away just as Trey's dragon kite, with the notes to another lost father and husband, disappeared with them beyond the horizon.

Then Kara turned and walked with Trey

toward him, her eyes as wet as his, but a smile on her beautiful face.

"Ready?" he asked.

"Ready," she answered.

Sax took her hand in his left, Trey's in his right.

And together the three of them walked back up the cliff.

Toward home.

# ABOUT THE AUTHOR

**JoAnn Ross** lives with her husband and two fuzzy little rescued dogs in the foothills of the Great Smoky Mountains. Visit her Web site at www.joannross.com.

The employees of Thorndike Press hope you have enjoyed this Large Print book. All our Thorndike, Wheeler, and Kennebec Large Print titles are designed for easy reading, and all our books are made to last. Other Thorndike Press Large Print books are available at your library, through selected bookstores, or directly from us.

For information about titles, please call:
   (800) 223-1244

or visit our Web site at:
   http://gale.cengage.com/thorndike

To share your comments, please write:
   Publisher
   Thorndike Press
   295 Kennedy Memorial Drive
   Waterville, ME 04901